JETT

KNIGHT EMPIRE
BOOK 1

LILY ZANTE

AUTHOR'S NOTE

JETT is the first book in KNIGHT EMPIRE, a steamy billionaire series based around a family of six brothers and their cold and manipulative father. Each book is a standalone romance based on one brother.

The series begins with the prequel, THE DARKEST KNIGHT. The first book is JETT, followed by DEX, and then RIO.

Each book can be read as a standalone, and is about one couple, but it is recommended to read these books in order for the best reading experience.

THE DARKEST KNIGHT

JETT

DEX

RIO

ZACH (pre-order, releasing in February 2026)

CHAPTER ONE

CARI

"Cari!" My boss's voice slices through the air like a whip. I grit my teeth. My fingers pause on the keyboard and the words on the screen blur as my focus shifts to the storm brewing near me.

His door is ajar and I can't see him, but I can *feel* him: Jett Knight, my boss and my personal tormentor, is probably hammering away at his keyboard like the Neanderthal he is. I brace myself, knowing what's coming.

His door flies open and he storms out like a hurricane ready to destroy everything in its path. I prefer the Neanderthal version of him, quietly smashing his keys into submission. Not this version: Jett Knight on a rampage.

"I can't find the Morgan contract." His voice is low and dangerous. One hand grips his phone, the other swipes the back of his neck.

Devilishly handsome and smelling like temptation itself, he strides to my desk, and I brace myself. That Armani suit, the sharp, navy blue one worn with his crisp white shirt and the blue silk tie, that suit means trouble.

Thank goodness there's a desk between us because the smell of his aftershave, a mix of cedarwood and something dark and spicy, hits me and makes my pulse race. That scent, combined with the heat rolling off his broad chest, is intoxicating.

At thirty-three years old, this man is older than me by almost a decade. There's something about an older man, about his commanding air, about the power he wields, that turns my insides to mush. That's why it's dangerous for me to even be within sniffing distance of him when he's in this kind of mood. Because I'm scared I'll give my feelings away.

"Find it." His cold blue eyes lock on me, and if looks could kill, I'd already be in the morgue.

"Okaaaay." I hesitate to get up, hating that he's pulling me away from my work, barking orders at me while he's on the phone with someone else. All he has to do is look through his filing cabinet and he'll find it. But patience isn't his strong suit, and he can be an ogre a lot of the time.

Yet he has a gentler side, the caring side that comes out when his little girl is around. Then he turns into a big teddy bear. Can't do enough for her. I see the pain in his eyes when he looks at her sometimes, like she reminds him of his loss. And then there's the fact that he's also extended his kindness to me in many ways. Especially during my mother's illness. There were many moments where I got to see the tender Jett, now that I look back on that darkest time of my life.

"Speak to you later, Dex. There's a shitstorm brewing over here," he says to his brother before sliding his cell phone into his pocket.

His jaw tightens as he glares at me. "I need it *now*, Cari. Not next year." His words drip with sarcasm, and I should know better. I should have dropped everything and jumped to attention, like he expects me to, like I used to. Though lately, I can't do it anymore. Something about the way he stands there, all tension and power, gets under my skin now where before I used to marvel at his commanding presence and his air of authority.

I'm sick and tired of being treated like this by him. Especially when I see him with his girlfriends, or when I have to pick up trinkets or sexy lingerie from a store for him to give to them. I am so sick of this; pining for him when I should know better.

"Bear with me, Jett. I'm only human. I can't multi-task like a computer." I force myself to stand, pressing my palms into the desk as I rise and take a few deep breaths to ground myself. I walk toward his office. "It's in the folder labeled—"

"I don't care where it is," he snaps, cutting me off. "Just get it." I whip my head in his direction, startled by his viciousness even though I should be used to it.

"Someone's in a very bad mood this morning," I say, loud enough for him to hear before I storm out of my office and to the filing cabinets in his, putting distance between myself and this gorgeous, sexy, commanding monster. Yes, I have an office. All to myself. Though I don't have an actual room to myself where I can shut the door if I need peace and privacy. It's more an open plan space off a hallway, but it's enough.

Unfortunately, Jett's office is only accessible through mine. But he's usually away on business or in meetings around the building where his brothers and father have their offices.

My eyes almost bulged out of my head when I came here for an interview three years ago. I'm a personal assistant to one of the three legitimate sons of Paul Knight, the billionaire patriarchal head of Knight Enterprises. He is a man I try to avoid at all costs. The head of a sprawling, diversified, global conglomerate with stakes in multiple industries, and a man who doesn't have an ounce of warmth in him. He's driven by the desire to make more money, even when he's got more than enough and could solve all the world's problems with his fortune.

Jett follows me in, and starts pacing around his office as he takes another call. I wonder who it is this time. From what I can make out, it's not Alicia, or one of his brothers. Or the Italian Knights, who are the other three sons Paul Knight had with a mistress. I can't remember which of the assistants coined that term, but it has stuck.

"It's probably where it always is, if you'd bothered to look properly," I mutter under my breath as I rifle through the filing cabinet. I find and pull out the file. It was there all along. Filed under M. Any idiot could have found it.

I place it on his desk.

"I need to go. I have a meeting. We can pick this up later." He hangs up and slams the phone on his desk. "A meeting with my father. The last thing I fucking need," he groans.

The mention of his father sends a shiver through me. Paul Knight is a force to be reckoned with and he rules with an iron fist. Every time he calls a meeting, Jett becomes even more unbearable than usual. His father has that effect on him. He has that effect on all his sons, really. Though Dex and Zach appear to be relatively calmer and nicer than their older counterpart.

"It was exactly where it was supposed to be." I can't help myself, and I immediately regret my words. This is not the time to push buttons. Not when Paul Knight is breathing down Jett's neck.

"Easy for you to find, then." Jett barely looks at me, let alone thanks me, as he sits down in his executive chair. But now his gaze flicks over to me, the intensity in his bright blue eyes taking in my appearance for a second longer than necessary. My heart does a small somersault in my chest and my eyes go to his silk tie. Sometimes in my moments of delusion I dream about undoing it and …

He moves his mouse around on its mat then growls. "I can't find the fucking link to the meeting. Can you find it?" he snaps, just as his phone goes off again. He stands up, stepping back from his chair and expecting me to sit down and solve his problem instantly.

"I'm sure I can," I say, tightly. I stare at the screen, unsure of what exactly it is he expects me to do. I slide his coffee cup to the side and out of my way. "Where is it?" I try to keep my voice level. I'm not so sure he wants me to go snooping through his mailbox. Unless he wants me to look in his online calendar.

He hovers over me, his bicep inches from my face as I find myself squeezed between the desk and him. Then he leans in, dipping his head as he reads the computer screen. His breaths stir the loose strand of hair by my ear and I'm tempted to tuck it away, but I'm frozen in this moment, because his scent and body heat blanket me, holding me hostage, making my pulse race. My breathing turns choppy. My senses are overloaded and I become hyperaware of his every move; his every breath, his quiet inhale and exhale, the glint of his oversized black-and-silver watch face.

His capable fingers drum on the desk.

"It's in this inbox, somewhere." He's clearly irritated, and I'm not surprised that he hasn't yet found it.

His body brushes against mine as he shifts back slightly, our hands touching for the briefest of seconds. Every nerve in my body lights up like a firework. This man is all hard muscle, and my skin tingles where we touched. I'm not sure if he even noticed, but I'm too stunned to move. It reminds me of that time he comforted me, when he wrapped his arms around me and held me in my darkest moment.

Eliana would kill me if I told her about this. My best friend and roommate has been telling me to quit for over a year. She knows the full extent of my Jett-induced condition.

I *will* leave.

I have to.

For my sanity, if nothing else. It just hasn't happened yet. I've been grieving, unable to step out of my comfort zone and do something new. Take the next step. Up until a few months ago, it was sheer torture just to get out of bed and get myself to work.

I miss my mom so much, but I am slightly better now. I can make it to the office and back, sometimes without thinking about her during my workday. She still haunts me at night, and there are mornings when I wake up and think she's still here.

It was really for my mom that I stayed on here. I needed this job because it allowed me to put my mom on my health insurance. And Jett was really good about letting me have time off when I needed to be with her. He has his good moments, and he's really not so bad.

Despite his arrogance, despite how infuriating he can be, I've seen glimpses of his heart. He adores his daughter, Brooke, and seeing him with her was enough to keep me tethered here, even when everything in me screamed to run.

"I've found it," I whisper, pointing to the screen as Jett continues his conversation with his brother. I glance up at him as he bends down, his gaze flicks ever-so-quickly to my lips.

Oh my goodness. He really did that. It's too much, him being so close, looking at my lips. My heart leaps inside my ribcage and I spring up out of his chair, knocking the coffee cup over in my haste.

My insides deflate in dismay just as quickly as the dark liquid bleeds across the desk, seeping into the edges of his desk diary. "Shit."

"Cari!" He lets out a frustrated cry, but there's something else there, something weary. "What the hell?" He looks down at the spill, his expression blank, but I hear the disappointment in his voice loud and clear.

I can be such a klutz sometimes.

"I'm sorry." I scramble to fix the mess, my fingers trembling as I burn with humiliation. I always turn into a quivering wreck in front of him. He's so mature, and so composed. I can't do anything right in his eyes. If only I were as cool and as glacial as Alicia. Heat tinges my cheeks like a pubescent teen and I'm horrified by what I've done. In my panic, I grab the edge of my dress and use it to frantically mop up the coffee. *Brilliant move, Cari. Brilliant.*

I glance up to see Jett staring at my exposed leg. He quickly clears his throat and looks away, not saying a word. He's already back at his computer as the meeting with his father starts.

Paul Knight's voice booms through the speakers, setting the tone for what I know is going to be a long, painful day for Jett.

And probably for me, too.

CHAPTER TWO

JETT

MY ASSISTANT CAN BE A BIT DITZY AT TIMES, BUT SHE'S
usually very efficient, and she's the reason I function as well as
I do. She organizes and fixes things for me. I rely on her too
much.

Then there are moments when she gets distracted. Her
mom's passing six months ago hit her hard. I understand it,
though. I know what it's like to grow up without a mother.

I was right there by Cari's side after her mother lost the
fight for her life. I'd been awful to her. A huge deal I
desperately needed was stalled at the last moment because she
missed something, and I unleashed my fury on her. I should
have picked up on what she missed because she was going
through such a tough time. I had no idea that her mother was
lying in the hospital sick with an infection which spiraled into
sepsis and took her life. I rushed to the hospital only to see Cari
fall apart.

I'm usually the last person to offer comfort, except to

Brooke, my beautiful little girl. But that day, I couldn't bear to watch Cari wrapping her arms around herself, as if she were trying to keep from falling apart. Tears streamed down her pale face, and I couldn't stand there and do nothing. I pulled her to me, and she melted against my chest. I hugged her tight and tucked her head under my chin. She was so small and fragile in my arms, and she broke into pieces while I held her.

That day is etched into my brain forever.

I don't yell at her for fun. She probably thinks I do it more since her mom passed, but that's not what's going on. There are moments where I see Cari drift off to another place. I know when it happens because I see grief crawling over her, winding its heavy vines around her and rooting her in sorrow. In those moments I try to do something, *anything*, to evoke an emotion other than the heartache and suffering she's feeling. It works, because I see it. I see how my words and my moods incite a spark back into her eyes. They make her react, give her a fire and animation that's a million times better than her drifting around the office with a blank expression. I will take Cari's anger any time over her bottomless misery.

So I do my best to elicit a reaction, because anything is better than seeing her heartbroken.

But she is a dichotomy. One moment she's a super-organized tower of efficiency who I'd be lost without. But some days I get the *other* Cari. Like the one who just tipped over my coffee cup and then mopped it up with her dress.

I didn't need to see her bare leg. Not as I'm about to start a meeting with my overbearing father. At times like this I need to be on my A game, and sometimes, Cari knocks me right off it.

I stare at the computer screen, at my father's cold face, and I listen. But my office smells of coffee, and it's hard to focus.

"I don't like it," my father says, pulling me back into the meeting. Thankfully, Zach is also in on this call.

"What's not to like?" I try to mask my irritation. I caught the gist of what he was saying. Our father distrusts everyone and everything. Hell, I'm the same way, probably more like him than I'd care to admit. Alicia once said that, along with every other woman I've introduced to the old man.

"I don't trust them, but that's because I don't know them. *Yet.* Is that the time?" my father grumbles, glancing at the corner of the screen.

"It's almost ten in the morning over here," Zach says helpfully, ever the diligent son out of the three of us—six, if you count the Half-Knights. Brothers by another mother. The secret family that upended our world and our mother's.

Of us all, Zach is the one who seems desperate for our father's love and attention. He's the only one who calls him "Dad." The rest of us don't call him anything, if we can help it. We meet every so often at the Knight family dinners that our father hosts at his place, with me and my brothers and the other Knights. We all sit around the table, eating and talking shop. It's a painful evening for everyone. Except, possibly, our father. He relishes the torture of putting us all together. I'm certain that he insists on it, not because he cares for unity, or about us being a family, but because a united front is vital to keeping his empire intact.

"I'm looking at AO Eletronica. The owner, a hugely successful businessman, is worth billions. I like their business, it's in the telecoms and electronics space, but I need to get to know him better as a person to see how we can help one another. Wine and dine him and his management board," our father says. "And until I do that, I don't trust them."

You don't trust anyone.

"Don't worry. I'm sure you'll suss them out, Dad." Zach reassures him again and I nod in agreement, my contribution minimal. Why isn't Dex on this call? I was just talking to him earlier. The smart guy probably wised-up and found something to keep him busy. No one likes a meeting with Paul Knight, but a morning meeting just sets the day up wrong.

"Are we done?" I ask, feeling a tightness at the back of my neck.

"For now." Our father hangs up.

"Speak to you later," I say to Zach, and hang up, before standing up and stretching. The tension in my shoulders ease with a satisfying crack. The air smells like coffee and wet fabric but my desk is spotless now, thanks to Cari.

I step out of the office to find her. She's standing at the copier with her back to me, still wearing that same damp dress. The soft hum of the photocopier fills the room. I clear my throat, but she doesn't turn around. I wonder if she's ignoring me on purpose?

"Isn't that still wet?" I ask, making my way toward her.

She jerks her head toward me, cheeks flushed. She's always been terrible at hiding her emotions.

"Your dress," I explain, gesturing toward the fabric clinging to her. "It's still looks wet."

Nose up in the air, she swipes her photocopied sheets and swans away. "I'll live."

She's been quieter lately, and it doesn't sit right with me. Normally, we trade banter; her sharp comebacks, my dry humor. Direct orders work best with Cari. She responds to those.

She sits down, placing the pile of papers on her desk before continuing with her work. She doesn't engage in small talk. I talk; she works.

"Go buy yourself a new dress." I pull out my credit card and offer it to her. Just as I expected, her brown eyes flash with defiance as she glances at the card, looking at it like I've handed her a dead rat. I don't understand why she looks confused. I've given her the card before, to pick up gifts, jewelry, and lingerie for my girlfriends; things I don't put on the company credit card.

"I have my own money, Jett." Her voice is low, almost wounded.

"It's just a suggestion," I huff, trying to shake off the tension. It certainly wasn't my intention to make her feel like she couldn't afford it herself. She shakes her head, and I slip the card back into my wallet. "Have it your way. But *that*," I motion at her outfit with my hand, "is a bad look for the office, especially if a client walks in and sees that."

"I'll dry it with a hand dryer in the washroom." She goes back to her work, still not meeting my eyes. Come to think of it, she's been off for a while now. Even when I sent her to pick up those earrings for Alicia from Cartier, she didn't throw her usual quips at me. I miss the barbed comments, the verbal sparring.

I miss the old Cari.

"We're leaving early tomorrow," I say, changing the subject. I'm going on a short business trip to Monaco, and when Alicia heard about it she wanted to come along. So, we're going a few days early to have some time to enjoy the sights. I don't care for it much, but Alicia says she could do with a break. "I won't be in the office for the rest of the week."

"Enjoy your vacation," Cari mutters without looking up.

"It's not a vacation." I grit my teeth. "It's business." Of the seven days, five are for business, meetings with investors and shareholders, then more meetings with a couple of startups I'm interested in. Plenty of things to keep me busy.

She meets my gaze, and something flickers there—something dark, simmering beneath the surface of those russet-brown eyes, something that has me feeling instantly restless and edgy.

"Okay then ... Enjoy your business, Mr. Knight."

I'm about to make a comment. She doesn't usually call me Mr. Knight, but recently, in prickly moments, she has been.

***

"DADDY!" MY LITTLE GIRL'S CHEEKY SMILE WELCOMES ME.

I open my arms, and she rushes towards me in her pink unicorn nightshirt, her damp hair still smelling like shampoo. "Gotcha, sprout," I say, settling her on my hip as she wraps her arms around my neck.

"Anything I should know?" I ask Anna, my live-in nanny.

"She's been waiting up for you, Mr. Knight. She's had dinner, and a bath, and we've done some coloring, and the homework school sent. She didn't want to go to bed without seeing you."

"You did the coloring without me?"

"You weren't here, Daddy. I never seen you 'till bedtime."

I nod to Anna. "Thanks, I'll take it from here." After a hard day at work, the best thing in my life is coming home to my girl. We live in a four-story townhouse-style apartment in the heart of Tribeca. Me, Dex, and Zach. We each have an apartment on a separate floor, each accessed by a private elevator.

This works for us, because it keeps us close but separate. Gives us privacy when we need it, but a chance to easily meet up if we need to. Naturally, being the oldest, I have the top floor penthouse. Dex and Zach have the lower floors, and we have a pool, sauna, and gym on the ground floor.

Unlike the office block we share with our father and the Half-Knights in Midtown Manhattan, we have our own living space, away from the boys who live in SoHo. I like that distance between us.

With my girl in my arms, I swirl her around in the air. Brooke giggles. "Daddy, stop!" So, I do, and sit on her bed with her still in my arms. Soon she'll be too big for this. She's no longer the chubby toddler I used to know. Now she's all long legs and skinny arms. She's only four, almost five.

Brooke snuggles into me, and I sit down on her bed, holding her close. She's growing up too fast. "I'm sorry I was late for dinner."

"You're going tomorrow. Anna said you're going for a long time."

I make a face, feeling genuinely wretched. I hate leaving her, but business comes first, for the moment. I would happily have taken Brooke with me, but her teacher said a week was too long to be out of school. She said Brooke needs stability, and consistency. I already took her skiing with us a few months ago when I pulled her out of her class for ten days, so I guess she has a point. "It's not a long time, sprout," I tell her gently. "It's not weeks and weeks and weeks. It's seven days."

Her face scrunches up just as her eyes widen. "That's a long time, Daddy!"

"I'll be back before you know it."

"But *when* will you come back? It's my party, 'member?"

"I do remember. How could I forget such an important date?" I drop a kiss on her forehead. Because of Brooke's birthday, I tacked a few days onto the start of the trip, not the end. There's no way I'm missing this milestone. She beams me a smile that melts my heart and I rush to reassure her, stroking her damp hair. "I'm sorry things are so hectic, that I'm always so busy. But one day soon, things will slow down and we'll be able to spend lots of time together."

"You promise?" Her eyes fill with hope.

"I promise." But I feel like a liar saying these words, even though a part of me wants them to be true. We're always working, doing deals, traveling, and expanding our empire. It seems as if our father thrives on all of this, but I'm becoming aware that I'm missing the chance to see my little girl grow up. She's already without a mother, and I need to be a better parent. I need to be a father *and* a mother, but I'm doing a lousy job at the moment.

This addiction to money that afflicts my father, I once had too—until Brooke was born. But I was forced to slow down and enjoy what little happiness we got to share as a family—Sophia, Brooke, and I. And then when Sophia died, I got caught up again in chasing deals and money. More as a distraction, than anything.

Brooke frowns as if she doesn't believe me. "Anna's not gonna be there," she says.

What? I huff as I start to remember. Of course she isn't. She's going away that weekend on a bachelorette party. I forget whose. Might even be hers, for all I know. "You're right, she isn't."

"You forgot, didn't you?" She stares at me accusingly. How did she get so clever?

"No, no." It's not technically a lie, since I knew,, but I just forgot this week. The meeting with my father was unnerving, and Alicia has been a distraction. "I know it's your party."

"Is Cari coming?"

My stomach drops. Fuck. Something else I forgot to do. I forgot to ask her. I beam a smile at my girl but she sees right through it.

"Did you forget, Daddy?"

I sure did. "I've been busy, sprout. Don't you worry, I'll sort it out."

"I want Cari there."

"I'll talk to her," I promise, knowing I'll have to call Cari as soon as we're in Monaco.

Brooke adores her, and I can't imagine the party without Cari being there. Alicia and my previous girlfriends have commented on their unusual connection, but I've brought Brooke to the office many times over the years. From what I remember, Cari met her during her first week on the job and took a liking to Brooke straightaway. Brooke seemed to bond with Cari, too. What I find most perplexing is how an only child like Cari can be so good with children, when she doesn't have any siblings of her own?

But Cari has so many endearing qualities, and she's got a big heart. Her smile is infectious, as is her laughter, even though I haven't seen much of these things in the last few months. "I can ask her, but she might be busy," I forewarn my girl.

Brooke grins, already content with my answer. Any mention of Cari has that effect. I owe my assistant so much. "I'll ask her, and let's hope she can make it."

My little angel nods, and I press a kiss on her cheeks, first one then the other, then a kiss on her forehead, nose, and chin. She giggles. "How about I read a book to you?" I offer, wanting to end the night on a good note. I want her to be happy with me, and to feel loved and cherished.

She races to her bookshelf and grabs her favorite bedtime stories. As she curls up beside me, I kiss the top of her head, guilt gnawing at me. My daughter deserves more than a distracted father and a carousel of girlfriends who take up what little free time I have outside of business.

Business comes first most of the time, but I'm determined to fix things. I'm taking Brooke to Bermuda for a long vacation soon. It's a business trip, but I'll make sure I spend quality time with my little girl.

CHAPTER THREE

CARI

Just as I'm about to flip my fried egg, my phone buzzes and my heart sinks to my ankles when I see the name on the screen: Jett Knight.

I freeze.

My boss is FaceTiming me from Monaco.

That's never happened before. Panic squeezes my chest as I smooth down my hair, feeling a slow wave of paralysis. Should I answer? Is this about Brooke? What if it's an emergency?

I swipe to accept the call.

Jett's familiar, intense gaze widens slightly, and he tilts his head; his classic tell that he's surprised or caught off guard. I've spent enough time around him to know his every microexpression. "Hey." His voice is rich and smooth, like velvet wrapping itself around me, leaving a trail of heat in its wake.

Damn him.

Even from thousands of miles away, he manages to scramble my insides and effortlessly pull me under his spell.

I hate that he has this power over me. I hate that he does it while lounging in a luxury apartment half a world away, with his girlfriend draped around him like an accessory. "Did you mean to call me?" I ask, keeping my tone flat, hoping it hides the traitorous warmth creeping up my neck. I hate that he has this effect on me even when I'm in the comfort of my own home and out of his kingdom.

His brows furrow as he studies me, probably trying to figure out where I am. "Yes, that's why I called you."

My stomach flips. "You've never FaceTimed me before," I blurt, my mind whirring. Monaco ... He's in Monaco and the time difference must be ... what, six hours ahead? I smooth my hair again, stepping away from the kitchen and into the hallway, out of earshot from Eliana.

"Sorry to disturb you at home." He shifts slightly, and behind him, the sky is painted in hues of gold and pink. It's the kind of sunset I love. I could just stare at it and be happy. But I also feel a pang of envy. I know exactly where he's staying, because I made the booking. It's a place with seven-star service and spectacular views. He doesn't own a place in Monaco. Not yet, but it's just a matter of time before the Knights stake their claim there, too.

I know everything. Where they're staying, his meetings, even the restaurants I suggested for his precious downtime. It was torture planning this trip and there were times when I couldn't help but imagine myself there in place of his girlfriend.

"I was talking to Brooke. She FaceTimed me, which is why I didn't think before calling you."

My irritation melts at the mention of his daughter. Brooke is everything Jett isn't. She's sweet, warm, and full of joy.

"Is everything okay?" A flicker of worry gnaws at me. She's back home with her nanny in that sprawling apartment. I wonder if she's lonely.

"She's fine. She reminded me of something I meant to ask you." He sighs, rubbing the back of his neck. "I've been so busy—"

"You're always busy." My words come out sharper than intended. He just nods like that's a fact of life. "What is it?"

Before he can answer, my gaze drifts to the background again, where Alicia is lounging on the balcony wearing nothing but his shirt. The oversized fabric swallows her, but it's impossible to miss the half-buttoned front. I grit my teeth. She's tall, leggy, effortlessly stunning, and there's no doubt what happened before she slipped into his clothes.

He clears his throat, drawing my attention back to him. "I should have asked before, but ... Anna's going to a bachelorette party this weekend, and Brooke's birthday is—"

Of course. I knew this was coming. He forgot. And now, like clockwork, here I am. His go-to fix-it girl. "You want me to help out at Brooke's party," I finish for him, my voice tight. It's always something with him. Always asking for more.

"No." He shakes his head so vigorously, I'm scared he'll give himself whiplash. "No, it's not that at all." He pauses, keeping me on edge. If it's not that, then why is he calling me?

"Brooke was upset. She's growing older now and becoming more aware, and she told me she's really sad that her mommy is never there."

"Oh." I put a hand to my chest. I've always had a special place in my heart for that little girl. Ever since I found out how young she was when her mother passed away.

This year especially, Brooke's misfortune sits heavier on me. I was twenty-three years old when my mom passed away.

Brooke was two. I'm certain she doesn't even remember her mom. "I'll be there," I tell him. I don't need to hear the rest. Jett doesn't need to convince me.

"I'll help out, if I'm needed," I offer. Anything to make Brooke's party so amazing that the little cherub won't even have time to feel sad. Besides, I have ulterior reasons for wanting to be there, because I got so carried away with the planning of her party. I took it right out of Anna's hands when Jett told me that she was making a half-hearted attempt at organizing the event.

Brooke not having the party she dreamed of was something I couldn't live with. If she had a mother, her mother would have done it. I offered to take it on and ended up planning the entire thing. Now I'm itching to see how the party ends up.

Before I can respond, Eliana sidles up next to me, and I can already sense her annoyance when she sees Jett's face on my screen. She steps away and mimes hanging up, rolling her eyes in disapproval. She's never liked how much Jett leans on me— or how I let him.

"Why's he calling you at home?" she mouths, shaking her head.

"Sorry, what?" I miss Jett's last words, distracted by Eliana's exaggerated gestures. She doesn't like my boss, and what she hates even more is that I can't often say "no" to him.

"I'm going to a concert that day," I tell him.

"You are?" His brows push together. "With whom?"

"The Mayflies," I blurt out.

"With *whom*?"

"What?" I don't understand the question.

"Tell him you can't babysit his daughter or work extra hours, no matter how tempting he makes it for you," Eliana hisses directly in my ear.

Jett's face turns somber. "Hey, look, then don't worry about it. I'll tell Brooke you had other plans—"

"No! Don't do that. Do *not* do that." I can't, I *won't* let Brooke down. I'd hate to disappoint the motherless, sweet, and cute little girl who deserves to have a wonderful birthday. Especially if she's becoming aware that she's probably the only one in her class who doesn't have a mother. My own loss, so raw and so recent, makes my heart bleed for that child.

"But you have plans. A concert, no less," Jett says.

"I'll make it in time for the concert. You don't have to worry about that, and you're arriving in the morning," I remind him. I hope he'll be at the party on time. I told him that it was the day of Brooke's party when I booked the flights, and reiterated that he was cutting it close landing the same day. He told me he had an important meeting that morning, one he couldn't possibly miss. He assured me that he would be back on time.

"I am, *we* are. I'll be at the party on time." He stares at me. Even though he's looking at me through a phone, I feel as if he's right here. In my kitchen. Standing close by. Sometimes his gaze is so intense, my breath hitches in my throat.

Eliana jabs her finger at me. "What if you're late for The Mayflies?" she hisses.

I won't be, I mouth back.

"Is he deaf? You're busy," Eliana says, loud enough so that Jett will hear. "We have tickets! What can't he understand?"

"I already told him that," I say, accidentally speaking that into the phone.

"Told me what?" Jett's bright blue eyes settle on me.

"Can you check on my egg?" I whisper to my friend, desperate to get her off my back.

"It's burned to a crisp," Eliana mutters, before disappearing.

"Sorry. That was my roommate." I have a sneaky feeling

that Jett's heard most of that. Eliana doesn't hide her contempt for him, and she's pissed off that I still work there. I've been trying to leave.

Trying.

But so far, it's not going to plan.

It's in moments like this, when I see Jett with his girlfriend in the background, that I wish I'd never walked into this man's life. It's sheer torture being in the office, being around him. Ordering gifts for his lovers, booking plane tickets, making reservations for tables at the top restaurants, the best hotels, for him and someone *else.*

"I'll pay you five hundred dollars for the trouble," Jett says.

I choke in surprise. Five hundred dollars? Neon dollar signs flash before my eyes. That's almost half my rent. Eliana is at my ear again, hissing, "Don't fall for it. He always does this."

"No. I won't take any money for coming to Brooke's birthday party."

"But I feel like I've guilt-tripped you into coming," he says, "It's just that Brooke wanted me to ask you, and I promised her I would. Please take the payment, Cari. This is a weekend, and you deserve your time off. You shouldn't be at my beck and call on your free time."

His words send a shiver down my spine. "I'm not at your beck and call, Mr. Knight."

He raises an eyebrow, as if he's not sure why I've reverted to calling him Mr. Knight. This is also a new thing, ever since my mom died and Jett was there for me. We shared a moment. He was at my mother's bedside not long after the monitor flatlined and she passed away. When I was all alone, Jett held me in my time of need. After that, something shifted.

I call him Mr. Knight only when he strikes at something and I don't care to analyze it. It's usually when he's annoyed me, or he's said or done something that causes an inappropriate image to flash through my mind.

"Take the money, Cari."

"I will not. I'm honored that Brooke invited me. Please let her know that I'll be there."

One day soon, I'll have to find the strength to walk away from this man.

But not today.

CHAPTER FOUR

JETT

I'VE MESSED UP AGAIN. I'M AN HOUR LATE FOR MY LITTLE girl's party.

I'm the only parent she has, and I should have done better. I should have *been* better. I should have come back a day earlier, like Cari said, instead of being adamant about attending an important meeting this morning.

I walk into the opulent hotel lobby, carrying two big bags of gifts, scanning for Brooke. The hotel is elegant, fancy but whimsical, just like my little girl wanted. Cari has done a great job. We follow the hotel receptionist as she leads the way, her cheeks flushing a shade of pink when she realizes who I am. Now she seems slightly flustered.

"This way, Mr. Knight," she says, breathlessly.

"How long do we have to stay here?" Alicia asks, already putting a damper on the day. It's not the reaction I want my girlfriend to have, not when it comes to my daughter. We had a few good days to unwind, but lately, I'm starting to realize she's never satisfied. All my girlfriends seem to follow the same pattern. They start out sweet and understanding, then slowly, inevitably, become more demanding. They don't show it so much at first, but over time I see how they avoid doing things with Brooke. Alicia and I have been together for almost seven months, and it's usually around this time that I start seeing the cracks.

The women I date want *me*, not my daughter. But my daughter is my life and she's always number one in my world, even if I'm still adjusting to this "single dad" role. I want her to have the best of everything, because I feel so bad that she doesn't have a mother. I try to make up for that loss and vow that I will be better, but there's always another deal or the lure of more money.

"You can go now, if it's too much for you." I don't even look at her.

She squeezes my hand. "Don't be like that."

The receptionist opens the door to the large room, and the sound of children's laughter and excited chatter fills the space. My eyes widen.

The room is magical. Elephant decorations, and elephant-shaped lights are strung across the ceiling, and a dreamy pastel color scheme that makes it look like a fairytale. Brooke wanted a Cinderella theme, with elephants, and Cari made it happen. My little girl sits in the front row with her back to me, her long brown silky hair cascading down her back. She's wearing a sparkling blue dress, her tiara perched perfectly on her head. She really thinks she's Cinderella today. My heart aches. I hate that I wasn't here from the start.

"Holy shit," Alicia murmurs, sounding awestruck. "*This* is your daughter's party?"

There's a pastel-colored balloon arch, a popcorn stand, a cotton candy station, a chocolate fountain, and a candy buffet. I wonder if Cari was inspired by Tobias Stone's Christmas party. This is magnificent. There's an elephant pinata suspended in the air. A woman paints children's faces, and a wizard entertainer, complete with a pointed hat, does magic tricks at the front.

"Isn't she just five?" Alicia drawls. Her voice lacks warmth and there's something bitter laced in there.

The wizard calls Brooke to the front, and she eagerly jumps up, her eyes glittering with excitement as she runs over carrying her beloved tattered elephant. I facepalm. She takes that plushy with her everywhere. We bought it soon after she was born. To this day, it's Brooke's favorite toy, though it looks all battered and tattered now. She has a butterfly painted on her cheek, and the sight of her joy brings a smile to my face. The wizard makes balloon animals for her, but each time he hands one to her, it pops, and Brooke bursts into laughter, joined by the other children. My heart swells. She's everything to me.

"She is. Cari did well," I murmur, my gaze sweeping across the room as I look for a place to leave her presents. I've been taking note of everything Brooke said she liked, and I bought her everything.

My father says I shouldn't spoil her, and that kids who have everything grow up to be brats. My brothers and I didn't have big parties, or get lots of presents. No cars on milestone birthdays, or expensive watches. Yet ours was still a privileged life. I realize that now. We lived in expensive homes, had the best education, and we didn't want for anything.

Except maybe love from our father. It was the important things he skimped on, like giving love and spending time with us. I'll never deprive Brooke of the former, and I'm trying to get better with the latter.

It was our mother who gave us the most special and priceless of things. She would spoil us with days out creating memories, moments I hold onto even now. She'd insist on baking our birthday cakes and spending the entire day together, just my brothers and my mom. My father was always absent. He was too busy building the Knight empire.

"Who?" Alicia asks.

"Cari."

"Your *assistant* did this?"

"Yeah."

"Doesn't she already have a full-time job working for you?"

"She does, but somehow she manages it all." The words come out with a hint of awe. Cari has pulled off something truly special. How did she find the time to do this? A thought crosses my mind: maybe I should give her another raise. Though I just gave her one a few months ago. Another one might make her suspicious.

I glance around the room, but I don't see her. Did she decide to skip the party and go to the concert instead? Did she have a date, maybe? I shake the twisted thought out of my head. No. Cari wouldn't do that. She's dependable, more so than anyone I know. I didn't check in with her yesterday to confirm her attendance because I was in meetings all day, but I didn't think I needed to. It's Cari, and she's completely reliable and trustworthy.

"Where is she?" Alicia asks.

I set my bags down and scratch my neck, feeling uncomfortable. Cari would never let Brooke down, but she doesn't seem to be here. "I'm not sure."

Then I spot her by a table piled high with gifts, carefully arranging them. I never see her out of her usual office attire, and she looks so different. Effortlessly casual. Relaxed and beautiful. She's casually dressed in jeans that fit her perfectly. She's wearing a gold chain with a black oval-shaped gemstone dipping down the front of her dark green satin top. Naturally, my attention goes there. She looks less like my assistant in her usual pencil skirts and blouses. Even from here, I see the flustered blush of her cheeks and that long, loose red hair that's usually tied up is now tumbling around her shoulders.

There are days when I find myself thinking of her more than I should. She pauses to fan her face, looking a little overwhelmed.

I'm about to head over when Brooke sees me. She's still with the magician who's now creating an elephant out of balloons. The huge smile on her face fills me with joy, but in the next instant, her eyes fill with tears. Her lip wobbles, and my heart plunges into my belly. She's going to cry. I feel wretched.

I caused this.

She's sad and so painfully aware that her mother isn't here on her special day, but me? I let her down. I don't deserve this precious angel.

You're no better than your own father.

The wizard's balloon pops again, and she bursts into laughter. Relief washes over me as I watch her laugh.

"Hey." Dex's voice interrupts my thoughts. My middle brother nudges me in the ribs. "I can't believe you made it back on time."

"This isn't him being on time. He's late." Zach rolls his eyes. "Hey, Alicia. How was Monaco?"

"Fantastic." She snakes her arm around my waist.

"Good," I add, trying to peer around Zach's head. "Did you guys get here early?"

"'Course we did." Dex grins.

"What happened to the nanny?" Zach asks.

"She's at a bachelorette party she couldn't miss," Dex answers for me. "That's why Superwoman over there is on it."

"Who?" Alicia asks.

"Her." Dex jerks his chin toward Cari. "The woman my brother can't function without."

I clear my throat, an odd feeling settling in my chest. "I hope you guys were helping." With Anna not being here, and my brothers referring to Cari as Superwoman, I hope they've not sat back and relied on her to run around doing things. Though I have a feeling that Cari would step in if needed. For Brooke, she would do anything.

"There wasn't anything to do," Dex says. "Superwoman took care of it all."

Typical response. I walk toward Cari, not in the mood for my brothers' commentary.

"This is amazing, Cari!" I set the gift-filled bags on the table.

"Daddy! Daddy, you're here!" Brooke comes barreling past Cari, her little arms reaching for me. I scoop her up, holding her close to me. Her laughter rings in my ears, washing away the stress of the last few days.

"I'm here, princess," I say, breathing her in. "And here," I show her the bags, "are all the things you wanted."

"Thanks, Daddy. But you're late." She pouts, making me feel worse than I already do.

"I came as soon as I could. I'm sorry, angel, but the flight was delayed."

"Delayed?" Cari asks, a hint of disbelief in her voice. She's watching me closely. It's the first time I see her displeasure so clearly. Usually, she hides it well. "Your flight was delayed?" she asks again.

I don't like the stone-cold edge in her tone. "You sound as if you don't believe me, and I don't blame you. But yes, it was. Something about a hydraulic leak."

"I did remind you that it was cutting it close," Cari points out. She seems to gloat in reminding me of my shortcomings.

"I couldn't leave Monaco any earlier because of a meeting that couldn't be moved," I say, wearily. "Maybe I should have missed it, but then I'd have the wrath of my father to contend with." I scratch my jaw, wondering why I put up with his shit. My daughter should come first, and it's about time I started making sure she does. As far as my father is concerned, family doesn't matter. Money. Empire. Legacy. That's all he cares about, but maybe some things need to change.

Cari shrugs and fiddles with the gemstone on her chain. "Okay, Jett. Whatever you say, but you let Brooke down. You need to make her understand and make it up to her."

"I came as fast as I could," I tell her. Brooke clings to me, her tiny arms tight around my neck. Despite all her friends, the magician, the popcorn, and the balloons, she just wants me.

"I chartered a flight out when they told us it would take at least two hours," I announce, looking at Cari as if I'm expecting brownie points.

She doesn't give them.

She looks unsure. If anything, her expression remains cool, her eyes distant. I clear my throat. "My brothers are calling you Superwoman."

"Why?" she remarks, as if she's clueless about her superpowers.

"Because you always get things done, and you're good, but you're here as a guest and I hope you haven't been helping too much."

A smile spreads across her face. "I've been having fun."

"I bet my brothers have been no help whatsoever."

"They were here on time, which is more than I can say for you."

Ouch. She's really mad at me, even though I explained. At least she's calm and collected, even if she can't bring herself to look at me. I side eye her, taking in her gorgeous tresses which

I'm only seeing now, up close for the first time. The way she's dressed down is so refreshing. I like her like this.

"It wasn't my fault, Cari." Maybe she's a little off because of that concert she's going to later. I offered to pay her for today, but maybe that's not the point. Especially since she's not taking the money. I don't care what she says. I'll slip it into her paycheck as a bonus, because she always comes through for me and for Brooke.

"The magician wants you back, Brooke," Cari says. I let Brooke down gently and see the way she takes Cari's hand, giving Cari no choice but to walk her back to the front of the room.

Cari is like a diamond in a sea of mediocrity. She's dependable, smart, and irreplaceable. If I could clone her, I would. I'd have one Cari as my assistant, and one for Brooke. No one else can be trusted. No one else gets things done without being told twice. She's a rare breed in a world where people seem to have stopped thinking for themselves.

Though I'm starting to find her brittle tone and her frosty demeanor unsettling. I don't know when it happened, when I started to care so much more about her opinion of me.

CHAPTER FIVE

CARI

"I have things to do, babe. I need to go," Alicia's arm snakes around Jett's waist, possessive and casual all at once. His arms remain folded, his body rigid like he's holding something in.

"You want to go now?" His voice was cool, but I can't quite read his expression from behind them. Their body language, though, tells me everything I need to know. After a few days in Monaco together, I expected them to be inseparable. Yet, the lack of any passionate, completely-in-love vibes make me wonder if all is well.

"It's not my scene." Alicia leans in, kissing his cheek, but her attention already seems elsewhere. "I've got to unpack. There's so much to do."

"It's Brooke's birthday," Jett reminds her, his voice a little sharper, a hint of frustration slipping through. He rarely lets that mask crack, but there it is, just for a second. She smiles then kisses his cheek again.

"Let's take her out for dinner tonight," she offers, brushing it off like it's nothing. It's not a question. It's her solution. As if this can fix the disappointment in Brooke's eyes. Jett doesn't respond, and my heart twists.

I spot a little girl sitting by herself at the edge of the room, looking lost and I go over to see her.

"Hey, sweetheart. What's wrong?" I ask softly.

"I need to go to the washroom, but I don't know where it is," she whispers, her big eyes full of worry.

Phew. At least it wasn't the kids ganging up on her like I'd feared, or any drama like that. "No problem, I'll show you." She slides her tiny hand into mine, and I lead her out.

We reach the washroom, and I bend down to her level. "There you go. I'll wait for you right here, okay?"

She nods and disappears inside, just as the door flies open. Alicia walks in, her expression faltering when she sees me standing there.

"Oh." She stops in her tracks and her eyes flicker with something I can't quite place. Is it surprise, or annoyance? It's like she wasn't expecting me here.

"You're not staying?" I ask, already knowing the answer.

"It's not my scene." She chews her lower lip. "That makes me sound like the wicked stepmother, doesn't it?"

Stepmother? Is there something brewing?

Her fingers thread through her silky dark hair. It falls perfectly over her shoulders, framing her face, softening her sharp features. All I can do is stand and stare as envy pours over me. I wish I could look as effortlessly stunning as she does. It's a far cry from my practical, barely-there makeup, freckled face, and frizzy hair.

"No, it just means you're busy," I offer politely. But the image of her in Monaco, lounging on a balcony in nothing but

Jett's white shirt, cuts through me like a blade. My heart twists. I wish I didn't care so much. I wish it didn't sting.

But it does.

And that is why I need to leave.

Someday soon.

Like next week.

I'm going to do it.

"I adore Brooke, truly," Alicia says quickly. "She's a sweet girl, but she won't miss me. Besides, I have a huge case next week and it was impossible to prep for it properly while on vacation." She gives a naughty giggle, and I immediately think of her and Jett together. They make a stunning couple, an unstoppable duo. They must make heads turn wherever they go. Me? I'm a plain Jane with red hair, freckles, and I'm on the short side. Ridiculous fantasies swirl in my head, but that's all they are—fantasies.

"It's understandable then, why you can't stay," I manage to say, though something in my chest tightens. Not only is this creature jaw-droppingly beautiful, she's also brainy. I've noticed that Jett often falls for women who have brains. Why does that surprise me? They are beauties, but they are also professional women. Fashion buyers, attorneys, doctors, CEOs.

I'm just a pathetic assistant. Hopefully, a florist one day, and the CEO of my own little kiosk. Though it's hardly in the same league.

"You did a fantastic job with the party, by the way." Her compliment is as polished as she is, but I can hear the edge in her voice. "Jett says you took care of everything."

I blink and smile. "I just wanted Brooke to have an unforgettable birthday."

"So sweet of you." She reapplies her lipstick. "I'm sure she did. It was good of you to make such an effort. Jett was in awe." Her voice trails off, and she gives me a thoughtful look.

Does she know? Can she sense my feelings for him? My useless, delusional, pathetic crush? If she suspects, has she voiced her suspicions to him? I imagine them laughing at it over a bottle of expensive champagne.

I don't know how to respond. I glance down at myself, feeling small and inadequate next to her. The little girl returns, reaching for the faucet. "Here, let me help," I say, turning it on for her. She's on tiptoes to wash her hands, and I smile.

"You're so good with kids," Alicia observes, touching up her concealer. Her reflection catches mine in the mirror. "It's no wonder Brooke adores you."

"Brooke's my friend," the little girl says shyly, as if that explains everything.

"And that's why you're here, at Brooke's party." A bright red smile flashes across Alicia's face. Her eyes glint with something I can't place. Then she leans closer to the mirror, reapplying her lip gloss with precision.

I don't like her tone or her patronizing comment to the little girl. "'Bye," I say to her, before leading the little girl back to the party. My mind races as we reenter the room. Brooke's face lights up when she sees me, her earlier frustration with her father forgotten.

But I haven't forgotten. She'd been sullen this morning, upset that Jett hadn't been here from the start. And the way her face crumpled when he and Alicia strolled in late, it hurt to watch.

The day hasn't been terrible though. Brooke is happy now, and that's all that matters. Jett seems to be impressed with the party, and I'm excited about my evening plans. The Mayflies concert is just what I need to unwind. I just need to get out of here.

I head towards Jett. He's leaning against a wall, watching Brooke playing games with her friends. He's not in his signature Armani suit, but he still looks so eye-catching and sexy. He's wearing an expensive, casual blazer over dark jeans and a white shirt with the top two buttons open. It hurts to look at him.

I refocus on the concert this evening and I try to get in the right mindset for it. "I should head out," I say to him. "Everything's under control, and your brothers can help you wrap things up."

He pushes off the wall. "You're leaving?"

"Yes, Jett. I'm leaving. I have a life away from you." My insides roil at my words. Heat creeps along my neck. "The party's in full swing and the kids are going to start eating soon. You and your brothers can supervise," I say quickly, hoping he doesn't notice the wobble in my voice. I gesture toward Dex and Zach, who are standing by a table, laughing, talking, and oblivious to the chaos.

Jett blinks, looking utterly lost. "You want me to ... *supervise*?" He looks around as if it suddenly registers that there are no parents here, and the Knights are the grown-ups. The parents will show up at the end of the party to collect their kids. Suddenly, he doesn't look like a hotshot billionaire. He looks lost.

I shake my head. This isn't going to happen. He's not going to reel me in to help. "It's simple enough. You'll be just fine, Jett, but I need to go."

"Okay ..." He sounds reluctant for me to go and looks around helplessly. There are no parents around by design, because Jett doesn't like to mingle with the other parents. He thinks they might want favors or money. He doesn't trust people he doesn't know, apart from the Stones.

Most of the kids in Brooke's class are the children of rich parents, but most people, apart from the Stone family, aren't in the same league as the Knights. "Get your brothers to help," I suggest. "You're good at ordering and delegating."

"They know about as much as I do about getting thirty kids to eat," he mumbles, shifting uneasily from one foot to the other.

"They're five years old, Jett, not babies. You can handle it." I try to stifle a laugh. This man runs so many successful businesses, and he's panicking over a children's party.

"Do you have to leave now? I can get my brothers to help, but it would be good to have you around."

"I have a concert to go to, remember?" I glance at my watch. It's two o'clock. I'm supposed to go home and get showered and ready so that Eliana and I can leave by five to make it to the concert which starts at seven. "I don't want to be late."

"Of course. I'm just sorry to see you go …"

I weigh his words and try to gauge what he's thinking and feeling, because he suddenly seems softer. Not the demanding tyrant I'm used to in the office.

He clears his throat. "Thanks for coming, Cari. It means the world to Brooke," he adds quickly. "I appreciate you so much. You know that, don't you?" Those blue irises gaze at me with such intensity that I'm forced to look away.

"I need to tell Brooke I'm going." I get her attention and beckon her over briefly. She's watching her friend get her face painted. "Are you having a good time, sweetie?" I crouch down to her level. She nods, her face lighting up, before turning sad when she sees my handbag on my arm. "Are you going?"

"Yes, sweetie, but I'll see you soon, okay? Don't forget to open the presents I got you."

Before I can stand, she throws her arms around my neck, catching me off guard. She buries her face in my shoulder, squeezing tight. My heart stutters. Brooke's always sweet, but this, this is more than I expected.

"Thanks for coming." Her small voice is muffled against me. "Can you stay with me for a bit when we eat? Like mommies do."

My throat tightens unexpectedly. I kiss her on the cheek as we pull apart, my heart full and heavy all at once. "Oh, sweetie." There's no way I'm walking out of here and leaving this little girl alone. I can do this for her. "Of course I'll stay. I would love to. Shall I just hover around? You'll want to sit with your friends—"

"I want you to sit with me."

"Okaaaay," I say slowly. "Then I'll sit with you." She rushes off in a blaze of happiness. Clearly there's more to the story, and I need to dig deeper. I need to speak to Anna and Jett. Something's going on in Brooke's life that we need to get to the bottom of.

"Told you it would make a big impression on her if you came." Jett's voice slices through the moment, snapping me back to reality. I think he heard what Brooke said. I straighten up, emotions quickly replaced by the desire to find out what's going on. I'm about to voice my fears to him but decide that now is not the time. "I'll stay for food, because Brooke wants me to."

"What about your concert? Won't you be late?" This is so not like Jett Knight. The man is worried about me missing my concert. What's come over him?

"It's only two o'clock." I glance at my watch again. "I can stay for a little while. Half an hour, an hour at most."

"Thanks, I appreciate it."

"I'm doing it for Brooke."

Maybe my tone is sharper than I intended because he looks

taken aback. "I know, and I appreciate it. I'll call you a taxi when you're ready to go."

"You don't have to do that, Jett. I'm quite capable of—"

"I know you are. You are more than capable of most things. Please, Cari. It's the least I can do."

THE KNIGHT BROTHERS SUPERVISING A LUNCH FOR THIRTY hungry children is a sight to see.

They don't have to do much because the servers take care of most of it. The most the brothers have to do is pour glasses of juice when it runs out, and serve slices of pizza when the kids want more.

Given that they're not used to getting their hands dirty like this, I think they did well.

As soon as the food is cleared away, the magician launches into a few last tricks for the kids. The party's winding down and I'm about to slip away, when a server materializes beside me with trays of brightly colored party bags. "Hi, Mommy. Please can you make sure the kids each get one?"

I blink, stunned for a second. "I ... I'm not ..."

The server has already walked away, leaving two trays of party bags, one for boys, and one for girls, sitting on the table in front of me.

My heart sinks.

"Are we giving those out now?" Brooke cries. She takes hold of my hand, looking up at me gleefully.

I glance toward Jett, who's standing a few feet away, deep in conversation on his phone. I scan the room for backup, but his brothers are nowhere to be found. It's just me, the servers, and the magician, who looks like he's already mentally checked out.

I glance at my watch in shock. It's three o'clock. I can still go home, shower, and get ready for my night. I can still make the concert, but I won't have time to wash and straighten my hair. All is not lost.

"Yes, we are. C'mon on. Let's get it done quickly, sweetie."

The magician gets the kids to form a line, thank God, and they wait patiently as Brooke helps me hand out the bags. She's smiling and happy, and that is worth every minute of me being here.

The parents trickle in right on cue, perfectly punctual, perfectly polished. Brooke hugs me tightly and tells me it was the best party she's ever had. Those words mean everything to me.

Then Jett calls me a taxi and I walk out, finally heading home to get ready.

I JOLT UP WITH A START. THEN RUB MY EYES AS I LOOK AROUND the room.

I fell asleep.

In a panic, I jump up from the couch and find my phone.

I have eight missed calls from Eliana. My stomach twists. There are no texts, but the voicemail icon mocks me for missing the calls.

I don't bother getting changed. I haven't showered, but I slip on my boots and rush out, flagging down a taxi. I pray I can still make it. The concert starts soon. No time for pre-show drinks now, but maybe I can still salvage the evening.

Sliding into the backseat, I hit play on the first voicemail. Eliana's voice fills the silence, sharp with irritation.

"Hey, it's me. You're not picking up. Why are you not

picking up? We have a concert to go to, or has being in Jett Knight's orbit turned your brain to mush again?" she snaps.

She's pissed. Of course she's pissed. I check the timestamp. She sent it at four o'clock. I scroll to the next voicemail, sent twenty minutes later.

"I knew this would happen. It always does! Why aren't you answering your phone?"

Her frustration is louder now, cutting deeper. My stomach knots. The final voicemail plays, the one that confirms what I already know.

"That's it. I've had it with you, Car. I didn't hear back, so I'm taking Bianca. I can't risk you bailing on me. She'll pay you for the ticket, even if she doesn't like the music, but she's a good friend, so she's coming. You have fun with the Knights."

I slump back against the seat, my jaw dropping. She didn't wait. She really didn't wait for me.

A text message pings as I stare blankly out the window, but I already know what it's going to say.

> I'll pay you back for the ticket. When it comes to Jett, you always pick him over me.

She thinks I stayed at the party because of Jett. Nothing could be further from the truth, and yet her words hit like a punch. My jaw tightens, guilt swirling with the anger already simmering under my skin.

But she's not completely wrong. God, I hate that she's not.

CHAPTER SIX

CARI

My gut churns. Bats, not butterflies, dance inside my stomach.

Why is this so difficult?

It's Monday morning, and I'm back at work, my fingers trembling as they hover over the smooth white envelope. Inside is my resignation letter, the one I finally wrote last night. After everything that's happened, I have to hand it in. I have to be done with this.

I should be furious, not nervous. After missing the concert, I should be storming in there.

Technically, this wasn't Jett's fault. I can't blame Brooke. She didn't hold me to ransom. I feel for her, and I see now that not only do I have an unhealthy attachment to her father, I also have one to Brooke.

But I'm only human, and I'd have to be a monster to not feel for that child. The truth is, I let my best friend down. I hate that I hurt Eliana and missed this concert that we'd been waiting fourteen months to see. If I'm not careful, I won't have a best friend at all. And then I'll truly be alone.

My fingers trace the edge of the envelope like it's a lifeline. And then I see him, striding into my workspace, wearing yet another one of his dark blue Armani suits that fit him like it was designed by the gods themselves. This suit is one of the ten he has in the exact same style and shade, all of them tailored to perfection. I've taken them to the dry cleaners myself more times than I can count. But somehow today, he looks even more devastatingly handsome. Like he knows exactly what he's doing to me.

He stops in front of my desk. This is not how it's supposed to go. He's supposed to breeze past me, muttering his usual distracted "good morning" without so much as a glance, heading straight into his office like every other day. That's the plan. I'm supposed to walk into his office, hand him the letter, and walk out with my dignity.

My heart skips. I can't do this now.

No. No. No.

I slide the letter under my diary, out of sight. My pulse races, betraying me.

He's too close and I can smell his aftershave again, a scent I recall each night I lie tossing and turning in bed. Spicy and intoxicating, it surrounds me like a spell I can't shake.

My heart slams against my ribs. I wish I had more control over myself when I'm around this man.

"Thanks again for coming to Brooke's party. I appreciate it." His voice is low, smooth, and it catches me off guard.

I glance up, forcing my eyes to meet his. "You already thanked me."

"Anna's back now, but you being there really made Brooke's day."

His tone is casual again, and the soft-hearted man from the

party is gone. The business-minded Knight is back to make my life miserable. I try to keep my voice steady. "I'm glad it did." I want to talk to him about Brooke, but this isn't the time.

"How was the concert?" he asks, again surprising me. This man is hardly ever interested in my life outside of the office.

"I missed it."

"What? How?" A shadow crosses his face, momentary but noticeable. His voice dips. "You told me you could still get there on time."

"I should have left earlier." I bite the inside of my cheek. *Don't say it.* Don't tell him you fell asleep on the couch, missed Eliana's calls, and woke up too late. Don't tell him how she went with another friend.

He shifts slightly, his hand resting on his hip. His watch glints in the light; expensive and sleek, just like everything else about him. And that aftershave completely fills the space between us, making my heart flutter.

Damn it.

I shouldn't still be attracted to him. But I am. Not just because of how he looks in a suit, or the way he smells when he walks past my desk.

It's more than that.

I remember moments. Him with Brooke, tender and protective. The way he cradles her when she's upset. Then there's the side of him that infuriates me. His temper and his sharpness when things don't go his way. But months ago, just after Mom passed, he did something kind for me. That memory keeps me tethered to him in ways it shouldn't. I keep replaying it in my mind; Jett with his arms wrapped around me as my body shook with sadness.

He was there for me when I lost the most important person in my life. That's what is imprinted on my mind more potently, more vividly than ever. I had a tiny crush on him before. Who wouldn't? You'd have to be made of stone for this man to not have an effect on you.

My earlier crush was manageable. It didn't mess with my head the way it does now. Now, it's like a part of him is attached to me forever.

"I'm sorry to hear that," he says, pulling me back to the present. "But I don't understand. Why did you miss it?"

His continued persistence to dig deeper starts to annoy me. Irritation bubbles hot under the surface. I'm tempted to snap a short answer. I've raised my voice at him before, once or twice, in moments of pure frustration. No one else dares to, but I have. And I've gotten away with it because he lets me. He treats me differently, and I don't know why.

I'm annoyed at myself, and I feel for Eliana and our now-precarious friendship. "I was just tired after the party," I say, my voice tight. "I should've had more energy, but I didn't." I need to give him my resignation. My obsession with this man is unhealthy. Brooke's also becoming attached to me, and I feel more torn than ever.

He looks genuinely disappointed. "I'm really sorry."

"It wasn't anyone's fault." *But mine.* I try to hide my anger. The Knights spell trouble and I need to find the strength and walk away. My hand inches toward the envelope hidden beneath my diary.

Just give it to him.

End this now.

But then he throws me completely off guard. "You always take on too much, Cari." His voice is soft, but it feels like he's scolding me. Like it's my fault.

But it is my fault I missed the concert.

Still, I can't believe what I'm hearing. "Maybe that's the sort of person I am," I snap, before composing myself. "I went because Brooke wanted me to come; that's what you told me."

He pinches the bridge of his nose. "I shouldn't have told you that. I feel like I put too much on you, and I'm sorry."

I blink a few times. Did this man get a heart and brain transplant over the weekend?

"You handled everything as brilliantly as you always do. The party was outstanding. Visually, it was a masterpiece. Brooke couldn't stop talking about it all weekend."

I'm not used to him heaping praise on me. I'm also not used to losing my temper. I can usually school my expression quite well, but right now I feel like we've switched personalities. "I'm glad she loved it." I'm reminded of why I did this in the first place.

"You took charge because Anna was busy, but … " He snorts derisively. "You're my assistant and not my nanny. I need to remember that."

I startle at his words. Did he really just say that? He's finally voicing the exact thing I've been telling myself over and over. I'm his assistant, not a babysitter. Not his personal fixer.

"Look," he sighs, wiping his large hand over his face. "I know how much you were looking forward to the concert. What can I do to make it up to you? Let me at least buy you some more tickets."

"You can't buy any more tickets," I scoff. "They were sold out within hours of going on sale over a year ago." Every time I think of the concert with Eliana and Bianca there, I feel more disgusted with myself.

Jett steps back and peers down at me, looking all smug as a hint of a smile plays on his lips. "I can *always* get tickets. How many do you need?"

"I don't need your money or your tickets, Jett." I want to scream. He doesn't get the point. These Knights are always about money, but this isn't about that. It's about my obsession with him, and how it always misfires on me. I hate that he riles me up. That he has such an effect on me. This man is bad for me. Because of him, I make decisions that are detrimental to my well-being. I can't do this any longer. I won't.

I'm just so mad at myself.

And I'm still not doing the thing that needs to be done.

Coward.

Chicken.

Weakling.

My hand twitches toward the envelope again. This is it. This is my chance to end it.

Before I can pull it out, Paul Knight strides in. His presence is like a storm, overwhelming the room. Big, booming, larger than life. He doesn't even acknowledge me. He never does. He's all business, all the time.

"You're back." He locks eyes with Jett. "We need to talk. *Now.*"

This man barely calls his sons by name, and they never call him Dad. They call him Father or old man, depending on the situation. I've never heard them talk about him in loving terms. It's always business with him, because nothing else matters.

"You missed Brooke's party." Jett's voice is tight, his face flushed with barely contained anger. I see the tension in his posture, the way his fists clench at his sides. The way his hand grips the handle of his black leather briefcase.

Paul scratches his nose, dismissive. "I was busy."

"She's your granddaughter. Couldn't you make time to show up?"

He eyes Jett like a hawk, sharp and cold, and looking as if he's about to swoop in for the kill. There's no warmth in him, no apology, no love. "I'll make it up to her. I had things I couldn't get out of." He brushes past the conversation.

"You should've made an appearance," Jett snaps, his voice rising.

"I couldn't." He's heading back out into the hallway. "I'm sure the kid didn't even notice I wasn't there. Come into my office, I need to talk to you about something important."

He disappears, leaving Jett standing there, his jaw tight, frustration radiating off him. With a heavy sigh, he follows his father, still holding his briefcase.

My resignation letter stays hidden, tucked safely away.

For now.

CHAPTER SEVEN

JETT

I FOLLOW MY FATHER INTO HIS OFFICE, MY FOOTSTEPS ECHOING in the cold, sterile space. The walls are lined with dark wood shelves, displaying trophies of power—artifacts from deals that broke men and made him richer. His massive desk commands the center of the room, a monument to his authority. There's no warmth here. It's all business. Behind him, clearly visible through floor-to-ceiling windows, the city stretches out.

He drops into his chair with a weary sigh, irritation etched into every line on his face. "Tell me about Monaco." He sounds like he's bored already.

I don't sit. I stay standing, arms crossed, jaw tight. "I was in the middle of a conversation with Cari." My voice is sharper than I intend. I hate that I followed him here, like I always do, like I'm still that obedient son chasing his approval.

But I'm angrier at Cari, at the way she snapped at me earlier. She's never talked to me like that before. I thought offering to buy more tickets would fix it, but she was pissed about missing that concert of hers. And yet I couldn't help but notice how she came alive when her temper got the better of her. A fire blazed in her eyes that made me take notice. Usually she sits quietly working away, head down. But seeing her all worked up, her breaths coming faster, her chest heaving a little in anger, I couldn't help but feel a lick of something tingling down my spine. Whatever it was, the unexpected arrival of my father poured water over it.

The man doesn't even blink. "Monaco," he repeats, his voice cold.

"You want to talk about Monaco?" My arms tighten across my chest. "How about you explain why you couldn't make it to Brooke's birthday party?"

His face doesn't change, but there's a flicker of something in his eyes. He pulls out his wallet, slips a hundred-dollar bill out, and slides it across the desk toward me. "Tell her Grandpa sent this."

I stare at the bill like it's poison. This man taught me that money solves everything, but I'm beginning to see that it's not true. He wants me to accept that this bill makes up for his absence. I leave it sitting there. "Monaco worked out. The contracts were solid, and I signed the deal."

"Good." He leans back in his chair, looking like he's finally gotten what he was after. "That's what I wanted to hear."

I stand there, silent. Waiting for him to ask about Brooke. To ask how the party went, or hell, to even ask about her in general. But he doesn't. He never does. He's shown about as much interest in her as he did in us when we were growing up.

"And you went with that ... that oncologist?" His voice drips with condescension.

My jaw clenches. He doesn't even know her name. Also, he's about two girlfriends behind. I dated the oncologist before

I met Dina. "Alicia," I say, teeth grinding. "Her name is Alicia. Try saying it. And she's an attorney."

He waves me off, like it doesn't matter. "You always go for the brainy ones. Is it serious?"

I bristle at the pointed interest in her, every cell in my body preparing for battle. Something is up. "What's it to you?"

"If it took you that long to answer, it can't be serious." His cold, steel-grey eyes hold mine.

My patience snaps. "Whatever it is, it's none of your business."

My father's eyes narrow, his voice lowering to that icy tone I know too well. "If it's just sex ..."

I flinch, my muscles locking up. That word, coming from him, makes my skin crawl. We don't talk like this. We don't talk about anything personal, *ever,* and certainly not about sex. It's very rare for this man to care or ask about our personal lives. Paul Knight is only interested in brokering deals and growing the Knight empire. An uneasy feeling in the pit of my stomach warns me that there's something behind his inquiry.

I exhale sharply. "I don't care what you're thinking. Whatever it is, I'm not interested."

"Arminio Oliveira." He throws the name out like it should mean something to me.

I frown, thrown off by the quantum jump in his conversation. "Who?"

"He's the head of a telecoms empire in Brazil. You recall my visit to Brazil recently? I met with him, and I truly believe that we could do wonders if we join forces."

What the hell? I try to connect the dots and fail. "Join forces? Are we going for another hostile takeover?"

His lips twitch into something resembling a smile, but there's no humor behind it. "He has a daughter. A beautiful,

Brazilian heiress. Unmarried. Not a dried-up spinster. Even I wouldn't do that to you."

A stone lands in my belly and sinks slowly as I stare at him silently, loathing taking up space inside me. No. I already know where this is going, and I'm not playing along. "No," I reply as it all starts to make sense. This is about money. It's always about money. A deal.

Another way to grow Paul Knight's empire. I want no part of this. I'm not averse to making money. We—Dex, Zach and I, and the others, Rio, Matteo, and Enzo—we all like making money. It's what we know, what we've been taught. "Whatever you're thinking, forget it."

"She's young and beautiful—"

"Stop." For one, I'm not in the market, two, I'm not interested, three, he keeps saying *young* but I'm thirty-three. "No. I said *no*." I growl. My pulse thrums in my ears. This is what he wants me to do. "I'm not interested."

"Think about it. Brooke needs a mother." His words hit me like a sledgehammer, knocking the breath from my lungs.

"A mother, not a mail-order bride, or whatever the hell this is."

"Think of it more like an arranged marriage. She's beautiful, smart and business- minded. She studied in college here, and now works in her father's business. You would have a lot in common. Our businesses could thrive. And … more importantly for you, Brooke would have a mother."

"You think someone that young is ready to become a mother to my daughter?" I glare at him, rage boiling under my skin. "As if you give a damn about Brooke."

"We could form an alliance. The Knights and the Oliveiras."

I'm intrigued at why he wants to make this match. "Why

not just a straight up hostile takeover?" We've done many of those before. The Knights often favor that approach.

"It wouldn't work as well, not in this situation. We don't know the market, or the country. We're foreigners in that world. It's better to have those people in place there while we take care of things here. When it comes to profits, we'd share them equally, of course."

"Profits?" I scoff. "What about people? And feelings? Don't they matter? And what exactly do you mean by *those people*?" He's already deciding the terms and conditions. I bet he hasn't even run them by the Oliveiras yet.

Dex hinted to me that the old man was up to something. Turns out he was right.

"It would be an easier way to get the same result."

"Easier, how?"

"Marry her. Keep it simple. You get a mother for Brooke and a wife for—"

"Keep it simple?" I bellow. "For fuck's sake." I slap a hand at the back of my neck.

"Brooke needs a mother," the old man says casually.

"As if you care what my daughter needs," I hiss.

His eyes flash, but his voice stays calm, controlled. "How dare you say that?"

"How old is she?" I challenge. It should be an easy question, given her recent birthday.

"Twenty-three, or twenty-four, something around that age—"

"Brooke," I bite out. "How old is *she*?"

Discomfort crawls in his eyes. "Six? Seven?"

My stomach turns. "She just turned five." My words are ice. I stand up to leave, needing to get the hell away from this man. If I continue to do what he wants, I'll end up no better than he is.

A ruthless, philandering, monster who is hell bent on growing his billions with no thought for people. Our family is broken. I can't end up like him, but at this rate, I'm on track to do just that. Brooke deserves so much more. I head toward the door.

"I'm not done with you, boy," he snaps, but I hear desperation, not strength, in his voice.

"I'm done," I growl. "You wanted to know about Monaco. Now you know."

"I'm not done with you!" he shouts as I open the door.

"There's nothing more to say. Don't talk to me about any *alliances.* I'm not interested. I'm very much in love with Alicia." It sounds odd even saying it.

"Love? Don't confuse sex with love," he screams after me.

"Like you did?" I throw back as I storm out of the door.

"You'll regret this," he snarls. That old son of a bitch.

I storm out. "I'm done with you," I mutter under my breath as I head back to my office. I don't give a damn about his plans, his alliances, or his twisted idea of what's best for Brooke.

I walk past Cari's desk and into my office. Slamming the door shut, I close my eyes and rest against the door, glad to be away from that monster who is my father. I don't love Alicia. I never have. We get on. She's good company and the sex is great, but I'm not in love with her. These feelings were hiding in my periphery, but the confrontation with my father has brought them to the surface.

I call Dex. He answers on the first ring.

"I just had a meeting with the old man," I tell him.

"Lucky you."

"I swear he drains all my fucking energy."

"That's why I stay out of his way as much as I can."

"Who the fuck is Arminio Oliveira?"

"He told you about that?" Dex sounds surprised.

"You knew?"

"Yeah. The old man wants you to marry his daughter as part of a business deal. Have an arranged marriage."

"When the fuck were you going to tell me?"

"I've been trying to get you to meet me for a drink," my younger brother shoots back.

I massage my temple gently, feeling a throbbing headache coming on. "I've been busy. Monaco, then Brooke's birthday."

"It's insane. We live in the same building."

He has a point. "So, you knew?" I ask, still in disbelief.

"Yeah. It's part of a business alliance. He thinks it would be good for both companies. An arranged marriage between the guy's daughter, and only heir to the fortune, and one of us."

"Of course he does," I mutter, my anger bubbling over as I lean against the door. "What the hell is wrong with him?"

"Since you're the oldest …" Dex drawls.

"Shut the fuck up." I hate the sound of this. Our father can't dictate the course of our lives. Not forever.

"Want to meet over a drink?" Dex offers.

"Maybe. Not today. I'll call you."

"There you go again, always too busy to meet me, brother. What if I came up to your place with a few bottles of beer? And a bottle of whiskey?"

"I want to spend time with Brooke. Maybe some other time." I hang up and sink against the door closing my eyes but all I see is Paul Knight. My father. The man I loathe.

A man who has no heart.

CHAPTER EIGHT

CARI

I'VE BEEN FILING PAPERS FOR THE LAST HOUR, MINDLESSLY going through the motions. It's dull, repetitive work, but my thoughts are elsewhere. I'm going to do it. I'm going to quit today. The decision pulses through me like a heartbeat, constant and unrelenting.

As soon as Jett gets back, it will happen.

The office has been unusually calm since he left for that meeting with his father. The peacefulness is short-lived because I hear Jett's heavy footsteps from down the hall. Without seeing him, I can already sense his mood. My stomach tightens and I brace myself because a storm's coming.

Sure enough, Jett barrels into view, his expression thunderous. His face is flushed, jaw clenched tight, and those eyes are as hard as steel, flashing with fury. He's in full hurricane mode, and I know better than to get caught in the middle.

He doesn't even glance my way, just storms past my desk.

The door to his office slams shut with a heavy sound that reverberates through me. I flinch, my fingers tightening around my resignation letter.

My well-thought-out but overdue plan just crumbled to ash. This isn't surprising. Jett and his father don't get along. None of the brothers do with Paul Knight, and for good reason. He's a manipulative bastard, always pulling strings behind the scenes. I steer clear of him, and thankfully my job doesn't overlap with anything that involves Paul directly.

Still, whatever just happened between Jett and his father has left him rattled. And Jett doesn't rattle easily.

I should just do it. Right now.

I look down at the letter in my hands. Maybe this is the perfect time. He seems off balance. With his defenses down, he might actually hear me. He might not fight me on it, not like he would on any other day.

But then doubt creeps in, and I hesitate. My pulse quickens, each beat telling me to just get it over with.

I inhale sharply, grab a pile of letters he needs to sign, and slip my resignation on top of the stack. My heart pounds as I march toward his office with a steely determination.

This is it. I'm going to hand it in. I walk into Jett's office and stand at his desk, just like I always do, but my heart hammers against my chest, erratic and loud.

This is my moment. He's not on the phone anymore, and it's finally quiet. I open my mouth, but the words refuse to come. My throat is so dry it feels like sandpaper. All I can hear is the boom of my heartbeat, growing louder, drowning out every thought.

"I can't sign anything right now," Jett growls, his voice low and rough, the kind that sends shivers down my spine. It's like a storm brewing, intense and swift, the way it always is when he's angry. He gets up and shrugs out of his jacket, tossing it onto the back of his chair, and I freeze, my mind going fuzzy. The way his broad shoulders move, the way his crisp white shirt stretches across his chest. It's ridiculous how I can't think straight when he looks like that. And the slight dusting of stubble on his jaw just makes it worse.

"Then I'll just leave them here, but there's something I need to—"

"Do something for me." He interrupts me as usual, and now he'll give me an order he expects me to follow without question.

Sitting back in his chair, he tilts his head slightly against the headrest. Something shifts in his expression. His eyes are a darker blue now, and glinting with mischief. "I've ordered something for Alicia, from Cartier. I need you to go pick it up."

Cartier, and Tiffany & Co. That's where he buys gifts for his girlfriends. I've been to these places so many times, collecting extravagant gifts for his parade of girlfriends. And now it's Alicia's turn. Of course, it is. "Not Tiffany this time?" I retort.

"I'd be asking you to go to Tiffany if that was the case."

"That is true." How I manage to keep my voice level is a miracle.

"Diamond and sapphire earrings," he says, as if he knows I was wondering. But I wasn't. I don't ask anymore. I never need to. It's always something sparkly, expensive. Just another trinket to keep them happy.

"Could you go now?" He glances at his watch. "Oh, and book us a dinner reservation at Lafont & Moreau for around seven."

The request feels like a slap, and the ache in my chest deepens. Dinner at Lafont & Moreau. Jewelry from Cartier. Alicia gets the diamonds and the fancy dinners, and I get the errands.

She no longer sounds like just another girlfriend. She's

getting more from him than any of the others ever did. My mind spins, doing the math. He's bought her the most gifts. Spent the most time with her. Taken her away more.

This is serious.

He's serious.

And then it hits me like a punch to the face.

He's in love with her.

And I recall how she referred to herself as the wicked stepmother in the washroom at Brooke's party. My stomach churns and I want to disappear, but I stand rooted to the spot, letting the feeling drench me. I have had enough.

"I'm about to go to lunch, Jett. I have plans to meet my friend." I don't, but he doesn't know that.

He sits up taller, clearly not expecting this reply. I've done his bidding for too long now, thinking I was weak and pathetic, believing I had no backbone. I follow orders and run his life, then pretend it doesn't hurt. But it does.

No more.

I'm out of fucks to give. I clutch the papers tightly in my hand.

"Pick up the earrings first." He dismisses me without even looking up and starts banging away on his computer, just like I knew he would.

I stare at his dark, silky hair. "Before I go, I have something for you." I'm determined that he knows.

He is forced to look up and then at the letter in my hand.

"I told you. Just leave it here." He motions to a space on his desk and goes back to his typing.

I set my letter down then turn on my heel and leave. Inside, my stomach churns, but it's not a crumbling, debilitating feeling, like I'm about to vanish into myself. This feels like roaring flames of a brightly burning fire.

And I feel like a phoenix rising from it.

All because I've finally done the thing that has taken me so long, *too long*, to do.

I've handed in my resignation and I finally feel free.

It's liberating.

Which is strange, because Jett doesn't even know what I've given him. I'm smiling from ear to ear when I flop back in my chair, feeling like a slab of concrete has been lifted off my shoulders.

The emotion is so profound that I start to laugh because I see glimpses of my future, of the flower shop I used to think about opening. I am now free to do something for me, for once.

The door to Jett's office opens and he peers out, his brows pushing together. He opens his mouth to say something, but words seem to fail him. He must find this *so* strange.

I quickly reach for my bag and make to leave. "I might be gone for a few hours," I tell him, suppressing my happiness. "It's going to be a looooong lunch."

His stony face is expressionless. "Enjoy," he says, before closing the door and vanishing from my view.

LATER THAT EVENING, I WALK THROUGH THE DOOR OF THE apartment I share with Eliana. She's waiting for me, her face lighting up the second she sees me.

"Did you do it?" She practically bounces with excitement.

"I did!" I pull out a bottle of fine champagne. I splurged a bit, because I have good reason to celebrate.

"You did it, hon!" Eliana screams, putting her arms around me. We jump up and down like kids, the champagne bottle still in my hand.

"You finally did it."

Eliana squeals and throws her arms around me again,

hugging me so tight I can barely breathe. "We have to celebrate! This is amazing! The first step you've taken to regain control of your life." She pulls back, beaming. "That man has worn you down, Car. You're finally breaking free."

I hand her the bottle, before taking off my jacket and collapsing onto the couch. "I took a long lunch," I tell her, as she begins to peel the foil and metal cage off the top.

"Yeah?"

"I called up the other assistants and they leapt at the chance to join me."

"Did you drink much?" Eliana asks, as the cork pops and I jump, feeling energized. Feeling like I want to pop myself.

Why does this feel so freeing?

"Nothing. Not when I'm working. We also didn't talk about work." I steered the conversation away from the Knight brothers because I didn't want to know what was going on behind the scenes. I was also afraid that I'd secretly let slip that I'd resigned, and I didn't want the news getting out before Jett discovered it for himself.

I want my resignation to hit him like a wrecking ball.

I've been so miserable working for that man. Not always, I remind myself quickly, because I've had some good times. Happy moments. I was good at my job, and paid well for it.

"To Cari Summers, the woman who finally found the courage buried deep within her." We clink glasses.

"To the best friend a love-drunk fool like me could have. Am I forgiven?" I plead.

"For missing the concert?" Eliana asks.

"I'm so sorry," I whisper.

"Don't you worry, babe. You're free now. You have your life back and we're going to celebrate!"

We both drain our glasses dry before Eliana refills them.

"Did Bianca have fun at the concert?" I ask. But Eliana has

turned the music on, and is blasting The Mayflies. We start dancing, moving around the room, jumping up and down.

She's recreating the concert I missed.

I love this girl so much.

We dance until we're sweating, refilling our glasses until the bottle is finished. Eliana pulls out a bottle of sparkling white wine from her handy stash in the fridge.

We dance and drink, and lose ourselves in the moment. For me, this is the best release from all the frustration that has burrowed deep in my body. I feel so free, and maybe it's because I'm leaving all that unrequited lust and the simmering tension behind. At least, I will in one month's time.

I fall back onto the sofa and think about my future. Plans start to form in my mind. Things that were seeded during the awful times at the hospital with my mom.

Eliana plops down beside me, her energy buzzing in contrast to my stillness. She doesn't know how far away I feel right now.

"Aunt Scarlett called," she says, referring to her as if she's her own aunt.

"Oh, shoot. I had a missed call from her."

My heart fills with warmth. Aunt Scarlett is my mom's younger sister. She's only a few years older than Jett. With her cute little pixie cut hairstyle, her tattoos and carefree life, she always checks in on me from whatever adventure she's having somewhere around the world. She's had a checkered history when it comes to relationships, which is why she's never settled down, but now she's happy going around the world on her motorbike with her new young stud.

"That's why she called me. She was worried when you didn't pick up."

"Is she okay?"

"She's fine. She was just checking up on you."

I love her so much. I love the women in my life: Aunt Scarlett, Eliana, Bianca.

"She says she might come by soon and wanted to know if you were here."

I roll my eyes. "Where else am I going to be?"

"You can be anywhere you want to be, hon. The sky is your limit. The world is your oyster." Eliana turns to me on the couch, tucking a leg under her. Holding her glass of sparkling wine. "Why so solemn, Car?" She picks up on something I can't name. A feeling of sadness lingering in the edges of my heart. "I know you've got it bad for your boss, but it's affecting you too much and your head hasn't been in the right place for a while. I'm glad you're leaving that toxic situation behind."

I flinch. I wouldn't call it a toxic situation, but my life has been stuck in limbo. First with my mom's illness, then with my obsession with Jett.

"I'm looking forward to the future." The thought of my resignation letter on Jett's desk where he will be sure to find it, has given me wings.

I just wish I could be a fly on the wall when he reads it.

CHAPTER NINE

JETT

As far as dinners with Alicia go, this one was definitely the most unexpected. Instead of going home for some hot sex, we are no longer together.

Of course, this all happens right after my disaster of a dinner with her, the one where I was supposed to give her the earrings. The ones I had Cari pick up for me.

I don't even know why I bought them. A desperate attempt to feel something, to pretend we were fine. Especially after my father told me about his batshit idea to marry the daughter of a Brazilian heiress for the sake of increasing our wealth.

When I pulled out the little red box, Alicia went pale. Fear flashed in her eyes, and I knew right then what she wanted to avoid. She didn't even try to hide it.

"I'm not ready to be a mom," she said.

"They're just earrings." I handed her the box. She hesitated to take it. Not exactly the reaction I'd hoped for, but it confirmed my gut instinct.

I took the box back before she could open it to see for herself, realizing in that moment that Alicia and I were over.

I bought the earrings out of some twisted form of protest, trying to prove to myself that I didn't have to follow my father's ridiculous plan of marrying for convenience. I didn't need the South American alliance, or whatever business venture he wants to rope me into. Maybe I was trying desperately to prove that I was unavailable faced with my father's proposal for me to marry someone I didn't know.

I had an idea that Alicia and I were drifting apart. I just didn't expect it to end so suddenly.

I'm not ready to be a mom.

Her words hit me harder than I expected. They opened my eyes, making me realize how far apart we really were.

It wasn't the earrings she rejected. It was Brooke. I knew it, deep down in my gut. I think I've known for a while now. The truth is, I wasn't in love with her, and nor was she with me. We were simply good together, and we had a good time. Unless we're away on a vacation, sipping fine wine and champagne, enjoying life and relaxing in a pool at an expensive resort, she doesn't want to be a part of my world.

She wants me, but not Brooke. It's like this with most of the women I meet. They don't want the whole package, but I don't come without Brooke. She's my world. My life. My everything.

Still, being with Alicia helped me in other ways, mainly that she kept me distracted from Cari. Helped me to keep my assistant out of my head. Alicia was never going to fit into my life long-term, but it was good while it lasted.

Because I didn't love her, it didn't sting too much. Her shock was almost comical. "You're getting the bill? We haven't even ordered the main dish!"

"You're right. This isn't going to work. I've lost my

appetite." I waved over the server, paid the bill and walked out, not looking back as she called after me.

I'm done with her.

And honestly? It's a relief.

I head towards our office building, needing to get some files. This day couldn't get any worse, because my father hit me with an unexpected trip to put some pressure on partners in Sacramento.

I have a feeling he's doing it to piss me off. I told him I need more notice as I don't like springing these trips on Brooke, but now I'll be glad to get away for a while and clear my head. It sucks to be away from Brooke so unexpectedly, but I'm going to make it up to her soon. I'll tell her tonight about the surprise I have for her.

I'm shocked when my father, Dex, and Zach walk out the revolving door. It's late in the evening and I have no idea what they're doing together. I wait for them, needing to know if there's a Knight family dinner tonight that I've forgotten about.

"Hey," Dex slaps me on the back. "What're you doing going back to work so late?"

"Yeah." Zach looks at me quizzically.

"Is there a dinner tonight?" I ask.

"You'd know if there was," my father replies.

"Then?" I feel oddly left out. What am I missing?

"Nothing much. We were discussing plans for expanding into foreign markets with the online learning sector," Dex explains. He's always so perceptive. He can sense my unease, and the question bouncing around in my head. What business are they talking about without me? With a slight shake of his head, Dex dismisses my concern. I wonder if the old man has been talking to them about the same marriage arrangement he's trying to force me into.

I don't even know if Zach knows about it.

"Are you set for Sacramento?" my father asks.

"You're going to Sacramento?" Dex looks disappointed.

"Got no choice. But yeah, I am. For a few days."

"We'll get those drinks when you get back," he says.

"What drinks?" Zach's gaze flits from me to Dex.

"You can come along too, little bro," Dex says in a Papa Bear voice, putting his large arm around Zach's shoulder.

"You didn't ask me, now you're just inviting me out of pity," Zach retorts, gruffly. Typical of Zach to feel left out. We all look at the ground because no one asks our father. I loosen my tie, feeling claustrophobic in the awkwardness.

"I only came back to pick up some paperwork." I make a move to go through the revolving doors.

"Come for dinner," Dex suggests. I school my face so that I don't look completely shocked out of my skin. They're having dinner with our father? On what is *not* a mandated family dinner night? Why the fuck would they put themselves through such torture? I'd rather have my toenails ripped out.

"I'm paying," our father says. "Roberto Vasquez is at The Resort this week."

"I don't have a fucking clue who he is," I mutter. But I have a feeling he's some famous chef my father adores, and The Resort is one of Manhattan's top restaurants.

"Wagyu beef." Zach licks his lips, trying to tempt me. He looks as happy as a puppy whose been handed a bone. Like this is a normal dinner with a normal family, and a normal father is going to treat them.

"I had dinner with Alicia." I smile and tilt my chin, locking eyes with my father.

"Don't forget what we talked about," my father says. I feel my brothers' questioning stares on me.

"We'll have a beer when you get back." I sense that Dex knows what this is about.

"I'll call you." Because I'm suddenly eager to find out what's so important that Dex is voluntarily agreeing to have dinner with my father.

Back in my office, I rip off my tie and open the top button of my shirt. Sliding off my blazer, I head towards my wet bar and pour myself a glass of whiskey.

What a fucking day.

Sinking into my executive chair, I let out an exhale before taking a big sip of the amber-colored nectar. I close my eyes and let it go down, warming my insides, providing the comfort I so badly need.

It's too much. Alicia. My father. The marriage plan. Going to Sacramento. I should go home to Brooke. I should get the hell out of here. Taking another sip, I decide to quickly gather the paperwork I need, but my gaze falls on the pile of letters Cari left behind earlier.

I move it closer to me, see the letter at the top, and quickly rummage through the rest. They're just letters I need to sign. But this ... the white envelope, is different. I pick it up.

JETT KNIGHT

is written on the cover in Cari's neat writing.

My heart trips a little. This feels personal. Intrigued, I rip it open in a rush to read what she says.

Dear Mr. Knight,

Please accept this letter as official notice of my resignation.

I will work my one-month notice period at the end of which I leave. In effect this makes my departure date to be August 17th.

Sincerely,
Cari Summers

She's leaving me?

I spring out of my chair. What. The. Fuck? I slap my hand to my forehead, the letter still in my hand as I pace around the room in shock. My stomach hollows out as I read it a second and third time.

I think back to our earlier interaction when she handed it to me. I was still worked up from the meeting with my father but she was perfectly fine.

How is that possible?

Me?

I'm not fine.

I can't wrap my head around the idea that she wants to leave me. How the fuck am I going to function without her?

I run my finger over her signature.

Cari Summers

When did she write this?

Why?

Where is she going?

Why is she going?

And why the fuck didn't she tell me in person?

Because I had her running around to pick up Alicia's earrings.

Then I made her book dinner for me and Alicia.

All that time this has been lying on my desk.

I drain my glass dry and pour myself another before sinking

back into my chair, thinking that just when this day couldn't get any worse … my world imploded.

CHAPTER TEN

JETT

"I told you about this months ago, Mr. Knight. It's my sister's wedding! I have the invitation to prove it. You said it was okay for me to take the time off."

I press the phone tighter against my ear, irritation bubbling up. I've had a brutal few days in Sacramento. My father knew exactly what a snake pit he was throwing me into. The management team hasn't been doing its job well, and sales are in the toilet. I think I've managed to figure out why, and put together a plan to fix things.

I wish I could say the same about the problem with my nanny. "But *three weeks*?" I try not to yell. "We're supposed to be going to Bermuda for three weeks."

"I haven't had a vacation since last year, Mr. Knight, and I told you."

Damn. I pinch the bridge of my nose, trying to think. I forgot. Of course, I did. And Cari didn't remind me. I've been in the Sacramento office for a few days now, maybe that's why. I rely on her for so much, and now everything's spiraling.

"You went to a bachelorette party recently," I retort.

"Yes. That was my sister's bachelorette party and I just went for the weekend."

"Can you at least come back straight after the wedding?" My voice edges on desperation.

"My entire family is flying in from all over the world, Mr. Knight. There are some things money can't buy."

I grit my teeth, frustrated. "You've put me in a difficult position, Anna." I have Bermuda coming up, business there that can't be delayed." I don't need more crap on top of the mountain of shit I'm already dealing with.

She doesn't say anything, but I can tell she's annoyed. Seems like a lot of people get annoyed when I talk to them. People like Anna, and Cari.

Cari.

I squeeze my eyes shut, not having slept well the past few nights. My assistant has left me in the lurch with her resignation. I spoke to her a few days ago about some files I needed her to scan and email over, but I didn't mention a word about the resignation letter. I want to ask her what the fuck she thinks she's doing, but that's a conversation I need to have with her face to face.

"If you go and you don't return by next week, Anna, I cannot guarantee that your job will be available when you come back." I can't lose my nanny too, so I threaten her hoping she'll relent. She'll have attended the wedding and seen her family by next week, and she can return in time for us all to leave for Bermuda. Does she really need to spend so many weeks with her family?

"You'd do that?" she scoffs, sounding defiant.

"Of course I'll do that. I run a business, not a summer camp."

"Mr. Knight, I put up with a lot. You're not the easiest person to deal with, and I know you'll struggle to find someone to replace me quickly."

"It's not impossible," I toss back, furious.

"Well then, I quit."

She hangs up. Just like that.

I stare at the phone, stunned. What the hell just happened? "What the fucking fuck?" I toss the phone down on the desk with more force than necessary.

I run a hand through my hair. Great. Not only has my assistant resigned, but my nanny has quit, too. I now have no childcare for Brooke. Just when I'm supposed to head to Bermuda for three weeks. My patience is wearing thin.

The phone on my desk rings. I grab it, barely holding in a sigh. "Yes?"

"Mr. Knight, the board meeting is about to begin," says the receptionist. I force a breath out, my frustration threatening to bubble over.

"I'll be there in five." I hang up, dragging my hand down my face.

With Anna quitting, I'm staring at another problem. I can't leave for Bermuda without Brooke. I won't do that again. She's getting older, and she notices these things. She said it to me the other day, with that look in her eyes, "Daddy, I don't see you a lot."

It gutted me.

Now, without childcare, I'm backed into a corner. There's only one person I can count on to pull me out of this mess. One person I can always rely on. One person who has one month left to work for me.

Cari.

CHAPTER ELEVEN

JETT

MY ASSISTANT IS THE LAST PERSON I WANT TO TAKE TO Bermuda for many reasons. But I have no choice. Anna's quit, and I don't have time to hire someone new on such short notice. Certainly not someone I trust with Brooke.

I step into the office, unfamiliar tension coiling in my chest, something I haven't felt in a long time. I pull my usual act together, striding in like I own the universe, but inside, I'm anything but steady. My mind is on overdrive. I've been burying thoughts I shouldn't have been having for months now. Ever since Cari's mother passed, she's become a different version of herself. Stronger, but more vulnerable. It's messed with my head, and now I'm stuck in this impossible situation, and to make matters worse she's handed me her resignation letter. I had no idea that she was unhappy working for me. It hurts more than it should.

I haven't been able to sleep properly in days, trying to figure out why she wants to leave a well-paying job with good perks. I brace myself as I come out of the elevator and walk down the hallway that leads to her office space. Walking past her desk daily to get to my office just adds to my torment as does having to see her numerous times a day, while also knowing that she's sitting just outside my door.

It's becoming harder to shut her out of my mind.

She's standing by the tall filing cabinet, her back to me, and wearing a charcoal gray pencil skirt with a black satin sleeveless blouse. Her hair is pinned up in that neat, tidy way she always does.

It shouldn't affect me, but it does. I try not to think about what it would look like if she let that auburn hair tumble over her shoulders.

But I do.

Damn it, I do.

The idea that she's leaving me gnaws at my stomach. She has such a good deal here, better than she could get anywhere else, but if she wants to go, I can't force her to stay.

Except … I *don't* want her to leave.

She turns around, and her eyes lock on mine as she catches me staring. I freeze for a second, cursing myself. She blushes, her cheeks turning the lightest shade of pink.

"Y-you're back," she stammers, her voice shaky. "I wasn't expecting you until tomorrow."

"Nice to see you, too," I say, my tone too casual, too easy, because I'm pissed she caught me ogling her.

I grit my teeth, forcing myself to focus. The situation is fucked, thanks to Anna. I won't drag someone Brooke doesn't know into this trip, not when she's been through enough change already. It's not fair on my little girl.

"I've got too much shit to deal with, and I need last year's Marsh report," I say, sounding more clipped than I mean to.

I've got a mountain of work to deal with in Bermuda, and I can't afford distractions.

She hesitates for a second before nodding and rushing to get it. I walk into my office and exhale. I've been walking a tightrope with her for too long.

There's something between us, something I've buried under the guise of professionalism. I've been harsh, deliberately so, to keep that distance, but it hasn't worked. She's been in my head for months, and now, the idea of asking her to come to Bermuda with me doesn't feel so smart.

I take a deep breath, pushing the thoughts aside as she knocks on my open door. I order her to enter. She steps in, holding the report, her expression composed, but her eyes quickly scan my face. I'm already on edge, and seeing her only sharpens it.

At some point we need to talk about that resignation letter.

"That was fast," I murmur, slipping off my jacket and throwing it over the chair. I turn to look out the window to collect my thoughts.

"I didn't want to give you an opportunity to yell at me." There's a hint of humor in her voice, though I can sense some tension lurking beneath it.

When I turn around, she's watching me, the same way I was watching her earlier. There's something in the way her eyes linger, a brief flicker of heat that she quickly hides. It seems like this is something we both feel. Even if it's true, I know I can't act on it.

All morning, I've tried to come up with a solution to get around this. I want Brooke to come with me, and the only way I can do that is if Cari comes too.

"The Marsh file," she says, placing a folder on my desk.

"Sit down." I clear my throat and force myself to look away.

I shouldn't ask her what I'm about to ask, but I'm really stuck, and I have no other option.

CARI

JETT CATCHES ME OFF GUARD WHEN HE WALKS INTO THE OFFICE looking as though he owns the world.

He's wearing a tailored suit that hugs his broad shoulders, the crisp white shirt open just enough to make my heart skip. He's effortlessly gorgeous, and the way he moves, it's as if nothing in the universe could ever touch him. Confidence radiates from him like he's untouchable. The master of everything.

I bet he proposed to her.

That thought punches me in the gut, hard. The image of him handing Alicia a ring burns in my mind. He asked me to pick up earrings for her, but I wouldn't be surprised if he already bought the ring. I've convinced myself that's why he's walking in now looking so smug and relaxed, like his life is falling perfectly into place.

I'm so glad I handed in my resignation letter. There's no going back now. I've had this stupid crush for far too long. I've occasionally caught him looking at me in a way that makes goosebumps prickle my skin and every hair on my body stand on end. It electrifies me, and takes my breath away. Sometimes I've let myself believe that look is for *me* but then he coughs or averts his eyes, or orders me to make yet another dinner reservation, and reality slams back in place.

My crush is not reciprocated. It never will be.

"That was fast," Jett says, his tone as condescending as ever.

"I didn't want to give you an opportunity to yell at me," I reply, keeping my voice as steady as possible, though inside, everything is spiraling. I'm waiting for him to say something about my resignation letter.

He shrugs out of his jacket, and I try not to focus on the way his shirt clings to his body as he eases into his chair. There's no way this ends well for me if I let myself linger on how good he looks. My mind is scattered, trying to hold onto my purpose, but his presence makes it so hard.

The muscle in his jaw flexes, and it confuses me because I sense that he doesn't like something. I'm suddenly fearful that I have a booger on my face, or a muffin crumb hanging off my lip. I'm self-conscious again, and I'm so sick and tired of being sick and tired of the feelings I have for this man.

I place the folder on his desk. "The Marsh file."

"Sit down," he orders, his voice controlled but laced with something else unfamiliar. Softness.

I hesitate. I won't be ordered around by him. Not now that I'm officially leaving.

"Sit. Down," he says again, more firmly. "We need to talk about your resignation letter."

I reluctantly do as he says. "I wondered when you were going to bring that up."

He steeples his hands together, looking clearly surprised. "I'm disappointed you didn't tell me face to face. You owed me that much, at least."

My insides almost empty. Why does this sound so personal? I owed *him?* I'm his assistant. That's all I am to him. "I handed you the letter last week and I tried to tell you, but you had me running around doing Alicia errands."

"*Alicia errands?*"

I fold my arms. "The name fits, no?"

"Why are you leaving? Do I not treat you right?" I'm slightly bewildered that he's more concerned about this and hasn't asked me what an Alicia errand is.

"I need to leave, Jett. I've put up with your arrogance for too long." The words tumble out of my mouth, and for once, they sound strong and certain. Stronger than I feel. I cross my arms, bracing myself.

"My arrogance?" He sits up straighter, his eyes narrowing as if I've just thrown him off balance. His face drains of color, and suddenly, I feel like I've hit him with a sledgehammer. "I'm your boss. I don't know what you mean by my arrogance." His reaction is completely different from what I expected. I thought he'd be annoyed, maybe even indifferent. But he looks hurt.

"A bit of appreciation would have been nice."

His mouth falls open, before he quickly composes himself again. "I've always appreciated you, Cari." The telltale muscle flexes along his jawline again. "Why?" His eyes lift to mine.

"I've been wanting to leave for a while now." I hold his gaze, even though I'm falling apart inside.

"You have? But why?" He sounds genuinely surprised and confused. And he's white as a ghost. Dear God. What is this? This isn't the reaction I was expecting. I thought he'd be shocked, maybe thrown off balance for a few seconds. I'm great at my job. I help him with his work and sometimes his private life. But I am replaceable, and for a man like Jett, replacing me should be relatively easy.

I have no idea what to tell him because I most certainly can't tell him the truth. "I need a change of scenery," I mutter, knowing how pathetic that sounds.

"Then take a vacation."

I want to get away from you.

"I don't need a vacation. I need a new job." One where my boss respects me and treats me with decency. Even as I think these thoughts, I know they're not true. Jett Knight does give me respect, even if he's coarse and demanding. The real reason is something I can never tell him. And now that he's going to marry Alicia, I can no longer put myself through the torture of buying lingerie for her, or picking up trinkets worth more than my rent for a year.

I cannot do that to myself any longer.

He looks stunned, like he can't process what I'm saying. "You're doing an exceptional job, Cari. I don't understand."

I feel the tension radiating from him, and it's almost too much. This isn't how I thought this would go. He's not supposed to care this much.

"I'm leaving, Jett. I've given you my one month's notice."

"You can't leave." His voice is firm, but there's an undercurrent of desperation I've never heard from him before. This is so new to me, Jett Knight looking lost and bewildered. I almost feel bad for him. "And I don't accept your resignation."

"What do you mean you don't accept it? You have to!" But I understand it then. He's proposed. This means that he'll need me to coordinate the celebrations. I laugh, more in disbelief than amusement. "I can leave, and I will."

He leans back, his eyes searching mine, as if trying to figure out what's really going on. "What can I do to make you stay?"

The question throws me completely. This is not the Jett I know. He never asks. He orders. But now ... he sounds almost vulnerable.

I sit back, stunned. I expected him to accept it and bark out more chores for the day. He seems to *care*. As if this news has, dare I say it, made him sad.

"There's nothing you can do. I need to move on." The

words hang between us. I am perplexed by the turn this has taken. "Mr. Knight?"

He looks up at me and the corner of his lip curls upwards. "You only call me Mr. Knight when I've pissed you off." Mischief swirls in those blue irises. "It can't be a change of *scenery* or *environment*." Clearly, he's having difficulty believing me. He has good intuition for a man. "Don't I pay you enough? I've given you two pay raises each year."

Which, as Eliana told me, was a lot.

"Money can't buy everything," I say. "I want to leave. I *need* to leave, what with everything going on ..." I look away, because I don't want to share my plans with him. What I intend to do for myself. The florist kiosk seems like an escape route from this. From Jett. A new start after a very tough time.

"I know you're going through a hard time. It's been a difficult year for you, and the last six months ..." His voice trails off, but he looks at me earnestly. His face turns apologetic, as if he's sorry for bringing back my sadness. "If you need more time off, Cari, I'm happy to give it. Take as long as you need."

It's not about taking time off.

It's about getting away from this man who messes with my head.

"Are you still having your counselling sessions?" he asks.

"They stopped last month." I've been going every week for the last six months, and it has helped, but I don't want to depend on anything like a crutch. I'm grateful that I had them, but I need to start living my own life rather than dwelling on the past and if I'm going to be serious about opening my own little flower kiosk, I need to get away from Jett.

"I can—the *company* can—pay for more. Whatever you need. We take care of our employees."

If he's hoping to dangle that in front of my face or scare me into thinking that I won't have the same perks and benefits elsewhere, it's not going to work. "I'm good, thanks. I just need to leave. It's what I want."

He stares at me for a moment, his jaw tight, then he stands and turns to the window, the silence between us heavy. When he finally speaks, his voice is somber. "I need you to do one last thing for me."

Here it comes. I knew it. He's only holding onto me because he needs something. I sigh in dismay, and force myself to stop staring at his back. At those wide shoulders, and the body that tapers to a perfect V at the hips.

"What now?"

"Anna quit."

"Anna quit?" Though this isn't surprising.

"She can't just take off for weeks—"

"I'm pretty sure she let you know."

"She's gone and I need you to come with me to Bermuda. I have a lot of business to tend to over there and I can't reschedule. I can't find childcare for Brooke on such short notice. We leave next week on Tuesday, and I don't know anyone else Brooke would want to stay with."

My heart sinks. Of course, it's about Brooke. "I'm not your babysitter, Jett. I'm your assistant."

"I know what you are to me." He grits his teeth together, hissing in a tone which startles me.

"Can't you ask Alicia?" I can't hold back the bitterness in my tone. "Surely she'll jump at the prospect of yet another vacation to an exotic island?"

His eyes widen at my insolent tone. "We are no longer together."

I sit up straighter, his words making me jolt. "Oh?"

His eyes meet mine, and I see something in them that I

didn't expect. It's not hurt, but hardness. "The only person I can think of ... to fill that role ... is *you*."

The air vacuums clean out of my lungs. It takes a moment to steady my breathing. To process his request. To understand what it means. He and Alicia are no longer together. And now he's asking me to go on this business trip with him. Me and Jett, with Brooke. Away from work. On a beautiful island. Somewhere hot and exotic. For three weeks.

I cannot go. No way. "You can find a replacement," I rush to assure him. "You just need to hire a nanny. You can afford it."

"It's not about the money."

"It's always about the money with you," I throw back. Because I know I'll be leaving, I've lost control over my mouth.

He looks genuinely hurt. "I can't leave Brooke with someone I barely know, not while I'll be in meetings and tending to business overseas. Especially somewhere that she's not familiar with and doesn't have family around her."

"Why not ask Alicia to help out, if you're so desperate?" I suggest, examining his face for signs of trauma, wanting to know more about that situation. Why did they split up? And when? This has come as a complete shock to me. He seemed quite taken with her. Who broke it off? Inquisitive thoughts circle around in my brain like vultures.

"I just told you. We're no longer together." He lifts a piece of paper from the desk and pretends to read it. I know he's pretending, because it's an address. A scribble. Nothing of any importance.

But I'm dismissed, it seems. That's his usual way of letting me know I can leave.

"You didn't propose?" The words tumble out before I can

stop them, my mind spinning. I've spent the last week lying in bed, imagining it all. Jett proposing to Alicia, the perfect romantic scene, and the sinking feeling that follows every time I think about it. Each scenario is more painful than the last.

His head snaps up, and his sharp gaze locks onto mine. His expression is a mix of confusion and something that almost says, *what the hell are you talking about*?

"Propose?" he repeats, his voice tinged with disbelief.

Heat rushes to my face, a blush creeping across my skin. "I thought … maybe … you went to dinner, and then … well, you didn't come back to the office." My words sound ridiculous even to my own ears, but I can't stop them.

"I had business in Sacramento." His tone is clipped, and he shakes his head like he's trying to piece together my jumbled logic. "We spoke, you and I. I needed you to scan some contracts and email them to me, remember?"

I nod, feeling utterly foolish. Of course, I remember. But I also assumed she might have jetted off with him, like she usually does. Unsurprisingly, my imagination just ran wild, spinning out a narrative that wasn't real.

"You feeling okay?" Jett's voice softens, his brows furrowing as he watches me.

My heart does an awkward flip, and suddenly everything shifts. The realization crashes down on me.

He's single.

He's not with Alicia anymore.

Can I really trust myself to go on this trip with him? To spend that much time around him?

"I didn't want to ask you," he says, looking away for a moment, almost like he's searching for the right words. "But I doubt Alicia would want to take care of Brooke."

There's a bitterness in his tone when he says her name. He mutters something under his breath, something like, she doesn't give a damn about her. It's clear now that he's not with her anymore.

But he also didn't want to ask me.

I feel a strange mix of emotions. Part of me wants to be annoyed, to be angry that he's putting me in this position. He's just a selfish, stubborn, controlling man. But another part of me, one I don't like to acknowledge, starts to feel sorry for him. This man is in crisis mode.

I sigh. "Okaaay. I'll do it," I say, begrudgingly. "But on one condition. You accept my resignation."

His eyes snap back to mine, and he seems to hesitate, as if he's feeling uneasy. As if he doesn't like my condition.

"I'll accept it when we get back." His voice is measured, almost calculated.

The words confuse me. I frown, trying to make sense of them. When we get back? "No, Jett. I now have three weeks left, on account of you going away to Sacramento. I handed in my resignation last week."

"We leave in five days. I will need time to find a new nanny, and with spending so much time in Bermuda, I won't be able to do that effectively. Just start the clock from when we leave, please? It gives me a week when we get back. You'll be leaving, my nanny has left. I'm going to be a wreck."

I know he is.

I look at the calendar on his desk, pretending to make a difficult decision. At least I have a week before we leave, which means I can go shopping for a few things this weekend.

"Unless you have another job lined up. I wouldn't want to mess up your new start date," he says, sounding miserable.

"No. It works." I cup my chin thoughtfully. I don't have a start date to consider because I'm not looking for a new job. I have other plans.

He looks shocked, then composes his expressions instantly.

"Of course, while in Bermuda, you'll be expected to look after Brooke on the weekdays, but you'll have the weekends and evenings to yourself to do as you wish. It will be a vacation for you. A change of environment and scenery that you seem to want so badly." There's a prickliness in his tone.

He picks up a pen. "I'll double your wages for the trouble," he adds, his tone now brusque and businesslike. It's like he's flicked a switch and returned to the Jett I know. The one who's always in control, always one step ahead, and always transactional.

"You've already increased my wages," I murmur, still thrown off by the moment we just shared. After Mom's diagnosis, he quietly gave me a raise. I noticed it on my next paycheck, but he never mentioned it. He took care of me even when I didn't ask him to. Then after she passed, he gave me another raise. When I questioned it, he told me I was due as I'd been working so hard, even under my difficult circumstances.

"I will give you a little bonus for the trouble, for you having to go to Bermuda and having to delay the start of your notice period."

"If you insist." Who am I to argue with that? I'll have more money saved up, and I have no idea how long it will take to start up my business.

"Deal," he says after a long pause. He holds his hand out to me. For a moment, I'm stunned. Then I take it, feeling the warmth of his skin. His hand is firm, strong, and his fingers curl around mine, sending a jolt through my entire body. It's like holding a live wire.

I pull my hand away, but the sensation lingers, and my heart races. The muscle in his jaw flexes as he watches me, his eyes darkening for a second. He doesn't want to take me to Bermuda. I know it. But he doesn't have a choice.

He looks down at his papers.

"Thank you," I say, my voice quieter now. "I appreciate it."

He nods, still focused on whatever paper he's scribbling on. "Close the door on your way out."

I turn to leave, my mind still spinning from the conversation. I glance back at him but he's already moved on. He's back to work, as if our conversation didn't faze him.

CHAPTER TWELVE

CARI

How is it that I've resigned from my job, but now I'm going on a three-week trip to Bermuda with my boss and his daughter?

How did this even happen?

How will I explain this to Eliana?

I think back to what Jett said, that he *didn't* want to take me, but he had no other option. His words keep replaying in my mind, over and over, along with the other bombshell. He and Alicia split up. I was so convinced they were celebrating together in Sacramento. I imagined everything, but I was wrong. He was on a business trip, and now he's single again.

And I'm going to Bermuda with him, for three whole weeks.

I freeze when I open the door to my apartment and hear laughter from the kitchen. That voice, it belongs to my aunt.

She's here!

A surge of happiness swells in my chest. "Aunt Scarlett!" I

rush into the kitchen, my heart light with excitement. I can smell chicken and dumplings. Something wholesome and hearty and just what I need.

Eliana is chopping vegetables at the counter, and Aunt Scarlett is stirring a pot on the stove. It smells so delicious.

My mood has made a one-eighty flip at seeing two of my favorite people. My aunt grins as she turns to me, enveloping me with a hug so tight that we hold it and stand like that for a few moments. I breathe her in and smell my mom. Reminders of her come flooding back—comfort, love, home. A bittersweet wave of happiness and grief washes over me. There are similarities in their faces and mannerisms that make me yearn for my mom. I feel happy and sad all at once.

"Cari, my sweet girl, I've missed you." Aunt Scarlett squeezes me tighter.

"I've missed you, too," I murmur into her shoulder. I've always loved Aunt Scarlett. She was there for us, for me and Mom, through everything. She finally releases me, and I step back, my heart feeling fuller. Aunt Scarlett is the adventurous one, always off on her latest journey, but she's never far away when I need her.

"How are you doing, hon?"

"I'm good," I reply. "How about you? How was your trip?"

She smiles, her eyes twinkling. "Finished the Appalachian Trail. I'm heading out again soon, but I wanted to see you first."

"We're making dinner," Eliana announces proudly, shooting me a playful look. "I told her you resigned."

My aunt throws an arm around me, grinning. "Well done! I'm so proud of you for doing what's best for *you*."

Guilt creeps up my spine. She doesn't know about the crush I have on Jett. Sure, she overheard me once, after Mom passed. I told Eliana about how Jett had shown a different side to him that day. How he was gentle, kind. Ever since then, my feelings for him have shifted to something deeper. But that's not something I can talk about. Not in front of Aunt Scarlett.

"About time, too." Eliana steps forward, beaming. "I bought some more wine when I heard Aunt Scarlett was coming, so we're going to celebrate some more tonight!"

I chew my lower lip, wondering how to tell them. "Something happened."

Eliana tilts her head as if she's bracing for the news. My gaze ping pongs between her and my aunt, who goes back to stirring the pot.

"What happened, hon?" she prompts gently.

"I … I …" I can't get the words out.

Eliana's eyes narrow at me. "Tell me you resigned. Don't tell me you lied to me."

"I did resign, of course I did!" My heart pounds in my chest. "But now … now I'm going to Bermuda with Jett for three weeks to take care of Brooke. Anna quit, and he doesn't have anyone else to look after her so I have to go." The words rush out of me.

Eliana's jaw drops. She stares at me, her expression one of disbelief. "You don't have to go. You're an assistant, not a nanny."

"Who's Brooke? Who's Anna?" Aunt Scarlett asks, clearly confused but still stirring the pot like everything's fine.

"Why am I not surprised?" Eliana mutters, her voice thick with disapproval. She sets the knife down on the counter, her expression hardening.

"Let's eat. Dinner's ready," Aunt Scarlett says, sensing the tension.

"We can't eat, Aunt Scarlett!" Eliana cries. "Didn't you hear? Cari's going to Bermuda with her *boss*."

"She's still working for him, and she still has to work out

her notice period," my aunt says, ever the diplomat. She sets the pot on the table.

"She's in love with him! She has been for months, possibly years. He breaks her heart every day she goes into that office. This is bad, Aunt Scarlett."

My mouth falls open. Eliana looks guilty, as she should, ratting on me like that. I know she did this out of love and concern, but I didn't want her to burden my aunt with that news. Also, I wanted to keep it between me, Eliana, and Bianca. Now my aunt will worry even more.

"You must be hungry, hon," my aunt says, a slight grin on her face making me wonder if she already knows.

"She's hungry for Jett Knight." Eliana grumbles under her breath, her arms crossed over her chest.

My aunt shoots her a warning look. "Let's just enjoy dinner. I'm back on the road soon, and I want to spend time with you girls before I head out again."

I step closer to my aunt, grateful for her warmth and presence. She makes me feel like I belong to something, like I still have family. Eliana is my best friend, but there's something about Aunt Scarlett that makes me feel like home isn't so far away after all.

Aunt Scarlett uncorks a bottle of red wine, and pours glasses for all of us. We sit and eat, I feel full already because my heart is content. Sitting around me at the table is proof I am not alone.

Unlike Jett.

My thoughts drift to my boss. When I lie in bed tonight, I will wonder how I'll survive the Bermuda trip.

"This is good!" I say, savoring my meal.

"Ummm hmmmm." Aunt Scarlett licks her lips and sighs. "I miss this." She places her hands over mine and Eliana's. "I love sitting down and having you girls to come back to. Being on the road all the time is fun, and coming back is the best, but …" She pauses, and stares at the table, as if trying to compose herself.

"I know," I say softly. The void is hard to fill. We all carry the emptiness in our lives after my mom's death. "I think of her all the time, too," I say, a tear rolling down my cheek.

She presses her lips together and inhales a deep breath, as if reaching inside for reserves of courage. "Your mom would like this, us all sitting here together, having dinner. I just wish …" She nods and looks away, unable to continue, and when she looks up, her eyes are shiny.

"She would," I croak. I don't know when the pain of this loss will subside. My wound is still raw. "You know we love it when you come back, Aunt Scarlett." I manage a smile.

My aunt put her freelance work on hold when mom was ill. Now she's away a lot, which means that mom's old apartment stays empty most of the time. I still go there occasionally, when Aunt Scarlett is away, to soak in the fading but familiar scent of the place my mom occupied. I love that my aunt always pops up in my life, often unexpectedly. She's more like an older sister to me than an aunt. There was such a big age gap between her and my mom. She never wanted to settle down, get married, or have a family. She's a maverick, wild and carefree and her life always sounds like an adventure.

Eliana's face is hard. She's eating quietly and drinking wine as if it's water. We finish the meal in silence.

"How handsome is this boss of yours?" Aunt Scarlett asks, sipping daintily from her wineglass. I blush, hoping the wine is what's making my skin heat.

"Handsome enough that your niece has been crazy about him for years. Years, I tell you," Eliana says.

"Is that right?" Aunt Scarlett eyes me, the corner of her lips turning up.

I shrug, hating the interrogation.

"I saw him at a Christmas party, and he's ... not bad," Eliana admits, reluctantly. "Dark hair, strong jaw, mesmerizing eyes. Built. Wide shoulders. The man looks pretty sharp in a suit. He's tall and—"

"Sounds to me like you've also got the hots for him," my aunt shoots back, mischief swimming in her eyes.

"I absolutely do not," Eliana protests. "But I can see why Cari's obsessed with him."

"I'm not obsessed!"

Eliana tsks, shaking her head. "You're so far gone, babe, but you are. Bianca and I have dissected your behavior, and we wholeheartedly can confirm that you are indeed obsessed."

Aunt Scarlett chuckles, then sips her wine. "He sounds pretty delectable to me. A hot boss. Mesmerizing eyes. Tall and built. What's not to like?"

"Aunt Scarlett!" Eliana slaps the table. "You're not supposed to encourage her!"

"Why not?" Aunt Scarlett winks at me. "Why can't a girl have some fun?"

Eliana's blinks furiously. "Because he's ten years older than her and—"

"Experienced." My aunt nods, approvingly.

I spit out my wine, and grab a napkin to wipe my mouth.

"He has a daughter!" I retort.

"I heard. And his wife died a few years ago."

I blink as my aunt recounts this news. "How do you know?"

"Your mom told me."

"My mom told you?" Something tells me that Aunt Scarlett has an idea about my crush. "How? When did mom tell you?"

She sets down her glass. "Toward the end, hon ... toward the end, your mom told me that your stories about work entertained her, but she was also worried about you. Though, she seemed to think that your boss was a good man, and he'd been good to you." Her mouth twists as if she's about to say something.

"What?" I frown, because I sense she's hiding something.

"Your mom was very lucky to get onto that clinical trial so quickly, and it was a miracle that there were no extra costs. I mean …" She pauses.

"What, Aunt Scarlett?" That trial was the breakthrough we'd needed. It was our last hope, especially when the surgery didn't remove the whole tumor and the chemo after didn't entirely kill it off. This was a new clinical trial, in early stages of development, but within a week she was on it. I didn't think about it much at the time. I'd assumed it was just luck.

"The doctor said a kind benefactor made a huge donation to the hospital and certain strings had been pulled. Seems like your mom was one of the lucky ones."

I sit back in relief and shrug. "There are plenty of philanthropists in New York."

She nods. "There are."

I swallow the lump in my throat when I think of my mom. I used to tell her about Jett Knight, but I never told her outright that I had a crush on him. I guess instinct told her. It hurts to know she was worried about me. That's the last thing I wanted.

"He's always dating," Eliana adds.

Aunt Scarlett waggles a finger at me. "You can't go there if he's attached."

"Oh, I wouldn't worry about that. Cari has no plans to get anywhere near him, even if he was attached!" Eliana cries. "Our girl likes to wallow in the misery and torture of unrequited love."

I fix my friend with a pointed stare, irritation crawling along my spine at the poor opinion she has of me.

"He's unattached at present." I lift my wine glass smugly.

Eliana snorts. "He's ... *what*? What happened to Alicia?"

"Who's Alicia?" Aunt Scarlett asks.

"A hotshot hot attorney," I reply. At this they both look at me like I am nuts.

"I hear you on the misery and torture." Aunt Scarlett points her wineglass at Eliana.

"They broke up recently," I clarify.

"Sweet!" Aunt Scarlett points her glass at me. "You can have some fun now, if things progress on vacation."

I want to fan my face, but dare not with four eagle eyes trained on me.

"Aunt Scarlett! Do not encourage her. A man like Jett Knight would eat her for breakfast and spit her out by lunchtime," Eliana protests.

"Then she'll surely enjoy the breakfast." My aunt winks at me. Eliana howls with laughter, thumping the table as she doubles over.

"Aunt Scarlett!" I am shocked.

"She's right." Eliana has a shit-eating grin on her face. "You've handed in your resignation, and he's taking you on vacation—"

"He not taking me on vacation. He's taking Brooke. He promised her, but Anna quit. Anna is Brooke's nanny," I explain to my aunt.

"That man can't keep the nannies around for longer than a year, but Cari's been there for a few years now. This might be your chance to get him out of your system," Eliana says to me, "because, boy, do you need to get this dinosaur out of your system."

"He's not a dinosaur," I protest. "He's only in his thirties!"

My aunt and Eliana exchange looks.

"Told you," Eliana says.

Aunt Scarlett opens a second bottle of wine and refills our glasses. "When are you leaving?"

"On Tuesday."

Eliana bangs her wine glass down. "Tuesday! You don't have much time to get prepared."

I need to buy some clothes this weekend, because I don't have anything suitable to wear in Bermuda. I'm not sure what Brooke and I will do, but I'm assuming it will involve going to the beach. I'll need a new swimsuit and something suitable to wear if we're invited out in the evenings.

"Look, my sweet girl," Aunt Scarlett says. "You've resigned. You're an adult. He's an adult. If you want to have fun, go for it."

I shake my head because this is the most ridiculous thing my aunt has ever said. Even if I fantasize about these things, reality is something else. Jett Knight is certainly not interested in me. Even if I were the last woman on earth.

"I was going to go shopping for a few things," I murmur.

Aunt Scarlett claps her hands together. "We're going shopping, *together*. I'll be back in a few days, and then, girls, we're going to make a weekend of it."

"I don't need *that* many clothes," I say.

"Don't you worry about that," Aunt Scarlett says, giving herself another helping of the chicken and dumplings.

CHAPTER THIRTEEN

CARI

I'VE NEVER FLOWN FIRST CLASS BEFORE, AND IT FEELS LIKE
I've stepped into a different universe.

Not only is Jett's bodyguard traveling with us, but
everything is sleek, luxurious, and intimidating. Even Brooke
seems to sense I'm out of my depth. She looked at me earlier,
wide-eyed, when I asked her if they always handed out noise-
canceling headphones to everyone. They look like they cost
more than my grocery bill. And when she told me the seats
turned into actual beds, my mouth fell open.

"Is this your first time on a plane?" she asked, her innocent
voice cutting through me.

"No," I replied, though the truth is I haven't flown much.
Just once, when I was ten. Mom and I flew to Hawaii to visit
Aunt Scarlett who was living there at the time. I was so excited
about the whole trip, the plane ride, the time with my aunt, the
beaches, everything. It was also the time I nearly drowned. And
when we came back, I remember being just as thrilled to get

back on that plane, but we had a lot of turbulence. I got scared. People screamed when the pilot told us to fasten our seatbelts. I still remember the fear in my mom's eyes.

That was the last time I flew anywhere.

Now, here I am, completely out of place. From the moment we boarded, the flight attendants have pampered us, offering things I didn't even know you could get on a flight. I feel like I don't belong in this world. Like I've stumbled into a life that isn't mine.

We fasten our seatbelts and prepare for takeoff. As the plane glides along the tarmac, I start to have palpitations. Beads of sweat break out along my hairline. My insides hollow out. As the plane speeds up, Brooke looks out of the window, marveling when the plane leaves the ground and ascends into the sky. I close my eyes and grip the armrest as fear engulfs me. I relive that last flight and the screams are loud in my head. My eyes squeeze shut and I see my mom's scared face again. I'm deep in my own private hell trying to breathe through it and find a place of calm.

But then I feel something warm on my hand and I hear Jett's voice. I must be dreaming again.

"Did you remember to bring the Steele reports with you?" he asks. I slowly peel my eyes open, and am shocked to see my boss. He's crouching on the floor, staring up at me, his eyes filled with concern. His fingers are softly placed over my death-grip on the armrest. "Wh-what?" I manage to say, wondering what he's doing here. I'm shocked to hear him talking about work.

"Sir, we're still taking off. Please return to your—" A flight attendant hovers by us.

Jett barely glances at her. "I'm in the middle of something. Please leave." Her mouth falls open, but she returns to her jumpseat. It seems everyone does as he commands.

My breathing is fast and shallow. "Did you … ask me for a … *report?*" Or did I imagine that?

His blue eyes lock onto mine. "The Steele reports. I need them tomorrow. Did you bring them?"

My mind rushes to the list he gave me, and I'm certain I packed everything on it. I nod. "I'm … I'm sure I did." But now he has me second guessing myself and I try to remember what I packed.

"Daddy, is Cari scared?" Brooke asks.

"She's fine, sweetie." He smiles at his daughter.

"You look sick," Brooke says, stroking my arm, completely unaware of the panic I'm trying to cover.

I breathe in slowly, then out slowly. "I'm … okay." My voice is shaky and unconvincing.

"She's going to be fine," Jett assures her. "The report, Cari. Think. Did you bring it? Because I need it to present to the CEO tomorrow."

My mind rushes back to the office, and now I'm worried. I never forget anything, and he's never had to ask me something like this. He knows I'm organized, that whatever he asks, I do. "I did. I'm pretty sure I did."

"And the MacPherson binder?"

I try to recall the list of things Jett asked for. I nod. "I'm pretty sure I—"

"The Hogarth files?"

He's bombarding me with so many questions and I try to think, worried that I might have forgotten something. No, I packed everything he wanted. "I did. I got everything."

His sleeves are rolled up, and his forearms flex slightly. Hot damn.

Is he stroking the back of my hand?

I glance down, and find that he is.

The seatbelt sign turns green, and I hear a message saying

we can unfasten our seatbelts. "Look Daddy, clouds!" Brooke points out of her window.

"Pretty cool, huh?" Jett gets up off the floor, moving his hand away from mine. "Relax," he says, pinning me with his gaze. "We're up in the air now. It's going to be okay."

My jaw drops and I watch as he brushes his hand over his trousers, removing the dust, not that I can see any. His cologne wafts over me again and I watch, dumbfounded, as he ruffles Brooke's hair and tells her he needs to get back to his work.

I watch him walk away to his seat a few rows in front of us. He's so tall and commanding and I notice the female flight attendants ogle him without even trying to hide it. Just before he sits down, he turns and glances at me. My heart leapfrogs in my chest and I look down at my lap, hating that he caught me staring at him again. I mentally go through the list he gave me yesterday and try to remember if I got everything he needed.

What a thing to ask me, now of all times.

JETT

DEX NEEDED THE FAMILY JET, SO HERE WE ARE, FLYING FIRST class. I hate flying commercial. I hate being cramped, surrounded by strangers. It's suffocating. I made sure the seat next to me is empty. I paid for it to remain empty because that's the only way I can tolerate a commercial flight.

With my brother off handling business in London, I had no other choice. Still, the flight isn't too bad. Cari's not in her usual office attire. She looks different; more relaxed, less buttoned up. Like she did at Brooke's party. Something about seeing her like this, out of the usual professional setting, catches me off guard.

I glanced over to check that she and Brooke were okay during takeoff, but I saw Cari, her face pale, her eyes closed, gripping the arm rest as if her life depended on it. She has a fear of flying. I didn't think she had a fear of anything.

I rushed to her side instantly and tried my best to distract her. With Cari, I know that means talking about work. Making her think she might have forgotten something important.

It seemed to work.

So far the trip is going smoothly. My little cherub has been on cloud nine ever since I told her Cari was coming. She hasn't even asked about Anna, which worries me. Anna took care of Brooke for over a year, and yet my daughter doesn't seem to miss her.

Maybe that's on me. I've had a different nanny for Brooke every year since Sophia passed. Three years, three different people. That can't be normal.

My exes used to tell me I'm too demanding. Too demeaning. An arrogant, patronizing asshole to the people who work for me. Maybe there's some truth in that, but I can't focus on it now. Every nanny I've hired eventually gets fed up and leaves for an easier life. I'll deal with hiring someone new once we're back. I'll have to choose more carefully this time. I'll ask Cari to handle the interviews.

I look over at Cari and Brooke again. Brooke wiggles out of her seat to explore the plane, passing me and planting a kiss on my cheek as Cari dutifully follows her, like she always does, reliable and steady. One of the few constants in my life.

I'm halfway through my report when Brooke taps my arm. "Daddy, the washrooms are fun!" Her little face glows with excitement.

I blink at her, momentarily thrown by the joy radiating off her. "Fun?" I ask, trying to shift my attention to her.

"Yeah! The doors are bendy!" Her eyes are wide with wonder, as if this new discovery is the most exciting thing in the world.

I can't help the small smile that tugs at my lips. She's so innocent, so free from the burdens of adult life. No worries about business deals, shareholders, or family drama. She doesn't know how complicated the world can be. She doesn't have to deal with the moron who is her grandfather, as she doesn't see him often. She only knows that she has me, and my brothers.

But is that enough?

That thought gnaws at me, keeping me up at night. I ponder where the past five years have gone, and how before I know it, my angel will be a teenager. How am I supposed to help her navigate those years?

My father's words echo in my mind, no matter how much I try to ignore them.

Brooke needs a mother.

I look at her now, so happy and carefree, and it hits me how little time I spend with her. Yes, I see her every day, but it's fleeting. Just moments. This trip is supposed to be different. I promised myself I'd make more time for her, that I'd be more present. This is supposed to be our time together.

"She's obsessed with the toilets," Cari says, her voice soft as she approaches me. The pen I'm holding slips from my fingers, falling to the floor. Before I can reach for it, she bends down, scooping it up.

I wish she hadn't. The way she leans over gives me a glimpse of her pink satin bra. My throat tightens as I tear my gaze away.

"Here." She hands the pen back to me with a slight smile,

looking relaxed for once. Her hair's down, falling in soft waves around her shoulders, not pulled back into the neat, businesslike bun she usually wears. It makes her look softer, more approachable. Beautiful.

I glance at my report, desperate to refocus on numbers and projections, anything to distract myself from the direction my thoughts are heading. This trip is going to be a problem. I knew it the second I asked her to come. I should've hired someone else. Anyone but her.

"Can you stay close to Brooke?" I ask, my voice rougher than intended.

Her expression falters and she nods before going back to Brooke, her presence lingering long after she's gone.

I feel like a complete idiot.

Cari didn't want to go on this trip. She tried to get out of it, and I practically forced her into coming. I dangled her resignation in front of her and used it to push her into agreeing. What kind of person does that?

Someone like me.

A selfish moron who uses people.

And, because of that, the last person I should be on an island with is coming to Bermuda with me.

CARI

Brooke is obsessed with the washrooms.

She keeps running back and forth, fascinated by the sliding doors and the way the toilet flushes. It's strange for a kid to be so excited about a washroom, but I get it. I was excited about everything the first time I flew, too. Even though this isn't her first time flying, I wonder if it's her first experience on a commercial airline. Jett usually takes the family jet.

The family jet. I can't even begin to imagine what that's like. A private plane with rooms, sofas, and tables, like an apartment in the sky. That's Jett's world. A world I'll never fit into.

I went shopping with Eliana and my aunt and bought a few outfits that will hopefully be fine, given that I don't know what to expect on this trip. Whatever happens, I'm definitely not taking any of Aunt Scarlett's advice.

Instead, I'm just thankful that I'm going to spend most of my time with Brooke. Jett says she likes to spend time at the beach.

But I'm better prepared now, having picked a good, sturdy tankini top and shorts as a bathing suit. My aunt and bestie, however, sneaked the tiniest, barely-there bikini into my suitcase. I already had some nice dresses, but they made me buy a couple more.

I lean against the wall while I wait for Brooke and let my imagination run wild. Replaying a completely fictional scene in my head, like I am prone to do, heat creeps up my neck. In my mind, Jett cups my face, gently unbuttoning my blouse. It's ridiculous, really. Mom always said I had an overactive imagination.

"Hot?" Jett's voice breaks into my thoughts, startling me.

I whip around, my heart leaping into my throat. Holy hellfire.

"A little," I manage to say, lying through my teeth while my heart beats wildly in my chest. This man is so up and down. I didn't like the tone he used on me earlier, asking me to stay close to Brooke.

His eyes trail down towards my collarbone, before quickly

snapping up to my face. "Odd. The AC's blasting. You sure you're not coming down with something?"

"No. I'm good." I raise a hand to my neck, trying to steady myself. The fantasy of Jett unbuttoning my blouse vanishes in an instant, replaced by the all-too-real version of him standing in front of me, hands in his pockets, and looking way too good for my sanity.

This is dangerous. Being thousands of miles away from home, with him, without Eliana's sensible advice to keep me grounded, is going to be torture. I can already feel myself slipping, letting my imagination take over. If Jett hasn't figured out my feelings for him by now, he will by the end of this trip. I turn toward the washroom and knock on the door, eager to escape. "Brooke, hurry up, sweetie."

But instead of Brooke, a pretty young woman walks out, tall and svelte, flashing me a dazzling smile. "Oh, I'm sorry, I thought …" I stammer, spinning around in embarrassment, only to see there's another washroom directly across the aisle. Of course. I rush over, but it's empty. My heart sinks.

Where is she?

I dart back to our seats to find Brooke, sitting happily, coloring like nothing happened. "Brooke," I breathe, relief flooding me, especially after her father told me to stay close to her. I don't seem to be doing a great job of that. "I thought you were still in the washroom."

She barely glances up. "I was."

I feel like a complete fool. I've lost my mind, and we haven't even landed yet. Just as I'm settling back into my seat, Jett walks over, a frown on his face. I shrink further into my seat.

"There you are," he says to Brooke, his voice light with relief.

I force myself to meet his eyes, knowing I messed up. "Sorry. It won't happen again."

"It's a plane, Cari. She can't go far. Relax." His tone is calm, almost soothing, but it doesn't stop the embarrassment from burning through me.

Then, the pretty woman who came out of the washroom appears beside Jett. "I see you have an empty seat next to you." She nods in the direction of where he was sitting.

He smiles politely. "I do."

She gives him a flirtatious smile and sashays past us. Has he already found a replacement for Alicia?

"I'll come by later, sprout," he says to Brooke, and leaves us.

My stomach twists as I watch him. My torture begins, causing my mind to spiral as I imagine all sorts of scenarios: Jett, the pretty woman, the mile-high club.

Great, just what I need. More fuel for my overactive imagination. I let out a long breath. This trip is going to be a disaster. I can feel it already.

CHAPTER FOURTEEN

JETT

A WOMAN WHO SEEMS TO THINK SHE KNOWS ME IS HOVERING around my seat.

She's vaguely familiar, though I can't place her face or remember her name. The last thing I need right now is small talk. I hate interruptions. I hate people being familiar and forward. Huffing out a breath, I walk back to my seat. Her eyes slide to the vacant spot next to me and she gives me that overly familiar smile. "Mind if I join you for a bit?"

Irritation prickles under my skin. "I was working on something."

She flashes a smile that's meant to dazzle, but it only grates on me. I almost shake my head, ready to give her a what-the-fuck-do-you-want look, but she keeps smiling. Coy, flirty, but something about it feels manipulative.

"Ah, come on, Mr. Knight," she coos, sliding into the seat beside me without waiting for permission. "You can't be working the entire time."

I grit my teeth. "Actually, I can."

Thankfully, first class seats have a good amount of space between them, so I'm not crammed up next to her. But she's still too close.

She orders a martini from the flight attendant, while I try to ignore her presence and focus on the report in front of me. The flight attendant turns to me with a smile.

"Can I get anything for you, Mr. Knight?"

Every woman smiles like that.

Except Cari.

A knot forms in my chest at the thought of her. I should've just let Brooke down gently, told her Cari couldn't come. Anything would have been better than this tension I'm going to have to endure for the next three weeks.

"Tomato juice with some Worcestershire sauce," I mutter.

The woman beside me giggles. "Teetotaller, huh?"

"Just for this trip," I reply tightly.

"I haven't introduced myself." She launches into an introduction that goes in through one ear and out the other. Her name slips past me and I pick up my pen again, my fingers itching to return to my report. Cari's right, I can be rude. I know that. I've heard it from enough people to know there's truth in it.

But she's taken the brunt of that more than most. I've been short with her more times than I can count and she just takes it in her stride, calling me out on many occasions. My red-headed spitfire is the only one who'll stand up to me.

The woman beside me keeps talking, but I have no interest in the conversation. I turn to her as she babbles on, something about her job. There's something vaguely familiar about her face, but I don't want to engage enough to figure it out. Then it hits me like a punch in the face. I met her at a gala dinner. She's a journalist.

"Please leave." I cut her off mid-sentence.

Her eyes widen, clearly shocked by my bluntness. The martini glass dangles in her hand, her long lashes fluttering. "I'm just being polite, passing the time—"

"I told you, I'm busy." I know how these people work. Eliciting stories, taking snippets of conversation out of context and making a fictional story. I avoid them at all cost.

She huffs, her lips tightening. "So rude."

"So nosy," I shoot back, waiting for her to get the hint and leave. But she just sits there, sipping her martini like she belongs by my side.

I stop typing and square my gaze at her. "You're sitting in my seat."

"It's empty," she says, as if that justifies her intrusion.

"Just the way I like it."

Her mouth opens, but then snaps shut. I lean forward, my tone dropping. "If you don't move in the next thirty seconds, see that man over there?" I nod in the direction of my burly bodyguard sitting a few rows over.

A flash of uncertainty crosses her face as she looks at him.

"I'll have him move you," I say flatly.

Her cheeks flush pink. "You wouldn't."

"I would. I've done it before. Do you want to make headlines on social media?"

Her lips part, but she doesn't say a word. She stands up, still holding her martini, and slinks away, clearly embarrassed.

I sink back into my seat, exhaling in relief. Peace. Finally. I return to my report, letting the steady rhythm of typing calm me down. A moment later, my bodyguard comes over.

"Everything okay, Mr. Knight?"

"It is now," I mutter, not bothering to look up.

Once I finish a few more lines of the report, I stand up and glance toward Cari and Brooke. They're sitting together, heads close, focused on something. Brooke's coloring, and Cari's probably smiling at her in that effortless way she has of making my daughter feel so at ease.

For all my grumbling, I did the right thing in bringing Cari. Brooke adores her. Cari always makes an effort with her, and she's just so good with her. I need to make sure I don't piss her off enough that she bolts before the trip is over.

My mind drifts to why Cari wants to leave her job in the first place. After everything with her mom, maybe I pushed too hard. She didn't give me a good reason, just that vague "I need a change of scenery" line. I didn't understand it at the time.

But now, it's starting to click.

She wants to get away from *me*.

I've been too demanding, too rude. Maybe on this trip, I should try to be nice.

CHAPTER FIFTEEN

CARI

"I'M SO SLEEPY, DADDY," BROOKE MUMBLES, RUBBING HER eyes, her voice heavy with exhaustion.

I had to wake her to get her off the plane. She must have been in a deep sleep because rousing her was a challenge. It was only a short flight, but we had to wake up early this morning, and Jett said she went to bed late because she was so excited. Now, she's clinging to her father, her little body limp with fatigue.

"Come here, princess," Jett murmurs, scooping her up effortlessly.

A few people swarm around us as soon as we step off the plane. One of them grabs Jett's laptop case and briefcase. Another offers to take my backpack, but I wave them off. It feels strange to have someone offer to carry my things. "Where are we going?" I whisper, glancing around. "Don't we need to get our luggage?"

The thick, salty air of Bermuda hits me like a wall. It's hot and humid, and I instantly feel sticky. Brooke's face is flushed, her hair messy and damp from the flight. I must look just as bad, maybe worse, but I don't care.

Jett, on the other hand, looks completely unbothered, like he didn't just step off a flight. His sleeves are still rolled up in that casual, effortless way that drives me crazy. I glance around, half expecting to see the woman from the plane, but she's nowhere in sight. Good.

"Pleasant flight?" Jett asks, leading me down the steps.

I force a smile. "Great," I lie. I lost my appetite and didn't eat much, nor did I have any breakfast before we left. Now I'm exhausted, hungry, and completely out of my element. I'm just overtired and crabby, but I made a decision while watching Brooke sleep like an angel. I'm going to make the most of this trip. I've never been to Bermuda, and I'll probably never go again. I looked it up online, and it's one of the most beautiful places on earth. I'm going to soak it all up and enjoy myself, just like my mom would have wanted me to do.

"Where's your friend?" I blurt out before I can stop myself, the words slipping past my filter.

Jett glances at me, confused. "What friend?" he asks as we get into a sleek black SUV with tinted windows.

I feel stupid now. I've never asked him about his women before, but already I feel a change in my mood. Like Aunt Scarlett says, I've resigned and I'm leaving. While I most definitely won't be taking her advice to *go for it*, I'm not going to be careful with my words around Jett. "The woman who sat next to you on the plane," I say, trying to sound casual.

Jett raises an eyebrow but says nothing as the doors close behind us. I try not to squirm under his gaze. Brooke is still nestled against him, half asleep with her head resting on his shoulder.

"Shouldn't we go to baggage claim?" I glance around,

realizing we didn't follow the rest of the passengers. "For our luggage?"

"Someone will handle it." His tone is calm and assured, as if this is just how things are done in his world. "Trust me, it's taken care of."

I blink. Is this what it's like in first class? People just handle things for you?

"But ..." I'm worried. I'm on an island with a man I barely know outside of the office, and I don't know anyone here. I feel safe with him, but ...

As if reading my thoughts, he reassures me. "The luggage will be brought to us within the hour."

A driver opens the door for us, smiling at Jett like they're old friends. "Good to see you again, Mr. Knight." The driver and Jett exchange brief pleasantries and then we step into the car.

I feel even more out of my depth. This world of drivers and people whisking bags away is far removed from anything I know. I hesitate for a moment, feeling a knot form in my stomach.

"You okay?" Jett's voice pulls me from my thoughts.

"Yeah," I mumble. "I just ... I'm not used to this."

His gaze softens for a moment. "Relax, Cari. Everything's taken care of. You'll get used to it with time."

Brooke stirs, her little face scrunching up in frustration. "I wanna sleep," she whines, clearly unhappy about being disturbed.

"Then sleep, princess," Jett whispers, smoothing her hair back, and just like that, she's out again. When her head lolls to the side he gently pushes it to the center so that she doesn't cramp her neck.

My heart clenches at the sight. This side of Jett, the gentle, caring father, is the one that gets to me every time. It's the side I like. It's the side that makes me feel something more than just attraction.

He catches me staring, and I quickly look away, embarrassed. He tilts his head, studying me. "What friend?" he asks again, and I wish I hadn't brought it up. I feel silly now that we're in the cool air-conditioned car.

"The one who sat next to you."

He scoffs, shaking his head, but doesn't offer an explanation. That tells me everything I need to know. He got her number. He'll probably hook up with her while we're here. The thought makes my stomach twist. I remind myself that when I come back from this trip, I'll have a week left at Knight Enterprises, and I won't have to see this man again. I won't have to be tortured. I won't be hurt. I won't have to sit there crying, dying inside, as my heart shatters into a million pieces watching him with his latest lover.

He looks at me. "Did you get any sleep on the flight?"

I can't tell if he's being nice or mocking me. "No. I didn't realize it was such a short flight. I was reading."

"Anything interesting?"

I hesitate. Do I tell him about the domestic thriller that I'm racing through? No. This is already too weird. The two of us, sitting here with Brooke asleep between us, driving to a mansion in Bermuda. It feels too intimate. Too much like something I've imagined in one of my daydreams.

"Nothing you'd like," I finally say.

Amusement flickers in his eyes. "Try me."

His voice sends a shiver down my spine. Oh, dear God. We never used to have these kinds of conversations back in the office, not even when he'd ask after my mom while she was really sick. Unless I count the day she passed. That day was different.

But before I can answer, the SUV comes to a stop. Brooke

stirs again, still groggy. Jett picks her up effortlessly, and we step out into the warm Bermuda air.

A group of staff greets us, smiling warmly at Jett and marveling at how big Brooke has gotten. They talk to him like they've known him for years, and I stand off to the side, feeling like an outsider.

I glance at the mansion in front of us. It's massive, like something out of a celebrity magazine. But it's not the size that has me in awe. It's where its situated. The home is nestled near the coast, overlooking the turquoise waters of the ocean where pristine white sands turn the scene before me into something that could be a postcard. This is a multi-story mansion, and its coral-hued limestone walls glow softly under the bright midday sunlight. The roof, painted white, gleams against the vivid blue sky.

A circular driveway leads up to a grand entrance, where towering mahogany doors are flanked by bright pink flowers spilling down the walls.

As we walk closer, I see a white limestone plaque mounted on one wall with the name *Aurora* elegantly carved and painted in a soft shade of gold.

I take a deep breath, feeling more out of place than ever. Jett introduces me as Brooke's nanny, and doesn't say anything about me being his assistant. I guess it's not relevant, especially since I'll be leaving the firm soon after we return.

We step inside and my breath steals from my lungs. The inside is as spectacular as its exterior. I look around at the polished marble floors and the sparkling crystal chandelier that casts shimmering light across the room. My gaze takes in the sweeping staircase with wrought iron railings leading to the upper levels. The walls are adorned with elegant, understated art. Pictures of flowers, the sea, houses.

"I'll show you to your room," Jett says, cutting through my thoughts.

"I can do that, Mr. Knight," one of the housekeepers offers, but Jett shakes his head.

"I'll do it."

I follow him, feeling like I've stepped into a dream. The house is beautiful, grand, and so different from my apartment back home.

Brooke's room is huge, with an adjoining door that leads to what I presume is my room.

Jett lays Brooke gently on the bed, brushing a strand of hair from her face. "She's exhausted," I whisper, not wanting to disturb the moment.

"Completely," he agrees, but his phone rings before he can say more. He holds up a finger, excusing himself as he steps out to take the call.

I'm left standing in the massive room, looking out at the view. I groan inwardly. I'm going to be sleeping here and waking up here. I'm going to be surrounded by Jett twenty-four seven for what now seems like such a long time. Once, this would have been the stuff of my dreams, being dropped into some billionaire's fairytale.

But now, it's not a fairytale.

It's real, and I'm not sure I like it so much.

CHAPTER SIXTEEN

JETT

I HANG UP ABRUPTLY, PUNCHING A BUTTON TO END THE CALL with my finger.

The old man never lets up. We've barely arrived and he's hassling me about an email he sent.

Have I read it?

Can I give it some consideration while I'm here?

This is important.

I didn't read his email. I skimmed through it late last night.

He's offering me ten million dollars if I agree to this arranged marriage, and he wants my answer by the time I return to New York. It sounds like he's in a rush.

It would be a real marriage, he says. But with no strings attached. Something fake that we'd need to do for a year, but the specific terms of the deal could be ironed out to suit me.

I shiver in disgust.

I couldn't do that to Brooke.

But she would have a mother.

I don't want a mother for Brooke to be *bought* or temporary. This isn't what she needs, and also, I don't want someone like that in *my* life. It's the first time it hits me that money can't buy everything.

My father's demands echo in my head, and no matter what I do, it's never enough. He always talks business, pushing me into meetings I don't need, deals I've already wrapped up. When it comes to control, the man can't help himself.

I exhale, rubbing my forehead. I'll deal with this when I return. There's no point reasoning with him when I'm so far away. I'll kill this plan when I see him next.

As I glance out the window, I feel the heat from the afternoon sun, its rays shining over turquoise waves. This trip should feel like an escape, but it's already turning into another battlefield, just in a different setting.

I check with my bodyguard. "Has the luggage arrived yet?"

"Yes, sir. I've already moved it upstairs."

"Thank you."

I head back upstairs. Brooke is still sound asleep in her bed, her little chest rising and falling in steady, peaceful breaths. I lean down, brushing a kiss on her cheek. She doesn't stir. Good. She needs the rest. Tonight's barbecue might be more than she can handle.

As I turn, I notice the adjoining door is open. Cari's standing by the window, staring out at the ocean, completely unaware of me as I observe her. She seems lost in thought, with a dazed expression on her face. I can sense that she feels out of place here, and this might have been too much to put on her. I should have just accepted her resignation instead of binding it to a favor.

Every time we're in close quarters, something shifts between us. The walls I've built around myself are crumbling piece by piece. I clear my throat. "I trust the room is fine?"

She spins around, startled. I didn't knock. I should have, but there are times when I feel an unspoken connection between us, and I feel it now, on this trip. Sometimes, she just knows I'm there before I say anything. There are too many moments like that lately. Moments I shouldn't dwell on.

"It's wonderful." Her cheeks turn pink like they always do when she's flustered.

"I gave you this room with the connecting door to Brooke's. Figured you'd want some privacy, but you'll still be close enough to check on her."

Her smile is tight, a little awkward. "This is great. Thank you. It's … it's a beautiful place.".

She's not wrong. The Knight mansion is one of those rare gems; it looks like a spectacular show home but is very much lived in and loved. The tropical blooms, swaying palm trees, and manicured gardens stretching towards the ocean give it a light and airy feel and inside the grand and opulent home is filled with precious memories of a much loved childhood.

We spent many happy summers here and it makes me think of time spent with my mom, Dex, and Zach. Unfortunately, those memories are faded and blurred. Nothing is in sharp focus. I can barely recall my mom's face or fine features. It's all based on what I've seen in old photographs. I remember that mom was happy here, as were we. But all the pictures are of her and us, and our father is not in any of them. There's also not a single picture of the two of them together.

Cari lets out a soft, nervous laugh, her hand brushing a stray strand of hair behind her ear. "What's so funny?" I ask, tilting my head.

"It's … just that ... what's not to like? My entire apartment could fit in this room." She gestures around, her eyes wide and filled with that disbelief I've seen so many times.

I remember her apartment well. "You think so?"

She gives me a wry smile. "You have no idea how most people live, Mr. Knight."

Her bluntness catches me off guard, though it shouldn't. She's always spoken her mind, about business, at least. But she never comments on personal things. On relationships. On me.

I bite back a sharp retort. "I see the luggage is here," I say, redirecting the conversation. "Good. You'll need a change of clothes for tonight."

She frowns. "I will? For what?"

"We've been invited to a barbecue."

Her eyes widen in surprise. "A barbecue?"

I nod. "One of my old friends is hosting us. I've got some business to handle."

"Oh." She hesitates, her voice softer now. "I didn't realize you would start working straightaway."

"I know this year has been tough on you. And I haven't exactly made it easier." Hell, I've probably made it worse. I was so stressed about the Vanhelm deal, and it brought out the worst in me, in the way I treated her. I've been trying to make up for it ever since.

She blinks rapidly, like she's processing my words, but then she changes the subject. "Sorry, I'm jetlagged and overwhelmed and hungry."

"Jetlagged after such a short trip?" It was just over two hours. Brooke has probably worn her out, when she was awake. "Get some rest. If you're hungry, just go down to the kitchen and get the house staff to make you something."

She looks at me as if I've asked her to land on Mars. "Get them to make me something?"

"They're here for whatever you need."

"I'm not used to asking people for things."

"You're not used to this kind of life," I say, a half smile

forming on my lips. "But get used to it. No one's going to let you make your own sandwich here."

Her expression changes, something in her eyes rejecting what I've just said. *She's not like the others, Jett. Remember that.*

Most women I know, hell, most women I date, are already part of this world. They get it. They thrive in it. But Cari? She's different. She's always been different. And it's becoming harder to ignore.

"Are you okay?" I don't want her to be uncomfortable here.

"I will be once I've gotten my bearings. Do I really need to be at the barbecue?" Her voice sounds a little too hopeful. I sigh. Of course she'd say that. We don't spend time together outside of work. We don't socialize. I didn't think this through. "You do, because of Brooke."

Her shoulders sag, then she nods like she's defeated. "Okay."

I turn to leave, but I can't shake the feeling that I've said all the wrong things today. Or maybe it's not what I've said, but what I haven't.

***

CARI

I SHOWER, THEN STRETCH OUT ON THE OVERSIZED, LUXURIOUS bed, but my eyes stayed wide open, fixed on the ceiling. I was waiting for Brooke to awake from her nap.

Every so often, I sit up to stare at the ocean through the huge windows. The view takes my breath away each time because it's just too beautiful to be real. Being here feels like stepping into a dream, until Jett's face pushes its way into my thoughts again. Then it all fades.

There's something happening between us, something strange. I keep saying things I wouldn't normally say, or overstepping boundaries I shouldn't. But it's not just me. Jett's been ... off, as well.

He mentioned my mom, touched on what a hard year it's been for me. He even admitted that he hasn't been easy to be around. For sure he hasn't. He's been an absolute pain in the butt.

Since my mom passed, I've felt numb, muted. That numbness is probably the only thing that's kept me from breaking under Jett's sharp tongue. But here I am now, trapped in the Knight mansion. Trapped in *Aurora*. What a pretty name for a house. Being here feels too close, to him, to all of this. I can't seem to get far enough away to breathe. It's dangerous, being around him all the time.

I miss home. I miss Eliana. I miss Aunt Scarlett.

I hear a patter of footsteps before Brooke bursts into the room, her face lit with excitement. "Cari, can we go to the beach now? I asked Daddy, but he's in a meeting." She stops her sentence with a pout.

A meeting? Already? So much for him spending time with his daughter. I intend to make sure Brooke has the best vacation, even if Jett Knight can't live up to his promises. I'll make sure this little girl has the vacation of her lifetime. "Sure we can! Let's get ready." I've unpacked her clothes and put them away, so I pull her cute pink swimsuit out of the drawer.

"I can get ready by myself," Brooke insists, snatching the swimsuit out of my hands.

"Good. You do that, and I'll get ready, too." Just before I leave, I pull out the big bottle of SPF fifty sunscreen from her bathroom. "We need to put this all over us or we will burn. Wait for me. I'll do it."

She nods obediently, racing to get ready. I head to my room, deciding a quick swim might be nice, and a good way to explore the area near the house. Opening my suitcase, because I was too lazy to unpack my own clothes, my fingers brush over the plain, conservative swimwear I bought with me. It's a black tankini top that covers me down to my navel, and has matching shorts to go with it.

"'Your nun's habit," Aunt Scarlett said, sniffing disapprovingly.

"Packed your chastity belt?" Eliana quipped, before the two of them burst out laughing. I had to shoo them out of my room so that I could pack my suitcase without their eagle-eyed observations.

As I pull out the swimsuit my eyes land on the bikini Aunt Scarlett made me buy.

"You said you wanted to have fun," I murmur to myself, recalling my resolve from the plane. Before I can talk myself out of it, I slip into the hot pink bikini.

I turn around, inspecting myself in the mirror. It's scandalously skimpy, hugging my curves and leaving very little to the imagination. The bikini might as well be painted on. It offers next to no coverage, the vibrant pink fabric barely conceals my breasts, and that ridiculous teeny triangle just about covers my private parts.

Good thing I got that bikini wax. No stray hairs peeking out from the teensy sides.

Flustered, I turn my back and gaze at my reflection. And blush. It's not quite a G string, as thin as dental floss, but it still exposes a *lot* of my bottom. I squirm in dismay. I might as well not wear anything.

But ... I have a good figure. My breasts are perky and don't look as small as I thought, and the halter-neck gives them a lift. My stomach is flat and my legs are toned. I'm glad so Eliana coaxed me into going running with her in the evenings.

I tie my hair up in a messy bun, then toss some towels into the oversized beach bag and grab a sheer cover-up for some semblance of modesty. But I hear a shriek from the other room.

"Brooke?" I rush out in a panic, and abruptly freeze in my tracks.

Jett is there, crouched beside Brooke, rubbing suntan lotion all over her. She's giggling because it tickles. Then he turns to look at me, and his gaze locks on mine before trailing downward, slowly, deliberately. His eyes darken, shifting from piercing blue to something deeper, hotter, in the span of a heartbeat.

Time slows to a crawl and I clutch the cover-up in my hand. *Great help that's going to be.*

His gaze feels like a physical touch, and my skin prickles in response. My nipples harden under the thin fabric, and I fight the urge to cross my arms.

"I-I t-thought you were in a …" I manage to say.

Meeting. Brooke said he was in a meeting.

"Y-you're … going to the beach," he remarks, his usual smoothness replaced by a stutter. Jett Knight, thrown off his game, unreal.

"Brooke wanted to." My chest rises and falls quickly. I pray he hasn't noticed, or heard the beating of my heart, because his sunscreen-covered hands have stilled.

"Daddy, hurry up!" Brooke chirps. He's suddenly pulled back to focus on her.

"Almost done, sweet pea."

I stand there, watching. Wondering what he's thinking, knowing I need to put my cover-up on, but I'm still frozen by the thought that my boss has seen me almost naked. *Almost.*

It excites me more than it should.

"Put some on Cari, Daddy," Brooke chirps, oblivious to the tension crackling between us.

God. No! "You don't have to. I c-can do it myself ..."

"She'll burn if she doesn't, Daddy!"

Jett stands, towering over me, and I still can't move. His expression is unreadable as Brooke thrusts the sunscreen bottle into his hand.

"Here, Daddy."

"I can do it," I say quickly, reaching for the bottle, but Jett moves it out of my reach.

Brooke shrieks. "Her back! She can't reach her back, Daddy!"

I frown, trying to figure out what's going on. Why Jett won't give it to me, why the space between us feels so charged.

"She's right. I need to do your back. You have the type of skin that's at risk." His words send shockwaves through me.

"Where's Elephant?" Brooke wails, looking around hopelessly.

"I think he's on the stairs, sprout."

She runs out of the room.

"Turn around," Jett orders.

My heart pounds as I turn my back to him, and I'm aware that it's just the two of us alone. I wish Brooke would come running back. My breath catches as his fingers touch my skin. Cool lotion meeting warm flesh. He rubs the sunscreen in slow, deliberate circles, one hand steadying my shoulder as the other works its way down my spine. My senses go into overdrive. I'm as conscious of his hand resting on my shoulder as I am of his other hand slathering lotion on my back. I bite my lip to suppress a shiver as the space between my legs begins to throb, and my nipples harden even more.

My breasts feel full and heavy as he rubs the lotion into my skin, his touch firm but careful as his hands move over my neck and shoulders gently before skating all over my upper back, then lower, and lower still.

This is exquisite. Jett's hand on my body feels intimate. It's what I've dreamed of for months. For years. And now my body betrays me. Heat pools low in my stomach, as I squeeze my eyes shut, praying I don't let out a moan.

"There," he says, "All set."

"Found it!" Brooke yells, running into the room with her tattered toy in tow.

"Great!" I manage to say. I don't want to turn around. I dare not. Jett will see my nipples through my tiny bikini.

His hand reaches over my shoulder, as if he somehow senses my dilemma and gives me the bottle. I wonder if he's packing some wood, too. "You need to put it over the rest of you."

"Th-thank you, Mr. Knight," I stammer, grabbing the bottle and rushing into my room before I can embarrass myself further. I close my bedroom door and press my back against it, struggling to catch my breath.

What just happened?

"Won't be long Brooke," I yell out.

My body hums with arousal, every nerve ending alight. My heart races, my mind reeling with the memory of Jett's touch. I debate whether to swap the bikini for the safer, nun-esque one. But Brooke's voice pulls me from my thoughts.

"Cari, come on! Daddy says we can only go for an hour!"

That settles it. I throw on the sheer cover-up, hoping it's enough to tone things down, and I pray that Jett will have had the decency to have left.

But when I step into Brooke's room, he's still there, almost like he was waiting for me. His gaze traces over me for a quick second before he pointedly looks away, shoving his hands into his trouser pockets. I glance down instinctively and catch it—the unmistakable bulge in his pants.

He felt something too.

My face burns. I'm so flustered I can barely think straight.

"Let's go!" Brooke calls, already bouncing toward the door. I follow, my pulse racing, aware of Jett just behind me. His presence is magnetic and I feel pulled to him.

It's the heat, I tell myself. That, and the flight, and the shock of being here.

But who am I kidding?

CHAPTER SEVENTEEN

CARI

My heated body needs to cool down, especially after Jett touched my skin and slathered suntan lotion all over my back.

Unfortunately the warm water doesn't give me the respite I need. Still, it feels better being out of the same building that Jett is in. I glance over my shoulder. Not knowing much about the layout of the house, I don't know where his study is or whether he can see out, see us, see *me*. Because upstairs, he saw every inch of me. I get goosebumps thinking about it even now, my body still tingling from his observations.

Up close, the sea is a beautiful, shimmering aquamarine-blue, the foamy waves washing over pastel-pink sand. I wade in with Brooke, taking care not to go in too deep, only where my feet can reach the bottom.

Brooke and I spend more time walking along the beach, which stretches out behind the mansion like it was made just for the Knights. These people seem to have the best of everything.

The sun beats down on us, and I wonder whether I ought to be here in such strong sunlight, and then I remember Jett's comment. It went over my head at the time because I was so fixated on his hands all over me. *You have the type of skin that is at risk.*

It felt so intimate, him saying that. It's a casual observation anyone who's seen me could make, with my auburn-colored hair and pale skin, but somehow it feels even more coming from him. Like he's been watching me, knows me, cares about me.

Feeling conscious of the time, I tell Brooke we need to get back. Luckily, she's been my distraction, and when we've been chasing each other in the water my thoughts didn't drift to my boss again.

We return to the house and I help her into the shower, then offer to help her get dressed. She wants to do it herself, though, which I've started to notice happens a lot. I'm not sure if it's just with me, or if she also did it with Anna, but she seems to want to be older, more capable.

I leave and go downstairs to make a few sandwiches for us both, but one of the housekeepers swoops in. She practically insists on doing it for me, smiling softly the whole time. It's blatantly clear that I'm not going to be needed for much here, other than to look after Brooke.

We eat, and she casually recounts how last year she had a tent set up here with lights and a nicely made-up bed inside, all snug and cozy. She asks me if we can set it up again this time. I agree and make a mental note to ask the staff.

Brooke is my distraction and, goodness, do I need one here, with my boss so close. But she's more than that. I love being around her. She's fun, and spending this much time with her, instead of the little slivers of time when Jett brings her into the office, means that I'm getting to know her better.

She's excited about the barbecue tonight. I'm not. Her energy's already returned after our time at the beach and her sandwich but for me this day already feels so long and my tiredness starts to set in.

I'm struggling with what to wear tonight. What does one wear to a barbecue here? I presume that Jett's friend is at the same insane level of wealth as the Knights. Thank goodness I went shopping with Aunt Scarlett and Eliana and updated my wardrobe a little. I settle on one of the dresses I bought with them. It's an orange sleeveless dress, in a soft fabric that flows as I walk. It looked good when I tried it on in the fitting room, and Aunt Scarlett commented that it showed off my figure and my hair.

I ask Brooke what she wants to wear, but she wants to see what I'm wearing first. When I show her, she picks out an orange-colored dress from her closet too. I wonder if she's mimicking me on purpose. It's endearing.

We meet downstairs in the expansive, marble-floored foyer, and the same driver from earlier is waiting for us. Jett comes into sight and Brooke rushes to him.

"Daddy!" she squeals, throwing her arms around his legs.

Jett smiles, brushing her hair back. "You look pretty, angel." His voice softens like it always does when he talks to her. He glances at me, his eyes tracing over my dress slowly while his gaze lingers. I feel it burning through me already and quickly look away, heat crawling up my neck. Did I nod? I can't even tell anymore. Every time he looks at me lately, I feel off balance.

Brooke slips her hand into his and beams up at her father, clearly happy to have more time with him. How precious this must be for them.

He looks different. The sun has kissed his skin, giving him a faint tan. When was he outside? This man never stops working. And when he does, it's either for Brooke or some woman.

"Shall we get in the car?" he asks, breaking the silence and walking away with Brooke. I follow.

We settle in, Brooke chatting away about all the things she's excited to do with him. She's looking forward to days at the beach, swimming in the pool, exploring, and going on boat rides. Things she must have done before. I'm amazed that she even remembers her last visit here. "We can do that, sprout." He agrees to her every request.

"It's going to be so much fun, and you're going to be with us all the time, Daddy!" Brooke cries excitedly.

"I'll be with you as much as I can, angel."

She's convinced this whole trip is one big vacation just for her.

And Jett? He lets her believe it.

Then he tells her that she's been invited to a lunch at her friend Madison's house. "You remember her, don't you? Last year, she had an elephant and a camel at her birthday party."

"I remember!" Brooke would never forget seeing an elephant. But having an elephant and a camel at a party? How rich are these people? I assume the girl must be of similar age to Brooke.

He turns to me. "You'll take her. Noon tomorrow. I'll have the driver bring you for lunch with the kids. Their mothers will be there too. I told Abigail, Madison's mother, that you would be coming."

The hairs on the back of my neck stand on end. He was so casual. So matter-of-fact. Giving me just the information I needed, and nothing more. He feels nothing like the man who saw me practically naked and ran his hands over me earlier.

"Cari's coming with us everywhere, isn't she Daddy?"

I freeze at the mention of my name, my gaze shifting to Jett.

Each glance is like a secret thrill-seeking missile, making me feel things I need to forget.

He opens his mouth to respond, but his cell phone rings and he answers, quickly falling into business mode while Brooke turns to me, her eyes wide with excitement. She recites everything her father just told her. This is likely the longest stretch of time he's ever spent with her. Usually, he's in meetings, on calls, flying in and out of the country. Even when he's around, he's not really present, so I can already see how this trip is so different for Brooke. I can tell it means the world to her.

The car pulls up to an impressive house. It's large but not as grand as the Knight mansion. This looks sleeker, where the Knight mansion is more cozy, more old world, and has infinite charm. This place is a large, modern, beachfront villa with whitewashed walls and large windows. An infinity pool stretches toward the horizon, seamlessly blending into the sea. The backyard has a large deck with lounge chairs and is surrounded by beautiful, landscaped grounds.

I step out, already feeling wary and out of place, as I wonder who this friend of his is. Brooke has her hand in Jett's and I follow behind, looking around me and taking in all the sights and sounds.

The barbecue is set up on the villa's ocean-facing deck, and the sea breeze carries the faint tang of saltwater. The air is thick with the scent of grilling meats, the sounds of laughter and conversation filtering the air under a rose-colored sky. Some people sit at tables set out on the grass, while others mill around with drinks in their hands, deep in conversation. Servers in white uniforms walk through with serving trays.

A few people approach Jett, shaking hands. Warm hugs are exchanged, and they fawn all over Brooke who stands there, shyly, looking as if she wants to disappear behind one of Jett's legs. I stand back, happy to be in his shadow.

A younger man, around my age, seeks me out.

"Are you hiding?" He seems friendly and offers me his hand.

Jett turns around instantly.

"I'm not hiding," I tell him, but it feels wrong, even though I'm being civil and just answering a question. I can somehow sense that Jett doesn't approve, even though this is normal. "I'm with Mr. Knight," I say weakly. I don't know what else to say.

"Hey, Jett," the guy says, breezily. His blond hair is short at the sides, with longer, curling locks on top. With his tanned skin and green eyes, he wouldn't look out of place in a boy band.

"Jacques." Jett's tone is clipped.

"Good to see you again," the young man continues, then, "Hey Brooke." He squats down and shakes her hand, pretending to act all business like. She giggles. He stands up and turns to me again. "I don't believe we've ever met."

I shrink back because he's a little forward for my liking. Jett answers before I say a word. "She's Brooke's nanny for the trip, and she's looking after her tonight."

The guy blinks, clearly thrown by Jett's sharp tone. "Okay. Well, when you're off duty, there's a bunch of us hanging out over there. Come over." He points towards a fire pit further out, near the sea.

Jett looks displeased. "She won't be. She's taking care of Brooke. Remember, I just told you that?"

I stand there, heat flushing my cheeks, utterly humiliated. Why does he have to sound all bossy and patronizing?

Jacques frowns and stares at Jett as if he's suddenly developed a split personality. Come to think of it, I'm wondering the same thing. My boss has turned into a possessive, territorial beast, only I can't work out what the territory is. Is it me, or Brooke?

Jett crouches down to Brooke's level. "You have fun, okay? I'll be right over there." He points at a table nearby then walks away, heading toward a group of men sitting at what I can only describe as a power table—cigars, whiskey tumblers, and too much testosterone.

Jacques hasn't moved. "I'm sorry about that," I whisper, not wanting to talk about Jett in front of his daughter. "I don't know why he said that."

"He's known for being grouchy," Jacques replies. "But, if you do manage to escape, we'll be over there. I'm Jacques. Welcome."

"I'm Cari." We shake hands.

"My parents are hosting this barbecue," he explains.

"Oh. I didn't know. I don't know anyone here." I look at the sea of strangers around me.

Jacques' smile is pure American apple pie. Sweet and wholesome. "I figure you probably won't want to talk business, so if you're in the mood for fun, just come over. Don't be shy. He leans in and whispers in my ear, "Even as the nanny, you're allowed to have some fun."

"Thanks." But there's no way I'm going against Jett's orders. Jacques heads back to his friends, and I survey the couples and older people milling around. My heart sinks. This is not going to be a barrel of laughs for me.

Brooke is gazing at a group of girls around her age, and tugs me to go to them. As soon as they see her they fuss over her. A few older women come by and greet Brooke, then ask where Jett is. I might as well be invisible.

After a while, it's just a few girls and Brooke. I sit alone and watch them play with hula hoops.

The deck is decorated with string lights that cast a warm

glow as the sun begins to dip below the horizon. Lush tropical plants surround the edges, their leaves rustling softly in the breeze, creating a private, cozy atmosphere despite the open expanse of ocean before them.

A long wooden table is set with colorful ceramic plates and glass tumblers and spread out along it is an impressive spread of food, complete with labels. Platters overflow with freshly grilled seafood. Lobster tails, shrimp skewers glazed with honey-lime sauce, and charred mahi-mahi fillets. Bowls of tropical fruit salad glisten with pineapple, mango, and papaya chunks. A crisp green salad tossed with avocados and a zesty citrus vinaigrette makes my mouth water. On the grill, thick steaks and marinated chicken thighs hiss as flames lick at their edges. The smoky scent of barbecue sauce, spiced with a hint of island rum, perfumes the air. This is an incredible feast, and the delicious aroma fills the air. I'm torn between whipping my cell phone out and taking pictures, filming a video, even, to send to my friends. But common sense prevails. Bianca and Eliana would drool and wish they were here—and how I wish they were here, too, but the people here are used to this. This is a normal everyday experience for them. They'd probably look down on me for filming it.

The guests are gathered in clusters, their laughter blending with the soothing sound of the waves lapping against the shore. Some lounge on cushioned rattan chairs with drinks in hand, while others drift toward the pool, where lanterns float like tiny stars on the water's surface. Brooke skips across the deck, a plate of grilled corn in her hands, her laughter ringing like a bell as she chats with other children.

I linger close by, watching her, and enjoying the breathtaking view. I marvel again that I'm here. Really here, in paradise. I wish Eliana and Bianca could see this. I wish Aunt Scarlett could see this. I wish my mom had lived to see this.

I look around to see where Jett is, and that's when I see her, the pretty woman from the plane. She's talking to Jett, laughing at something he's said, her hand brushing against his arm. She flips her hair, her eyes locked on his in a way that makes my stomach churn.

It's always someone else. Bermuda feels like paradise, and yet every time I think of Jett I'm far from relaxed. I remind myself that I'm here for Brooke and I sit up straighter as I remember the promise I made myself on the flight over.

I'm here to have some fun.

A month from now I won't be working for Jett Knight anymore. I'm only here to help him because he was stuck.

I'm doing the man a favor. I stare at where Jacques and his friends are. As long as I'm looking after Brooke, Jett Knight can't dictate how I spend my evening.

CHAPTER EIGHTEEN

JETT

THE EVENING DRAGS ON. I'M SURROUNDED BY MEN WHOSE IDEA of a deep conversation is comparing yachts or private jets, as casually as most guys talk about their cars. It's all just a pissing contest, and it's getting old.

Someone laughs, recounting how he had to explain to his wife about an expensive trip he took with his mistress. The others chortle, their laughter bouncing around the table like it's all a big joke. I don't join in. Cheating grates on me, gets under my skin. It's unacceptable. I don't see men who cheat in the same way once I find out. I don't care to do business with them. If they can cheat their wife, think what they could do in a business deal. People reveal who they are by their actions.

My mother's face flashes in my mind. I don't remember her clearly anymore, but the pain of what happened hasn't dulled. Did she die in the accident? Or did my father kill her spirit long before? His affair with that Italian woman wasn't just an affair. It tore our family apart. The resentment Dex, Zach, and I feel towards the Half-Knights runs deeper than anyone's willing to admit.

But I shove those thoughts aside as the conversation finally shifts. Now it's about business and making money. Their real passion.

Mine too.

Work has been my lifeline since Sophia died. I had six months of grieving before I threw myself back into the business with a ferocity that left no room for emotions. It kept me sane, kept me focused. Helped the business, but I need to fix my work-life balance, especially now that Brooke is growing up so fast.

"How long are you over for this time, Jett?" Raphael asks, breaking through my thoughts.

"A few weeks." I lift my glass, taking a slow sip.

"Fighting fires?"

I tilt my head. "You know how it is. We fight fires, and then we build something bigger from the ashes."

Raphael's eyes slide toward Cari, standing with Brooke in the distance. "She's cute."

I nod, absently. "She's growing up fast. Just turned five."

He smirks. "I meant the nanny."

A sharp, hot flash surges through me. The punch in my gut is immediate, and I fight to keep my composure. "She's probably only a few years younger than your daughter," I snap, disgust twisting in my stomach. Raphael is in his fifties, with grandchildren, for fuck's sake. Dirty bastard.

I stand, excusing myself from the table, pretending it's business as usual. But inside, I'm seething. I never planned for this. Being around Cari outside of work, on a fucking island for three weeks, is not something I expected to deal with.

It's been impossible for me to erase the image of her in that pink bikini, and seeing her in that dress is yet another image

I'm struggling with. The way it looks on her, bringing out the rich color of her hair and the golden tint of her skin, make it impossible for me to keep my eyes off her. I'm not hiding it well, and it's no wonder that Raphael has noticed. Cari's turning heads and its fucking with my brain. She's been on my mind for most of the time I've sat here.

I glance at them. Cari's sitting on a bench, Brooke and some girls playing with hula-hoops. I walk toward them, but someone steps into my path.

"Fancy seeing you here." It's the journalist from the plane. Her voice is sugary sweet, but there's an edge to it, like she wants to have her say because of the way I dismissed her. Over her shoulder, I can see Brooke laughing with her friends. Cari sits on her own, watching. This is a good time to check on her. My gaze shifts to the journalist, and forcing a tight smile, I say, "Fancy that."

"We got off on the wrong foot," she purrs, playing with a strand of her dark hair.

"Maybe don't sit in someone else's seat next time." I raise my glass, trying to figure out how best to extricate myself from this leech, but then I see Cari take Brooke's hand and they walk in the direction of where Jacques is.

My stomach tightens, a slow burn turning into a full-blown blaze. Why the hell does that bother me so much? It shouldn't. But it does.

"I apologize for that. Can we start over?" the woman asks.

"Sure," I say, watching Cari approach a group of young people. Jacques comes over to her and they start talking. He's sniffing around her like a dog and now I have two reasons for losing my shit. The journalist before me and that guy standing too close to Cari.

The woman before me still twitters away, her voice blending into the background, but my attention is firmly on

Cari. Jacques hands her a cocktail, and the sight of it makes my blood boil. I came here to get away from Raphael, and now his son is pushing my buttons.

I clench my jaw, watching as Cari stands, her dress flowing in the soft night breeze, looking stunning. She's a far cry from the woman who organizes my life at work. Here, she's someone else entirely. Someone I shouldn't think about.

In the office, I had control. I could wind her up, push her away. Send her on errands to buy gifts for my lovers, lingerie for someone else. I had strategies for keeping her at a distance. But here? No walls. No rules. No boundaries.

I stand here, pretending to listen to the woman in front of me but not only do I have to put up with this shrew who bores me to death with her inane conversation, I have to watch a younger guy make a move on Cari.

She laughs at something he says, and that's the final straw. "Excuse me," I mutter, brushing past my unwelcome leech. "It's past my daughter's bedtime."

I stride toward Brooke and Cari, planting myself between Cari and the guy. "You're drinking?" I ask, my voice harsher than I intended.

Cari looks startled, her eyes wide with confusion. "It's a virgin piña colada. No alcohol." She sounds defensive, and she should be. I'm acting like an ass.

"That's right, Jett." Jacques blinks at me, his voice smooth. "It's a virgin cocktail."

"I wasn't asking you," I snap, glaring at him.

"I'll catch you later," he mutters to Cari, walking off, tail between his legs.

I turn back to Cari, my frustration bubbling over. "You're supposed to be looking after Brooke."

From my periphery I see Brooke lift her head up at me.

She's still holding Cari's hand. "What's wrong, Daddy?" She detects my tone.

Cari's expression hardens, and she thrusts the drink toward me.

"Nothing's wrong, sweetie," Cari answers, reassuring my daughter. "Daddy's confused." She lifts her chin up at me, defiance blazing in her eyes. "I don't drink when I'm working. It's a virgin cocktail, Mr. Knight. Here. Taste it. Or maybe you'd rather have it tested."

I deserve every bit of her biting, sharp tone.

"There's … there's no need for that." My thoughts are all over the place. I can't focus. My body is reacting in ways that are anything but rational. I shouldn't have stepped in. What was I thinking?

"Are you sure?" Her words hit me like a punch, and I'm about to fire back, but then I see Brooke. She's standing there, looking at us with wide, innocent eyes. I stop, my anger dissolving.

"It's time to go," I say quietly, guilt twisting inside me.

We gather our things, say our goodbyes, and head to the car. Brooke falls asleep almost immediately, but the silence between me and Cari is deafening.

Her face is turned toward the window, l and she seems lost in her own thoughts. I've made a mess of everything and now, we're both stuck here, too close for comfort.

CARI

THE RIDE BACK TO THE HOUSE IS SILENT, PAINFULLY SO. THE tension between us is thick, and every second that ticks by feels like an eternity. Jett carries Brooke inside, her little arms wrapped around his neck, and even in sleep, she looks peaceful. Meanwhile, I'm anything but.

One of the house staff steps forward. "Shall I take her up, sir?"

"No, I'll do it," Jett replies, his tone cutting. He's so angry, and he doesn't even glance at me.

I follow behind, still reeling from what just happened. He humiliated me in front of everyone and now I feel like a schoolgirl who's been given detention. It hurts more than I want to admit.

One moment he's kind and caring, like in the plane when I got scared, and the next, he's storming over and accusing me of drinking on the job. I was too shocked to even respond at first.

I can't do this. It hasn't even been one night, but I don't think I can suffer this man any longer. I can't see how I'll survive a few weeks of this. This trip is nothing like I imagined. It's not an escape. It's torture. Being here, in paradise, with Jett Knight, is my personal hell.

This has been an excruciatingly long day and we walk up the stairs in silence. The quiet between us is heavy, suffocating. I open the door to Brooke's room, watching as Jett gently lays her down on the bed, his movements surprisingly tender.

"I'll take care of her," I say, my voice barely above a whisper. I just want this night to end. I want to be out of these sandals and this dress, out of this whole situation.

"I need to explain what happened back there," Jett says, his voice low as I step into my room.

A familiar knot of frustration tightens in my chest. I don't want to hear it. I don't want his explanations. "Just leave it," I mutter, kicking off my sandals as I yank the earrings from my ears.

But Jett doesn't leave. He stands there, hovering in the doorway. "I don't want to leave it. We need to clear the air."

There's something in his voice that makes me stop. Something personal. Something deeper than his usual detached tone. It's unsettling, and my body tenses, instinctively on edge.

"No, we don't." I face him, crossing my arms. "I know why you're mad. Brooke gets in the way of your love life, and so do I. You could have stayed at the barbecue. I'm perfectly capable of watching her without you hovering over us." I gesture toward Brooke's room, then turn away, desperate to end this conversation. "We're home now, safe and sound. You can go back there. I promise not to get drunk while I'm watching over Brooke."

"I don't want to go back there."

I barely suppress a scoff. My disbelief must have been obvious because I see the way his eyes narrow at my response. "She'll still be waiting for you," I add, unable to help myself.

"Who?"

I roll my eyes, incredulous. "Your friend from the plane. You know, the one you were all too happy to laugh with while I was taking care of your daughter? You can run along now."

Run along now?

He tilts his head as if he can't believe what I've just said. To be honest, I can't believe what I've just said, either, because although I'm not a wallflower when it comes to dealing with this man, this is a personal matter, and I tend not to comment on things like that.

Now I'm starting to wonder if that really was a virgin cocktail because I'm being more daring than is good for me.

Jett's brows knit together. "I don't care for that woman."

"Sure looked like you did." The words spill out and I regret them instantly. This isn't me. I don't talk to Jett about his women, or his love life.

"I didn't care for her on the plane." His eyes lock on mine. "She might have been digging for information, or maybe she wasn't, but she's a journalist and I'm always wary about people like that. I told her to leave or I'd have my bodyguard remove her from the seat."

I blink, thrown off by the intensity in his voice. I'd seen them talking, laughing even. She wanted him. That much was obvious.

He frowns, noticing my hesitation. "What?" His voice drops an octave, but there's still an underlying edge to it. "What's going through your head?"

"It looked like you two were getting on just fine." I fold my arms tightly across my chest.

His expression changes, darkening. "You were watching?"

I nod, biting the inside of my cheek, suddenly feeling foolish. But why should I? He made a scene at the barbecue, humiliated me in front of everyone, and now he's acting like he's the one who's been wronged.

"Why are you so mad about me talking to Jacques?" I shift the conversation back to safer ground and note that his jaw clenches. "The guy I was talking to," I explain.

"I know who you mean." A muscle ticks in his jaw, the way it does when he's barely holding back. "I have to be extra careful out here. I need to be vigilant around Brooke."

I exhale sharply, disbelief washing over me. "But you know the guy! He told me his parents hosted the barbecue."

Jett's lips purse together, like he's fighting to contain himself.

"We were at a barbecue," I continue. "I was talking to a guy. What do you want me to do? Ignore everyone and keep my eyes glued to Brooke the whole time? You said this trip was supposed to be a break for me. You told me I wouldn't be working the entire time. In fact, you said I would have the weekends and evenings to myself to do as I wished."

The muscle in his jaw tightens again, and still he doesn't say anything. This is most unusual. Jett Knight never backs down. Never accepts defeat. He always has an answer.

He nods, then. "I remember, and I'm sorry."

My eyes widen. I must be staring at him in shock because an apology from him is unheard of.

"I'm sorry, okay?"

"You made me feel like a fool. You humiliated me."

The way his gaze ping pongs from my eyes to my lips and then back up again, sets my heart aflutter. "I'm sorry for making you feel that way. I was wrong, and I'm sorry."

Not only has he apologized, but he's admitted he was wrong. This moment deserves a drumroll. But he doesn't stick around. He leaves and I let out a breath, trying to steady the whirlwind of emotions swirling inside me.

This man is so unpredictable. Just when I thought I knew him, he does something that completely throws me.

Now, I'm stuck in paradise, and I feel like I'm drowning in a flood of emotions. I can't be emotional, not now. Not here. Not around my boss.

At least Jacques and I exchanged numbers. He said he'll call me soon, and I'm looking forward to it.

CHAPTER NINETEEN

CARI

I HARDLY SLEPT LAST NIGHT. MY BODY ACHED FOR REST, BUT my mind refused to shut off. I told Jett it was jetlag, but of course it wasn't. It couldn't have been. We were barely up in the air long enough.

I'm feeling unsettled and it's because of my boss. Being around him is harder than it's ever been.

Thankfully, when I wake up, he's nowhere to be found. A feeling of relief washes over me. Without him looming in the background, sucking the energy out of me, I feel good. Refreshed, even. Maybe it's the space, the chance to breathe without his presence weighing on me like a boulder. Making my heart hurt.

But it's not like I've forgotten what happened last night. The barbecue, Jacques, Jett humiliating me. It plays on a loop in my head, messing with my sense of reality. I keep wondering what was real and what I misread. Why did Jett act so possessively? Why did he apologize? He's never like that. He never apologizes. He's so concerned about Brooke. She's his everything. He was just being extra vigilant for her sake.

I shake off the thoughts. I don't have time to dwell on him, not when I have Brooke to take care of. So, I throw myself into the day.

Jett has sent me a message, informing me that we need to be at Brooke's friend's house by noon for lunch. That gives us a bit of time to explore the house and the surrounding grounds.

There's so much to do here, and Brooke's in her element. We explore the house, and to my delight I see that there's a big library, a bar, and numerous other rooms I soon lose track of. Brooke turns her nose up when we step inside the library. I quickly take in the deep oak shelves stretching from floor to ceiling, the plush armchairs, and a stone fireplace. I make a note to revisit this place later on.

We explore the gardens outside, a lush expanse of brightly colored blooms and palm trees. Nearby a turquoise-colored pool shimmers under the sun. It's surrounded by lounge chairs and shaded canopies. A winding stone path leads to a gazebo, its white pillars framed by climbing ivy. Further up, near the sea is an oceanfront terrace overlooking the Atlantic, with steps leading down to a private stretch of beach.

This truly is paradise.

I see Ruby, one of the house staff, and ask her about the tent Brooke mentioned. She tells me she'll have it sent up to Brooke's room later. I tell her that Brooke and I will put it up, since I like the idea of having a little project for us both to work on.

We get ready to go to her friend Madison's house, with the driver and bodyguard in tow, of course. I text Jett to let him know that we're on our way, wanting to keep him updated since he seems to be so concerned about Brooke. I don't expect much of a reply. He's been buried in back-to-back meetings since we arrived, and I can only imagine how exhausted he must be.

Madison's house is another sprawling mansion, with manicured lawns and a large shimmering pool. As we arrive, Madison's mother, Abigail, greets us with a practiced smile. She's a glamorous blonde in a tight dress, dripping in jewelry.

"You must be Cari," she says. "It's so nice to meet you. Brooke! My, how you've grown. Madison, Brooke's here!" she cries out to one of the girls in the pool. "Would you like to join the other moms?" she asks me.

"I'll stay close to Brooke and keep an eye on her, if that's alright."

Her relief is almost tangible. "Of course. The kids are free to dip in and out of the pool. Please make yourself comfortable, and help yourself to the buffet." She waves her hand at a large table near where a group of women are sitting. They're all staring in my direction.

I quickly glance at the food and murmur, "Thank you."

"The children are having their lunch inside." Another wave of the hand in the direction of the house. I notice the way she glances at me when she thinks I'm not looking. She leaves me with another smile and goes back to her friends.

I help Brooke get into her swimsuit, but I catch the other moms huddled together, whispering, their eyes flicking toward me. I know exactly what they're thinking.

I'm the help.

And you know what? I don't even care. I'd rather be labeled *the help* than sit with those women, gossiping about who knows what.

Brooke gets into the pool and in no time at all she's having the time of her life, splashing around and playing tag with her friends. Her laughter rings out, bright and carefree. It's a sound that makes the day easier to bear.

Jett hasn't spent much time with her since we arrived, and I wonder how Brooke really feels about that. She was so excited to be here, thinking she'd see her father more, but he's been too busy to even see her after the barbecue. It's good she has friends to keep her occupied, but I still feel bad for her.

The girls come out of the pool and Abigail implores them all to get changed into dry clothes so that they can have lunch and watch a film. At this a chorus of excitement goes around the group like a wave.

Because I'm always by Brooke's side, I inadvertently end up overseeing the girls. There are about eight of them sitting on expensive leather bar stools eating lunch, pizza and fries, in the sleek marble-topped kitchen.

A housekeeper brings out more hot, freshly cooked pizzas, and I keep replenishing the girls' empty glasses with more juice.

"Are you not eating?" I turn to see an older woman, much older than the others, walking towards me. Her eyes are as warm as her smile, and she has an aura that lowers my guard.

"I'm not feeling hungry."

"Not feeling hungry, or too scared to get to the table?" She gives me a knowing grin. "I'm Celine." She smells of lavender, and I immediately feel peaceful around her.

"I'm Cari, Brooke's nanny."

"I thought you might be, on account of how you won't let her out of your sight. Can I get you some food from the adult table? I sense you're more than capable of getting it yourself, even if you have to cross that group to get it."

"If I needed food, trust me, they wouldn't be in my way." The truth is, breakfast in the morning is a banquet with plates of fresh fruit, pancakes, bacon, and cereal, as well as freshly baked croissants and pastries. I more than ate my fill this morning.

Celine chuckles. "Brooke has grown," she says, fondly, surveying Brooke as a proud grandmother would.

"She just turned five."

"Five," she says, wistfully. "How times marches on. And how is Jett?"

I immediately force myself to think of Jacques in order to keep my face from blushing and keep my thoughts in check. "He's ... very busy."

"Busy. As always." Celine nods, folding her arms and watching the girls, her gaze going to Brooke often.

"How do you know Brooke?" I ask, curious to discover more. I wish I'd seen her earlier, because I would have sat out with her while watching the girls in the pool. Now we're about to go and watch a film in the cinema room, wherever that is.

She surveys me for a few seconds more than is normal. "Brooke's grandmother was a very good friend of mine."

My mouth falls open. "Oh ..." I am all ears, wanting to know whatever I can glean.

"Aurora Knight was as beautiful inside as she was on the surface." Celine's eyes turn misty. "I think of her a lot, especially when I see Brooke. Or Jett, Dex, and Zach, whenever the boys are here. Though when it's business, I don't see them at all."

I don't even know what to say. But I have a question. "You didn't mention Paul Knight."

"No. I didn't."

"You're here with ...?" I ask politely, sensing that she doesn't want to talk about Paul Knight.

"My granddaughter, Zara." She points to a pretty little girl sitting between Brooke and Madison. "Her mom, my daughter, is about to give birth, so I'm helping out."

"Awww. She's lovely. They appear to be getting on really

well." I've noticed that Brooke seems to stick close to Zara's side.

"They're friends. When she was born, Sophia came here for a long break, more than a few months, and Zara was also a newborn then. We used to spend so much time together. I often think of how proud and happy Aurora would have been to see Brooke, her first grandchild, at least, the first one we know about." She mutters these last words to herself, and I am still processing that when she adds, "We only see Brooke once a year, if that, but I'm always astonished at how quickly these youngsters can continue their friendship. It's like they've never been apart."

Sophia. Jett's wife. "There's something to be said for that," I murmur. Children don't hold grudges the way older people often do. They let bygones be bygones.

"I need to go pick up something for my daughter. Would you mind keeping an eye on Zara for me? I'm sorry to lumber you with this, given that you've ended up taking care of—"

"It's really not a problem." I rush to ease her worry. "I would rather be here, with the girls."

"Thank you." This woman is so lovely. I want to spend more time with her. "I'll be back shortly."

"Take as long as you want, and please don't worry about Zara."

"With you around, I know she's in good hands." She winks at me. "I hope Madison won't be too upset with her. Zara adores Brooke. She's missed her." She leaves quickly, and I feel all alone again.

The girls finish their lunch, and Abigail seems pleased that I'm keeping an eye on the children. She asks me if I'll be okay to watch a movie with them, then informs me that a staff member will put on the film once I've herded the girls into the cinema room.

Before I can ask her where that is, she's already walking back to her friends.

"Who's ready to watch a film?" I ask the girls.

"I want to show them my designer doll collection," Madison announces, sliding off the stool.

They follow Madison upstairs and into an enormous room that's the size of the apartment Eliana and I share.

On one side of the room, a glass table exhibits the most exquisite dolls, with perfect features. They are dressed in gorgeous clothes that look expensive, made from velvet, silk and satin. There is nothing cheap and trashy here.

I've never seen anything like it. The girls *oooh* and *ahhh* over the collection.

"Don't touch!" Madison yells.

The girls whip their hands to their sides again, obeying Madison's order.

"Shall we start the film?" I need to get them away from this expensive-looking collection quickly.

"Yes!" They cry out in unison.

"Show me the way to the movie room!" I say to Madison, rather dramatically and with a flourish of my hand. She looks at me with suspicion.

Beside me, Zara and Brooke giggle. They're holding hands, and I see Madison's face twist as she notices this.

"Follow me." With her nose in the air, she leads us into a movie theater. As we walk in, I almost choke with surprise. It's a small movie theater with seating for about fifty people. But this is the real deal. A thickly carpeted floor. Spacious, wide seats with leg rests that raise up with the touch of a button. The armrests have trays that contain boxes of popcorn, candy, and slushies which one of the staff has finished setting out.

The girls take their seats, the lights turn off and the movie plays.

It's the *Barbie* movie.

Even I'm delighted as I sit behind Brooke.

During the film, a few of the girls get up and go to the bathroom, which is at the back, but still inside the theater. When Brooke needs to go, I go with her. It's not just one toilet in there, but five.

My eyes widen, and I take a quick video of it to send to Eliana later. I'm still trying to wrap my head around where I am, and what I've seen, and I can't wait to tell her everything.

When the film finishes, it's time to head home.

I remind Brooke that we need to thank Madison's mom, and we make our way over to her. Abigail is all smiles, but I can't shake the weird tension from earlier. It's like I've been under a microscope all day, judged for not belonging.

Just then we hear the loudest wail.

"She broke my doll!"

Everyone whips their head around, to see Madison holding one of her beautiful dolls, snapped in half. She's pointing at Brooke who shrinks against me.

I place a protective hand on her shoulder.

Madison's mother rushes over. "What happened?" she asks her bawling daughter.

"Brooke broke my doll!"

"I didn't." Brooke protests, and bursts into tears.

I'm horrified. "Don't cry, sweetie. You didn't do anything." I say it loudly so that everyone hears.

"She broke my doll!" Madison insists.

I try not to glare at her. "She did no such thing."

"Don't you dare talk to my daughter like that!" Abigail shrieks.

"Brooke did no such thing," I say to Madison calmly, remembering the warning Celine gave me earlier.

"Madison, baby." Her mother bends down and takes the two

parts of the doll. She gets up and looks at Brooke with a horrified expression on her face. "How could you?"

"Brooke didn't do that," I protest, my nostrils flaring.

"How do you know?" Abigail asks.

"How does Madison know? Where is her proof?" I push back. "Your daughter can't make accusations without backing them up. Brooke did nothing of the sort. I've been with her the entire time."

All of the mothers have come over to witness this spectacle with a better view.

"She went to the bathroom!" Madison yells, her face an ugly grimace as she glares at Brooke. I keep my hand firmly pressed against Brooke's shoulder, letting her know I have her back.

"I accompanied her." I narrow my eyes at Abigail, hating her intensely for siding with her daughter without giving Brooke any benefit of the doubt.

"Mommy, she broke my doll. I hate her. She's come and now this happens." The child throws her arms up in the air, like a diva.

With her daughter's face buried in the skirt of her bright yellow summer dress, Abigail eyes me icily. "These girls are around each other's houses all the time and we've *never* had this problem before."

I place my other hand on Brooke's other shoulder. "Brooke is a well-behaved child, and she would *never* do something like this. You and your daughter owe her an apology because she's been in my sight the entire time. It's appalling that you would make such an accusation without a shred of evidence. I assure you, Brooke hasn't touched those dolls."

"Who's to say you'd tell the truth anyway?" Abigail hisses.

"Pardon me?" I fire back. "What do you mean?"

"Why should I believe *you*?"

There's an accusation there. A sliver of something nasty.

"It's the truth, and I don't care whether you believe me or not." This is personal. She doesn't know me, and she's referring to me being the help, and not part of her clique. I wish Celine were here because it feels like the mob has turned on me and Brooke with pitchforks. "Come on, Brooke. Let's go home." They obviously don't believe me, and there's nothing else I can say, so it's better to leave.

Brooke is somber on the way home, and I feel terrible for her. I tell her that she's done nothing wrong and shouldn't feel bad. I still feel awful for her, because Madison seems to be popular. And because Brooke isn't a regular member of this club, it's easier to vilify her. Celine did warn me, and I wish I'd taken her number. I have so many questions I'd like to ask her. I'd also like to know more about Jett's mother.

At least, I've now learned that this house was named after her. As we head back, Brooke remains downcast, but I'm determined to cheer her up. Entering her room, I see a few large boxes on the floor and big folded heap of material.

"My tent!" Brooke cries. It's the first burst of excitement I've had from her in the last hour.

"We're going to put it up right now!" I want to cheer her up fast and make her forget all the ugliness of the day. Quickly opening the boxes, I discover fairy lights, a large fluffy blanket, and some pillows.

"Can I help you put it up?"

"I'm not doing this alone."

Her smile reaches her eyes now, and I feel so much better. The tent is easy enough to erect. Lots of pieces connect with a click, and in no time, we've put up a large dome-shaped tent.

"I love it!" Brooke cries gleefully, crawling into it.

"It's pretty cool." I can see how much fun this would be. We lay down the fluffy blanket and put in the pillows. Once inside, I string up the fairy lights.

We both lay on the blanket, looking around us.

"Feels like a magical little place, doesn't it?"

"I love it. Please can I sleep here tonight?"

"I don't see why you can't." If she doesn't like it, she'll climb into her bed.

She turns and hugs me, burying her face into my chest as her small hands press against me. I kiss the top of her head. The memory of her being accused of breaking the doll, of Madison being so nasty to her, fills me with rage, and I hope the tent being up will wipe that nasty episode from her mind.

Still, something niggles me. Why would Madison only blame Brooke? She seemed so sure of it, but Brooke wasn't the only one to leave and go to the bathroom. As I ponder the reasons behind this deviousness, Brooke crawls out, reappearing seconds later with her tattered elephant and a few books.

We snuggle in our own fairy-lit kingdom as I read to her.

Later, Ruby comes up and tells Brooke that her Daddy is home and would like to have dinner with her. "And you, too, Miss," Ruby says, as I head towards my room.

"Oh, I'm not too hungry yet."

I am hungry, because I didn't have any lunch, but I would like Brooke and Jett to have time together. Also, I'm not too keen on joining him for dinner. Last night put a sour taste in my mouth and I want to limit my contact with him.

I respond to a text from Jacques. He texted me about a pool party on Saturday night.

It could be fun. I don't know him, but he seems pleasant enough, and from our short conversation the other night, we seem to like the same movies and TV shows and read the same authors. My gut tells me he's a good guy. So, why not?

Why not go to a pool party in Bermuda and enjoy an evening off?

I call Eliana and tell her about my day and what's been going on. I tell her about the private home cinema after sending her the pictures. She says I'm making her jealous.

"Anything happen? Anything we should dissect or analyze?" she asks, with a hint of mystery in her tone.

"Nothing," I reply noncommittedly.

"How's vacationing with your boss?"

"Ugh–haven't really seen him much. He's busy working." No point telling her about the cocktail incident at the barbecue.

But my plans for a quiet evening are interrupted when there's another knock on my door. It's Ruby. "Sorry to disturb you again, Miss, but Mr. Knight needs to see you in the library."

"In the library?" I frown. It's not dinner then.

"The library. Yes, Miss."

"I've been summoned," I tell Eliana.

"Exciting." She giggles, obviously having overheard. "Isn't that what you've always dreamed of?"

"Not really." I rub my temple trying to make sense of the sudden invitation.

Why now? Why to the library?

Then it dawns on me.

He's already found out about what happened at Madison's. How, I don't know.

"I'll call you later," I say to Eliana then hang up.

Smoothing down my unruly hair and my dress, I check my reflection in the mirror, making sure I look somewhat presentable. Then I head downstairs and straight for the library, a heavy stone turning in my stomach. I haven't seen Jett since last night, since he apologized to me. I'm beginning to prefer it that way, because it makes things easy.

Even being at Abigail's, with the other moms talking about me, was bearable. Meeting Jett in the library is not.

I used to dream of moments like this, but now it feels weird. This is not a world I could inhabit. I miss Eliana, and suddenly, I miss my mom. I really miss my aunt. I feel the urge to call her later, but if I do, she'll just get worried, and I don't want to worry her. She already worries enough about me.

With a deep breath, I walk in. It's the library, not his office, so I don't knock. Our eyes meet and my heart flips.

He's having that effect on me.

Again.

Even now.

CHAPTER TWENTY

CARI

"Close the door behind you," Jett orders.

Ouch.

I face him, already knowing that this isn't good.

"When were you going to tell me about what happened at Abigail's?" He starts pacing around with his hands in his pockets, his brow furrowed.

"I didn't have time to think about that," I reply, truthfully. As I watch him, I start wondering who called him. As far as I was concerned, I was trying to cheer Brooke up. Her well-being was my main concern, then we put up the tent and then he called her down to dinner. I didn't have time to tell him. *Yet.* "I would have told you, eventually," I say, feeling as if I'm to blame, when I'm clearly not. I hate that he makes me feel like this.

"But you didn't. Instead, I found out because Abigail called me." He walks over to a wooden desk near the center of the room. A green banker's lamp stands on one side, but with his rolled-up sleeves, his bare forearms steal my attention. He presses his hands on the desk, flexing. All I see are his thick veins. It's enough to kickstart my fantasies.

I drag my gaze back up to his eyes, forcing myself to focus.

"Abigail said you were out of order. You've been described as being accusatory, rude, and defiant."

Trust her to call Jett to whine. "I'm not surprised," I retort.

"Neither am I."

"She and her daughter accused Brooke of breaking her doll—"

He cuts me off. "She didn't say anything about that."

"What?" I gasp. "She didn't?" I search his face for clues. "Why did she call you, then?"

"Because you obviously made an impression," he answers, dryly.

"This isn't about the broken doll?"

"What broken doll?" he growls.

I sink back, wondering what game Abigail is playing. "She knows who broke it," I say, feeling smug.

"I don't know what you're talking about, but you can't be rude and shoot your mouth off when you're here." I listen to him, frowning in disbelief. "Here, you must talk to people with respect. Abigail alleges that you were rude to her and her daughter, and that your behavior was threatening."

"But she didn't mention anything about the doll?"

"I heard nothing about a doll! She said the girls had a disagreement."

I chortle. "Jett. You've only heard half the story, and without the context—"

"You do not know these people, Cari—"

"I know enough about them."

"There you go again! You cannot lose your temper, or insult them, no matter what the disagreement is about."

"You only have half the story."

"Cari." Here it comes. This man is pissed and gritting his teeth together. "You were a guest at their house. You are here as a nanny. You have no right to talk to Abigail like that."

"Her daughter made Brooke cry!" I raise my voice.

He stops and blinks. "What?" His eyes narrow to slits. It's the first inkling I have that he's realized there's more to the situation than he's been led to believe.

I slap a hand to my forehead. "She really thought she could complain to you about me and I wouldn't say a word in my defense? Of course, I'm going to tell you what really happened. How incredibly stupid," I mutter. I have a feeling that the doll problem has solved itself, because Abigail has found out the truth. And it probably doesn't paint her in a good light. "Do you know what happened? Why I told Abigail that she and her daughter needed to apologize to Brooke?"

"You said that?"

"I sure did," I say proudly. "I told her that she and her daughter needed to apologize to Brooke for making such unjust accusations without a shred of evidence."

He takes in a breath. A popped vein throbs along his forehead.

"Her daughter alleges that Brooke broke her prizarnd designer doll." I go on to tell him everything. "But Brooke didn't. I was with her the whole time. And when they accused Brooke in front of everyone, Brooke started to cry. I wasn't having any of their blatant lies and accusations," I roar, outraged as I relive that moment.

His cell phone rings, he answers it. I walk around the library and start looking at the bookshelves.

"Oh, hi. Yes. Yes. Oh. Is *that* what happened? I see. You're sure?"

His tone makes me turn around and gape at him. He scrubs

his hand over his face. "You have proof, huh?" His face turns white. I feel jubilant. "No, Brooke is fine. She's been excited about a tent, apparently. She and Cari put it up after they got back from Abigail's. Yes, Cari." He looks at me. "That's not quite the word I would use to describe her, but she does grow on people."

He's talking about me. I fold my arms and wonder who he's talking to. It doesn't sound like it's Abigail who's called him with her forked devil's tail between her legs. He gives a restrained laugh. "Thanks for letting me know, Celine. Yes, we'll have to meet if possible. Goodbye."

Celine.

I wish I could talk to her.

Jett hangs up and lets out a long exhale, as if he's letting the tension seep out of his body.

"What did the lovely Celine have to say?" I ask.

"You met her?"

"She was at the lunch."

He shrugs. "She wasn't there when it happened—"

"She had to get something for her daughter."

"Right. Zara, her granddaughter, told her what happened, and how Brooke was upset and started crying. She claims that Madison was nasty to her—"

"She was. I told you that."

"Right." He scrubs his jaw, looking sheepish. "Celine remembers that they have cameras on in the house and she insisted they check the footage. Abigail wasn't too keen on it, but Celine put her foot down. Zara was upset that Brooke was crying."

I love Celine. I want to hug her. I want to ask her to meet me for a coffee. "Go on," I say, smiling because I know Celine would have had Brooke's back. Not that Jett didn't, but he was just played by a woman who wanted to make me look bad.

"The footage showed that it wasn't Brooke who broke the doll."

I waggle my finger at him, my anger overflowing. I don't care if Jett Knight has to bear the brunt of my wrath. "I know the cameras didn't show Brooke breaking it. You know why? Because I trust your daughter, and I was with her the whole time. Moreover, even if I weren't with her the whole time, I know Brooke would never do something like that. I don't even spend that much time with her, but I know she's a lovely little girl. Unlike Madison ..." My lips press together as I fight to keep my words to myself. I recall that conviction on her face, the accusation that came a little too easily.

"The video footage showed that Madison went into the room before you all went into the cinema, and she snapped the doll in half," Jett says, wearily.

"I'm not in the least bit surprised," I say with smug satisfaction. "I hope Abigail and her daughter will make a great big groveling apology to Brooke, and I hope you'll be man enough to sit Brooke down and tell her that you're sorry you didn't ask for her side of the story before siding with Madison's mother. Abigail didn't call to tell you about that part of it. She called you to complain about me."

The color drains from his face. "I'm sorry for accusing you of being rude to her."

"You don't have to apologize to me, Mr. Knight. I'll always do the right thing by Brooke. I don't expect you to stand up for me, I am more than capable of standing up for myself, but I'd stand up for Brooke in a heartbeat."

"I'm sorry." He lets out another loud exhale again, and his shoulders sag. He pinches the bridge of his nose, and I notice the dark circles under his eyes. He looks tired. "I had meetings all day with my father, then various other CEOs. I wasn't thinking straight."

"No, Jett. You weren't thinking at all, and this woman fed you facts out of context. The least you could have done was ask me what happened."

"I'm sorry for not believing you."

The long day, coupled with my anger at the injustice Brooke faced and now with Abigail's call, has wiped me out. My filter is off. "It's funny how in New York, I don't hear that word from your mouth, and in Bermuda, you've said it to me twice in twenty-four hours. What's going on?"

He stares at me blankly. "I don't know myself."

I turn to leave.

"Have dinner with us," he says.

"Thank you, but no. I have friends to call."

His face hardens. He didn't like me saying that. I can read him like a book. "Celine thought you were refreshing," he says, as I open the door.

"I think she's lovely." I walk into the hallway, ready to ascend the stairs, longing for the peace and quiet of my room, when Brooke runs towards us.

"Daddy says we're all going on a trip tomorrow," she chirps, clearly thrilled by the idea.

A rock lands heavy in my chest. "We're doing what now?" I glance at Jett, who's watching me with an unreadable expression.

"We're going on a big boat! Just the three of us."

I blink. "I don't have to come if you're going with your Daddy."

Brooke's face falls. "But I want you to come."

I force a smile, trying to hide my unease. "Then I'll come. We'll have so much fun."

CHAPTER TWENTY-ONE

JETT

It's clear that Cari doesn't want to be here.

Part of me doesn't want her here either, for my own sanity, but I want to make it up to her for being such an ogre. Especially after messing up spectacularly yesterday, falling for Abigail's story without consulting Cari.

The atmosphere between us seems especially tense as we step onto the yacht, a trip I've done countless times. The plan is simple, to sail to a private beach, dock, and enjoy a lovely lunch. Brooke's practically bouncing with excitement in her little swimsuit, though she's thrown a frilly pink skirt over it for some reason. She wasn't keen on wearing the life vest, but I insisted.

Then Cari walks aboard, and I realize why.

Brooke's copied her. Cari's covered up, with a sarong tied around her waist and a white linen shirt buttoned up to her neck. There are no signs of that hot, sexy number I saw her in the other day. I still haven't recovered from it. It's probably good that she's not wearing that, though it's hot out here and she's dressed for anything but a day on a yacht.

"You'll bake in that." The words slip out before I can stop them.

Cari doesn't even flinch. "I'm sure I'll be fine," she says coolly.

"Look, Daddy, I have a skirt too!" Brooke gushes, twirling her little pink skirt with a grin.

"Nice, sweet pea."

"Yours is prettier." Cari flashes Brooke a warm smile, but the way she shuts me down with just a glance is ice cold.

I glance back at the horizon and get my phone out, thinking I'll check a few emails while we're sailing.

"Daddy! No work today, remember?" Brooke's voice is sharp with disapproval.

I sigh, putting the phone away. "Just checking a few things, sport."

"If you're going to work, I could've brought her here without you." Cari's voice carries an edge that makes me bristle. It's dismissive, like I'm just in the way. I don't like it.

I put the phone away and join them, leaning back against the railing. Brooke's brought along her beloved elephant, as well as some dolls and coloring books, though she's now holding up her elephant and a couple of dolls, making them "look" at the sea.

"Do they like it?" Cari asks, smiling as she watches her.

"They love it!" Brooke beams.

"Then it's a good thing you brought them." Cari's eyes light up as she interacts with my daughter. She's so good with Brooke.

Too good.

She's great as my assistant and I'm going to struggle without her. The thought shakes me.

Brooke faces the water, lost in her world, holding her dolls up toward the sea. Cari undoes the top buttons of her shirt, and I can't stop staring. She's overheated, she must be, but she's keeping her clothes on.

Good. I'm not sure I could handle seeing her in anything more revealing. I shift in my seat, glancing down at my own outfit, a light linen shirt and swim shorts. Perfect for a day like this. Cari walks up to me, hovering close as if she has something on her mind.

"You don't have to include me in every outing when it's just you and Brooke. I'm sure she would love to have you to herself," she says in a lowered voice while Brooke is busy playing with her dolls.

"Brooke insisted. Glad you came, though?" I ask, wishing she could look happier about being here. She's still sour about last night. And the night before. I've been such a jerk and we're only a couple of days into the trip. But I've apologized. What more does she want from me?

"I guess."

Not the answer I wanted.

"I appreciate you being here," I try again. "I'm sorry about … just sorry for …" For being a jerk on two consecutive days. It's hard to say it, in the cold light of day. Cari's right. Apologies don't come easy to me, and I've already said sorry twice. "It won't happen again." I keep my words deliberately vague. "But Brooke loves having you around. Maybe I should just hire you as her nanny instead of my assistant." I say it jokingly, but Cari would be brilliant in that role. She's brilliant no matter what she does.

Her face hardens. "You'll need to be more open with the next nanny. Nannies aren't replacements for mothers. It's still a job, no matter how much they care for her. They have lives outside of this."

There's a bite in her tone, but she's right. I feel like she's giving me advice I need to take. I've gone through so many nannies since Brooke's mother passed. None of them stayed long enough to make a real connection. Cari would be perfect for the role, but this isn't what she wants to do, and I can understand that.

If only I could clone her. She's so good at everything. I look at people like Alicia, and while they have brains, they lack so many other important qualities. Cari can run rings around most women.

"I might need you to do the interviews for me," I say, jokingly, though a part of me means it. She would be able to weed out and find the perfect nanny for Brooke.

A crease lines her brow. "This trip was included," she reminds me. "I'm still working while I'm here and then I leave a week after we get back, remember?"

"I remember." How could I fucking forget? I only have a week in New York to get my act together. Then life begins without Cari, and it's going to be hard. My eyes burn into hers. "I need to find someone as good as you, as amazing as you, and it's not going to be easy."

She moves away and slips into the seat opposite me. "You'll have to make it happen. I'm sure you'll be more than capable of finding someone you can rely on."

"Thank you for agreeing to come. This," I gesture around the yacht, "is the closest I've come to feeling like a family again. I know we're not," I add quickly, "but days like this are rare for us. Brooke is usually only with a nanny, and her world has been … fractured. I grew up without a mother. I know what that's like."

Cari's eyes soften, turning glassy like she's going to say something, but before she can, Brooke's excited voice interrupts us.

"Daddy! Cari! Come look!"

We head over to where Brooke's pointing, and my breath catches. Dolphins leap through the air, dancing in and out of the water with effortless grace. Brooke squeals in delight, and I grin at her joy.

Cari's beaming too, her shirt now fully unbuttoned, hanging open to reveal a tankini underneath. I let out a breath, grateful that she's not in *that* bikini.

The dolphins follow us for a while before disappearing, and we sail on toward a hidden cove. The water here is impossibly blue, almost fluorescent, and I order the captain to stop the moment I see it.

Brooke bounces on her feet. "Can we go in the water, Daddy?"

"Of course. Let's go." I toss my shirt aside and dive in, the water warm and inviting as it envelops me. Brooke jumps in right after me, darting around like a little fish.

"Come on, Cari!" she calls.

Cari shakes her head, staying on the deck. She's obviously not comfortable stripping down any more than she already has.

Brooke splashes me, and I splash her back. We play, laughing as the sun beats down on us, the day slipping away in the warm embrace of the water. Brooke is an amazing swimmer, flitting away from me only to be scooped back up in a fit of giggles. Her tiny fingers dig under my armpits, tickling me until I'm yelping and letting her go.

"Catch me, Daddy!" she shrieks, swimming off again.

After a while, Brooke swims up to me, her eyes drooping. "I'm tired now, Daddy. And I'm hungry."

I chuckle, hoisting her up onto the ladder. "Alright, sport. Let's get back on the yacht."

Once we're back on deck, Cari's waiting with a towel, drying off Brooke. As I climb up the ladder, I catch her giving me a quick glance, and I swear her cheeks flush pink. Feeling a surge of confidence, I puff out my chest a little, rubbing the towel over my skin with more flair than necessary. *Why the hell are you posing, idiot?*

But Cari turns away, focusing all her attention on Brooke. She's taking her sweet time drying her off. "No point getting her bone dry. We're stopping again soon," I tell her.

Cari doesn't respond, but I feel it once more, the quiet, invisible thrum of something between us. I tap her shoulder gently. "We're having lunch. That alright with you?"

She startles slightly at my touch. "Yes, sure." She seems wary, and I wonder what's going on. She didn't want to swim, and I didn't push her. Her movements are jittery, almost like she needs something to do with her hands. Is it my imagination, or is she a little too jumpy around me today? Maybe it's the first time she's seen me shirtless. Hell, maybe it's the first time I've seen her this way—in swimwear, on a yacht, out of the office.

She could be hungry, so it's a good thing we're stopping for a bite to eat. I bend down to Brooke. "How hungry are you?"

"I could eat a horse!" she exclaims, her face lighting up.

"I don't have a horse for you, sport, but how about hot dogs?"

"Hot dogs? Where, Daddy?"

I point toward the stretch of sand ahead. "Right over there. See the tent?"

Brooke squints, then her face lights up. "Hot dogs!" she cheers.

Cari glances over, shading her eyes with her hand. "Are those *people?*" She looks at me, confused and curious. But there's a hint of a smile on her face.

CARI

WE COULD'VE BROUGHT A SIMPLE PICNIC HAMPER, BUT NO, JETT Knight has to take it a step further. He sent two of his kitchen staff ahead on a speedboat to cook for us. I shouldn't be surprised. I should be used to him and his extravagant ways by now.

It's sweet, the effort he's making for Brooke, to make each moment memorable. I give him the side eye and my insides turn mushy. He is a good dad, and Brooke is lucky to have him.

By the time we reach the shore, there's a tent set up. The smell of grilled hot dogs, shrimp, and fish floats toward me, making my stomach growl.

"This is … over the top … but amazing," I say.

Jett's eyes search mine. "Not too much?" he asks, like he's seeking my approval.

"You did well," I whisper to him.

He smiles.

"Hot dogs!" Brooke squeals, running ahead. "Thanks, Daddy!"

We could've managed with a hamper, but this is his world; one where everything is excessive and exaggerated, and I'm learning to sit back and enjoy it. "It's lovely," I say, watching Brooke race toward the familiar kitchen staff. They all know her by name.

There's even a small table set for three. It's elegant, yet simple, a far cry from what I'm used to. But that's the thing with Jett. He knows how to make moments special, especially for Brooke. It's touching to see this side of him, the softer, more thoughtful side. So different from the man I work for. This version of him is calm, kind, and careful. This is the side of him that came out when my world collapsed.

"This really is so amazing," I repeat, genuinely in awe of the day he's crafted.

We eat quickly, silently, enjoying the food and the moment. The food is delicious, the setting picturesque. It's been a perfect day. One I'll remember for a long time.

And then there's him. I can't stop thinking about him in those swim shorts, especially when he climbed back on deck earlier and crouched beside Brooke, smoothing sunscreen on her back.

Earlier Brooke reminded me to do Daddy's back.

So I had to.

This time the roles were reversed, and I got to spread my hands all over his wide shoulders and back. Squeezing out the milky lotion and rubbing it into his skin felt so erotic. I could barely breathe. I tried to swallow a few times, but my mouth was dry. It caused the familiar heat to build between my legs, and I wondered if this excited him the way it excited me.

When he came back out of the water, dripping wet, his body gleaming, it was impossible for me to look away. His tanned, sculpted chest gleamed in the sunlight. His abs look like they were carved from stone and the water trickling down his chest, clinging to that dusting of dark hair, tipped me over the edge.

I had to bite my lip, and hide what the sight of him did to me. That was before my gaze fell to navy swim trunks hanging low on his hips, clinging to every ridge of muscle, and dipped lower before I could stop myself.

And what I saw told me that this man is *big* down there.

Huge.

I mean, I'd *suspected* it, but seeing that bulge confirmed everything. The worst part? He caught me staring. I turned red, completely mortified. I had to look away, focus on Brooke, on anything but him. Thank God for the food, because I've been able to distract myself with that. And thank God he's put a T-shirt back on.

After lunch, Brooke is busy building sandcastles, her laughter filling the air. I sit back, sipping on sparkling water as I watch her. "She'll treasure this day forever."

"As will I," Jett replies, his voice contemplative. He seems lost in thought, staring out at the water. I glance at him, wondering what's running through his mind. He's hard to read in these moments.

"You're doing a great job with her," I tell him. "You really are."

His brow furrows slightly, and he stays silent for a moment. I'm not sure if I've upset him or if he's just deep in thought. "Growing up without a mother is something I wouldn't wish on anyone."

I shift in my seat, sensing something heavy behind his words. "I know it's hard," I offer quietly, not sure how much to say.

Jett sighs, running a hand through his hair. "Brooke needs a mother. But it's not that simple."

I blink, caught off guard by the personal turn in the conversation. "Did you think Alicia was the one?" The question slips out before I can stop it.

He gives me a long, unreadable look. "It's not about that."

There's a pause, thick with unspoken tension. I know this is personal, but I also feel like I'm treading in dangerous territory with the ground constantly shifting beneath my feet.

"You need to be more open with the next nanny," I say, trying to steer the conversation back to safer ground. "You can't just expect them to know what you're thinking, and you have to listen to them."

"I listen to you."

I chuckle, but my heart jumps inside my ribcage at

something that sounds like a compliment. "I don't really give you advice."

"Don't you?" His voice is soft, his gaze intense. I let out a nervous chuckle.

Before I can respond, Brooke calls out, "Come help me with my sandcastles!"

"Go on," I say, encouraging him.

"I'm not doing this alone. I haven't built a sandcastle since I was a kid," Jett protests.

"All the more reason to help your daughter now."

"You're coming too." He grabs my hand, and the moment his skin touches mine, a jolt of electricity shoots through me. But he doesn't seem to notice. He pulls me up, leading me toward Brooke.

We all join in, building sandcastles together. Brooke's happiness is infectious, and for a while, it's easy to forget everything else. I've opened the buttons to my shirt, and I do feel silly wearing it. I might as well be in a firefighter's outfit for how ridiculous this looks. Kneeling as I am, my loosely tied sarong has come undone and when it falls off, I let it because I'm not wearing a skimpy thong underneath.

I'd never have the guts to do that again, not in front of Jett, and him seeing me was a pure accident. I still feel naked in my shorts and tankini top though. It's so hot out and I want to shrug out of my shirt, but it feels like too much exposure.

Something has shifted since lunch. I feel more relaxed, and Jett doesn't feel like my boss. Come to think of it, that commanding, dominating man has disappeared. I like this softer, more playful Jett, and when he said this feels more like family it made goosebumps erupt all over my skin.

If only.

I shake my head, dispelling those crazy thoughts of a stupid, crazy fairytale. He laughs freely, with gusto, more than I've ever seen him. It does feel nice. Like I belong here. Like we're a family.

We get carried away, building an entire village of sandcastles, complete with towers and moats. They are all spread out on the shore. Then Jett decides to build different sized sandcastles on top and we all make a second tier.

By the time we're done, we've created something incredible. It feels like a snapshot of what life could be like, if things were different.

"I wanna swim!" Brooke exclaims suddenly, breaking the moment.

Jett shrugs. "Okay, let's swim."

He peels off his T-shirt, and I force myself to look away. He heads toward the water with Brooke, then glances back at me. "Come on."

I shake my head, focusing on the sandcastle I'm rebuilding.

"The water's great," Jett calls over, wading deeper into the ocean. When I don't move, he comes back, walking out of the water towards me like he's in an advert for expensive cologne. His biceps flex as he raises his arms and smooths back his hair, and his chest, with those ridges and valleys of muscle, are a blur as I hastily look away.

"You're missing a lot of fun." There's a determined look on his face that I've seen in business meetings. "It's warm. You'll love it."

"I'm good," I mumble, feeling my heart race.

He frowns, crossing his arms over his chest. "Can you swim?"

"Of course I can swim," I snap, feeling defensive.

"Then what's the problem?"

I hesitate. It's not that I can't swim. I just that I don't like deep water. I don't like the idea of being out of control.

"Okay. I'm coming," I say reluctantly, more to get him off

my back than anything. He turns and walks back to the water, and I quickly strip off my shirt and wade in behind him, keeping my eyes on the horizon and not on his perfect form.

The water is warm, just like he said. Refreshing, even. But I can't go near him. Not with the way my body reacts every time we're close.

Brooke makes a game of swimming around us, splashing us with water, her laughter filling the air. She's an impressive swimmer who puts me to shame. The water is shallow and my feet pad across the soft sand. Soon, we're swimming further out, and it is so much fun. The water is shallow, my feet touching the soft sand beneath. It's impossible not to get caught up in the fun, even as I try to keep my distance from Jett.

Once or twice, in a bid to get away from Brooke, I accidentally bump into Jett. He's all hardness.

"See, it's not so bad," he says, water trickling down his face. His lips are wet, and I feel the urge to lick the water off.

I feel the urge to do more than that, so I swim away, needing to put physical space between us. Our bodies have brushed a few times, an electric spark zapping in my heart each time. It's too intense, causing the space between my legs to pulse. The water hides my arousal, but I feel my breasts turn heavy, so I swim out further than I intended. When I stand up, I can't touch the ground.

I glance back, seeing Jett and Brooke a distance away, and that's when it happens.

I go under.

Panic surges as water fills my mouth, and I thrash, trying to get my bearings. I go down once, twice, three times, and this time everything happens in slow motion. I take in mouthfuls of water, and I fear this is it.

I'm going to die.

I will drown in paradise and everyone will laugh. Jett will

laugh. The Knights will talk about this at one of their dinners. Or maybe not. I don't suppose an assistant drowning on vacation would make the cut for dinner conversation.

The more I struggle, the more I go under. Everything slows down and water fills my lungs. I'm sinking, sinking, sinking …

I flail and panic, struggling to keep afloat. Then strong arms grab me, pulling me up, holding me tight. I gasp, sputtering, my hair plastered to my face as I inhale sharply.

"I've got you." Jett's voice is calm and steady and his eyes are locked on me. But I begin to choke. He offers me soothing words, and I wrap my legs around his waist, clinging to him like a barnacle, until he tells me I need to get upright so that he can help get me back to the shore.

I blink, still disoriented, but I feel safe. Jett is here, with his arm around me, strong and steady and holding me close until we reach the shallows. Once I can touch the ground again, I stop, still shaking, my chest heaving with breath.

"You're safe now." He brushes my hair away from my face.

I'm trembling, and the humiliation burns through me. Jett keeps his arms around me, grounding me, reassuring me. I don't know why I do it, but I wrap my hands around him, feeling gratitude that I didn't drown and die. I press against him, feeling his strong, hard chest against mine. And then I feel it; something hard pressing into my stomach, and instinctively, my hands slide lower and I cup his bottom.

It just happens. It's unwarranted and wild, but we stand there, chest to chest, and I stare up at him. His eyes are locked on mine, and in this moment, everything else fades away.

CHAPTER TWENTY-TWO

CARI

I LIE ON MY BED, MORTIFIED. I MADE AN ABSOLUTE FOOL OF myself yesterday. I groped my boss after he saved me from drowning. What was I thinking?

Did he know what I did? I mean, *of course* he did. He must have. I had a good grope, in my panic induced stupor. Is he going to fire me for it? Would I even survive the humiliation of seeing him again?

The way I'm feeling right now, I can't trust myself to face him.

The ride home was painfully silent, and I didn't sleep last night, tossing and turning in the suffocating heat. I didn't even go down for dinner. He didn't summon me either. Instead, I wandered aimlessly around the house until I found myself in the library. I curled up on the couch, eventually falling asleep there. Somewhere in the early hours, I tiptoed back to my room, where I've been hiding ever since.

Today, Jett was nowhere to be seen. After spending a few

hours in the sea, Brooke was content to play in her tent all day. We read and she played with her beloved elephant and her dolls. She loves the tent, and I do, too, because it's a place where I can hide, and disappear from the world. And from Jett.

THE WEEKEND IS UPON US ALL TOO SOON. I'M LOOKING forward to the pool party tonight. Jett has plans with Brooke, which she told me after breakfast.

I still haven't gone downstairs, preferring to have my meals in my room. I wait until they leave, watching the black SUV pull away from the house.

Only then do I feel like I can finally exhale. Going downstairs, I grab a plate of fruit and sneak out to the beach. I settle far from the mansion to have my breakfast alone, book in hand.

But I can't focus on reading. My mind keeps dragging me back to the beach, to the moment Jett pulled me out of the water. The memory hits me like a tidal wave of embarrassment.

Did I really do that? Did I really wrap my legs around his waist like a desperate woman? I clung to him, panicking until he had to pry me off, telling me he couldn't swim like that.

And then, when I choked on too much water, he stood me upright, holding me steady until I regained my footing. When my feet finally touched the sand beneath us, I felt such overwhelming relief that I threw my arms around him.

We were chest to chest.

I don't remember if he wrapped his arms around me, but I was clinging to his waist, shaking, overwhelmed. And that's when I felt it. That hard pressure against my stomach. Was it …? Could it have been?

I shake my head, embarrassed at my own thoughts. It must

have been my imagination. I was disoriented, in shock, overcome by his strength, his muscles, his ... *everything*.

But then I remember how my hands slid down and how I cupped his hard, sculpted and beautiful bottom. I hide my face in my hands in shame.

What must he think of me?

Jett dates women like Alicia; glamorous women. Meanwhile, I'm here groping him like some love-struck intern. Thank God I've already resigned. If I hadn't, he'd probably fire me.

I let out another embarrassed groan and hide my face under the pillow but my phone pings, pulling me out of my misery. It's Jacques.

> Are you still on for tonight?

I am most certainly on for a night out, away from Jett. Away from his presence which seems to infiltrate every cell in my body, even when he's not around me. Going out with Jacques and his friends feels like a necessity now. An escape I so badly need. I text back:

> Looking forward to it!

By six, I'm dressed and ready. I opted for a dark green off the shoulder dress that fits me snugly. It leaves very little to the imagination, but because it doesn't expose much, apart from one shoulder, I feel comfortable in it. I've never worn anything off the shoulder before but Eliana and Aunt Scarlett insisted I try it on when we went shopping. I reluctantly did, and it looked good, I must say. It complements my hair color nicely.

I stop by Ruby on my way out, letting her know where I'm going. She smiles warmly and tells me I look gorgeous, wishing me a good time. I call a taxi and head to the address Jacques has given me. It's at a hotel, not someone's house, and that brings me some relief. I don't relish the idea of bumping into Abigail or her friends again.

I haven't brought my swimwear with me, partly because I don't want to get into the pool. I just want to have a few drinks and talk to people. Take my mind somewhere else, and not think about Jett for a change.

As I walk out to the pool at the back, I hear loud music. A DJ is set up on one side, lights flashing around his area, and people are on the dance floor. Others are in the pool, or sitting on recliners. There's a buzz in the air, an electric force that fizzles with potency. I feel energized being here and it's a big change from the intense atmosphere around Jett.

Jacques comes up to me, greeting me with a soft kiss on my cheek. He's wearing swim shorts, but it only reminds me of how Jett looked in his.

"You can change over there." He points to a door which leads to washrooms.

"I didn't bring my swimsuit." I make an apologetic face.

He looks dismayed. "No? But at least you're here. Off duty, right?"

"Off duty?"

"No childminding."

I laugh. "No childminding. I could do with a night off."

"I thought as much. Let's get those cocktails in!" He whoops with excitement.

IT'S PAST MIDNIGHT BY THE TIME I GET BACK. JACQUES AND HIS friends kept me out later than I'd planned. We had drinks at a bar in the hotel, then he introduced me to lots of his friends.

Every now and then, we'd dance. It was fun, and the people I met were nice, but my mind wasn't there.

Despite being around younger people my own age, I couldn't enjoy myself. Not fully. I kept thinking of the day with Jett and Brooke. It had been perfect until I ruined it in the water. Now, everything feels off. Jett's probably going to send me home early. Or maybe he'll just fire me outright. The thought gnawed at me the entire evening.

By the time I let myself back into the house with the key Ruby gave me, I'm a little tipsy. Not drunk, not like I was at the Christmas party, but enough to stumble a bit as I tiptoe through the hallway, my heels dangling from my hand. My throat is parched, so I head to the kitchen for water, gulping it down in the dim light.

As I walk down the long hallway, heading towards the stairs, I pass by one of the rooms. I think it's the bar. The door is slightly ajar and light spills out into the hall. I step closer and peer in. I notice a polished mahogany counter and vintage brass fixtures. Shelves behind the bar are stocked with a huge display of multi-colored concoctions.

Jett is sitting inside, a whiskey glass in hand. He looks up, and his eyes lock onto mine. "What time do you call this?" His smooth voice is edged with something sharp.

I freeze, my shoes slipping from my hand and clattering to the floor. His stare is hard, more intense than I'm used to. He's dressed casually, in loungewear that hugs his body, and the sight sends a tingling sensation through me. It's not what I need right now.

"You're s-still up," I stammer, feeling a little unsteady from the cocktails. "What are you doing here?"

"What do you think?" He takes a sip of his whiskey, his gaze moving over me slowly, deliberately.

I shift uncomfortably, tugging at the hem of my short dress

and suddenly feeling very exposed, especially when his gaze settles on my bare shoulder. "Isn't it late?" I ask.

"For what?" His brows push together in irritation.

I scramble for something to say. He looks annoyed. He's going to say something about what happened in the water. And he's going to fire me. I crossed a line, groping him the way I did, and now I must face the consequences. "To … be … drinking by yourself," I say slowly.

"Where were you?" His eyes are dark now, like an angry thundercloud.

"I went to a pool party with Jacques and some of his friends," I mumble, suddenly feeling like a teenager caught sneaking out.

"A pool party?" he snarls, as if he's having difficulty wrapping his head around the idea. "And you decided to come home now?"

"You said I could have weekends off," I remind him, trying to stay calm, even though my heart is pounding.

"I still need to know where you're going," he growls. "I'm responsible for you."

"I told Ruby. I didn't think you'd care."

He takes another sip of whiskey, his eyes never leaving mine. I've never seen him like this, drinking alone, late at night. It feels like I've caused more trouble than I even realized.

"Which bikini did you wear?"

His question shocks me, like a bucket of ice water thrown at me. "W-what?"

"Was it the stringy, pink one? Or the army regulation one?"

My mouth opens but words fail me. I wish I hadn't had so many cocktails because I feel floaty and light-headed, like this is a dream and not real. "Why do you care?"

"I need to know."

"Need?" The cocktails have given me a little courage. His need to know feels dangerously flirtatious.

He takes a swig from his whiskey tumbler.

"How much have you had to drink?" I ask.

"Not enough." He drains his glass, his gaze heavy on mine. "Why not stay out all night?"

"Because I wasn't having that great of a time," I admit, my voice quieter now. I don't know why I'm being so honest.

He tilts his head, watching me carefully. "You weren't?"

"No." I shrug, trying to seem nonchalant, though the tension between us feels like it's growing by the second.

He looks me up and down again, his eyes lingering on my bare shoulder, then sliding lower. "You look beautiful." His voice is almost a murmur, and I don't think I heard him right. Heat flushes through me and I nibble on my lower lip, unsure how to respond.

"Thanks."

"I like your hair up." It's strange how his tone is so casual, and his gaze is so intense.

I reach up, touching my hair self-consciously. I didn't do the tidy updo I usually wear at work, but something looser, more tousled and with wisps falling along the sides. "It's so hot here. I didn't want it sticking to my neck."

"Let it down."

I blink. "What?"

"Your hair. Let it down." He's never spoken to me like this before. There's a wildness about him. He's not as smooth and as polished as he usually is. The slick Armani veneer has gone. In his loungewear, with the fabric hugging his body like a second skin, he seems bigger, more built, and I can't stop myself from checking him out.

Without thinking, I reach up and do as he says, pulling the clip from my hair and letting it fall loose around my shoulders.

His gaze rakes over me, making my heart race as I feel the heat of his gaze.

Am I dreaming?

It's like he's looking at me differently; as if he sees every part of me. He's saying all the right things. He's talking to me as if we're at the same level. As if he wants me. My heart races, and the atmosphere between us turns electric.

Every nerve in my body is alive.

I wish I hadn't had so many cocktails. I don't know if this is really happening or if I'm imagining it.

"You didn't answer my question about the bikini."

"I didn't go into the pool. I didn't want to. I just wore this." I wave a hand at my dress.

"Was that for him?" He tilts his chin towards me. There's a roughness in his voice which jolts me.

"What?" I'm confused, trying to keep up.

"The dress," he clarifies. "Did you wear it for him?"

"Why so many questions?" And when he gives me a pointed look, "No," I say quickly, shaking my head.

"Good," he mutters, before taking another sip of whiskey, his gaze never leaving mine. "You shouldn't waste your time on boys like him."

My insides turn into a fireball. I run through the words again, second guessing what I heard. "You think I should find someone ancient instead?" I joke. A couple of times, when he's riled my temper, I've made pointed remarks about his age. But he doesn't appear to have heard. He gets up and walks over to me, and now I smell the whiskey on him.

"I love the way this dress clings to all your curves. I love ..." His eyes trail over me again and he reaches out, his fingers hovering around my shoulder. I brace myself for his touch. It's like he wants to devour me. A low, thrumming vibration starts to build between my legs.

Heat rolls off his body. I feel as if wanton lust has spread all over my body like an essential oil. "If I shouldn't waste my time on boys like him, who should I waste my time on?"

"Someone who knows what he's doing. Someone who would make it worth your while."

"I didn't dress for him." His question has been buzzing around in my mind. He seems to despise Jacques, and the idea of me being with him.

"No?" His gaze darkens and the intensity in his eyes are like nothing I've ever seen before. I don't trust myself to breathe. "Would you dress for me?" His voice is thick with something unspoken.

The tension zaps between us, and a fire ignites inside me. Before I can stop myself, the words slip out. "I would dress however you wanted me to." In this moment, I would. In this raw and dangerous moment, I'd do anything this man asked me to do.

He drains his glass. My desperate confession hangs in the air like a challenge. Stupid girl. What did I go and say that for? More importantly, why is he asking me this? Intense and wickedly dirty thoughts flash through my head.

"I need more whiskey," he rasps, going behind the bar and pouring himself more.

"Shouldn't you go to sleep?" I'm trying hard to ground myself, to break the spell we seem to be under. I walk over to the bar stools because I need to sit down. My knees feel like they're made of jelly, and I'm scared they're going to give any moment now.

"No."

I set myself down and watch the amber liquid glinting in his glass under the low lights. Something has shifted. Jett is always so controlled, always in command, but tonight … tonight, he seems unguarded, loose, like there's something untamed lurking beneath the surface. The boundaries between us slip away in this moment and something feral unleashes. And for once, I don't care.

Though I should. I suddenly recall that I'm taking Brooke to the Crystal Caves tomorrow. My head needs to be in the right place. I'm a responsible nanny. "I should go." I slide down from the bar stool and start to walk away.

"Haven't you forgotten something?" he growls.

I turn around at the sharpness of his tone.

"Your shoes, Miss Summers."

"Oh." I take a step back and pick up my shoes, feeling foolish. Standing in front of him, holding my heels, I ask, "Is everything okay? You seem … different."

Also, he called me Miss Summers. He never calls me that. What is going on? He takes a long drink of whiskey, and I realize he's not himself. "You've had too much to drink," I say softly, suddenly worried about him. Has his father called? Or maybe he's missing Alicia.

Then another thought crashes into my head, bringing that humiliating moment back. I wonder if it's because of me. Because of what happened yesterday. I put him in a terrible situation. Without thinking, I drop my shoes and flop down on a bar stool. "I'm sorry about what happened," I blurt out.

His expression changes, his eyes narrow. "Sorry for what, exactly?"

I shake my head, feeling embarrassed. "For, um … the other day. In the water, when I-I—" I stop, unable to find the right words.

"Spit it out."

"I-I appreciate ... I mean I'm thankful that you saved me …" I begin, "but I mean … the part after that. The part where I —" I glance up at him and something dark burns in his eyes.

"Where I-I …" I begin to stammer again. Surely he knows what I am talking about?

"The part where I saved you from drowning?" he prompts.

"I appreciate you saving me. I mean … what happened *after* that."

His perplexed expression has me doubting myself. Maybe it didn't happen. Maybe I didn't grope him. He stares up at the ceiling and nods. "Not a problem."

Heat rushes to my face. He hasn't said it, but I'm sure he knows what I'm talking about. When I touched him. "I don't know why I did that," I whisper. "I'm sorry."

"I'm just glad you didn't drown on my watch, Cari."

"That would have been traumatic for Brooke to see."

"Traumatic for me, too."

"And bad for me," I say, trying to make light of the conversation which suddenly seems heavy.

"I was never going to let you drown." Whiskey glass in hand, his gaze smoldering, he says, "I can't lose you, Cari."

The way he says my name sends a shiver down my spine. My pulse races, my head spins, and I'm unsure of where this conversation is going.

His gaze trails down and lingers on my naked shoulder before dipping lower, and lower still, taking in all of me. I feel as if he's undressing me. He's never looked at me like this before and then his eyes meet mine. "Want some?"

A thrill charges through me. "What are you offering?" I tease, though I already know the answer.

He raises a brow. "Whatever you want."

My insides hollow out. What exactly are we talking about here? It feels intimate, secluded, as if this moment exists in a world all its own. Before I can answer, he says, "Whiskey, but I've got tequila, rum … whatever you like."

Drinks. He was only talking about drinks. I take a moment

to compose myself. "It's late for me to be drinking." But my gaze still flits across the array of bottles behind him.

"The night is young, Cari. You drank with your *boy-man*, surely you can have a drink with me?"

I blush as he looks down at me. Boy-man? Ouch. He really doesn't like Jacques.

"You're on vacation," he continues. "We're not back in the office, and you're not my assistant here."

I'm not? Then what am I? I try to loosen the knot that's stuck in my throat, as I struggle to make sense of his sinister and sexy words. Words that are almost an invite.

Have some fun, my sweet girl. It's been a tough year for you. My aunt's words spin around in my head.

"I've never had whiskey before."

Jett slides his glass across to me. I take it, inhaling a deep breath, steadying myself as I maintain eye contact with him. I turn the glass around, putting my lips on the same spot where his lips have been. His mouth parts slightly and I sense that he may not be as calm as he appears.

I know, as surely as I feel it myself, this is turning him on.

I take a sip. It burns like liquid fire at first, and I almost gag but I force myself not to, under Jett's watchful gaze. Then the smoky warmth rolls over my tongue with an unexpected sweetness, like burnt sugar.

"It's … *strong*." I wrinkle my face at the sharp, bitter edge that lingers.

"Like it?" Heat flares in Jett's eyes and his gaze dips as he watches me take another sip.

"I could get used to it."

This feels like a dangerous game we're playing. I lick my lips provocatively, feeling the dynamics between us shift. My actions are affecting him and it feels good.

"Do I get that back? Or should I pour you a fresh one?"

I cup his glass with both hands, hear the thudding of my heart and pray he can't hear it. "I'll stick with this, thanks."

Reaching for a new glass, he pours himself another whiskey, then lifts his glass to me. "What shall we toast to?"

"To ... a ... a farewell," I scramble to say the first thing that comes to mind.

There it is again, the telltale flexing of his jaw. "Why a farewell?"

"Because I'm leaving."

"So you keep reminding me." Anger darts across his face, lightning fast, but in an instant it's gone. "I don't want to talk about you leaving." He's a master at hiding emotion. I've witnessed this firsthand, seeing him with his father. He's trying to hide it with me now. "To a great adventure in Bermuda," he says.

"An adventure?"

"It can be. It can be anything you want it to be."

"Oh." In my head that sounds like an invitation, and when our glasses meet with a soft clink, it feels like more than a drink. It feels like an understanding.

For the first time, I feel like his equal. Maybe it's the way he looks at me, as though I'm someone other than his assistant. Like he's really seeing me.

And I like it.

CHAPTER TWENTY-THREE

JETT

Thank God I'm standing behind the bar where she can't see what she's doing to me.

When she drank from the place my lips had been, my cock twitched. Does she have any idea of the effect she's having on me?

I have a sneaky feeling she does. Her actions are deliberate. She means to torture me. Cari the assistant would have asked for a new drink. Maybe even something non-alcoholic. Vacation has made her carefree, happier.

Wild.

I like it.

I like that she's not in her usual pencil skirts and smart jackets with her neat little updos, putting me in my place and giving me icy put downs.

I like that she's here with me in the bar at midnight. Drinking from my whiskey glass. Fuck. I've never had to jerk off as much as I have since we got here.

That first day, seeing her in that tiny little slip of a bikini, having to rub suntan lotion into her skin. Fuck me. I had to cancel my business meeting and take a cold shower. I couldn't focus and I've had trouble focusing ever since.

Lately, every time I'm around Cari, I can't seem to keep myself in check. The pent-up frustration is unbearable.

When did it start? I know exactly when it started.

And now she's watching me, unsure of what to say next, her confusion palpable. Her lips part as if she's going to ask something. She looks so damn good.

"Are you going to send me home?" she finally asks, her voice soft but uncertain.

I set my glass down, wondering where this crazy thought of hers has come from. "Why would I do that?"

"Because … it was a moment of madness. I didn't mean to do it."

"You didn't?" I lean across the bar, not quite believing how this evening has unfolded. She's still consumed by what happened in the water. I know exactly what she's talking about, but I can also see she's embarrassed by it. I've tried not to dwell on it but she can't seem to let it go. I won't ever forget the way she wrapped her legs around me, clinging to me for dear life, and then later, how she grabbed my ass and pressed against me. Instant hard on. She must have felt it.

"No, I … I was drowning." Her cheeks flush again, and I try not to smile. But she can't think I'd send her away because of that. "I brought you here for a reason."

"What reason?"

She frowns, as if she doesn't understand. Or maybe she does, and she's just not sure what I'm thinking. We haven't seen one another since then, and I sense we've both been keeping our distance, but tonight the air is charged with a boldness, and a simmering, sexual attraction I can no longer hide.

She's crazy if she thinks I'd send her away. It's the last thing I'd do, but she's clearly rattled by nearly drowning. We never talked about her fear of water, where it came from. I always assumed she could swim, but she panicked the moment she couldn't touch the floor.

Maybe later, after more drinks or when we're lying in bed, she'll tell me.

Stop.

I shake my head at the intrusive thoughts that have plagued me since we arrived. Why did I think it was a good idea to bring Cari here? She solved my childcare issues, but now I'm plagued by this. Having a constant hard-one whenever I'm around this delectable creature.

But right now, she's standing there looking vulnerable and strong all at once, and I can't take my eyes off her.

"For taking care of Brooke."

"Yes. Yes," she says. "I just thought, you know, with what happened in the water that maybe you'd want me gone."

"You panicked." I try to keep my voice level. "You were scared. Where does that fear come from? Have you always been scared of water?"

She looks away, embarrassed. "I'm really sorry," she whispers. I notice that she doesn't tell me.

"Don't apologize," I mutter.

"But I feel embarrassed," she insists. "Humiliated, if you must know. I'll understand if you don't want me around. If you want to send me home."

"Cari, stop this. You worry too much."

"I … I touched you inappropriately, Mr. Knight." That sentence makes my cock turn harder. Not that I thought it was possible. I try to stay calm, to not acknowledge the raging current of need coursing through me.

Eyes filled with fear assess me. Cari only calls me *Mr.*

Knight when she's pissed off or making a point. I tilt my head. "Hmmmm." It takes effort to keep my voice casual.

"You don't remember?" Her cheeks are flushed as she lifts her glass to her lips but doesn't sip.

Don't remember? It's been looping around in my brain ever since it happened. I had to jerk off again as soon as I was alone. She has no idea of her effect on me. And now her lower lip looks plump and inviting. All I can think about is how badly I want to suck it, feel it between my teeth. Feel it on me.

"Maybe you should remind me." I find this amusing.

She hesitates, turning a deeper shade of pink. "I'd rather not."

"Ah," I say, my voice dropping. "You mean when you put your hands around my ass and squeezed? Or when you wrapped your legs around me?"

Her mouth falls open, making the thoughts in my head turn even more dangerous. I swear I can see her nipples hardening through her dress. My heart skips a beat. This is turning her on.

Why?

How?

She's such a beautiful young woman. I wish I were as young and as appealing in her eyes as that fucker she went out with tonight. But to her, I'm old, *ancient*, even, as well as pompous and a snob. I know because she's told me as much.

"Yes," she murmurs, barely audible, her eyes wide and unsure.

I lean across even more, setting the glass aside, my hands clasped in front of me. Filthy thoughts rush through my mind. A floodgate has opened, and I can't control it anymore.

"I would never send you back for doing that." My voice is full of dark promise.

Her eyes drop to my mouth and her glass trembles in her hand as she sets it down. My gaze keeps going to her bare shoulder and I'm so desperate to trace my fingers over her skin. To feel her softness. To drop a kiss or two on it. She's not wearing a bra. That much is clear.

"You're not wearing a bra, are you?" I ask, unable to stop myself. There are no brakes anymore. I can't contain my thoughts or my words anymore. Not around her.

She shifts back uneasily on the stool, clearly flustered. "Mr. Knight …" Her skin flushes a deeper shade of pink.

She must think I'm a monster. She obviously doesn't have these feelings for me. "I-I'm sorry," I say, panicked. I can't even think straight anymore. "You're right. I've had too much to drink. I only wanted you to know that you look amazing."

She licks her lower lip, the action sending a jolt straight through me. "Thank you, Mr. Knight." Her voice is shaky. "I just wanted to make sure you weren't going to get rid of me. Brooke is having a lovely time, out here. Apart from that episode with Madison and her mother, she's really in her element."

I love that she's so focused on my daughter, but this conversation is about us. "I don't plan on getting rid of you, Cari."

She laughs nervously, but I can hear the uncertainty in her voice. "You couldn't anyway," she adds with a chuckle. "I already resigned, remember?"

I hate that she's talking about leaving again. I don't want her to go. I've never wanted her to leave, but I can't say that.

"Why are you leaving?" I want the real reason instead of the generic one she gave me.

She looks down at her hands, avoiding my gaze. Her brow creases. I only realize that she's struggling to answer when she doesn't say anything.

"Tell me, Cari," I whisper, my voice hoarse. I move back a little, giving her space because I don't want to frighten her. My thoughts are X-rated, but hers won't be. She might even be scared of me.

This collision course I've been careening on for months has brought me to this moment. I tried to move out of her way, tried to block her out of my thoughts by sending her on various errands, but now I must face the truth head on. Because even though I'm her boss, I don't feel like it right now. I see her as a beautiful woman to whom I am ridiculously, impossibly attracted.

It's not just because of her looks. Cari is a beautiful person through and through. But she also keeps me in check. On my toes. She makes me better. When the bear in me comes out, she stares me down and puts me in my place. She has more power over me than she realizes.

"I need ..." She chews her lower lip again. I know she's nervous.

A ray of hope explodes inside me. Does she feel this? A buzz of anticipation fizzes through my veins. I know when a woman wants me, when she's interested. With Cari, I've second guessed myself but here in Bermuda, I feel a stronger pull to her than ever. I've tried to suppress my feelings for her, and the way I think about her, and how she's been in my thoughts for so long. I've tried and yet here we are.

Something keeps me bound to this woman. It keeps her in my thoughts no matter how hard I try not to think about her.

"You need?" I lean forward even more, stretching over the wooden countertop, hanging onto her words. If she needs more money, I'll give it. If she needs more responsibility, she can have it. But she looks somber, and now I'm scared she'll think I've overstepped my boundary. She fixes me with her russet-colored eyes. I fall deeper, mesmerized by the bursts of gold.

"I need to get you out of my system."

Her words hit me like a punch to the gut. My hands grip the

whiskey tumbler so hard, my knuckles are white. Before I can say anything, she stands, grabbing her things, and rushes out of the room, leaving me behind with my jaw hanging, my mind racing, and my dick harder than ever.

Again.

CHAPTER TWENTY-FOUR

CARI

I wake up with a start.

Last night, I rushed back to my room with my heart pounding and my pulse racing. I still can't believe what happened. After replaying what went on in the bar between me and Jett, I finally fell asleep. I slept blissfully, like a baby, for once, but now I'm wide awake again, and it's only five in the morning.

All I can think about is what happened last night. Did that conversation really happen, or did I imagine it? What did he mean? Did he seriously comment on my lack of bra?

No, that can't be right. I shake my head because the lines between wishful thinking and reality are blurring.

Not only did I have too many cocktails, but I ended up sharing another drink with my flirtatious, very-drunk boss. At least this time he's not sitting in my room keeping watch over me.

You're not wearing a bra.

My body reacts just thinking about it, but Jett Knight would never say those things, especially to someone like me. I'm not Alicia. I'm not some glamorous woman who turns heads when she walks into a room. I'm a simple girl who doesn't belong in Jett's world, and I don't possess the sophistication and beauty of the women he usually surrounds himself with.

I must have made it up. Imagined it. Also, he was bordering on drunk.

I peek out the door to check on Brooke. She's still fast asleep. We're going to the Crystal Caves today, just the two of us. I'm relieved that Jett won't be around.

It's still early, so I let her sleep and head back to my room, opening a window and breathing in the salty sea air as the early morning sunlight warms my face. The view is stunning. The turquoise waters of Bermuda glisten like liquid diamonds, stretching out as far as the eye can see. The ocean sparkles, catching the light in a way that makes it look like a living, breathing thing.

In the safety of my room, my mind drifts back to my boss and I try to recall what happened last night with some distance. The flirtatious words, the lingering looks … they kept coming, and I didn't want to leave. But there's no way, *no way,* he could be interested in me.

Is there?

A man of his wealth and standing would never see me as more than his assistant. The thought is strangely comforting, though mixed with confusion. He's older, and he's my boss; a man of the world. A billionaire. If he was flirting with me, it's because he's lonely, frustrated, and missing Alicia.

This is all in my head.

Wishful thinking.

Yet, we did talk. Like we've never talked before.

I remember he wasn't nice about Jacques, and he seemed annoyed that I'd gone out with him.

Still … I don't know. He was drinking alone, and he was moody and irritated; the way he gets when something's wrong. I wonder if his father has said or done something to upset him? Jett always gets like this after dealing with him.

I hear voices outside and look down, my heart tripping over my emotions. Jett is dressed in one of his immaculate suits, and I watch him climb into the SUV. It's a Sunday, but he mentioned something about having a busy day. Even in this heat, he wears a tie and looks as polished and perfect as ever. I don't know how he does it.

I hope his entire day is filled with meetings because I can't face him. As the black SUV drives away, I let out a sigh of relief.

Last night was fun, meeting Jacques and his friends. I drank too much, danced, loosened up. I got a break from everything back home, from my mom's memory haunting me here. Jett was right about one thing, this trip has done me some good. Except now, it feels like I'm on a slightly different trajectory. Like this is not just a trip to Bermuda to take care of Brooke.

I'm so confused. *So* confused. My thoughts spiral into a fantasy where Jett is magically interested in me, where we could actually have a future. But before I can lose myself in that fairy tale, Brooke bursts into my room. She's wide awake, bouncing around like she's been up for hours.

"Can we go to the caves now?" she asks excitedly.

I laugh, finding humor in her misplaced sense of time. "We can, but after breakfast, sweetie."

I'm looking forward to being out of the house and I'm desperate for a distraction. I need to stay far away from Jett, and I need to calm down.

And figure out how I'll ever face him again.

WE HEAD TO THE CRYSTAL CAVES RIGHT AFTER BREAKFAST. One of the drivers takes us there.

I'm secretly relieved to have the day to ourselves. It feels good, refreshing, actually, to focus solely on Brooke, pushing all thoughts of Jett out of my mind. Her innocent excitement is endearing. She makes me want to protect her and make her smile. I so much want her to enjoy this vacation, and I want the memory of the situation with Madison to fade away. I managed to get Celine's number from Jett and I'm hoping to call her at some point to arrange a play date with Brooke and Zara, but for now, it's just me and Brooke.

I tell her briefly what I know, what I've looked up about the caves which are an underground wonderland, formed millions of years ago. The air is cool and damp inside, and Brooke's eyes are wide as we stare at the underground lake at the heart of the cave. It's amazingly clear, the still surface reflecting the ethereal beauty of the formations above. Soft lighting illuminates the crystals, casting sparkling reflections across the water.

"Oooohhhh," she murmurs, reaching for my hand as we stand together, enchanted and in silent wonder. We observe the shimmering stalactites suspended from the ceiling like delicate chandeliers and the pointy stalagmites that rise from the cave floor, some almost meeting to form columns.

I feel as if I'm in another world down here. Brooke gazes wide-eyed, her voice echoing softly as she marvels at the natural artistry carved over millennia. We take our time going around slowly.

Later, we sit down at a picnic table, outside a small row of shops.

"They were breathtaking, weren't they?" I unpack some

sandwiches and open a plastic container of chopped fruit. Then I set out two bottles of water. "What did you you think?"

Brooke turns to me with those big, curious eyes of hers. "I wish you were my mommy."

The question slaps me hard. She didn't even hear my question, or even if she did, this thought must have been percolating around inside her head to come tumbling out the way it did. I blink at her, completely thrown off guard. "Oh, sweetie …" I want to tell her that only her mommy can be her mommy, but I'm scared she'll ask more questions, and I won't have the right answers.

"You're prettier and nicer than all the other mommies," she says innocently, her voice full of conviction.

My heart squeezes tightly at her words. What thoughts are going through her mind? She's so young, but she's growing up and is naturally curious. It's only to be expected that she'll have questions. Then, just as casually, she asks, "Do you know where my mommy is?"

I'm stunned and don't know how to respond. Has Jett told her about Heaven? Or has he told her something else? I'm so unprepared, and I didn't expect this conversation, not today, not here. I've always seen Brooke as this bright, happy little girl, but there's so much more going on beneath the surface. I try to gather my thoughts, but all I can think is that I need to talk to Jett. I smooth down her hair, plaster on a smile I don't feel and tell her, "I'm not sure, sweetie."

"Daddy doesn't tell me."

"Have you asked him?"

She nods, her big doleful eyes looking at me for answers. "He looks sad when I ask him, so I don't ask him now."

We can't avoid this anymore. Brooke's asking questions, and it's clear she deserves answers. I need to figure out what to say to her, which means I need to speak to Jett.

"Oh, Brooke." I hug her as she clutches her beloved elephant to her chest. She takes it with her everywhere, along with a small knapsack filled with some dolls. "I ..."

I wish I could give you the answers you deserve. But instead I say, "I was thinking that it might be nice for you and Zara to have a play date. Would you like that?" I avoid the subject like a coward.

She nods enthusiastically, her questions and worries zapped out of her mind. I feel like I've failed her, but I'm determined to talk to Jett about this. "Okay, sweetie. I'll see what I can do. Let's finish our lunch, shall we?"

After lunch, I call the driver. I've been granted the privilege of calling him whenever we need him. As the SUV pulls up, the driver steps out and opens the door for us.

We climb inside and my heart stumbles at the sight of Jett. Brooke lights up at the sight of him.

What is he doing here?

Brooke sits between us, and I feel a sense of relief. My heart thumps like I've just done a sprint. Jett looks at me, causing the air to be sucked right from my lungs. We acknowledge each other with only a nod.

I try to regulate my breathing as the memory of last night's flirtatious conversation buzzes in my mind. Jett, on the other hand, is cool as ever, like nothing happened. He greets Brooke warmly, pulling her into a hug, but his eyes linger on me for a moment too long. It's the same look from last night, and I can feel the heat rushing to my cheeks.

As always, he looks devastatingly handsome, still in his business suit. The air between us feels thick, charged with everything unspoken. Brooke's excitement barely cuts through the tension as she playfully sits on his lap, animatedly recounting our day.

I'm no Grace Kelly. I have no icy indifference to make me

appear nonchalant and cool. I'm more likely to trip over my emotions and lie face down in embarrassment. I'm an open book, as easy to read as a children's story; simple, with no hidden meanings.

Jett is distant and completely unattainable, like always. His face gives nothing away. I'm not involved in this conversation, and I might as well not be here.

Brooke chatters away happily telling him about the Crystal Caves. She twists in his lap to face me. "What were they called? Those pointy sticks." Jett's casual glance slides in my direction, making my insides electrify.

"The stalactites are the ones that hold *tight* to the ceiling, and the stalagmites grow up from the ground and *might* one day reach the ceiling." It's shocking that I find the ability to think with the heat of Jett's gaze on me.

He listens but still doesn't pull me into the conversation. It's as though last night never happened, like he's reestablishing the boundary, the one we blurred after too much whiskey and those late-night, too-honest words.

The two of them continue talking while I stare out of the window trying not to fall apart. As I lay in bed last night, I concocted fully fleshed out scenes of me and Jett. But now he's poured a bucket of ice-cold water over my sizzling dreams.

As he should.

When we arrive at the mansion, Jett opens the car door. Brooke bounds past him and jumps out first. I'm about to open the door on my side when I notice that Brooke has dropped her beloved elephant. We both reach for it at the same time and our hands brush. The fleeting, innocent touch sends a shock through me and I pull away, flustered, meeting his gaze. For a second, the world tilts as his strong and sensual cologne wafts over me. I let go of the toy, and notice Jett's lips twist like he's about to say something. He stares at the elephant.

"It's *fixed*. Who did this?" He sounds impressed.

"I did." I sewed up the holes and strengthened the stitching on the tail.

His eyes settle on me, turning soft. "You did this?"

"I can sew, Mr. Knight. The poor thing was falling apart."

"Thank you."

I nod.

"After you." His voice suddenly turns cold and businesslike again. The door on his side is open, and I obey, walking past him gingerly in a small space, trying my hardest not to touch him. But my heart pulls tight, like a drawn cord. Throughout the ride he didn't say a word to me.

But then again, I didn't say anything to him either.

I wonder if he's so angry with me that he can't face me. Maybe the man before me is the same miserable, turbulent man I work for. The one who hides his emotions behind a cool, detached exterior.

CHAPTER TWENTY-FIVE

JETT

I STROKE MY COCK AND GRUNT, REPLAYING THAT SCENE IN MY head again. Of Cari in that dress. Barefoot and sitting beside me on a barstool, telling me she'd wear anything for me.

When we got back, I told Brooke that I needed to freshen up and that we'd meet for dinner in thirty minutes. But the truth is, I've been hard for most of the day, trying to arrange the wood in my pants. Things just got worse after bumping into Cari. Even getting out of a fucking SUV is torture with this woman around.

My hand moves in long, hard strokes, helping to ease the tension that's been building in my body all day. Tension I barely managed to release as I left for work this morning.

I come hard, streaking the glass shower door with thick, white lines. All because of her. Groaning out the last of my release, I press my forehead to the tiles. Water cascades down my body, but I can't wash her off me.

I squeeze my eyes shut, wincing at the memory from last night.

You're not wearing a bra.

Who the hell says that to their employee?

She's been messing with my head and my cock. It started when we met in the bar. No, it was before that. When I saved her from near drowning. I can't forget the way her body clung to mine in the water, the way her legs wrapped around me, the way her hands rested on my bottom, the way her fingers dug in.

When I'm around her, my cock has a mind of its own. It stood to attention when she caged me between her legs in the water. I had to jerk off in bed that night as well, because I had trouble sleeping. I left the sheets a tangled, dirty mess, all because of the feel of her.

And then again last night, seeing her in that off-the-shoulder dress. Like I needed any more encouragement to think about her.

When Ruby told me Cari had gone to meet with friends, I knew instantly who she meant. The thought of her with *him* made me insanely jealous. Still does.

That tells me something.

She matters, more than I care to admit.

I sat in the bar waiting for her because I couldn't sleep knowing she wasn't back at the mansion. I feel responsible for her, especially here where she doesn't know anyone, and in a country that is new to her. I would have stayed up all night, but I was pleasantly surprised when she came home when she did.

I saw her on the security camera and expected her to go straight to bed. I wasn't going to confront her or anything, I just needed to know she was safe.

But she came into the bar.

That was her first mistake.

I would dress however you wanted me to.

That was her second. Why would she say that? Cari doesn't

care about my money or my status. I'm just a boring, old boss to her. So why say something like that to me, of all people?

She needs to go.

The most responsible thing for me to do is to send her home, and soon, despite what I said to her. I just can't be around her anymore. It's getting harder and more dangerous having her here, in this house, under my roof. It's easy enough to keep my business life separate from Brooke, but this mess with my assistant? That's hard, and if I'm not careful, I'll do something stupid, like earlier today when I couldn't help myself and ordered a gift to be delivered to her room.

Instead of going home after a hard day of negotiations, I asked the driver to take me to the caves where I knew they'd be. I was desperate to see Brooke, but I also needed to see Cari. And when I did, I couldn't bring myself to say a word to her.

On the way back, I watched her sneakily, trying to gauge her reaction after last night, but she didn't give anything away. Didn't say a word. She was quiet. She was probably thinking of her next date with that imbecile.

I didn't speak to her even though I wanted to. I couldn't, and didn't trust myself. But just being in the SUV was something. My sweet little girl sitting between us and chattering about her day helped, but the few glances at Cari told me she was miserable. I wanted to say something so much, but the logical part of me knew better.

Then as we left, we both rushed to grab Brooke's elephant, and my hand brushed hers like a feather. Having her so near me, caught me unexpectedly.

It made my cock jerk to attention.

I had no option but to jump into the shower. Not because I was hot or sweaty from work, but because I had to get her out of my head.

These last few days, I've gone over our interactions,

wondering if there's something I'm not seeing. I try to make her words have a deeper meaning rather than facing the truth for what it is; she's just a girl who'd had too many cocktails and was feeling brazen. She was tipsy and having fun. She's young, carefree, and still grieving her mom.

Send her home.

I should but … I'm not one for playing it safe. I'm a risk-taker and I have a surprise for her. I'm eager to see if she really means what she said.

CHAPTER TWENTY-SIX

CARI

True to form, my boss is back. He's ignoring me again, after thanking me for putting Brooke's tattered elephant back together.

After everything he said last night, the dirty, inappropriate things he whispered in my ear at the bar, today, he's back to being Jett Knight, the untouchable, impenetrable man.

But something's gnawing at me. If last night meant nothing, then why did he show up when we were leaving the Crystal Caves? I can't figure him out, not even when I think I've cracked the code.

Our hands brushed as we stepped out of the SUV, and an electric shock jolted through me, sharp and sizzling. My pulse raced, and I nearly gasped from the intensity. But Jett? His face seems always to be carved from stone.

I couldn't detect a flicker of a reaction.

"After you," he said, cool and collected, like he hadn't turned my world upside down.

I'm such a mess, as I rush to get Brooke to get ready for dinner, then I retreat to my room, needing the safety of solitude. There's no way I'll go down for dinner, no matter who summons me.

But when I step inside, a gold-embossed box with a black bow waits on my bed. A card rests on top, written in Jett's unmistakable handwriting.

This is from *my boss*.

My stomach lurches, heart pounding against my ribs as if caged. I freeze. My mind turns to mush. Do I open the envelope first? Or the box? I want to do both, but my hands tremble with indecision. I need eight arms for this moment. I lift the lid and my breath catches as a silky flash of red peeks out.

A scarf.

Perplexed, I gently lift it out, only to discover that it's actually a dress. A vibrant, poppy red, the type of red I'd *never* wear. The fabric is light and luxurious and slips through my fingers. I hold the dress in front of me. It's low cut, with a high slit at the front. It has a deep plunging V-neckline, with two flimsy bows that tie on each shoulder. I would *never* wear something like this, because I don't think I can carry it off. A dress like this isn't made for someone like me.

Clutching it to my chest, I walk over to the mirror, my heart hammering wildly, like it's trying to escape. My reflection stares back at me, my face is flushed, and the red dress? It suits my skin tone. I expect it would also reveal a lot of skin.

I walk back to the bed, excited and terrified as I glance at the card still inside the box. I'm afraid to see what he's written. Just as I lift the card out, I see that there's also a matching pair of red stilettoes.

I gasp. Thoughts run riot in my head. This is too much. All of my crazy fantasies are wrapped up inside this box. Heart thumping, I read the card:

You said you would wear anything for me. Prove it.
Meet me in the bar at 11 p.m.

My breath falters, and my pulse quickens. He wants me to wear *this*? This flimsy little thing that'll show every curve, every imperfection. That slit? It'll expose my entire leg up to my inner thigh. And the neckline? A plunging halter that leaves nothing to the imagination.

I'll be practically naked in this, with barely more than a few scraps of fabric holding me together. I press the dress tighter against my chest. It's so light, I could crumple it into one hand. But I don't dare. Not this. Not when Jett Knight expects me to wear it.

And I will.

I don't back down from a challenge, especially when it's from him, *the maddening, arrogant king of control.*

But what does this really mean? These gifts, this invitation? He's made a leap, a massive assumption. We've gone from simmering tension to this bold, brazen dare.

But I feel deliriously happy. Giddy, even. I slip my feet into the stilettos, and they fit perfectly. Like they were made for me.

How does he know my size?

"Can we have dinner now?" Brooke runs into my room. I quickly put the dress behind my back.

"I'm not hungry, sweetie. Do you mind going down to dinner? Your daddy is probably waiting for you."

Her gaze dips to my shoes. "They're pretty."

I smile, because I can't bring myself to say thank you. Because it feels strange that her father has given me these gifts. Brooke skips away. I have no appetite. My stomach feels queasy, and anxiety claws my insides.

I can't risk running into Jett. Not yet. I need time to think, to process, but how will I ever face him in *this*? He wants me to meet him at eleven. I don't think my nerves will have calmed down by then.

I go back to the mirror and hold the dress in front of me again. My breath catches as my reflection stares back at me. I'm starting to feel like a different person.

And then I remember our conversation. Why he's doing this. Because I said I'd wear anything for him. And now, he's daring me to.

Left with my spiraling thoughts, I call Eliana, but there's no answer. I call my aunt, but it goes to voicemail. Brooke will probably spend a few hours with Jett, so I have plenty of time to kill.

I try to read, but I can't concentrate. My heart races, my nerves fraying with every tick of the clock. It's not even nine o'clock.

I decide to do one of the high intensity cardio workouts Eliana and I sometimes do when we feel guilty that we're not exercising enough. I pull up a video to follow and for thirty minutes, I lunge, squad, do burpees and move around the room like I'm on steroids. It tires me out, and gets rid of my excess energy.

After, I shower and get dressed into a T-shirt and shorts. It's too early to wear the dress, which I've hung up on the outside of the closet for now. It stares back at me. Daring me. Teasing me. Scaring me.

What am I doing? This isn't wise. None of this is. Out here in the sultry Bermuda night, far from the rules of the office and the pressure of the Knight empire, it's easy to lose myself. Here there are no checks and balances, no people to rein me in. No Eliana, no clients, no girlfriends of Jett's to schedule romantic getaways for. No beautiful women to be jealous of.

Just me. And him.

I look at the dress again. There's no way I can wear a bra with it, but the fabric is so thin it might as well be translucent.

I might as well be naked in front of him.

My heart beats faster than ever.

Feeling restless, I pull it off the hanger and take it to the mirror, holding the dress against my body again. I can't deny it, it looks good against me. The color complements my skin tone and hair, better than I expected.

A secret thrill surges through me. I feel naked. Exposed. But there's a strange power in that.

My face falls as I remember something about Jett. He'll be disappointed. He likes women with curves, with cleavage. I've noticed that all his women have huge breasts. Whether they're fake or not, I don't know, but he's a breast man.

I can't compare.

But clearly, he wants me to wear it. For him.

Does this mean he likes me? Or is this just a frustrated man acting out?

This version of Jett, the one in Bermuda, is different. Maybe it's because he knows I'm leaving and I'll no longer be around to fix his life, personal or business wise. This could be a fling, a last-minute fantasy. There's a constant throbbing between my legs, and it's been there ever since he put sunscreen on my back.

I've fantasized about him during most of my working hours. Maybe I should take the leap and see where this leads.

Brooke comes up late, around ten, and is thankfully ready to crash. I've been a bag of nerves waiting for her. I wonder if her father did that on purpose, and kept her there to help bide his time.

After tucking her into bed, I get ready in my room. My heart races as I slip into the dress. The fabric clings to my curves, hugging me in all the right places. I stare at my reflection. The low back, the deep plunge. It fits like a glove, but it exposes so much skin. More than I'm comfortable showing.

This is insane. My nerves are pulled so tight they might snap. I reason with myself. I'm following his orders, that's all. I twirl in front of the mirror. The dress is daring, seductive, and shockingly beautiful. I pull my hair up, knowing how much he liked it when I took it down for him last night.

I'm a bundle of nerves, fanning my face with a magazine, trying to calm down. I don't think I can go through with this. But then I slip into the stilettos, and everything changes. It's like a magic switch has been flipped and I have an alter ego.

I walk around in my new shoes, which click against the floor with purpose. My hips sway as I walk and my calves are shapely; my entire body is transformed by these shoes. I glance at the mirror again and love what I see, because I look *amazing*. Chewing my lower lip, I feel a shift inside me.

I'm not Cari Summers anymore.

Tonight, I'm someone else.

Someone who can look Jett Knight in the eye with confidence, even if it means playing a part.

CHAPTER TWENTY-SEVEN

JETT

I TRY TO GET COMFORTABLE. AS COMFORTABLE AS A MAN CAN be with a raging hard-on.

I've changed into lounge pants and a T-shirt, whiskey glass in hands strategically placed, though a bucket might be better suited to hide the evidence.

I have no idea if Cari will do it; if she'll wear the dress. I don't know what's going through her mind, but I've been turning the possibilities over in my head ever since I sent her my surprise gift.

I wonder what she thinks of it all? Does she think I'm a pervert? Probably. But I need to know. I need to find out if she feels what I feel.

Doubt creeps in. Maybe she won't go through with it. Maybe she'll come down in shorts and a T-shirt and call me a disgusting old man. Or maybe she won't come at all.

The grandfather clock chimes. Its loud clang drowns out my thoughts and any other sounds in this cavernous room. But after it stops, I hear footsteps. The clickety-clack of stilettos on the marble floor grow louder with each step.

My heart lurches, and my cock stiffens painfully.

She's wearing the shoes. Which means ... *she's wearing the dress.*

My entire body reacts, a surge of desire so intense it's almost unbearable. My relaxed posture vanishes, and every muscle in my body stiffens. The door flies open and Cari strides in like a breeze. No, like a storm.

Confident. Poised. Powerful.

This isn't the Cari I know.

She's stunning. Sexy as hell. My mouth falls open, and I almost drop the whiskey glass. I should stand up because this moment deserves it, but I sink further into my wingchair, fearing that she'll see the evidence of my desire if I do.

She closes the door, her hips swaying as she walks toward me, stopping just inches away. My lips part, and I instinctively lick them, the urge to devour her overwhelming me. The dress clings to her curves, the slit teasing dangerously high up her thighs. And then I notice. No bra.

Fuck.

Me.

It's even better than I could have hoped for. Cari was made for this dress, or this dress was made for her. If she's as turned on as I am, she's soaking wet. I want to reach out and feel her there.

Stop. I suppress a guttural groan in the back of my throat. Biting down on my molars I let my eyes roam all over her freely. "You look fucking good enough to eat," I growl, my voice rough with need.

"Why, thank you, Mr. Wolf." Her chin tilts up, her eyes, those fuck-me eyes, defiant.

Mr. Wolf? I raise an eyebrow. If that's how she sees me, I

can't wait to fucking eat her up. "That dress was made for you."
I quickly down the rest of my whiskey, trying to buy time to
collect my thoughts. She's nothing like I expected.

She has surprised me.

Taken control of the situation.

Done the unthinkable.

"How did you know what size I was?" she asks, her voice
steady, not a trace of the shyness I'd anticipated.

She's not afraid. Not shy, not embarrassed. What the fuck
has gotten into her? I didn't expect this, this confident, bold
Cari. She's strong, just like she is as my assistant, but this ...
this situation is entirely different.

"I pay attention." My hungry eyes sweep over her, top to
toe. I want to tell her to twirl, but resist the urge. I don't want
her to think I see her as an object.

Her gaze pins me in place. "Why did you give this to me?"

I let out a labored breath. Easy. I've been rehearsing my
answer. "I wanted to see if you meant what you said."

"You're my boss," she purrs, sliding her tongue across her
lower lip, making my control slip another notch. "I'll do
whatever you say, Mr. Knight."

Fuck. Who is this creature? "Anything?" My voice is barely
a whisper. My breath hitches in my throat, stuck there like a
ball of clay, as the air between us thickens heavily with
innuendo.

My eyes travel down her body, over the plunging neckline
of that flimsy fabric, straining against her breasts. The peaks are
perfectly outlined, and I am so tempted to reach out, to slip my
hand inside, to kiss her, suck her, devour her.

Don't go there.

She did what I asked. She wore the dress. I didn't think she
would, but what now? What the hell do I do *now*? Talk to her?
Figure out what this means?

I finish my whiskey in one gulp, then stand abruptly and walk to the bar, needing another drink, needing distance. I pour myself another glass. "What'll you have?" I ask, more to break the tension than anything else.

"Nothing." She sits on a barstool, opposite me.

"Nothing?" It's an effort to keep my voice casual. This version of Cari unnerves me. I feel trapped and clasp my whiskey glass tight, feeling grateful that the bar is between us, hiding the obvious bulge in my pants.

"I need to talk to you. It's just as well you called me down," she says, her voice calm and steady. Nothing like the torrent of emotions spinning inside me. Still, I'm not surprised she wants to talk. Probably about what an ass I was on the drive back from the caves. "I noticed you didn't come down to dinner."

She tilts her head. "I lost my appetite."

I lost mine, too, but I doubt her reason is the same as mine. "Oh? Any reason for that?"

I see the gentle movement of her throat as she swallows. "Not one I can put my finger on right now."

"I thought you were avoiding me." I examine her carefully. Then, because she wore the dress, and she came, she obeyed me, I slowly make my way over and sit down next to her.

Her hair is up, and she looks like a goddess. It gives me a perfect view of her shoulders, and how the dress ties in pretty little bows. Flimsy bows. One tug, and it'll all fall away ...

"You didn't talk to me on the ride home," she challenges, her voice calm and composed as she leans back, perfectly comfortable. "Are *you* avoiding me?"

She's got me there.

I clear my throat. "I'm sorry. Brooke was excited and telling me about her day," I offer weakly. "You heard her chattering away. She had a lot of fun today, so ... thank you, for that." I ramble like a fool, trying not to look down at her dress, or focus on the way her thighs are exposed. "What did you want to talk to me about?"

"It's Brooke."

My sexy thoughts disintegrate.

"Brooke?" I lean forward, my attention sharp.

"She asked about her mommy. She wanted to know where she is. I didn't know how to answer that, so I wanted to check with you. What does she know?"

I stiffen, trying to mask my reaction. Brooke's questions have been more frequent lately, and it's become increasingly difficult for me to answer. She wants to know if she can ever have a mommy again.

"I told her that her mommy has gone to heaven," I tell Cari.

"I don't know what I'm allowed to say. What do you want me to tell her?" Cari gives me that look, the one that cuts through my defenses.

"Just reiterate what I've told you. Tell her that her mommy is in heaven and looking down on her."

"And what if she—"

"I don't want to talk about it, Cari," I growl. I can't talk about my dead wife. I can't have a conversation with Cari about my personal hell, about my past, about Sophia. Especially not when she's dressed like that and staring at me with her bedroom eyes. "You're very good with Brooke," I say, not wanting to sour the mood. "I appreciate everything you've done for her, and not just the little things. The thoughtful things, like fixing her elephant, you're just so good all around. You're the best nanny she's ever had."

"I'm not her *nanny,* Jett. I'm your assistant, and I'm helping out because you needed me to."

Fuck. The lines in my brain blur when it comes to Cari. "Of course you aren't her nanny. I'm not thinking straight."

Her gaze drops to my lips. "Why *this* dress? Haven't you already seen enough of me?"

My throat is so parched, it's like I've poured sand into it. I can't give her an answer.

"You were testing me." She nods, her eyes darkening as she whispers, "Did I pass?" Her voice is so low, I have to lean towards her to hear her words.

"With flying colors."

She watches me closely, her breathing shallow. I try not to look at the quick rise and fall of her chest. "Is something wrong?"

I reach over for the whiskey decanter and pour myself another drink. "The truth is, Cari ... *you're* the one bothering *me*."

Her eyes widen, and her lips part in surprise. "Me?"

I have to tell her. This might be my only chance. "I think of you in ways I shouldn't."

Her eyes turn darker. Her mouth falls open. Fucking hell. That delectable, delicious mouth. In my private moments, I have jerked off to thoughts of that mouth. The things I want to do to her, if only she'd let me.

Her tongue flicks out nervously. "Th-that's because you're here, without Alicia—"

"We broke up," I grind out. I hate that she's so fixated on my ex-girlfriend. "She's history. Do not talk about her. *Ever*."

She shrinks back. "Then it's ... because you're lonely out here—"

She couldn't be more wrong. "It's not because I'm here. It's not because I'm single. I've been thinking of you for a while now." The whiskey has loosened my tongue, removed my filters. I see the shock on her face.

"Thinking of *me*?" she asks, weakly.

It's now or never. Three glasses of whiskey, or maybe four,

have given me courage. "In ways I shouldn't be thinking of my assistant."

She frowns. Then looks down at her dress quickly before her gaze snaps to mine. It's as if clarity has suddenly dawned. "Is that why you asked me to come here with you? To Bermuda? Did you plan this?"

My insides feel like they've emptied. She's shocked. Worse, she's disgusted. I panic. "No! I swear. I didn't plan anything. I didn't want you to come here. I shouldn't have asked you to. I knew it was wrong, but Anna let me down, and if she hadn't, I wouldn't be in this impossible situation. You're the last person I wanted to come here with."

Hurt fills her eyes. I move closer, needing to explain. "It's dangerous, you being near me. Me being near you, away from the office where it's easier to push you away. Where I have a million other distractions. I think of you in ways I shouldn't, Cari, and that's why you're the last person who should be here with me."

She looks stunned. As if I've announced life-changing news, like she's won the prize in a multi-million-dollar lottery.

A range of emotions cross her face, giving me time to examine her features. Her russet-colored eyes, the light freckles on her nose and cheeks. Her luscious lips, and tiny upturned nose. Her pale, iridescent skin with a dewy sheen. Her rich auburn mane, thrown up into a loose bun, wisps framing her face. She's smart, sexy, sassy, beautiful, and has a heart of gold. Everything about her is perfect. Why did it take me so long to realize that Cari Summers is the whole deal?

"You really think of me like that?" she whispers. I can't tell if she's shocked or scared, if she feels trapped. I don't want her to feel any of these things.

Once again, the tiny voice of reason screams in my head. *What the hell are you doing?*

She deserves an answer, and now's my only chance. "You have no idea," I tell her, leaning in towards her just a little. "I feel like a dirty old man and this is wrong on so many levels, but you … you in that dress is an image I'll take to the grave with me. But—" I set my whiskey tumbler down.

She's much more than that.

I clasp my hands together in case I can't hold back, and I'm already so desperate to touch her. "There is so much about you that I admire. You're not just my assistant, Cari. You're not just a beautiful woman. You keep me grounded. You keep me in line. I love your smile and your infectious laughter, which I miss, because it's been a while since I last heard it. Though I understand why. I love your heart, and how you care. How you are around people. How you are around Brooke. Unlike me, you're not scared to feel your emotions. You don't hide anything. You're not afraid to feel everything, and you wear your emotions on your sleeve. I can often tell how you're feeling just by looking at you."

I close my mouth, fearing that I've said too much. Gushed like a sappy teen. This woman unravels me in a way that is unfamiliar and uneasy for me.

"Jett." She looks at me strangely. A faraway expression in her eyes. "Are you … playing games with me? Is this some sick joke?" Her voice is all choked up.

Damn. I've offended her. She'll sue me for harassment. I'm not thinking. This constant hard-on I seem to have all the time has affected my brain. "Don't hate me for this," I beg, feeling like I've lost her. She's revolted by my confession, knowing I can't take back what I've just revealed. I panic, not knowing why I've done this, not knowing what happens next. "But … it's not a sick joke. I thought I could handle being here with you, but I can't. You do all sorts of crazy things to me, and you don't even know."

She chews her lip as if she's contemplating things. "I've been thinking about you, too, Mr. Knight. For the longest time."

"What?" I can't believe what she's just said. "What did you say?"

"I've been thinking about you for the longest time. I can't even remember when it started. During my interview. A few days in. A few months in." She shakes her head. "I don't know the exact date, but it's gotten worse with time, this affliction I have."

My cock grows even harder, and I didn't think that was possible.

"Affliction?" I don't like the word she used.

"You asked me why I'm leaving. That's why. It drives me insane watching you with all your girlfriends. Watching you take them to dinners, having me book your restaurants and vacations, picking up the sexy lingerie and trinkets for them."

I'll be damned. "You've got to be fucking kidding me." I want to believe her. Cari doesn't lie, which means she's telling the truth, but this … this is unreal. I never, ever in my wildest dreams suspected this. She's snarky and direct with me. Up until a few months ago I thought she hated me. But recently, there have been moments when she's looked at me, that made me think perhaps this isn't just in my head.

"I can't work for you anymore, Mr. Knight. I have this stupid … *stupid* crush on you." She squeezes her eyes shut, then opens them again, and looks directly at me. "It's gotten worse since my mom died, and I can't take it anymore."

This news is music to my ears. It's a breathtaking, astonishing reveal that has the potential to ruin me or make me deliriously happy.

"You're not playing games with me?" I ask, disbelief sweeping over me. I have money and power, neither of which she cares for. She's young and beautiful, but she's intelligent and kind, even when I've been impossible to be around. She's also resilient and funny, and she has so much going for her, whereas I'm just a cynical and jaded bastard.

What does she want with someone like me? I'm older. I have a child. I have a ton of baggage, and I've been an absolute pig to her. It would be wrong of me to tarnish her with my darkness. She deserves someone as amazing as she is.

"What do we do now?" She bites her lip, and tries to lift up the flimsy fabric to cover her exposed thighs.

I don't know. I don't know what the hell I'm going to do with this news. "What do you want to do?"

She puts a hand to her hair and takes out her clip. I watch in awe, my pulse starts to race as her hair tumbles down and falls like gossamer around her shoulders. I gaze at her in dumbstruck adoration.

I pushed her out of my thoughts, I barked orders at her, and did everything I could to keep her at bay. And I succeeded, but it's only now that I have unfettered access to her. Now that she's in my space, inches from me, I can sit and freely observe her features. I can take my time with every curve and dip of her body.

And I love what I see.

There's still a trace of Cari Summers, my assistant, in the woman I see before me, but she is now a vixen. She's strong, bold, and unafraid, and she drips with sex appeal.

I want her so badly.

My eyes trail down her body, inch by inch, as if I'm discovering her for the first time, and she catches me.

"I excite you," I say, peering at her nipples which stick out like bullets beneath the dress. Fuck.

Instinctively moving my stool closer, I reach for her, wanting to touch her, but I resist and lay my hand on the countertop instead. My cock is so hard it's getting painful.

"You do that a lot, lately," she answers, shifting on her stool, her eyes lowered. It's the first sign that she's playing a part. Confident on the outside, yet deep down, she's nervous.

We're sitting so close, I can smell her perfume, light and flowery. A scent I have come to know. A scent that excites me.

"God, you are so beautiful, Cari." My eyes trail down to her shoulders, and I imagine untying those delicate bows. I want so much to slip my hand inside her dress and cup her breasts, but miraculously I manage to resist that, too.

"I want to touch you," I say, because I am steel hard with need.

Her eyes meet mine. "Then touch me."

Fuck.

My hand trembles as I tentatively reach out and cup her breast gently over the fabric, sliding my thumb lightly over it. Her nipple peaks even more. A low growl rolls in my throat. I've never had to exercise such restraint before.

This is torture, touching her like this. Her dress gapes apart at the slit, exposing her thighs again. My mind is a riot of confusion as debauched thoughts fly around in my head. Her mouth falls open. She's enjoying this as much as I am, and so far she hasn't asked me to stop. So I keep stroking her, hissing out a sigh, enjoying this first touch and taking pleasure in observing her reaction.

Maybe she wasn't fucking with me.

Maybe she meant what she said.

This wasn't just all in *my* head.

Is she as wet as I am hard? I'm tempted to touch her there and find out. I move my hand to her other breast, giving it the same careful attention. She's so perfect, in every way. Her nipple hardens even more, and I fight the urge to claim it with my mouth. I want to suck her hard, drawing it out to a higher peak, but I don't. I can't. I won't. And it's slowly killing me.

"You're a breast man, and I'm really small." She closes her eyes, as if she's ashamed to look at me.

Her words break the magic spell and my hand stills. I pull back. A breast man? She's so astute. I don't have an answer for her because I can't think straight. "What makes you think I'm a breast man?"

"Because your girlfriends are all gorgeous, and ... busty."

"I don't go looking for women who have big breasts."

"It's just an observation." Her voice is low, rushed, breathless. Sultry, sensual energy tension whizzes between us, making me hot and sweaty. "You've been paying close attention to the women I've dated." I shift a little closer, and she doesn't move back. She seems comfortable, and that reassures me.

"Hard not to when you have me arranging your vacations and dinner reservations. Not to mention the–"

"Okay. Enough about that." I don't need her to rub my face in it. I know what an ass I've been. "I've been a difficult boss."

"That's one way to describe it."

"But I've tried to do the right thing when I can."

"Meaning?" She peers up at me.

She won't know, can't ever find out, that I paid towards her mother's medical expenses. Or that I pulled strings to get her on the clinical trial. It was no easy feat. I also contributed toward the funeral, told the undertaker to give Cari a reduced price. I paid for her bereavement counselling. I've given her perks and bonuses and pay raises, even when they weren't due.

"I'd rather not talk about the women I've dated," I say, letting her think it's about that. But I see a pattern. I met Dina at an art gallery in Manhattan. Voluptuous and beautiful, she caught my eye as I people-watched, bored out of my brains. I met Alicia at a bar one evening, when my Vanhelm deal was sapping my strength. She was there, having just finished a court case. She had beauty and brains, and I don't recall ever looking at the size of her breasts but … now that I think about it, Cari isn't wrong.

I reach out and take a strand of her gorgeous red hair, feeling the texture beneath my fingers. Silky and soft, it glistens under the hanging Tiffany bar lights. "I don't go seeking women who have certain attributes, at least I didn't think I did, but …" My eyes instinctively dip to her chest before meeting her eyes again, "… it would appear that I've been fickle. You're not like that, Cari."

She looks affronted and with a toss of her hand moves her hair out of my fingers.

"You're different." I grab her wrist gently because I don't want her to leave. "You're different, Cari. I love—*admire*, I admire everything about you," I say quickly. "But it's your personality and your wit, and the way you stand up to me, that makes you stand out." I soften my hold on her.

She stares at me in silence, as if she's trying to decide if she believes me or not. I'm such a hypocrite. I couldn't stand to see her talking to that boy-man, and the thought of her being at a pool party with him filled me with rage. It was whiskey that dulled my senses.

I hate that she wants to leave, and her reason for it pierces me like a blade. I realize now that the non-related things I'd get her to do for me, the errands I'd send her on, just to put distance between us, must been torture for her. "I'm sorry I did that to you, but I did it to create a barrier between us. I did it for *me*. I hate that I hurt you." I thumb her lower lip, the one she often chews without realizing. She jolts at my touch. "This is new and unexpected, this revelation that you have feelings for me."

In the silence, we eye one another warily. I can scarcely believe what she's told me, and my hand moves to cup her face gently. Her skin is soft and warm, and lays against the palm of my hand as if it belongs there. I have imagined this moment for a long time, and now it feels like a dream from which I don't want to awaken.

She hasn't said a word, but she also doesn't stop me from touching her. "Whatever happened to that ... to that ..." I have trouble asking the question. "That ... guy who used to come and meet you after work?" I move my hand away, and rest it on the countertop.

Just the thought of her with someone else is hard for me to take. Hard for me to even say. And yet, she's had to see me with my girlfriends. I have so much to do to make it up to her.

"Rory?" She looks away. "I broke up with him when my mom was sick. He wasn't there for me during that time. He seemed to think we could continue going to dinners and going on dates, and ... for him, life continued as normal." She sighs. "I didn't need him in my life."

"He let you down?"

She looks up at me. "In more ways than I can count."

What a loser. He had someone so precious and he didn't value her. To think that when she was going through that tough time the one man who should have known better failed her. It pains me to think of her alone then, though I did what I could to help.

"I didn't have time for anyone but my mom back then," she continues. "I needed Rory to be my rock, my safe place, and he wasn't. The last thing I needed was for someone to irritate me. You know how I can't put up with nonsense."

That's my Cari. I smile at her, and she smiles back. "You put up with me," I say, wanting to take her mind away from her past.

"You were a challenge. And with you, it wasn't nonsense." She leans towards me now, and I shift closer. We're a tangle of legs, and I don't know how it happened, but her knee is between my legs and my knee between hers. The problem is, her thighs are exposed and it takes all my willpower to not lay my hands on them, to not dip my head a few inches closer and plant a kiss on her lips.

I keep my wits around me, lifting my whiskey tumbler, and taking a big sip. "A challenge, huh?" Though, I know I was more than that, I'm sure. A moody, miserable asshole.

"You kept *me* on *my* toes. I didn't want to get anything wrong when I was working for you, but I messed up with the Vanhelm deal."

"You never got anything wrong, and the Vanhelm deal? Well, I was despicable. You fixed everything, despite being under the most difficult of circumstances. You're the best assistant I've ever had, and I don't know what I'm going to do once you're gone."

She rests her hands on my knees. My body responds, like she touched me with a hot poker. I almost flinch, but I stay strong and try not do anything hasty. She looks at me as if she's daring me to make a move.

I set my whiskey glass down and give in to my desire. I place my hands on her thighs and can't help but hiss. Her skin is silky, and soft, and my fingers gently move over her. Fuck. My head drops to my chest, and I inhale a deep breath feeling my cock stiffen some more.

"You're ... uh ..." she whispers.

I lift my head to see her eyes on my package. The flimsy loungewear fabric hides nothing, and my erection looks huge.

"That's all you," I whisper. "You do that to me. I've been hard most of the time you're around, and if that sounds vulgar and disgusting—"

"I like it. I like that I do that to you." But her hands remain fixed on my knees, as if she can't trust herself to move them higher. My fingers, on the other hand, continue to trace over her skin, moving slowly towards her inner thighs.

Our gazes never drift. "You make me so hard that I need to take care of myself every night before I go to bed."

Her mouth falls open, and she chews her lower lip.

Fuck. There she goes, doing *that* again.

"Are you wet?" I ask, my voice raspy with need. "I bet you are."

"Drenched." Her hooded eyes turn darker. "Feel for yourself," she dares me, before closing her eyes and anticipating my next move.

I let out a groan, my hands stilling on her skin as I contemplate her request. But I pull back, because even in my addled state, I know I can't go there, to that place in my mind's eye, where my face is planted between her legs, my tongue lapping up her juices ...

"You should go to bed, before I do something I'll regret," I say.

Her eyes fly open, her lids shuttering as if she doesn't understand. The words don't match the mood, or the longing in our bodies. She looks pained. It hurts my heart when she slides off the stool and rushes out of the room.

CHAPTER TWENTY-EIGHT

JETT

SHE DISAPPEARS IN THE BLINK OF AN EYE. I COULD HAVE stopped her, but I didn't.

I've done the right thing. For once. But what the fuck happened between us?

All sorts of things.

I'm trying so hard to stop myself from crossing that line. Cari made it almost impossible by telling me she has feelings for me.

Now *there's* a revelation.

I cradle my whiskey glass between my hands, savoring our conversation, remembering the feel of her. The scent of her. Now I understand because it all makes sense, her wearing that dress, obeying me.

She *wants* me.

Fuck. I so badly want her, too.

I need to think carefully. I'm a cautious man. I have a

reputation. I could have taken her any which way tonight, and I know she would have let me.

Because this wasn't the commonsense Cari I'm used to dealing with.

The woman I saw tonight was a siren.

All I can do now is squeeze my frustration out in the shower, and hope I manage to sleep.

I TAKE THE DAY OFF AFTER HAVING LOTS OF MEETINGS yesterday. I deserve a break and I'm looking forward to having time with Brooke.

The breakfast table holds way too much food for three people—or two. I'm not sure that Cari will turn up after last night, even though the weekend is over. That's probably not a bad thing.

I'm still waiting for Brooke when my phone rings and I answer it instinctively, without checking to see who it is. I'm on autopilot this morning after tossing and turning in bed all night. Instead of sleeping, I was replaying the scene with Cari continuously in my head, and it has messed with me.

"Hello," I growl, irritation bubbling under the surface as my pent-up frustration builds.

"Jett. It's Bryce."

I mouth a silent *Fuck.*

If he were the last man left on the planet, I wouldn't want to hear from him.

"How are you doing, old sport?" he says.

I've been avoiding this cretin successfully up until now. He used to be one of my closest friends, but he turned into a real jerk when he made money from an investment in Lithium mines and turned greedy on a deal we were working on. Since then, I've steered clear of him.

"Good, good," I mutter, pressing my fingers against the bridge of my nose.

"I didn't know you were here."

"No," I say. *That's because I didn't want to tell you.*

"I'm having a small get together."

"Ahhh … sorry. I have plans."

He bellows with laughter. "I haven't told you when it is, old sport."

Oops. "Right."

"Don't be such a sour puss. My girls dote on little Brooke. How the hell is she?"

"She's fine. She's good," I mumble.

"Bring her."

"A get together for what?" I wonder if it might be the twins' birthday and he's downplaying it. They're around ten or eleven.

"I don't need a reason, old sport. I'm having a party for no reason. Because I can." There he goes again, showing off like the ass that he is. "Tonight, at seven. It's very informal," he continues. "Just the usual friends getting together. Otherwise, we'll never see you, old boy. You like to stay in the shadows."

When it comes to leeches like him, there's a good reason. I know what his "just a few friends getting together" will be like. It will be a show of abundance. A feast, with lots of drinks and guests. Nothing at all like a small get together, by any normal person's definition.

"Come as you are and bring Brooke. Bring whoever the hell you want. You with anyone? Gotten married or anything?"

"No. Nothing like that."

"Then you don't have any plans, old boy. Don't be an ass and deprive your girl of some fun. Tell her we still have the ponies she loves."

"I will." I really don't want to go to this asshole's get together. I hang up just as Brooke comes running in. "Daddy! You're still here."

"I am. I've cleared the entire day to spend with you." I love the way her dark blue eyes light up.

"The whole day?" She stands next to me, her tiny hands running over my five o'clock shadow. "Ouch, that hurts!" she cries and stops touching my face.

"I should shave, but I didn't want to waste time I could spend with you. Yes, the whole day." I tap her nose playfully.

"What are we gonna do?"

"Anything you want to do, sweet pea."

She wraps her arms around my neck and drops me a kiss. My heart fills to bursting. How many mornings have I missed with this adorable angel of mine?

Far too many.

We have weekends in our Manhattan apartment, but they are few and far between. Anna helps a lot, or rather, *did*, but I'm away often and haven't had as much time with her as I have on this vacation. Even on our vacation last year, when Anna came, we only spent a few days here and most of that time I was in back-to-back meetings. Brooke was asleep in bed by the time I got home.

It's unacceptable. We can't carry on like this, not now that she's getting older.

"Have something to eat," I tell her, pulling out a chair for her. She sits down, looking all bright eyed and smiling like an imp.

At least someone slept well.

I push her chair in gently, feeling happy that I get to spend a day with her. I notice that Cari still hasn't come down. I wonder why. I didn't tell her I'd be here. Has she overslept? Or has she heard me and is avoiding me?

What I did to her was bad. I made her think I wanted her, and I so fucking badly do. I made her wear the dress for me, and she did. But then I ruined it. I'll never forget the look on her face as she fled. I hurt her, and I hate myself for it.

"I want to go to the Blue Lagoon," Brooke says. "Zara said it's a nice place."

"Then that's where we'll go."

"With Cari."

"With Cari?" It's strange how attached Brooke is to Cari. Not once has she said anything about Anna.

"Yeah, with Cari," Brooke insists as I fill her plate with fruit and pour her a bowl of cereal.

"Did I hear my name?" Speak of the devil, and Cari comes bouncing in looking remarkably upbeat. Not anything like how I expected. She's wearing a tank top and shorts with frayed edges.

These days, she often surprises me. For a few seconds, my hand stills on the milk I was about to pour into Brooke's bowl. She must have heard Brooke and I talking as she came down the stairs, and after last night I would have understood if she didn't come down to breakfast at all. But she's here, pulling up a chair next to Brooke as if everything is fine. She's in my direct line of sight. I gaze at the slices of grapefruit on my plate.

"You want to go to the Blue Lagoon?" Cari asks, breezily, filling her plate with a mountain of fruit. "Sure. I'm up for that. Let's go."

She's all for it, but I'm not so sure we can be around one another. "Why don't you take the day off?" I suggest. "You worked yesterday, and it was a Sunday."

"So did you." She flashes me a sweet smile that confuses the hell out of me. If I was hoping for a flicker of recollection of last night, it's not there. "Going to the Crystal Caves with

Brooke isn't work." She smiles sweetly and I feel like she's up to something, and I'm not sure I like it.

"If you have other plans …" I offer.

"I do have plans, but not till this evening."

My jaw hardens. I can already guess.

"I'm meeting Jacques and the gang," she says, as if reading my mind.

Jacques and the gang. After what we shared last night, she's meeting him again?

"We've been invited to an informal get together this evening," I announce suddenly. Bryce has come in handy for a change. I turn to Brooke. "Do you remember the twins, Melly and Andi, and their cute little ponies?"

"I remember them," Brooke cries. "I love their ponies!" I'm amazed she remembers. It was only last year, but a year is a long time in little lives.

"Their parents have invited us over, and they want you to come."

"I wanna go! Will I get to ride a pony?"

I stab my fork into the grapefruit. "I'm sure you will." I pause and direct my gaze at Cari. "You and I will both go, sweet pea. Cari's got other plans." The idea of her spending the evening with Jacques screws with my mind.

Brooke's face drops.

"You and your daddy can have a lot of fun," Cari tells her.

"But I want you to come! Please come, Cari. Please."

Cari throws me a look that has the power to freeze my insides. I don't fully understand why she's so mad at me. "You know, what?" She picks up a banana, having hungrily devoured all her fruit. I marvel at her appetite, apparently everything is just fine and dandy in her world. I don't think she lost any sleep over what happened, or didn't happen, between us last night. "I'll just rearrange and meet my friends tomorrow."

"You can do that?" I snap.

"I can do that."

"Yay!" Brooke gurgles with happiness. "When are we going, Daddy?"

Cari slowly peels the banana and looks at me as she takes a bite. My train of thought derails.

"Daddy! What time?" Brooke asks, impatiently as Cari licks her lower lip, then takes another bite.

"Seven …" I hiss, feeling a familiar twitch in my pants. Cari chews slowly, her eyes on me the entire time.

"Daddy when—"

"Eat your breakfast … sweet pea," I say as calmly as possible given the situation.

"What shall I wear this time?" Cari eyes me like the devil she is as she peels more of the banana.

Fuck. Me. "Come just as you are." My eyes lock onto her mouth and the bite she's about to take.

"I might wear a dress," she says. "A red dress, maybe."

Why does it feel like this whole thing has backfired on me?

CHAPTER TWENTY-NINE

CARI

Last night was real, and not a figment of my imagination but it was simultaneously the most wonderful thing to happen to me and the worst. I wanted to believe I could have my own fairytale, even if it was just for a night. But a part of me now wonders if Jett is playing with me.

He told me things that sounded so believable. I remember the way he touched me. The way I touched him. We sat so close together, talked so intimately, our legs intwined in one another's.

He told me he'd been thinking of me in ways he shouldn't have for the longest time. In the moment, it sounded like he was telling the truth, but he blows hot and cold, and now I'm not so sure.

I tell myself I don't care, because I'm leaving. I can do this. I can have some fun, but not if it's for just a moment or a night, because I give my heart. And I can't give my heart to Jett

Knight. He'd likely chew it up and spit it out when he's finished with me.

He's lonely, and probably frustrated. I doubt he goes without sex for more than a few days. This must be torture for him, being stuck out here with me and Brooke, and no hot girlfriend to wine and dine or shower with gifts.

The man has been commanding and dominating and a brute. He says he has feelings for me. But does he?

After the incredible, surreal, stuff-of-my-fantasies proximity we shared, just when I gave him permission to touch me, he said I needed to leave before he did something he regretted.

He played with my mind and my body. His soft touches, stroking my thighs, turning me on, cupping my face, touching my lips, they come as easily as breathing to him.

I mustn't forget that he's a seasoned player. He's had more lovers in a year than I've had in my entire life. Rory was my longest relationship, lasting all of one year and two months. Before that, there were two others. Short-lived, six-month relationships. I'm not a virgin, but I'm also not in Jett's league. With him being a decade older, he's so much more experienced than I am. It turns me on as much as it makes me anxious. He knows how to make a woman feel. Sitting so close to him, with our legs entwined, he strummed my body so perfectly that I was willing to let him do anything. He could have played me any which way he wanted, and I would have let him.

But instead, he sees me as something he'd regret, and that hurts as much as being dismissed.

Men are so weak and pathetic sometimes. I remember Aunt Scarlett and my mom saying that about them, and I have to agree.

It took all my resolve and every ounce of courage I could find to come down for breakfast. Jett should have been at work, but apparently he's taken the day off. I was tempted to hide away from him, but why should I?

I won't allow him to make me feel bad.

He was uneasy during breakfast. He looked sheepish, too. I felt like I had the upper hand, like I did last night in the bar until he dismissed me.

My stomach twisted in knots as I walked in for breakfast, but Brooke's cheery, chirpy manner put me at ease. My confidence vanished when her father said we had to go to someone's house later this evening. I feel like he made it up when he discovered my plans with Jacques.

Apparently, Brooke wanted to go to the Blue Lagoon, but thankfully Jett persuaded her to do something else. He whisked her away to watch a film, and she was so happy that she didn't even remember to ask if I could tag along.

I'm so relieved. I wouldn't be surprised if he suggested watching a film just so that he wouldn't have to spend the day with me. I don't want to spend the day with him, or the evening at this so-called party. It'll be filled with obnoxious rich people, so I'll just focus on Brooke.

I would have given up my evening with friends for her, if it were true, but I made it up on the spot. After last night, I wanted to see if it would make Jett jealous. I think I did. I can read him just as well as he claims he can read me, and I know he didn't like the idea of me meeting Jacques and the others. He's jealous over the idea of me being interested in another guy.

Maybe there is some truth to what he told me. I kind of believe him. I like to think that he was open with me last night, when he confessed to his feelings. This man isn't a liar, and even though he's a pain in the ass and a brutal, arrogant businessman most of the time, when it comes to something like this, I think he'd tell the truth.

I understand it better now that I can think clearly. We're from different worlds. There's no way it could ever work between someone like Jett and someone like me. Even if it's just a summer fling. One night of passion, so that we can both get each other out of our systems.

All those times I wondered if that sizzle between us was just in my head, and he's now telling me it wasn't. That he's been feeling the same for a while.

But he still rejected me.

I need to leave with my head held high, and I intend to do just that. But before I do, I'm going to teach him a lesson. I'll show him.

JETT IS WAITING FOR US DOWNSTAIRS IN THE GRAND HALLWAY. I kept him waiting because I couldn't decide on what to wear.

He looks up, his eyes now bright blue and wide as his gaze trails down the length of me. Brooke and I hold hands as we come down the stairs together. He shoves his hands in his pockets, looking as debonair and charming as ever. I put Brooke's hair in pigtails, and they bounce as she races down the few steps to her father.

"Daddy, do you like my dress?"

"I love your dress, sweet pea."

"Do you like Cari's dress?"

I note the tight set of his jaw. I can tell that he doesn't want to look at me, but now has no choice. He throws a cursory glance my way. "It's lovely, but I like yours better. Come on, let's get going."

They walk on ahead of me. Hand in hand. It's a cute sight, and it warms my heart. I can already see how happy Brooke is on this trip. This means so much to her. As for Jett, were it not for the horny devil I met late at night, I'd say he was softer too. Different. Less guarded.

And for me, dangerous.

Brooke chatters away, talking about the ponies as we climb into the SUV. She seems obsessed with them and I'm happy to let father and daughter have their conversation as I stare out of the window.

Jett and I lock gazes every now and then. We're still distant with one another and haven't talked. We reach our destination, and Brooke gets out of the SUV first. I make to leave from my passenger door, when he grabs my wrist lightly, his thumb sweeping over my pulse point in soothing strokes that both excite and calm me. It immediately transports me to last night at the bar, and I feel that familiar throbbing between my legs.

"I appreciate you giving up your evening to come here tonight." He sounds a little gruff, as if it pains him to say it.

"I didn't do it for you. I did it for Brooke."

"I appreciate that. I just didn't want to mess up your social life," he adds.

"You haven't."

His nostrils flare and he looks like he's fighting to *not* say something.

I feel like ... he might really be ... *jealous.*

As if I need further confirmation, his blazing eyes pin me in place and I can't move. I know all his cues because I have studied this man for so long and stolen secret glances at him when he didn't even know he was being watched. I know his moods, when he's happy and sad. And my heart surfs along a wave of anticipation at the thought that he can't stand the idea of me being interested in another man.

I hold my breath, daring to believe that my wildest fantasy is coming true. Am I even ready for this? He says he has feelings for me, and if he gives in, what do I do? He's so much more worldly, mature, and wealthy. We live in different universes. I'm torn, feeling adrift and wondering if I should settle for someone like Rory, because I don't think I'm ready for a man of Jett's caliber.

But Aunt Scarlett's words bounce around in my head.

It's been a tough year. Go for it, Cari. Have some fun.

It *has* been a tough year, and I do need to get this man out of my system. He gave me that red dress for a reason. He seemed almost reticent, like a man fighting his demons, when he dismissed me. But I'm determined to have some fun. I deserve it. A week of our trip is already behind us. The next two will fly by in a heartbeat, and after that I only have a week left at work.

I'll be out of Jett's life for good. So, if he pushes me again, I'm going to go for it. I'm going to channel my inner vixen and live this fantasy before we head back to real life in New York.

We get out of the SUV, and I sidle up to him.

"There's something you should know," I tell him, with a confidence that is alien to me. Fear blankets his expression, and it makes me wonder what he thinks I'm about to say. I move closer and tiptoe so that my lips brush his ear. My heart thumps so loud that I fear he's going to hear it, but I say it anyway. "I'm not wearing any panties under this dress." I move my head away because I want to see what my words do to him.

What I see is pure, feral lust. A gasp escapes his lips.

Bullseye.

I walk away. I love that I have that effect on him.

But as he navigates his way through groups of people, I see the reaction he has on most of the female guests. The word must be out that he's single again. There isn't a woman on his arm, and though there are a lot of good-looking guys here, Jett stands tall above them all. I don't know if it's because of his height, or the way he carries himself with poise and privilege. It could also be that his slicked-back, dark hair and that commanding face, all square lines with a strong jaw, is hard to miss.

He doesn't have anyone. And he says he wants me.

Abigail, Madison's mother, comes up to him with a smile on her face and longing in her eyes. My heart sinks to see her here. She rests her arms on Jett's and leans in letting him kiss her on both cheeks. They talk and I watch, standing by like a third wheel. Alongside her is another woman, someone I haven't seen before. She's tall and beautiful, her hair scraped into a tight bun that shows off her stunning features. "So wonderful to see you," she gushes, moving in for her welcome kisses. "It's been too long, Jett. We've missed you. *I've* missed you."

I feel out of place in this beautiful world with beautiful people. I stick out like a sore thumb. Like a big green alien, but then I remind myself of how good I looked in that dress, when I finally plucked up the courage to wear it. It's all about perception, and maybe I've had too low of an opinion of myself. I'm the one who's made myself smaller, by making myself believe that anyone like Alicia and these gorgeous women here are better than me. Meanwhile, they're too busy enjoying themselves to even think about me.

"How are you, Tiffany?" Jett asks.

"All the better for having seen you." She playfully squeezes his hands. "So good to see you, Jett. Let's let it all be water under the bridge."

Jett's smile is so fake, but I doubt that anyone else notices.

"I see you brought the nanny," she says, barely glancing my way. Jett scratches his neck. It's a tell. He's unsure how to answer. He could say I'm his assistant, but on this trip, I *am* the nanny. I flash a dazzling smile at the woman.

A large, portly man comes over and talks to Jett. I look

away, observing the crowd, and seeing where and how I can escape with Brooke. She tugs on my hand and I bend down. "Yes, sweetie?"

"Can we go and see the ponies?" she whispers.

"Sure, we can." I was waiting to see if Abigail would say anything to me, but she hasn't so much as looked my way. I catch the big guy assessing me. "Who is this delightful creature?" he asks Jett, loud enough that I can hear.

I give him a dazzling smile, while thinking that he sounds like a sleazeball. I don't want Jett to see me looking miserable. "I'm taking care of Brooke," I reply. "Would you please excuse us? We're going to see the ponies." I nod at Jett and leave, reaching for Brooke's hand. I see some of the moms from that disastrous lunch huddled in a cluster, talking and whispering among themselves. I catch sight of Celine and wave to her. She leaves the group and heads in my direction.

"Let's say hello to Zara's grandmother," I say to Brooke. She happily skips alongside me as I walk toward Celine.

"Celine." I'm so glad you're here." My heart blossoms and I feel happy that I came, if only to run into this lovely woman again.

"Cari! Brooke! I'm so glad you're here. I wasn't sure if I'd ever get to see you again." She kisses the top of Brooke's head and gives me a kiss on the cheek. Celine radiates sunshine. She has an aura about her, something that makes me feel at peace.

"Is Zara here?" I ask.

"Sadly no. She was earlier, but her dad took her home." She makes a sad face. "We need to get you two together on a play date."

"That would be lovely." Brooke tugs my hand gently, reminding me that we were on a mission. "Celine, it's been lovely seeing you. Maybe I'll run into you later, but I promised Brooke we'd go find the ponies."

"Go, go! My grandchildren had rides on them earlier. Enjoy yourself, young lady." She smiles at Brooke.

We head off, but I don't know where I'm going, I have no clue where the stables are. We soon run into two girls who look so alike that I do a double take. They give Brooke a big hug and she seems enthralled. She obviously knows them, and through their conversation I discover that they are the daughters of the hosts. They lead us to the stables.

Brooke's excitement reaches a fever pitch at the sight of the two gorgeous ponies. They have glossy coats of dappled gray and chestnut, and prance gracefully around a ringed off area. They whinny softly, drawing Brooke's wide-eyed admiration.

"Can I ride one?"

"She did last year," one of the girls says.

I look at Brooke, then at the girls.

Can she? I don't know, but I don't want to go looking for Jett to ask him. "As long as she's got the appropriate gear," I say.

"She will, we promise!"

CHAPTER THIRTY

JETT

The moment I saw Cari coming down the stairs in that dress, I knew this evening was going to be tough.

My heart lurched at the sight of her. The black fabric made such a contrast with her golden-red hair, she was a striking vision to behold.

It was so *her*. No flimsy fabric. No slit. No plunging cleavage. And yet I want her in this as much as I wanted her in that red dress.

I shouldn't have come here. I wouldn't have. Bryce and I have bad history, a business deal that went sour when he turned on me and took more money than we'd agreed on.

I detest people like him. I like honest people, and Bryce is anything but honest. I have ulterior motives for coming here, and now I'm paying the price having to converse with people I don't even regard as my friends. I get to spend more time with Brooke, and she loves the ponies. She wouldn't stop talking about them last year. Anna brought her, because I was working on a big business deal during that visit.

But it's not just because of Brooke's love for ponies. I wanted to disrupt Cari's evening with Jacques. My blood boils at the thought of her seeing him again.

"Jett, old boy. I didn't expect you to show up." Bryce slaps me on my shoulder, and we shake hands warily.

"You asked me to come," I reply, casually, before sliding my hands into my pockets.

"So I did. I'm delighted to see you. And who is this delightful creature?" he asks, eyeing Cari like a predator. If she senses him being slimy, she doesn't show it and instead gives him a smile he doesn't deserve. I feel a muscle pop along my jaw. Before I can answer, Cari does.

"I'm taking care of Brooke." She can probably see right through him, and tells me she's taking Brooke to see the ponies, then quickly makes her escape. I chuckle to myself. She's always been a good judge of character.

"I don't remember her from last year," Bryce comments.

"That's because my nanny quit. Cari's helping out. She's my assistant."

"Your *assistant?*" Bryce winks at me. "She must be super fucking talented if she's an assistant *and* a nanny. And she's a hottie." Bryce gazes at Cari and Brooke in the distance. Pretty soon they'll be out of his line of sight. And mine. She looks gorgeous in that dress which contrasts so magnificently with her hair. I've never looked at her as intensely as I have here in Bermuda. In New York, I have ways and means of avoiding her, but sadly none of them apply here. And now not only is she wearing a dress and looking so damn fine, she's also not wearing any panties. My cock hardens some more. At this rate I won't be able to contain myself any longer.

I love how Cari is with Brooke. She genuinely cares and

wants the best for her. She could so easily be a nanny, as well as an assistant. She could be anything she set her mind to. That girl is just fucking amazing all around and I'm lucky to have her.

"Does it bother you?" Bryce pulls me back into the conversation.

"Does what bother me?" I ask, bracing myself

"Brooke. She's grown so much and she looks so much like Sophia."

The bastard. Trust him to bring up my wife.

"Why would it bother me?" I look away, hoping this fucker gets the message that I don't want to talk about this.

"Because, you know—"

I don't know and I don't care to find out. "Excuse me." I need to get away from this prick. "I should check in on them." I pat him on the shoulder, but he grabs my arm.

"Your daughter? Or the assistant?" He winks at me again. He knows. I need to be careful.

There's something happening between me and Cari. Something weird and wonderful. Something that can get me in trouble. I should hold back. I *should*. But I don't think I can.

I shake him off and walk away, swiping my hand through my hair as I head for the stables. What the fuck am I walking into?

I turn the corner to see Cari taking photos of Brooke and it makes me happy. I always forget to do that. My eyes linger on Cari longer than they should. I take in her curves, her slim waist, and remember how she looked in that red dress. I groan, and when my gaze dips lower, below her waist, I suck in a breath at the thought of her being naked underneath.

I'd rather be in the bar at home with her than here. I'd rather be talking to her than these people. Even though she's giving me the silent treatment right now, I deserve it.

I led her to believe that I had feelings for her, and then I told her to leave.

I would hate me too if I were in her shoes.

CARI

I KEEP SNAPPING PICTURES OF BROOKE TO ADD TO THE MANY I've taken on this trip. It was something my mom always did, even though we never really went on vacation. Just the one.

Mom used to snap pictures of me doing the most ordinary things. Eating ice cream. Watching TV. Looking up at her. The photo albums she lovingly put together have been a blessing these last few months. I have roared with laughter, and sobbed with heartache seeing the wonderful, beautiful childhood she gave me. She was a single mom who worked so hard, and I will never get over losing her.

My camera is full of moments with Brooke, and it seems to have been one non-stop rollercoaster ride. We've done so much and have been somewhere every day. At this rate, I'll need a vacation to recover from this one.

Right now, I'm glad to be away from everyone, including Jett. This corner near the stables, away from everyone, is where I plan to spend the rest of my evening. So much for having fun and mingling.

I snap some more pictures of Brooke so that she'll have memories to look back on when she's older. These are things a mother would do, and seeing Jett around his daughter, I'm all too aware that he doesn't take many pictures. I plan to print a book with photos from this trip for her.

"Daddy!" Brooke shouts. My insides turn to fire and I

glance over my shoulder to find him standing a few yards behind me. He doesn't look happy, though he plasters a smile on his face and waves to Brooke.

Something is bothering him, even though his adoring gaze is fixed on Brooke. He doesn't even look my way. I wonder if he's annoyed with me. It can't be me, because I gave myself to him on a plate last night, and he turned me down.

Maybe his father has done something. Again.

I decide to be the bigger person. After all, I'll never forget the hungry look on his face when I told him I wasn't wearing any panties. I'm discovering that it wasn't a good idea because I feel naked and exposed. I've been in a constant state of arousal ever since our interactions went up a notch.

"What's with the face?" I ask. The question makes his jaw muscles twitch some more.

"Why did you tell me that you're naked under that dress?"

This is an easy one to answer. Something about being aroused, something about the conversations we had, something about the look in his eyes when I wore that red dress for him has turned out my inner vixen. I smile sweetly. "I wanted to mess with your head the way you've messed with mine," I whisper. We're standing close now, almost turned towards each other, and I lower my voice, trying to keep this conversation quiet.

"How's that?" Jett's eyes pierce through me.

"I told you how I felt about you. I did what you asked. We were ... close last night," I say, struggling to find the right word. "And then you told me to leave before you did something you regretted. I don't know what to believe anymore."

"Believe everything I said to you last night."

My heart stumbles in my chest, and my knees go weak. "But you told me to—"

"Meet me tonight, when Brooke's asleep. In the gazebo out back."

When I don't respond, he leans closer and whispers, "I need to see you again. *Alone*." His words and his overpowering scent cast their magic spell on me, making my heart flutter.

Is he crazy for saying this to me out here? People might hear. I look around, but it's just us, with the children in the riding ring. But *still*. I seem to be driving this man crazy, and he can't contain himself.

It makes me feel *so good*. I bite my lip again, but standing so close to him makes it difficult to clearly process his words. I try to steady my breath as the knot in my stomach becomes even more tangled.

I quickly pull myself together. He's so slick with the art of persuasion. This man is a salesman. A negotiator. A savvy businessman. I'm just a pawn on his chessboard, and if I'm not careful, he'll convince me that he wants me. He'll make me do things just because there's no one else here who has caught his eye.

No girlfriend for release.

I'm just a substitute.

Someone to play with.

"You say all the right things, don't you?" I'm doing my best to stay strong, even though I can't control my need and desperation for him.

His brows push together. "The right things?"

"Like the things you said to me last night, before you rejected me and sent me away."

His eyes shut for a few seconds longer than normal, his face twisting as if he's in pain. He leans closer to my ear. "I was trying to do the right thing. Truth is, Cari, I want you so badly, it hurts all over."

Chills slide over my back and arms. He's whispering in my ear again, his words an arrow straight to my heart.

"Then don't push me away and make me feel like you don't want me." My words shock me. A month ago, I would never have believed I'd say such things, especially when talking to my boss. But something has changed. There must be something in the air here.

"Meet me," he begs.

Being in an unfamiliar territory, in an exotic location, has caused havoc on my sensibilities. But now there is a chance to do something about it.

He gazes at me with an intensity that makes my jaw drop before leaning towards me again. "I love touching you. I know you loved it, too."

I bite my lower lip again, trying hard to resist running my fingers across his face. I'm so desperate to touch him. I used to imagine these things in my daydreams, and now I want to reach out and do the unthinkable. I want to skate my fingers across that five o'clock shadow lightly dusting his face. He's not my boss here. And all the guardrails between us have disintegrated.

"Jett!" Someone calls out for him, but he ignores them.

"Meet me. At midnight," he says, a pleading tone in his voice. Then he leaves me standing there, feeling so aroused I'm almost giddy.

I try to take in a few calming breaths as I watch Brooke on her pony, but my thoughts are a jumbled mess. I feel like I'm on shifting ground. My boss has told me he wants me, and now that my fantasy has come true, I feel afraid and exhilarated.

When Brooke comes up to me and tells me she's hungry, I'm grateful to have a distraction so that I don't have to dwell on what Jett has asked me.

After getting Brooke to wash her hands, I take her over to

the buffet tables, making sure to keep her by my side. I don't want to be left alone to face Jett or the party guests.

I plate up some food for Brooke, but I don't have an appetite myself. Brooke sits at a table with the twins, who seem to think of her as a cute little plaything. I hear them gush about how they've seen her grow up, from a baby to now. From the sounds of it, she's been coming here every summer, while her father handles business meetings. She knows a lot of people, at least, and many seem to know her.

Jett holds court with a group of people nearby. He's surrounded by women who are smiling and laughing. They run hands through their hair, rearrange their postures. Smooth down their outfits.

For him.

So many crave him. Even married women, like tonight's hostess. She keeps touching his arm as she talks to him.

Brooke is clearly ravenous because she's cleaned her plate and wants more. We go up to the buffet together because she can't reach some of the platters. But she has no difficulty reaching the one with donuts. I let her, folding my arms and smiling at her as she picks up a donut and looks at me, before cheekily putting a second donut on her plate.

Jett walks over to us. "Daddy, these are delicious!" Brooke picks up another donut and hands it to him.

He takes a bite. Behind him, a couple of the women are talking amongst themselves conspiratorially, like they were when I took Brooke to the lunch play date. "Delicious!" He eats the entire thing, then sees me watching him. "You're not eating?" he asks.

"I'm not hungry." The air is too charged with anticipation. I'm simmering with want for this man, so no, I'm not hungry for food.

"Do you mind just running into the house and fetching some more drinks?" The hostess, the gorgeous woman with her hair tied up in a severe bun, asks me. Someone who looks like she might be her sister joins in. "Grab a couple of bottles of Moët, would you?"

They stare at me as if they're waiting for me to skip to the kitchen and do their bidding. I look back, stunned. The group of people behind them stop talking, and they're all looking at me. Jett included.

I wait for him to say something, to stand up for me, but he doesn't. "I'm keeping an eye on Brooke," I reply as calmly as I can.

The hostess waves her hand dismissively at Brooke. "Don't you worry about her. She'll be fine. The drinks are just on the kitchen table." She waves a slender, perfectly manicured hand at one of the tables. "We need more champagne there."

I stand my ground. "I'm not a server."

"Oh, sweetie." This time the younger woman talks. "Brooke's eating. Just run along and fetch the drinks. It's not a big ask."

"She's not a server. And if it's not a big ask, why don't you go and do it yourself, Nicole?" Jett's voice is laced with quiet fury.

I know that tone. It's the one he sometimes reserves for his father. Or the Italian Knights.

"What's the problem, old boy?" The big guy, the host, puts his arm around Jett. "The help is the help, eh?"

"Get your fucking arm off my shoulder," Jett growls. "Cari is not the help. She's here as my guest, and therefore as *your* guest. I'd appreciate you treating her with the respect she deserves."

Oh, my heart.

He's standing up for me. He's standing up to these people and putting them in their place. It can't be easy for him, but he's doing it.

For me.

And now my heart feels like it's going to burst.

CHAPTER THIRTY-ONE

JETT

"She's uppity," Bryce's wife says.

"Terrible attitude," her sister adds as we start to walk away. It's loud enough for me to hear it.

Unfazed, I turn around. "The only uppity, terrible people at this shitty party are you people," I growl. I don't recall Bryce, his wife Tiffany, and her sister Nicole being so despicable before. I don't think highly of Bryce, but witnessing the others' behavior leaves me feeling completely disgusted.

To think I had Cari go to Abigail's house, where these women were. And I wasn't there to protect her from any of this.

Brooke looks shell shocked, so I gently take her hand. "C'mon sweet pea, we're going home." The color has drained from Cari's face. I can't tell if it's surprise or shock.

We walk away but I hear a familiar voice chiding them.

"You knew exactly what you were doing. Shame on you people."

I look over my shoulder to see Celine. I feel reassured. If anyone is going to put those two divas in their place, it's Celine.

"I'm disappointed in you, Tiff," she says, wagging a finger at Bryce's wife. "This is beneath even you."

I chuckle to myself.

"Hey, hey, hey ..." Bryce starts on Celine, but Celine turns on him, her mouth set in a hard line. "I didn't hear you speak up, Bryce. You know they were wrong. You should have been a better host."

They're out of earshot now, but I make a note to call Celine tomorrow to thank her. The night ends on a sour note, though it wasn't so great when we got here.

"Slow down," I say to Cari, who seems to be in a rush to get away. I don't blame her. Celine rushes past me, calling out Cari's name. They hug each other.

"I'm so sorry you had to bear the brunt of that," she says to Cari.

"It's ... it's okay. Jett stood up for me." Not only can I see the admiration in Cari's eyes, I hear it in her voice.

"They were despicable," Celine hisses, looking the angriest I've ever seen her. "Jealous because you're young and beautiful."

"It's ... okay." I see the way Cari shrinks back, like she doesn't want to have this conversation in front of Brooke. It's true. My little girl seems a little scared, so I scoop her up in my arms.

Celine gently pokes me in my ribs. My mom's oldest friend surveys me fondly.

"Jett." She leans in and gives me and Brooke a hug. "Were you ever going to make plans to come and see me on this trip?"

I open my mouth, but don't want to lie.

"Daddy, this is Grandma's friend!" Brooke cries cheerily.

"Yes, she is. She is Grandma's dearest and oldest friend." I set Brooke down again and take Celine's hands in mine. An ache crawls into my heart and takes up residence there. "Scold me all you want, Celine. I have no excuse. I've been busy with business and spending time with Brooke."

"Make time in your schedule for old friends, Jett. It would be good to see you all."

"I will," I tell her.

Looking at Celine, I'm reminded of my own mother. It gets me thinking about how old she'd be now, had she not died. She would have been a proud grandmother, and would have been so happy with Brooke. It hurts to know how much she has missed, how much we've all missed, my brothers and I.

"It makes me happy to hear that you're spending time with Brooke," Celine says.

"We're having a wonderful time, aren't we, sprout?" Brooke nods enthusiastically. "I see that you and Cari have already met."

Celine lets go of my hand. "You're way behind, Jett. Cari and I are practically kindred spirits."

CHAPTER THIRTY-TWO

CARI

"Thank you, for standing up for me." As I settle into the SUV, I'm still blown away by what Jett did back there.

"I couldn't let them talk to you like that."

"I just didn't expect it. They're your friends—"

"Some friends."

Jett's face is tight, and I wonder if he regrets confronting the party hosts. I know he's not too fond of the man, but even so, standing up for me in that crowd can't have been easy.

The journey back is filled with silence, and Brooke, bless her, falls asleep, her tiny body tilting against Jett. He puts a comforting arm around her shoulder, and his hands brush my arm. I jolt as a zap of electricity zings through me. He moves Brooke towards him, so that there's no chance of him accidentally touching me again.

I stare out the window, needing time to reflect because so much happened this evening. The argument with the two sisters has soured the mood, and I wonder if Jett even wants to go ahead with our midnight meetup.

So much has changed.

If anything, it's only highlighted the difference between us.

Those people saw me as the help, and even though Jett defended me, his family would treat me the same. If I meet him at midnight, what am I doing? Walking into more heartache? The whole point of me resigning was to get away from him, from the torture of what I feel for him.

But this is different, my heart says, dismissing my brain. *He told you he has feelings for you, too.*

It's not a one-sided crush. I need to see what he has to say at midnight.

We get back and Jett carries a sleeping Brooke to her bedroom. I tell him that I'll get her into pajamas and tuck her in, and he leaves without a word. Brooke is tired, but she's such a good little girl that when I gently rouse her she doesn't complain. She gets up and brushes her teeth with no fuss.

I'll never go without panties again. I'm so wet down there and it feels uncomfortable. I'm about to hop into the shower because I need to cool down, but before I do that, I decide to go down to the library. Having finished my thriller, I'm in need of something new to read. I still have a few hours before I go to the gazebo.

My nerves are frazzled thinking about what midnight will bring, but reading will help to settle my mind. It used to help when I was with my mom in the hospital, or when I'd keep her company after her chemo sessions. She'd be out like a light, but I would sit by her bedside, crying and falling apart, willing her to get better again and imagining our lives going back to normal. The only reprieve I had from real life was to lose myself in books and stories.

When Mom didn't make it, it broke me.

I tiptoe down to the library, feeling anxious and on edge, already wound up like a coil. I dread to think how I'll feel as the hours pass. I open the door and walk in, instantly feeling calmer. There's something about books, and a hallowed space just for reading and quiet solitude. This place calms me and I walk around, inhaling the scent of old books. It takes me back to another era; one I never even lived through.

The sections are clearly labelled, and I easily find the old-world literature classics, picking up a copy of *Jane Eyre* and *Wuthering Heights*.

I run my fingers across a bookcase and there's not a speck of dust to be found. I marvel at how well this house is kept. At the Knight family's lavish lifestyle, how everything is taken care of. How this family has everything they want, and it's still not enough.

I doubt Jett reads much; only the financial newspapers, or memoirs and autobiographies of rich businessmen. He prefers to spend his time at the bar.

"You needed to kill the time, too, huh?" His voice rumbles through my body. I turn around to find him closing the door. He walks towards me. Being alone in a room with him again unnerves me, and the quiet grandeur of the library does nothing to still my beating heart.

"Are you up drinking?" I ask. He's not holding a whiskey glass, which is unusual.

"I haven't touched a drop. I need to clear my head."

"What are you doing here?" *Thud, thud, thud.* My heart beats like a drum as he stands before me. So close that the spicy scent of his aftershave wafts over me, making my nipples harden. I'm such a mess around this man. My body reacts in a way I can't control.

"I was restless." He stares down at me, his eyes dark now, in the dimly lit room.

I hold the books to my chest as a shield. "A-Are we still meeting at midnight?"

"You tell me. Are we?"

I frantically note that I haven't showered, and I'm not prepared, mentally or physically, for whatever is going to happen at midnight. "Thank you for standing up for me."

"You already thanked me."

"But I'm so grateful that you did. I felt so … alone in that crowd, and you surprised me."

"You didn't think I would?"

"I ... uh ... I wasn't sure. I wanted you to, but these are your people. Your crowd. I hope this doesn't mess your friendship up."

"Friendship?" he snorts. "Bryce Richards is no friend of mine. He stole from me, backstabbed me in a business deal, and he's a shady piece of shit."

"I could tell you didn't like him."

"How?"

"I can read your body language, Jett. I can tell just by looking at you, what you feel, what you're thinking."

"You see more than you let on," he murmurs, his gaze settling on my lips. A light, giddy feeling stirs inside me. I notice that he's showered and changed into his comfy loungewear.

"A lot of those women think of me like I'm the help. It was just like that when I took Brooke for lunch at her friend Madison's house."

"I'm sorry." He sounds weary. "You're not the help, and I despise them for the way they treated you, for the way they made you feel. You are *much* more to me."

This quick and direct jump in conversation startles me. I thought we'd do our usual verbal dancing around, talking about anything but the real reason we're meeting at midnight.

"I am?" I muster a smile, because I really am in awe. What he did for me speaks volumes about who he is, and how he sees me.

"You should know that by now. After everything I said to you,"

"Sometimes it feels like a dream," I whisper.

"And this ..." He takes a step, invading my personal space, making me lean further back against the bookcase behind me. "Does this feel like a dream?" I smell his lemon body wash, and I hate that I'm still hot and sweaty. I really need to shower before we meet, but he catches me off guard, deftly swiping the books I'm holding and sliding them onto a bookshelf.

I can't even breathe. When his fingers gently stroke my cheek, I swear my heart sinks into my belly. Is this really happening? His breath caresses my cheeks, and if I move my face a little, our lips will brush.

"I've dreamed of moments like this," I confess, because with him almost flush against me, his overpowering presence intoxicating me, there is no space left to think. Or to lie. There is only the truth.

"As have I, my little red-headed shortcake."

I'm his little red-headed shortcake.

I want to burst with happiness.

"You have?"

"Oh, yes." His voice is thick, and reverberates deep in my chest. When he cups my face, his thumb trailing down my cheek, I almost mewl with desire. I am so consumed by need for this man, I'm going to do something silly if I'm not careful.

"I-if you don't like that man why did you go to his party?" I ask, my curiosity getting the better of me. "Was it for the ponies? For Brooke?"

His lips purse together, as if he's grinding his teeth. "I'd forgotten about the ponies. I went ..." He pauses, his dark eyes blazing into mine. "I went because I wanted to ruin your plans to see the boy-man."

"The boy-man?" I'm confused. It takes a while for it to sink in. He's name-calling Jacques. This thirty-three-year-old man is as jealous as I thought. He hates the guy he thinks I'm interested in. "Why do you hate him so much?" I ask, all innocence.

"Because you like him. Because he likes you. Because he's young. Because you're seeing him tomorrow."

"I'm not. I lied."

Tension seeps out of his face and his features soften, as he rests his forehead against mine. "You lied to me?" His lips brush so lightly, like a feather over mine, that I'm not sure if it happened or if I've imagined it.

"I wanted to get back at you for telling me to leave that night, after I'd worn the dress for you."

Another brush of his lips against mine. I gasp, and we inhale each other's breath. It's sexy and intimate. The throbbing between my legs intensifies. I could orgasm just by standing and talking to him like this. "You looked so beautiful and sexy. So desirable. I couldn't look at you a moment longer and do nothing. I was scared I'd make the wrong move."

"Even after I told you how I felt about you?"

"You're not hearing me. I was trying to restrain myself. To exercise self-control while I could."

"You hurt me."

"That wasn't my intention."

"You made me feel less than."

He moves his head away. "You are *never* less than, Cari."

I nibble my lower lip as he places his hands on either side of the bookcase, caging me in.

"I'm not with Jacques. I'm not interested in him and never

have been. I wanted to tease you. I wanted you to think of me being naked under this dress."

His eyes widen. "You most certainly fucking did that."

I'm so wound up with desire for this man that he only has to touch me somewhere intimate and I would spontaneously combust. I was already full of need for him, but the way he stood up for me at the party makes me want him with unbridled desperation. I've never felt this way about anyone, and what I felt before is nothing compared to the hunger I have for him now.

I would do anything he asked me. *Anything.*

"I just needed to know that I could drive you crazy, Mr. Knight."

"You do, Shortcake. You fucking do," he growls. His eyes assess my lips like he wants to fuck me with his tongue. He presses against me and I feel his steel-hard cock against my stomach. "Feel that?"

I'd have to be a bookcase myself to not feel that. My chest rises and falls. To be caged by Jett Knight, to have him say these things to me, while his hardness pokes me … oh sweet Jesus.

"Yes," I murmur, feeling on the edge of something.

He thumbs my lower lip. "I already told you, but I'll say it again because I need you to believe me, I've had feelings for you for a long time. You're smart, and you stand up to me. I've been a bully and an ass to you, but I behaved like that to keep you at bay. In a world of liars and cheats, you're honest and real. You sparkle like a diamond, Cari. I'd have to be blind not to see you."

My jaw drops open in shock and his eyes fall to my lips again. He wants to kiss me. And I so badly want to kiss him. Instead, I slide my hand between us and rest it on his hardness.

Holy hellfire. The man is carrying enough wood to light a

bonfire. He moves an inch, giving me space to feel him up. "You do this to me every day, every fucking hour lately," he bites out, like I'm the one who is problematic, and not his dick.

I stroke him gingerly over his joggers, even over the thin fabric I can feel everything. The ridges and hardness. It's so big, my heart pitter-patters inside my ribcage in excitement. I feel a wetness at the tip and my eyes widen. Is he not wearing any boxers? "Have you gone *commando*?"

"Why don't you find out for yourself?" he dares.

Not one to back down, I slip my hand inside the elastic waistband and … I let out a choke. He's not wearing boxers.

"Two can play that game." His voice is gravelly with need. I close my hand around him, and stroke his thick, long length. I don't know if I can handle it. *Him*, inside me. I slide my thumb over his wet tip, making him groan. Feeling emboldened, I smear his wetness over him. He closes his eyes as I gently squeeze. "Fuck, Cari. What are you doing?"

"Something you like, evidently."

I continue to stroke him gently, and his tip leaks some more pre-cum which I smear over him, making him groan low and feral. His eyelids fly wide open. "My turn." He moves my hand away.

"May I?" he asks. I lean back against the bookcase and lick my lips.

"Touch me," I beg.

He doesn't need to be told twice. Bending slightly, he reaches the hem of my dress then slides his hand up my leg. I groan, then bite my lip as the anticipation builds. His fingers skate along my bare skin, making the dress ride up. Soon I'm completely exposed as the dress hitches on one side at my waist. His fingers reach my hip and his eyes pop open when he discovers that I am indeed not wearing any panties.

"Fuck," he growls.

"You thought I was just teasing you?"

"You tease me even when you don't mean to." His hand stays on my hip, his fingers splayed. If he moved them a few inches back, he'd be cupping my bare cheeks.

His thumb lightly rests along the crease of my hip and he groans as he gently strokes me there. I recognize the pent-up frustration in that sound, hear his breathing slow down. He rests his forehead against mine again.

"Fuck, Cari."

I wish he would.

I breathe, and wait with bated breath, desperate for him to feel me between my legs, where I've had a dull ache for weeks. My heart jackhammers in my chest and my knees threaten to collapse.

We both hiss, swallowing each other's breaths. My lips part, I feel as if I'm going to come already and he hasn't even touched me in my most intimate place.

"May I?" he rasps.

"Yes … do it… *please.*" It's a tortured plea. I don't even know what he wants, but I'm all for it. I sigh when his hand moves and he cups me between my legs. I sigh with relief. To be touched there, by him, feels like a small release.

"Fuck. You're soaking."

My breaths come fast and short. He tilts his head away, watching my reaction as he thumbs my clit. I groan in ecstasy as he slips in a finger, then another, turning me into a boneless, writhing wreck. I sink against the bookcase, throwing my head back, lost in the feeling. "Oh, oh, oh," I moan.

His fingers piston in and out.

"You're so wet," he murmurs.

"For you."

It's like my words have poured gasoline over his fire. His other hand slips below the hem of my dress, hitching it up and folding it entirely around my waist. He rubs my clit with his thumb and with his other hand slips in a third finger. I finally feel the fullness I've been craving.

Inside, I unravel.

Just when I can't take it anymore, he kisses me, lifting his hands to cup my face. I smell my arousal on him. His tongue sweeps into my mouth and he takes control, kissing me hard and feverishly, like a feral beast who can't be satiated.

My body jerks to his touch. I want his hands down below, not on my face. When I shake my head, hoping he'll get the message, he falls to his knees and plants his face between my legs. He nudges my knees wider with his elbows, and feasts on me like a man who hasn't eaten in days. His mouth, tongue, lips, and fingers explore my swollen folds, making me shudder with an intensity I can't contain.

"I'm going to … I'm going to … come …" I pant out, so close to the edge.

"No." He stands up, his face shiny. He kisses me again, and I taste myself. For a fleeting moment I recoil, but he's so masterful, so in control, that I lose myself in another hungry kiss. He pulls away, wags his finger at me. "Don't you dare come yet."

"But I can't—"

Before I can say anything, he grabs me gently by the wrist and leads me out, heading towards the stairs.

"We can't … Brooke is sleeping," I protest, afraid that he's heading toward my room. He doesn't listen, and tugs me up the stairs, but at the top he takes a different turn, walking down the hallway.

He pushes the door open, and I stumble inside.

Into his bedroom.

I barely take in the sight of a supersize bed, black-and-gray silk sheets, and warm light from a bedside lamp, before he pushes me up against the door and presses his hardness against me, caging me in again.

"Do you want this?" he rasps, his hungry eyes on me.

I want this more than anything. "Y-yes."

That's all it takes. His mouth crushes against mine. Every cell in my body sizzles. We kiss as though we've been starved for one another for years. This is certainly true for me, and I'm only just realizing that its true for him. He growls as he explores my mouth with his tongue. He swiftly turns me around and unzips me, pulling the dress down my shoulders and yanking it to the floor. Then he unhooks my bra, and I instinctively cover my breasts with my hands.

"Don't be shy," he husks, dropping a sloppy wet kiss on my shoulder. He sucks my skin and I bite back a moan. This is heavenly. He's up to something, and as I'm about to turn around to look, his hands lift mine off my breasts and I feel the wet tip of his cock against my back. He holds my breasts, tweaking and kneading, then moves one hand below, using it to slide his shaft along my butt cheeks.

"Fucking Christ. You feel so fucking good." He doesn't even sound like the man I work for. He sounds like a dirty, sexy monster. I buck against him, wishing he would fill me. Wishing he would fuck me hard. But he promptly stops, and holding my hand, leads me to the bed.

I sit on the edge and scoot back a little before lying propped up on my elbows, blinking furiously when my gaze dips to his engorged penis.

Feeling it was one thing. Seeing it is another. My mouth falls open in awe. In shock. I had an inkling about his size, but looking at it is something else. It's the biggest one I've ever seen. Its bulbous tip purple and glistening.

"I don't think I can ..." *Fit you in.*

I scoot back more towards the headboard feeling a little

scared. He'll rip me apart. And to make things worse, I haven't had sex for a while.

He moves over to his dresser, then takes out a foil packet, ripping it open with his teeth. He strokes himself as he walks towards me. Just seeing him do that turns me on. "This is how I've had to fix myself most nights. Because of what you do to me, Cari."

If this isn't one of the hottest things I've seen. Pre-cum glistens on his tip, and he smears it on himself, the angry vein in his forehead throbbing as if it's about to burst.

"You're so … incredibly … *huge*." I gulp, watching him roll the condom on.

"We can take it slow." He lies over me, supporting himself on his elbow, as one hand dips between my legs. "You're slick enough to take it." His finger hooks inside me, and I whimper as he hits the spot. But, just as quickly, he pulls it out.

His eyes are so dark now, filled with need. I sense the urgency for release. "Do you trust me?"

This man will never hurt me. That much I know. "Yes," I whisper, feeling safe with him. His mouth lowers to mine and we melt into another kiss, this one gentler, but full of need. Then he moves lower, his lips nuzzling my breasts. He takes one into his mouth and sucks hard, the sensation so overwhelming that I arch my back, savoring every moment.

I let out a deep groan, then sigh when he pays careful attention to the other breast. All the while, his fingers stroke my clit. I'm so wet and fully aroused, I can't hold it off much longer.

"Ready?" he murmurs, looking down at me as he shifts his body over mine.

I nod.

I feel his tip at my opening. He slides in a little, and … my head sinks into the pillow, feeling a thousand sensations all over my body. He slowly slides in further and I feel the stretch. Oh, this is … *beautiful*. He fills that dull ache and the emptiness so magnificently. I sigh, feeling every stretch as he slowly inches into me. The delicious friction has an edge of pain. Our bodies are slippery with sweat. In the heat of the night, so close to my release, I start to pant quickly. He stills, kissing me deeply, his lips sucking my mouth, his tongue painting my lips.

"Are you all in," I murmur, feeling full.

"Just a little bit more, Shortcake." He dips his head and sucks my nipple hard, tweaking the other one between his finger and thumb. "Ready?"

I groan, loving the way he worships my breasts.

He sucks harder, gliding in some more, before slamming all the way in. I cry out feeling pain and pleasure. I've never felt so full before. He holds, not moving, letting me adjust to his length, his girth. The pain doesn't last long because he kisses me again, claiming my mouth and my breast, alternating with each as if he can't get enough. Then he stops and stares at me. It's so intimate, him inside me, looking at me beneath him.

"You feel so good," I whisper.

"*You* feel so good." He pulls out slowly, then slaps back into me, making me jolt.

"Ahhhh." I let out a noise. "Don't stop," I beg, and he obeys, setting up a nice rhythm. I can feel the crescendo within reach, and I want to stay in this glorious moment forever. Every cell in my body is bracing for the peak, where I'll fall apart completely.

I'm almost there, but he lifts my leg, widening my angle. Part kneeling now, he slides out slowly and slaps back in hard and fast. Each time he does it, I feel loose and trippy. Like I'm coming apart.

This man is a master. I've been with guys, but now I'm being taken care of by a sex God.

He's right. There is a difference between a man and a boy.

Turns out there's a big difference.

He pumps into me hard and fast, the liquid heat setting my insides on fire. I'm already so close to coming, and when he bends down and kisses me, slamming into me, my head turns light as pleasure spreads over me. It's pleasure and pressure, my orgasm building to a wild crescendo. I cry his name out between gasps. He grabs my arms and pins them above my head, his eyes watching me as he slams into me hard. I like this roughness. This edge to his sweet softness.

"You like this?" he growls.

"I ... love ... this," I manage to get out. He pounds away, and then I fall apart, filthy moans falling from my lips. He grunts as he pushes in deeper, then holds, and I feel every beautiful inch of him filling me as I come undone.

CHAPTER THIRTY-THREE

JETT

CARI HAS UNDONE ME. I COME HARD, GRUNTING OUT MY release. This is what I've been thinking about, dreaming about, for so long.

I get up and take the condom off, throwing it away before I slide back under the covers with her.

It's a sultry night. We lie in bed, in the dim light of the lamp. She snuggles against me, her hand on my chest, her face near the crook of my arm. I love holding her. I love feeling her naked and damp against me. We're a carnal mess of sweat and sin. She lifts up on her elbow, lying on her side as she stares at me with her big golden-brown eyes and gives me a goofy smile.

"Wow."

My lips curl into a smile. "Wow?"

"I have no words." She runs her soft fingers through my hair, and I fucking love this. Cari in my bed, looking at me like that, her smile wide, her eyes shining. All that tension and gridlocked frustration has seeped away. I want this moment to linger forever. I want her like this, with me, alone in our own private heaven. Forever.

"That's most unusual, it's not like you to have no words, but ..." My hand skates over the dip of her waist. "Your sound effects more than made up for it."

She blushes. The color shoots to her cheeks, just like it did when she came, her mouth open as she let out the dirtiest, sexiest groan. I felt her muscles clench around me, and it felt so goddamn good. I watched as she blushed from her face down to her breasts, and all I could do was savor that moment, pausing before I let out my release.

"Don't feel shy," I tell her, tracing her lips with my finger. I want her again, and again and it feels like I'll never tire of her. This first time will stay with me forever.

Already I can see that things are different. Usually, I don't stay long enough to cuddle because something distracts me. My phone, or a message, or having to leave for a meeting, leaving my lover with nothing more than a kiss on the forehead.

But now, I want this woman in my bed all night. I tweak her nipple, and it stands to a peak. She's right. I am a breast man, and hers are perfect.

"I'm adjusting," she says. "This will take some getting used to, the fact that you're my—"

Boss. But she doesn't say it. I don't want her going there, allowing the office to encroach on our private haven. "You're so relaxed, and there's not a trace of anger in your face now." She adjusts her words as her fingers skitter over my skin. I'm doing the same to her, touching, stroking, examining. We're taking our sweet time getting to know one another. I don't want this to be just something physical. I want to hold her close, breathe her in. I want her to tell me her innermost secrets, her fears, her dreams, her hopes. I want to ask her a million questions and discover all the hidden facets of her.

"If I'm relaxed, it's because I came hard. We're talking months of tension here, finally releasing."

She giggles, and I swear it's the most glorious sound.

"You laugh, but ... I'm not kidding when I tell you that I've had to jerk myself off most evenings. I have painted those granite tiles white."

She scrunches up her face. "Mr. Knight!"

"I'm being honest with you. I like sex. Love it. I'm a physical man with needs and living like a monk was killing me."

Her face falters and I realize I've been too blunt. Truthful, but blunt. "This isn't just sex." I rush to say. She needs to know that. Months of fantasizing about her, and now finally getting to climax, have driven me insane.

Making love to her, I felt a connection I haven't felt for a long time. I twist a lock of her hair between my fingers. "What we shared just now was something else. It was incredible. It was on another level." I want to tell her that she's different, that this has blown me away. But I'm scared to tell her the truth, because it's not like me to gush or get excited, let alone talk about my feelings to a woman when we've been intimate.

I know Cari Summers. I know how she can doubt herself. She'll think I'm just exaggerating to make her feel better.

"It was the best sex I've ever had," she says.

"The best?"

"Oh, yes. Maybe there's some truth in not wasting my time on boy-men."

"Aren't you glad you took my advice?"

"A seasoned, experienced, *older* man is what I really need."

"I'm not a dinosaur, or ancient," I protest, sliding my hand between her legs again. Her eyes widen momentarily, and a tiny sigh escapes her lips.

"You do have a lot of energy. I'll give you that." She mewls again as my thumb circles her clit.

"An older man can teach you much. He can show you things … *do* things …" I slide in two fingers and her mouth falls open.

She often throws my age back at me because she knows it annoys me. It only annoys me when it comes to her, because of our age gap. It was another tool I used to keep her at bay. It's not just the age, but the fact that she's my assistant. This could get tricky and I don't know what comes next after tonight.

Fantasizing about Cari was the most I did. I never thought we'd end up in bed together. The unthinkable has happened, and we have two weeks left here. But then what? The old man won't take well to our liaison, and now that he's focused on an alliance with the South American telecom magnate, he won't like this at all.

I feel Cari's muscles clenching around me, and I pull my fingers out of her.

"It was on another level?" she asks, completely ignorant of the worries encircling me.

I nod, looking at her and still marveling that we took this leap into the unknown. "It absolutely was."

"Okaaaay, then ... I believe you, because I know how easily you lie. I've been privy to your business dealings, Mr. Knight, and I know the things you say about people behind their backs when you've been so nice to them to their face."

Trust her to call me out on that.

"It's the price of doing business." I lower my head and suck her breast again, my addiction to her growing stronger. She moans as I suck her greedily.

She lifts my head gently, breaking the suction of my lips to her nipple. "We were in the middle of a conversation."

I sigh with disappointment. "Okay. I own up to it. I can be

two-faced sometimes if it's warranted. But that's business. What we have here, now, it's private and personal."

"You've liked me for months?"

"Yes."

"That means you liked me when my mom passed, but you were still seeing people then. You'd just broken up with Dina and then you met Alicia."

She seems to be hung up on Alicia. That's my fault. I told her to make more restaurant reservations, and I had her go and pick up more gifts than with the others. It's as if I knew my feelings for Cari were getting stronger and I had to nip them in the bud. The Knight name has a certain reputation. "It's all about the brand," my father often says. "Tarnish the brand at your peril."

"You were off limits to me. I couldn't do anything with you even though you were in my head much of the time. I had to carry on living. I had to get through the day," I protest.

"Your relationships were ... transactional?" she asks, surprised.

I've been thinking a lot about that recently. This time away from the office, from my father, from my brothers, has finally given me the space to think. I realize that I haven't ever had a long gap between girlfriends. Apart from that year after Sophia died, when I could barely function and all I wanted to do was be with Brooke.

"They weren't transactional, exactly," I start to explain. "There was an attraction, both ways, with all my girlfriends. But I think I dated more to stave off the loneliness. Instead I was just making it worse."

"Worse?"

It's obvious she wants to discuss this at length, and I sense it's been bugging her. Just like being here in Bermuda has probably been aggravating, given the types of people she's had the misfortune to meet. I need to reassure her.

"Nothing ever felt right. I couldn't see a future with Dina, or Alicia, or the others."

I've said too much. She moves away and sits up, drawing her knees to her chest and folding her arms. Fuck knows why I said that. I didn't mean to talk about the future. It's the last thing on my mind, but sometimes, when I see Cari with Brooke, I get a whisper of what would make my life complete.

For Brooke, for sure.

For me, I'm not so sure.

"Don't listen to me. The blood has drained to below my waist and I'm not thinking straight." I sit up and gently move her arm away. "I don't want to scare you, Cari. I just don't know what this is."

She gives a nervous laugh. "We don't have to think about that. We just have to get each another out of our systems."

Is that what this is?

"You mean I have to fuck you out of my system?" I force a laugh, untangling her other arm from around her knees.

She gives me a rueful look. "That should do it."

This isn't about sex. No way. I take her hand in mine. "I was just building on the loneliness with those women because everything was superficial with them. I was too blind to see that at the time. It was about having someone on my arm at exclusive restaurants, and at luxury resorts. It was about what I could give them. Gifts I could shower them with. It was a mutually beneficial arrangement, but it wasn't enough."

I slide under the covers, and she does the same. We're both turned on our side, facing each other. I move her hair off her shoulder, exposing her neck, and I see the hickey I left there. I'm tempted to leave more. To brand her, claim her as mine. Being with her, even before tonight, maybe when I saw her close her eyes with fear on the plane, I realized there was so much more about Cari that I didn't know, and I wanted to.

I also realize that some things worth having, you have to chase. They don't just land in your lap, the way my previous girlfriends did.

I want more. I want warmth, stability, desire, and love all intertwined. Cari, looking at me, listening to me earnestly, giving me her undivided attention, is the person who can make that possible.

"Do you know what enough is?" she whispers in the dim light.

"Being here with you, is enough. I don't need anything more." I press a kiss to her lips. We're covered by a thin sheen of sweat and the room smells sinful. As hard as it is to leave the bed, I get up and open the windows some more. The gossamer-thin curtains ripple gently in the night breeze.

When I come back to the bed, she's turned the lamp off.

"Why did you do that?" I turn it back on again.

"Because ..." I sense the old Cari returning. My assistant. Now that we're not in the heat of the moment, post-sex reality seems to have hit her hard.

"I want to see you, Cari. Every inch of you. You're beautiful, as are these ..." I flip her over onto her back and start feasting on her breasts again. I lift my head, midway through a long, delicious suck. "They're perfect." She has an insecurity about herself, and I'm determined to erase that from her mind.

I slide my finger into her mouth and she sucks it willingly. I trace it along her lips, growing hard for her instantly. God. I want her again. But something comes to mind from earlier, something she said that bothered me. "You're not alone, Cari."

"Alone?"

"Earlier you said at the party, you felt so alone, and you

never expected me to stand up for you. You really felt alone, even with me and Brooke there?"

"You weren't there for most of the time, Mr. Hotshot. You were busy holding court with your female admirers."

"I was trying to *not* follow you around."

"Hmm." She appears to consider this.

"I'm sorry this has been such a chore for you. The moms' lunch and those hideous women tonight."

"Celine is nice."

"She's an old friend of the family." Cari stares at me expectantly, but I don't want to talk about the past. "Are you sore?" I ask, hating that I might have hurt her in any way.

"I don't think so."

"So, we can go again?" I waggle my eyebrows mischievously. I love the smile that spreads on her lips. She's been smiling and giggling and laughing so much more recently.

"I'm not ... I don't have as much experience as you ... and I haven't had sex in a long time." She sounds shy, embarrassed almost, but I'm over the moon happy to hear this. It means I can teach her things. Do things with her that she's never done before.

Be her first in a lot of ways.

I cup her face gently. "You should have told me. I would have gone slower and been more gentle. I tried ... but ..." I put my hands between her legs again and cup her there. "I couldn't resist this. You turn me into a beast."

Another full smile, before she lowers her head and kisses my chest.

"How many boyfriends?" I ask, my hand still between her legs.

She looks up at the ceiling, then at me. "Three, including the last guy. The one who sometimes met me at work."

I remember him. "The loser who wasn't there for you when

you needed him to be." What an asshole. During her mother's illness, she was so fragile, so broken. She'd cry a lot and try to hide it, but it was impossible to ignore her bloodshot eyes, or the way the trash can behind her was filled to the brim with tissues.

"Yes, and the two before him were very short relationships."

Three lovers? She has much to learn. There is a lot I can teach her. "Define short." She seems surprised at my questions. "I want to know all about you, Cari. I know a few things, that you like pepperoni pizza with a ton of olives, you also like turkey and avocado on toasted sourdough, you live with your best friend, you love The Mayflies, you're reading up about businesses—"

"How do you know that?"

I got carried away and said more than I should have.

"I saw some papers on your desk, some courses or something. The leaflets were just lying there," I say, rolling my eyes. "I snuck a peek. I didn't go through your mail. I would never."

"I've been doing some business courses in the evenings."

This only reminds me that she's leaving, and I don't want to think about that.

"How many lovers have you had?" she asks. Apparently she doesn't want to talk about her leaving either.

"You want me to count?" I protest.

"You expected me to count."

Fair point.

"After Sophia died ..." I try to think. I had a year of celibacy, and then I went wild. There were many, and I'm struggling to count.

A warm hand lands on my chest, stroking my skin. "We don't have to go there," Cari says softly, before pressing her lips to mine. I want to tell her. I want to share, but not this. Not yet. It's raw, and too soon, and I don't want my past to taint my present.

Her eyes assess me, like she needs to know that I'm okay. This is what I mean. This woman gets me. She knows what I need, what I feel, often before I realize it myself.

She grinds herself against my hand between her legs. I want her to feel good, because I'm grateful, I slowly slide two fingers in again, making her arch her back. She shudders as I glide in and out slowly.

Then she leans towards me and kisses me again, this time a long-lasting kiss. Her tongue explores my mouth as she bucks against my fingers. Breaking the kiss, she asks, "Can we go again?"

"I'm ready."

She reaches down and grasps my cock in her hand. "So you are." She wipes the wetness from my tip and smears it over the head, eliciting a dirty hiss from me. She continues to stroke me until I can take no more. Moving her hand away, I sit up against the headboard.

"I thought you liked what I was doing," she protests.

"I fucking loved it." But the intense pleasure she's giving me is turning painful. "Sit down," I order, like I have many times in the office.

"Sit?" She lifts up slowly, covering herself with the sheet.

"On my cock."

She gasps. "What?"

"You heard. Take control. Slide onto my cock. Slowly. Swallow me." I pull the sheet away, so she's naked. That familiar bite of her lower lips tells me where her mind is at. She's nervous and unsure, but she obeys, just like I knew she would.

"Can I turn the lamp off?"

"I want to watch you." My cock lies against my stomach

and she moves to straddle me, positioning my tip at her entrance. "You control it. Do it as slowly as you need to." I stroke her clit gently and watch her pupils grow. A sigh slips from her luscious lips. I love this cause and effect. I love watching Cari react to my touch.

"I should be used to it by now," she says, taking an inch of me in. She lifts up and rests her hands on my shoulders, dangling her pretty perky breasts in front of my face.

I grunt, because the friction between us is so good. She giggles nervously again, and then sinks onto me a little more. I let out a sigh as I slide into her wetness.

"Condom," I groan, suddenly remembering. She moves off of me as I reach into my drawer and pull out a foil packet. Ripping it open, I unroll it and hand it to her. "Put it on me." I lift myself on my elbows to watch her.

Her eyes flutter, but she takes it and rolls it on perfectly. Just watching her, hesitant and unsure, naked and straddling my thighs, is one of the biggest turn-ons of my life. This woman undoes me like no other.

"Perfect." I grit my teeth, letting her set the pace. Her eyes meet mine, but she looks hesitant again.

"What's wrong?"

"You don't have to wear that. I'm ... I'm clean. I haven't had a boyfriend for months, and I'm on the pill ... because I have heavy periods."

My breath hitches in my throat. No wonder she was tight. I could feel her stretching as I slid in. My hands rest on her hips. I shake my head. "You should never offer to do that. With *anyone*." I imagine someone like that man-boy sniffing around her wouldn't hesitate to take her up on that offer. "How do you know I'm clean? You don't. Don't risk things, Cari. Not for anyone."

The hurt in her eyes kills the heat of the moment and she

slides off me. I sit up and I cup her face. "I'm sorry. I care about you too much. I don't want you to do anything that puts you at risk."

Her eyes soften, and I think I have her back.

"Now, fuck me any way you want," I command, lying back down again. A hiss escapes her mouth as she eases herself on my length. I love watching my cock slide into her pussy. Love hearing her soft noises, her sighs of deep content.

Oh, Jesus.

Fuck. Fuck. Fuck.

Her face turns red, and her hips gyrate, causing her beautiful breasts to jiggle. I continue to stroke her nub as she moves up and down slowly, the sound of her soft sighs pure music to my ears.

I love watching her. Love seeing her come, getting her release with her muscles clenching around me. She moans my name, and hearing her say it, in the heat of her climax is even sexier. Her eyes closed, her lips parted, she collapses onto me. I run a hand through her hair, before flipping her onto her back, my hands bracketing her hips as I thrust into her, driving in hard and fast, sliding in deeper and claiming every ounce of pleasure I can from her beautiful body.

CHAPTER THIRTY-FOUR

CARI

I open my eyes in the creeping dawn as memories of last night come flooding back.

My cheeks turn crimson. Heat sears my skin.

I did that.

We did that.

I want to close my eyes and have my daydream linger just a little longer. I just don't know how Jett will react once he faces what we did. Maybe it would be easier if I left now, and we could pretend it never happened.

I turn to my side, wincing because I'm sore below. My eyelids fly wide open in shock when I see Jett watching me. He's also lying on his side, with a strong, muscly bicep curled under his pillow. I dread to think how long he's been watching me sleep.

He chuckles, watching my reaction. "Morning, Shortcake."

I love that he calls me that. "Good morning." I hold the sheet to me, and as I pull it, it leaves him exposed.

To my shock, the man is hard. *Again.*

"Are you taking something for that?" I ask, still in awe at the size of him. I'm shocked at how he is constantly hard.

"This is what you do to me."

I love that I have that kind of power over him, but it's a new day, and things are awkward. I don't know where we go from here.

"I should go." I make to stand up, plastering the sheet to me, leaving him deliciously and temptingly naked.

"Why?" He grabs a hold of the sheet, preventing my escape.

"Because … we can't wake up together." I'm surprised that he doesn't understand this.

"Why not?"

"Brooke. Sometimes she wakes up early and crawls into my bed."

"She comes into your bed?" His brows lift.

"Yes, she does."

"I'll wake you before that happens. Stay," he murmurs, his voice a low invitation. "Spend the rest of the night with me."

I want to. He looks so calm, so undone, almost dazed. He's relaxed in a way I rarely see, as though every defense is down. Not a trace of billionaire armor on him. "Won't it be strange?"

"Why would it be?"

"Given everything we've done."

He scoots over to my side of the bed and his hands move to my waist, fingertips pressing lightly as he tugs me closer. "I want to do more of it."

Oh. Electricity dances along my back. I love that he wants more of it. So do I. I have dreamt about this. So why am I in such a rush to escape?

Because of who he is. His reputation. He'll break my heart.

"Come back to bed." He pats the empty space next to him, and I dutifully climb back in, and turn toward him as we both settle against the headboard. He gently smooths a strand of hair from my face. "I want to talk. There's so much I have yet to discover about you."

I know the feeling. After years of pining for this man, we've reached the stage I could only dream about. I can't believe that this is real. I already know a lot about him, but there's a lot more that he hides. I want to unearth him, dig deeper, reach his core.

"I want to talk, too." It's only been a week since we landed but our time here has flown. Looking back now, we've done so much, but three weeks doesn't feel like enough. I could happily have forever with Jett and Brooke.

"I want to know how you are. I want to know how you're feeling, how you're dealing with things … after your mom. I want to know what else I can do for you."

"Do?"

"To make your life easier."

"I'm leaving soon, Jett."

"Don't keep reminding me."

He looks away, obviously not wanting to talk about that.

"I have good days and bad."

He takes my hand in his. "I worry about you. I wanted you here because I thought it might help. It hasn't been long since she passed."

He wanted me here? "You said you didn't want me here. That I was the last person you needed to be here."

"For good reason. I knew having you here would make things difficult, but it would also be a break for you, a chance to escape New York and the sad memories.

"It's been … *difficult*. I miss my mom every day. Wish I could've done more."

"You did more than most would," he says quietly.

"Thanks to you." He gave me so much time off, for all her

medical appointments, her chemo sessions, and time to work from home when I needed to take care of her. Now that I look back on it all, I wonder if there was more to it than him just being a supportive boss.

My heart tugs painfully. "She was my best friend. A single mom, young and big hearted. It's cruel that her life was cut short, not just for me, but for the future she could've had."

"Cari, my little shortcake." He lifts my hand and kisses it gently. "I'm so sorry that happened, to you and to your mom. The world is full of scheming, power-hungry bastards, and it seems that good people often get taken way before their time."

We sit quietly, reflecting. I imagine he's thinking of the loss of his wife. He looks away, and I see something deep in his expression. "I worry about Brooke. She's forgotten her mom now, but she was just two years old when Sophia passed."

He's opening up to me and I feel so privileged. This is the second time he's mentioned his wife. "I'm so sorry, Jett."

His face twists in pain. "It was horrible. She had a brain aneurysm, and it was all so quick. She was in a coma for a week and then she was gone."

"I heard."

"You heard?"

I pull a face. "I heard that it was sudden, but I didn't know what it was. We assistants talk."

"You gossip." He sounds half-amused, half-annoyed.

"You and your brothers are a captivating bunch." I hold my breath, wondering if he'll talk about his mom. That's one thing the assistants don't know much about. There's hardly anything about it online. I've looked. Paul Knight has the power to buy the media, and gets to dictate what gets printed and what doesn't.

He gives a rueful smile. "Are we?"

How does he not know this? The Knight brothers are intriguing.

"Brooke's been without a mother for so long. I should do more. Be a better father." His train of thought has veered someplace else.

I scoot closer to him. "You already are, Jett, especially on this trip. She adores you."

"This vacation is not what our normal life is like. I work way too much, spend too much time away from her. Leave her with nannies."

"You'll have to find a new one when we're back," I remind him gently.

Something shifts in his expression, a trace of tension. "Another nanny, and another assistant. Fuck." He turns to me and trails a finger along my lips, his tone softer. "I don't want to think about that. I want to focus on the time we have left, with my daughter and my ..." His gaze lingers, a confession hanging unspoken. I watch him carefully, wondering what he's going to say, but he doesn't say anything.

"Your *assistant.*" I finish the sentence for him.

"You're more than that to me." His thumb traces over my lower lip. "You're so good with her. You help out a lot, even when it's not something you've been told to do. I rely on you more than I should."

"You've only just realized?"

"I rely on you because I know I can." His voice drops to a murmur. "When it comes to my daughter, only the best will do."

My breath catches.

"You always go over and above what's expected of you, fixing her elephant, standing up to people like Abigail."

"That's not going over and above what's expected of me. That's just being human."

"That makes me a fucking robot."

I giggle. "A robot who likes to fuck."

"Very much so." He cups my breast, but I move his hand away.

"Let's just focus on talking for now," I say. I like that he appreciates and acknowledges what I do. "I just want Brooke to be happy. I want the best for her."

Something shines in his eyes. It's hard to label what it is. Admiration? But it feels like more than that. More profound. "And that's why …" He pauses. "That's why she lights up around you." I get the feeling that he didn't say what he meant to say.

Just thinking about Brooke pulls a smile from me. "I adore her. I have since the day I first met her." I think back to the sweet little toddler with wide eyes and a shy smile. In the years I've worked for him, Jett's had about six girlfriends, but none ever got close to Brooke. Somehow, I did.

"You're so good with her," he says, almost wistfully.

"This is the longest time I've spent with her. It just feels *right*."

He watches me closely, regret flickering in his eyes. "I wish we'd just arrived. I wish we were still in the first few days of our vacation."

"We still have time." But it pains me to think how quickly it's flying past. "You also need to work, Jett. You came here for business."

"You sound like my father." His expression turns somber.

"Sorry." I lean in and kiss him. "What are you stressing about now?" I stifle a yawn because I haven't slept much.

"Just ... I don't know how to handle the questions."

"Questions?"

"About us."

I blink, trying to make sense of his words. Us? Since when

is there an *us*? My mind spins, heart racing at the way he speaks like this isn't just a one-night thing. Part of me wants to remind him that there is no us, but something stops me.

"You're scared of the sea," he states.

"Is it that obvious?"

"Hell, yes. The way you hugged my buttocks, the way you wrapped your legs around me."

I want to die from shame.

"You liked what you felt, huh?" he asks, his eyes filling with amusement. The arrogant, handsome devil.

"Oh, yes, Mr. Knight. I loved what I felt," I say, breathlessly. My hand skates under covers and brushes over his cock. I'm not in the least bit surprised to find him rock hard.

"Tell me."

I frown.

"About your fear." He doesn't seem to want to let it go.

I exhale loudly. "It was when my mom and I went to Hawaii, that one time, to visit Aunt Scarlett. It was the first and only time I'd been on a plane." I stop to check his reaction, to see if he'd shocked, but he's not. His expressions is calm, not judging. He's listening.

"I got a cramp and my mom was talking to someone. Not Aunt Scarlett. She was lying on the beach. But I was in the water, and I got a cramp and I went under. I remember swallowing mouthfuls of water. My mom was still talking to someone, she had her back turned to me, and she didn't hear me. I went under, then, the next moment, I recall my mom pulling me to the surface. She and a few others managed to get me out of the water, then the lifeguard came over, and a paramedic was called. My mom felt so bad. So bad." I remember the day vividly. "She was beside herself and all I remember is her sobbing hysterically. She was so upset, thinking she'd lost me. She kept saying over and over again that she was scared she'd lost me. That has stayed with me more than me almost drowning."

"Have you ever considered swimming lessons, or therapy, to get over the trauma?"

I shake my head. "I don't need therapy for that."

Jett's hand slides over my stomach, and his fingers splay out, warm and solid. "You're always going to be safe on my watch."

I nod, because his words are comforting, and because I believe him. He could say anything to me in this moment and I'd believe it.

"We should do something special," he says, suddenly. "I want to make the most of our time here."

My heart skips. "This is already special."

"And where will it lead?" He cups my face as I frown, his touch soft, eyes intense.

I try to gauge where he's at, but he's talking as if this could go somewhere. "I thought we were just, you know, getting each other out of our systems," I say, trying to keep my tone casual.

A grin spreads across his face, wicked and knowing. In one swift move, he rolls me back onto the bed, his body pressing against mine, eyes alight with mischief. "Not a chance, Ms. Summers."

His eyes glint with mischief. I bite my lip, knowing exactly what's coming next. He flips me back onto the bed and places his body above mine. I am going to be so sore in the morning. Reaching for a foil packet, his gaze locks on mine as he opens it, rolling it on. "I'm going to need way more than one night to get you out of my system."

These words send a shock of dismay through me. Deep down, I know the truth. There's no future for us. Not beyond this place, not beyond this moment.

"Daddy!"

I hear Brooke's voice and her footsteps outside the bedroom.

"Hide!" Jett cries. I jump out of bed in a panic, and rush over to collect my clothes but I don't have time to get them.

"In there." He opens the door to his bathroom. I dive in just as he grabs the sheet from me, leaving me naked. He throws himself onto the bed and I close the door quickly.

"Daddy!" Brooke sounds panicked. "Cari's not here. She left!"

I suppress a giggle as I look around for towels. I dare not open the drawers, so I take the one tiny hand towel I see and wrap it around myself. It just about covers me.

"She's not?"

"She's not, Daddy. Did she go back home?"

"No, angel! She would never leave us."

"Where is she then?"

"She might have gone for a run, on the beach."

"Oh." How easy children are to convince.

"How about you go and brush your teeth, sprout, and I'll do the same. Then we can have breakfast together."

"Okay."

I hear her footsteps fade away, and in the next moment Jett appears, holding the sheet to him.

He locks the door, and drops the sheet.

I gasp as my eyes settle on his hardness.

"Can't let this go to waste." He moves towards me and rips my towel away.

"But ... Brooke ..." I protest.

He places his hands under my thighs and lifts me easily. My legs wrap around his hips and I drop a kiss on his neck.

"I need to be inside you," he rasps, his voice thick with need.

"But we don't have enough time—oh!"

He sets me down on the dark quartz counter next to the sink and the coldness hits me.

A vein throbs in the center of his brow.

"I need to fuck you." His dark eyes meet mine. Is he asking for permission? Because I have no objection to anything he wants to do, but I'm worried about Brooke walking in on us. His attention is riveted on my body, and he tweaks my pebbled nipple, making me sigh.

"Jett, we don't have—"

I stop when he pushes my feet up to lie flat on the counter. I'm so exposed and open for him right now, in a way I wasn't in bed, under the light of the lamp. Blood rushes south, below my belly.

"I want to do so much with you," he murmurs, a low satisfied sound falling from his lips as his fingers slide over my silky folds. I shiver involuntarily, opening for him easily. Then he kisses me, his cock pressing against me, teasing and tempting. I sigh, sucking his tongue, drowning in pleasure. When he slides inside me, guttural sounds come from deep in my throat. This feels so good, I wish we could be like this forever.

He pulls back and looks at where we've joined, slowly moving in and out, watching, mesmerized. I watch too, holding my breath, as he fucks me slowly.

"Oh, God." I swallow, feeling light headed. He fills me completely then holds, teasing my clit mercilessly, until I shudder and come, riding out the wave as I fall apart under his gaze.

As I start to slump against him, he lifts me up in his arms and places me against the wall, where he sinks into me, right to the hilt, and drives into me relentlessly.

CHAPTER THIRTY-FIVE

JETT

I CANCEL ALL MY MEETINGS FOR THE DAY, INCLUDING THE CALL scheduled with my father. I shoot him an email, letting him know I'm taking uninterrupted time with Brooke and that he shouldn't contact me unless he's dying.

He calls instantly, of course. I let it go to voicemail, fully aware that he's seething, but I don't give a damn. Though I'll probably pay for it later.

Last night was something else. What Cari and I shared, it's beyond anything I've felt before. I can't shake the feeling that she's *different*.

I've always thought this, so it shouldn't come as a surprise.

Something's been bothering me lately. Are all my relationships transactional? I think back to Dina and the easy, detached setup we had. Everything calculated, like it was part of a contract we'd both signed.

Alicia was something more. She was independent, smart

and successful. An attorney. She more than held her own. She could survive in the tempest of the Knight empire.

But the way she was around Brooke? That disqualified her.

And Cari? She's remarkable in every way. Just as I suspected she would be.

We spend the day at the beach, then grab lunch later in Tucker's Town, the exclusive enclave sprinkled with luxurious estates, pristine beaches, and world-class golf courses. The reason I wanted to come here is because of its breathtaking views of turquoise waters and the air of secluded elegance, both of which I know Cari appreciates.

The hours feel like they're suspended in a kind of quiet bliss. Brooke's giggles mingle with the breeze as we soak in the day. Cari captures moments on her phone, snapshots of Brooke covered in sand, of us splashing in the waves, of the unguarded smiles I can't seem to keep off my face.

That night, Cari slips out of her room and into mine again. We give in to the pull between us, as natural as the tide.

The next morning, we're out on the yacht, heading to another island. Cari steps out in the itsy bitsy bikini I saw her in that first day, and my mind goes blank. I lose track of whatever I'd planned to say, and for a second, it's just her standing there, watching me with a big grin on her face. Damn if I don't want her right now.

"Daddy, are we going to the Blue Lagoon today?"

I stare at Brooke for a few hazy seconds. "Uh … yes, sure, sweet pea." I don't dare look at Cari again, but I can't wait to get her back in my room tonight.

Luckily for me and my sanity, she puts on a sheer cover-up while we sail out to the Blue Lagoon.

My brothers and I learned to captain yachts and have all of the licenses and qualifications. Most of the women I've taken aboard have been impressed, but Cari has barely blinked. These things don't matter to her. Sewing up a tattered old elephant does.

I find a suitable space and drop anchor to moor the yacht. Like Brooke, Cari's now wearing a life vest, and we all jump off the yacht and swim around in the turquoise blue waters. Feeling safe now, she swims, and we play a game of tag with Brooke who is like a slippery eel gliding out of reach.

It's tiring work, playing in the water, and soon we set up a picnic on the beach and have a lazy lunch in the sand.

For this, Cari's life vest comes off, and it takes all my willpower to avert my gaze from her. It's not an easy thing to do when she's spreading out a blanket and bending down, then getting on all fours as she straightens the edges.

Jesus.

I have to physically turn away, but then she calls me over and together we unpack the picnic basket, letting Brooke dive into the food. Laughter follows. This feels like family time, and I can't get enough of it. Happiness shines on Brooke's face, and in her demeanor. It's easy to see that this trip has been good for her. As it has been for me.

Cari's phone is out again, capturing moments; Brooke with a cookie in her hand, Brooke snuggled up and asleep on the yacht, me putting suntan lotion on her. I take my phone and snap pictures of my girls. Brooke making sandcastles, posing with her sand-covered elephant, and pictures of Cari, sitting back, looking blissful. Our photos turn simple seconds into lifelong memories. All the while, Brooke's laughter rings across the beach with a joy that's as warm as the sun on my skin.

It's late evening by the time we head back. Cari and I slip stolen kisses when Brooke isn't looking, silent brushes of lips that only add fuel to the fire between us.

Cari helps Brooke shower, then I read Brooke a bedtime

story. After Cari tucks her in, she keeps watch over her until she falls asleep.

I can't shove her into my room fast enough, grateful for another night of debauchery. She giggles, trying to make it to the bed, but I grab her arm and stop her, my eyes trailing slowly over the fuck-me bikini she's been parading around in all day.

I want to ask her how she managed to pack two diametrically different swimsuits, but I don't have time for questions or answers. Within seconds, I've removed her top and bottom. She has her back to my chest and I know she can feel my hardness against her. Reaching back, she grasps me hard and starts to slowly stroke me.

I let out a growl because it feels so good. I'm in danger of coming in her hand if she carries on like this. What I want, what I need, is to be buried deep inside her when I come. I gently push her towards the bed, and she jumps on it, before turning around. She lays there like a provocative minx with her feet on the bed and knees up, giving me a peek of her glistening sex.

I don't know whether to eat her or fuck her.

I MUST HAVE DRIFTED OFF, BECAUSE WHEN I OPEN MY EYES, dawn is breaking and Cari tries to slip away. I slip my arm around her, holding her to me. I beg her to stay, and just like that, she's back beside me. She doesn't want to go either, but feels compelled to because of Brooke.

Dex calls a short while later. I hold a finger to my lips as I answer. Cari raises an eyebrow but mouths "I know" with a look of annoyance.

"What's up?" I ask my brother, keeping my tone casual.

"The old man says you've not been on your A game. You're slacking off."

"I don't know what he's talking about. I'm on top of things."

"He said you canceled a call."

"I'm spending quality time with Brooke," I say, firm but trying to keep it light.

"Word is, brother, that your nanny quit, and you brought Superwoman along." His tone is loaded, and I don't miss the hint of something more.

"That's right," I answer smoothly, unwilling to let him rattle me.

"Anything you want to tell me?" Dex's voice is casual, but I know him too well. He's fishing.

We're close, and usually I'd want to talk to him, but not like this, not over the phone, not with Cari lying right here beside me. "No, nothing. She's just ... good with Brooke. Great, in fact. That's all there is to it."

"Right," he says, skepticism dripping from the single word.

Cari gets up and slips out the door, and this time I make no attempt to stop her. I guess she doesn't want to hear this, and she's lying so close to me, she can hear everything Dex says.

"I'll be back soon. We'll talk then." I stare at my empty bed in disappointment.

"You're in a hurry to go."

"I was sleeping."

"Alone?"

"What is this?" I growl.

Dex chuckles. "We'll talk some other time. You get back to ... *whatever* you were doing."

I slam my phone down, unsure what I'm more pissed off about, Cari leaving, or Dex knowing more than he should.

There will be questions when I get back, and I don't know how to answer them. I don't know how much to tell, because I don't know where this is heading.

CHAPTER THIRTY-SIX

CARI

Dex's voice was laced with disapproval. I could feel Jett brushing it off, but it leaves me wondering … does he really feel what I feel, or is he telling me what I want to hear?

These past days with him have been everything. A fantasy made real, woven with stolen nights and whispered promises. I still can't believe this is my life. Up until that call with Dex, I was floating, wrapped in the warmth of it all. Brooke's laughter, our days spent out together, these perfect little memories we've been making, they've meant the world to me. They're priceless.

But now, doubts begin to creep in, slithering through the edges of my mind where I'd tried to lock them away. It's not just the age difference, though Jett is nearly a decade older and so wildly out of my league he might as well belong to another world. No, it's more than that. Jett is a man with experience, intensity … sexually, he's light-years ahead. Sometimes I wonder, am I just some passing fling for him, despite what he says?

This isn't business. This is personal.

That's what he said to me, but he's also admitted to lying, to telling people what they want to hear. Can I trust him? Can I really believe in this?

I'm tired. Slipping back and forth to Jett's room in the early hours is taking its toll, draining me. My phone blinks with missed calls from Eliana. She texted a few days ago, and I replied, planning to catch up properly, but I never did. We keep missing one another, but seeing her missed calls now feels like a pull back to reality, so I hit the call button.

The phone barely rings before she picks up, gushing with an apology. "I'm sorry. Sorry I didn't call you, but I'm only getting your missed calls and your messages now. I'm not sure what's going on with my service provider. How are you, Car?!" She sounds so happy to hear from me.

"I'm good! Great!" I smile as I say this.

"Busy with Brooke or ...?" She knows me too well to know that I'm happy about something else, despite how much I adore being with Brooke. I hesitate, feeling the pressure of the secret I've been holding in. But maybe it's time to let her in, to share some of it. "El, I ... I have something to tell you."

"Go on. I'm all ears." Now she's smiling as she says this. I can tell.

"I ... I did what Aunt Scarlett said. I had some fun."

"You go girl!

"With ... Jett."

"You did what?" Eliana screeches, and I have to pull the phone back.

"I had fun ... with Jett. Things ... just happened, you know?"

"No, I don't know! What *just* happened, exactly? Stop talking in riddles!" Her voice is sharp with disbelief.

I bite my lip. "We ... you know... we did the *deed.*"

There's a sharp intake of breath on the other end. Eliana goes silent, and I can almost imagine her fainting in shock.

"Say something!" I urge, a bit panicked now.

"You did the *deed*? Cari, that's not even you talking. What do you mean? What *deed*?"

I swallow, cheeks heating. "We … went all the way. Quite a few times now, actually." My insides heat just thinking about it.

"You had sex with Jett Knight? A few times?" Eliana's voice pierces my eardrums.

With a deep breath, I tell her; the main parts, anyway. I don't mention the red dress, or the bar, or any specifics because I'm paranoid that someone could be listening in at, or that the calls are recorded. Instead, I keep it broad, sketching out the main points.

"I can't believe it," she says, when I finish. "Jett Knight, your tormentor? The guy who drives you insane? The one you have a crush on and yet hate for the way he treats you?"

"Ah, but it's not just me. It's not been one-sided, El. He's had feelings for me all along."

"Is that what he told you after he slept with you or before?"

I don't like the sarcasm in her tone. "Don't make it sound so vulgar. It's not like that," I insist.

"You sure?" Eliana's tone doesn't soften. "I bet his girlfriend isn't there. Are you sure he's not just using you?"

"He's not! They broke up."

"How convenient." She doesn't sound impressed. This wasn't the reaction I wanted. I thought she'd be happy for me, even excited. But instead, I feel a dull ache as my best friend's doubts seep into my thoughts.

"I gotta go," I say, my voice wavering.

"Don't go!"

"I have to. Brooke's getting up," I mumble, ending the call and pulling my knees to my chest.

I feel a sharp stab of loneliness. This has been the closest I've ever felt to being in a deep relationship. Except it's not a relationship. I know I shouldn't even call it that because it's more like a whirlwind affair, an erotic fling in paradise.

Go for it, Aunt Scarlett told me, full of encouragement and warmth. She'd understand. Maybe she'd know what to say. I pick up the phone and call her, but it goes straight to voicemail. Her recorded message fills my ear, and just the sound of her voice brings a lump to my throat.

"Hi, Aunt Scarlett." My voice wobbles, and a tear slips down my cheek. She sounds so much like my mom, and I realize just how much I miss her. How much I wish I could talk to her, to ask her what to do. My mom would have understood, and she would have counseled me and helped me through this.

"I miss you so much," I whisper. "I just wanted to hear your voice." Another tear slides down. "You're probably busy, so I'll talk to you when I get back."

CHAPTER THIRTY-SEVEN

JETT

We go snorkeling later that day, or rather, Brooke and I do, jumping off from the yacht into the aquamarine water.

Cari hesitates, her gaze lingering nervously at the edge, so I don't push her to join. I know her fear of the water. The day she almost drowned is a day I'll never forget. Seeing her flailing and start to go under scared me to death.

I leave her sitting on the deck, with her legs dangling over the edge, watching us. But Brooke, with the boundless wonder only a child has, is fearless. It's one of the things I admire most about her. I live for these moments, showing her something new, seeing the thrill in her eyes. Every time she grins back at me, I feel a satisfaction that no business success has ever quite given me.

For the first time, it feels like we're a family. A unit. And I don't know if I'm ready to let it go. Waking up every morning and knowing we have the whole day together has made time slip through my fingers faster than I imagined.

After snorkeling, Cari's content to sit back, snapping photos of Brooke and me as we swim. Her smile is soft and steady, and her laughter blends with Brooke's as we play. We have a quiet picnic on the yacht as it glides through Bermuda's crystal-clear waters, cutting through shades of blue that shift from turquoise to sapphire. The coastline is dotted with pastel-colored homes, there is a vibrant coral reef beneath us, and tall palm trees sway in the distance against the endless sky. It's the perfect picture, almost surreal.

When Brooke finally falls asleep after lunch, it's just me and Cari. For once, no barriers.

I glance at her as we sink into the sofa, the faint hum of the yacht beneath us. There's a hesitation in her eyes now, a subtle distance that wasn't there earlier. I have a feeling it's about the call with Dex earlier.

"Look, I'm sorry about that call with Dex," I say, testing the waters. I hate when anything hangs between us unspoken.

Cari shakes her head, brushing it off. "You don't have to apologize. He's entitled to his opinion. Whatever he thinks you're up to … well, that's none of my business." Her voice is steady, but her eyes betray her.

"Dex and I are close," I say, reaching for her hand. "Zach and I … not so much. As brothers we've always stuck together. We had to, after our mother died." The words spill out before I realize it, slipping through a crack in my carefully built walls. It's something I don't talk about, not with anyone, except my brothers. But here it is, laid bare.

"I'm sorry that happened to you." She looks at me with her big doleful eyes, but she doesn't press me to elaborate. She just stays there, her hand warm in mine, gently stroking it.

"My mother's death … it's not exactly public knowledge," I murmur. "It's not something I talk about much. My father had it erased from the newspapers and silenced as much as he could."

"People can do that?" she asks, innocently. She has no idea what people can do when their insane wealth drives them to make insane decisions.

"If you have enough money, you can do anything."

She lets out a gasp, looking horrified. I go on to tell her how no one outside of this family truly understands what it's like to be the son of a megalomaniacal billionaire; a nasty, narcissistic, selfish self-absorbed man. The type of man who had a secret family on another continent. The type of man who, after his wife kills herself unable to deal with the revelation of his adultery, moved his mistress and their secret children to another country, to come and live in the same city as us. The type of man who called a family meeting a few months after our mother died, and introduced us to these people. We've never seen the mother—at least the old man spared us that—but I think she's still here, in the US. I don't know. We don't know much about the Half-Knights. Only business is discussed at the family dinners, and their mother is not part of those. If she had any sense she wouldn't want anything more to do with Paul Knight.

After meeting the Half-Knights face to face a few months after our mother died, we didn't cross paths with them until I turned twenty-one. My friends got yachts and cars, and ridiculous parties thrown for that milestone birthday, but for me and my brothers, it marked the day the panful Knight family dinners with our father's secret sons started. The old man knew what he was doing. He was preparing us to start working in the family business.

Dex was nineteen, and Zach only seventeen. The Half-Knights? They were still in their teens. Enzo, the baby, had just turned fourteen, we were told.

"I've never shared this with anyone, in such depth before. Not Alicia, or Dina, or any of the others."

Cari's eyes widen. It's so easy talking to her. Opening myself up to her, being so vulnerable. These awful family secrets were stored away deep in my heart, but getting them out, sharing them, makes me feel lighter. They're not secrets any more. I'm sure Dex and Zach tell people, and I imagine so would the Half-Knights. It's just that this news was kept out of the public eye for so many years.

"So, there you have it. My mother killed herself by driving off a bridge after she found out that the old man had a secret family for years."

"Oh, Jett." Cari clasps a hand to her chest, her eyes filled with shock. "That's so messed up. Not knowing your other brothers like they're a part of your family, and also losing your mom like that. A mom is irreplaceable."

A familiar ache dulls my body. Talking about it now, even after all these years stirs something raw inside me. I glance away, focusing on the gentle roll of the ocean. "It was a long time ago." My words catch slightly and I take a moment to compose myself. "I was thirteen when I lost mom."

"I'm so sorry." She rests her hand against the side of my face. The memory hits me, a sharp twist that hasn't dulled with time. The first moment I heard the news, a crack formed in my world I'd always thought unbreakable. Even now, it's a wound that hasn't fully healed.

"Now *I'll* worry about *you*," she whispers.

I try to smile, to shrug it off. "I'm all grown up now. There's no need to waste your time worrying about me."

"A hurt like that never goes away." Her hand is still in mine, her touch grounding me. Telling her feels as if a load has been lifted from my chest. I pause, reliving the moment I heard of her death all those decades ago. The knife to my heart is as raw now as it was then.

CARI

I FEEL LIKE JETT SHARED HIS DEEPEST, DARKEST SECRET WITH me. A part of himself he's never shown anyone and I feel a connection to him that is even deeper now. A connect that goes beyond the physical and emotional.

He opened up about his mother, and from what I've overheard in whispers between the other assistants, it's a topic the Knight brothers never really broach.

That his mom died by suicide breaks my heart in a way I didn't expect. It explains why he was so empathetic when I lost my mom. I had no idea of the depth of pain this man has endured, no sense of the scars hidden beneath that polished, arrogant exterior. It's a tragedy that feels unimaginable, and now that I know, I can't shake it. The pain of his loss presses into me, leaving me with an ache I feel for him and the boy he once was. Just as I go to hug him, Brooke stirs, then stretches, sticking her skinny little arms up. Her eyelids fly wide open.

I stop, and Jett stands up. "What now, sprout? What do you want to do next?"

She wants to go back in the water. So we do, and with my life vest on, I don't fear it as much.

We return home and go through the ritual of getting Brooke ready for bed. When she's snuggled up and her eyes start to droop, I know she'll be out like a light in no time.

I reach for Jett's hand and tug him towards his bedroom. Still in my bikini, wearing my sheer cover-up, and smelling of sea and salt, we stand in the middle of his room. I cradle his face, my fingers softly tracing his jawline. His skin is warm beneath my touch, and I lean in, kissing him deeply, trying to convey every ounce of the emotion welling up inside me. The world around us fades as our lips meet, slow and tender at first, then with growing urgency. The kiss becomes a promise of understanding and comfort, of everything I want to give him.

"You okay?" My fingers brush his cheek lightly. I feel an overwhelming sense of needing to care for him, especially after everything he shared with me.

He opens the clip that holds my hair up, letting it tumble around my shoulders. "I am now that you're with me." He presses a kiss on my lips.

"I know you worry about me," I whisper against his mouth, "You've been checking in on how I'm doing since my mom passed. But did anyone ever ask how *you* were doing?"

His gaze holds mine, as if stunned by the question. Then, as if all words have failed him, he answers with another kiss, one that ignites a slow fire in the pit of my stomach. My heart pounds as his arms tighten around me, pulling me closer, our breaths mingling in a heated silence.

I slipped out of his bed early this morning, feeling annoyed by Dex's intrusion. All day, I've kept my distance, staying aloof when normally we'd sneak a few stolen moments behind Brooke's back.

He noticed. I saw the flicker in his eyes earlier, a hint of frustration, maybe even longing. Now, here we are, just the two of us again, and I feel him hard and insistent against me, pressing through the delicate fabric of my bikini bottoms. I'm desperate for him, craving him in a way that blurs everything else.

His hand moves between my legs, his fingers push the wisp of fabric and slide it to one side. A shiver of anticipation races through me as his fingers trace my warmth, pressing, circling, each touch sending a cascade of need spiraling through me. A thought crashes into my mind unbidden. I want to take him again, ease onto him, feel every inch of him sliding into me.

"Sit on me," he commands, his voice low, his fingers sliding and slipping over my folds, fueling my need. He takes my hand and leads me to the bed. I want to. I want nothing more than to give in to this wild urge, to let go completely and lose myself in him.

But I have other plans. My fingers skate gently over his chest before sliding down, down, down. I peel down his swim shorts and note that he doesn't waste time stripping off his T-shirt. I'm still wearing my bikini, but he's completely naked now with his cock upright and ready. I gape at his member, my insides turning to heat because I know what happens next.

"Looks like I need to take care of something for you." Every part of me wants to take care of him, to hold him. I stroke his wet tip, my heart filling with love for this man who has suffered so much. I push him gently onto the bed, and start to explore his body, like he's been exploring mine.

He hitches a breath. "Sit ... on ... me," he says, but its softer now, not commanding, like he's enjoying seeing where this is going.

"No. I want *this*."

He leans back a little, on his elbows, his cock beautifully sprung up for me to feast on. I kneel in front of him, moving his knees wider, unable to take my eyes off his beautiful shaft. To think I was once scared of him being inside me, and now ... now I dream of us doing unspeakable things in bed together.

"You don't have to do this ..." He tries again, sitting up, but I can sense the urgency in his voice, like he needs the release immediately.

"I want to." My voice is almost a low growl because I'm already dripping wet with desire for him, my arousal starting to trickle down my inner thigh. I could so easily sit on him and ride him wildly so we would come together, but he needs taking care of first.

I slide my hands along his inner thighs, hear the way his breath hitches. Keeping my touch featherlight, I trace along his heated skin, letting my hands run gently over the hard ridges of his abs. His cock is in the way, but I ignore it for now, as impossible as it is. I touch and trace, eliciting growls from him that only give me more confidence.

I smell salt and the sea on him. It's a scent that will always remind me of passionate nights with Jett. Dipping my head, I rain tiny kisses under his navel, moving down slowly.

"Fuck," he groans.

"In time, yes. We will." I look up at him with a smile. Seeing the torture in his expression fills me with power, but I lower my head again and lick his skin along his lower belly. He rests a hand on my head and I suck his skin, wanting more, wanting to leave hickeys and branding him like he does me.

"Cari ..." he groans. I continue sucking, dragging this moment out longer than is comfortable. It's painful because the dull ache between my legs needs him inside me. But teasing him the way I am, so close to his cock and not doing anything to it, must be beyond unbearable for him. I move lower still, my head between his legs, skating my mouth along his inner thighs and making him groan again. Each sound he makes tells me I'm doing something right.

And I'm enjoying this. Clasping my fingers around his cock, I wipe his wet crest with my thumb. He jerks like he's been pinched, giving me the green light to continue.

I stroke him gently, then bend down and lick the tip of his cock, glancing at him to see his reaction. But he's tilted his head back, and his eyes are closed.

I did this for Rory a few times, but I didn't really like it. He was so rough with me. He'd force my mouth so that I'd gag.

Jett doesn't do that. I might not be up to the standards he's used to, but he's letting me do as I please and he seems to be loving it.

JETT

If Cari continues like this, I'll come all over her. I could come right now, but I'll force myself to hold on, because I want to bury myself and empty inside her.

She starts to suck, her gorgeous lips swallowing my cock slowly. I look at her, needing to see her mouth around me. She seems emboldened now. One of her hands teases my balls. She's wearing my favorite bikini, but I need to see her naked. "Take your clothes off," I beg.

She looks annoyed, like I'm breaking her rhythm, but she does it anyway. Quickly taking off the sheer cover-up, she strips off completely and my cock hardens even more. She sees it. Not losing another moment, she kneels back down, pulling and stroking me relentlessly, her thumb sliding over my wet tip, spreading my pre-cum all over me. When she makes eye contact, her lips wet with saliva as she swirls her tongue all over my cock, I jerk, and grind my teeth down, trying to keep it together.

"I'm going to suck you off. Would you like that?" she asks, going full on vixen-mode and making my resolve crumble.

Hell, yes.

The sunbursts in her eyes sparkle as she stares at me. "I didn't hear you." She's turned into the sexy minx again. Bold and confident.

"Very much," I manage to say, then watch as she swallows

me inch by delicious inch. I let out another groan. Seeing her like this, completely naked and on her knees between my legs, talking dirty to me, with my cock in her mouth, is a dream come true. Sweet, sweet ecstasy. She licks the length of my shaft, then closes her lips around the head. I lose my mind when she plays with my balls as she sucks me hard, her head bobbing wildly.

It's the most divine feeling in the world.

Fighting for control, I look at the ceiling. I'm desperate for release, and just when I think this can't get any better, she takes all of me in until I feel the back of her throat. I fist my hand in her hair, trying to not come apart, but when she sucks my tip, long and hard, I'm gone. I grit my teeth together, trying not to come inside her mouth. I want her tight, warm pussy for that. But she alternates, swallowing me whole again, doing it slowly, then licking me up and down.

"What the fuck are you doing to me?" I growl, trying to keep it together. I want to explode, but I'm trying not to. She looks up at me, her eyes shimmering under the light of the lamp. This image of her like this, is one I'll never forget; Cari with my cock in her mouth, her lips red and swollen, and those gorgeous, peaked breasts. If I could only reach out and suck them.

"I'm taking care of you," she says, innocently, before her tongue darts out and glides over my length again.

Just when I think I need to pull out, I lose control, grunting out my release. I'm so far gone, that it takes a few seconds before I jolt upright and see what I've done. I didn't pull out in time and I came. And Cari took it. She swallowed every drop.

I reach for her. "I didn't mean to come in your—"

She lifts up, her fingers brushing the side of my face, tracing the line of my jaw. "Did I take good care of you?"

This woman undoes me. "The best, my little shortcake."

She presses a kiss to my lips and I pull back, just enough to meet her gaze, my hand on her waist. I have so many words. So much I want to say, but she nods, smiling at me, as if understanding that this moment needs only silence.

We scoot back on the bed, and she presses against me, snuggling in the crook of my arm as we lie entangled in one another.

CHAPTER THIRTY-EIGHT

JETT

It takes a while for my breaths to calm down. I'm still feeling loose all over. "You've bewitched me," I murmur.

She moves away from me and props herself up on one elbow. I love the smile that pops up on her face. "You … Cari Summers, have captured my heart."

She rolls her eyes. "Trust you to say that after a blow job." Then she scoots off as if she's going to leave.

I grab her wrist, not willing to let her go, because I have other plans. "That was fucking amazing … *amazing* … but we're not done yet. The night is still young." I waggle my brows, making her giggle as I pull her back into my arms.

"The night is still young—" she starts to say, but just then my cell phone pings a few times. These notifications of messages or emails coming through are not something I want to deal with now. I've managed to block out the world, and I want to keep it that way.

"Jett," Cari whispers, her hand resting softly against my chest. "Check your phone. It might be urgent. The reason you came here was for business."

"And to spend time with Brooke."

"Yes, but your father … I know how demanding he can be. How hard he is on you all."

"Why are you so afraid of him?" I'm surprised by her words.

"I'm not afraid of him. I fear for you. I know he unsettles you."

"He's a bully, and a demanding prick." I pause. "I'm a lot like him."

"You can be. But you have a heart, Jett." She presses against my lips. "I'll be back. I need to shower because I've got salt in all my crevices."

"I'll happily lick it off," I volunteer.

She flashes me a smile. "I would love for you to lick it all off." She bites her lower lip, "but let me shower, and you can check your messages. I'll be back."

I reach for my phone and see a whole heap of emails. I'm not going to look at them now. This has been heaven, a much needed break. It's been bliss. Sheer paradise. It's everything I could ever have hoped for and more, and I don't want to go back home or into the office. I want to stay here forever.

I WAKE UP SLOWLY, DISORIENTED, MY MIND STRUGGLING TO grasp what day it is or why I feel so damn content. The bed is empty beside me, and for a second, I'm seized in panic.

Then I remember Cari and last night. What she did for me. The memory hits me like a tidal wave. The way she cared for me, her soft mouth, her lips, her gentle touch. I had plans for more, but we must have fallen asleep, and she never returned to my bed. Or she did, and I was asleep by then so she left me.

My phone rings. It's a sharp, rude awakening that jolts me back to reality.

"What are you doing?" Dex's voice booms the second I answer.

"Sleeping," I growl, my voice rough.

"You've been suspiciously quiet. What's going on?"

Nosy bastard. He means well, but this, whatever Cari and I have started, is too new, too precious for his meddling. The last thing I need is Dex poking around. But now I'm beginning to wonder if something's brewing back in the office.

"Like I told you, I've been busy. Spending time with Brooke," I say, and it's not a lie. I've spent the last few days reevaluating my life, realizing that the people I love are what matters. Not just chasing deals for the next empty high.

Dex snorts. "Read your damn emails. You can't be that busy." He pauses. "You met someone, didn't you?"

I ignore him and pull up my inbox, scrolling through a flood of emails. One subject line stands out like a flashing neon sign. My blood boils as I skim the threads, an angry exchange between my father and the legal team.

"What the hell is this?" I snap, already knowing the answer.

"It's a problem." Dex replies. "A big one. The acquisition deal with Pinewood is about to fall apart."

I sit up and take notice. This is a high-profile deal we can't afford to lose. Knight Enterprises is attempting to acquire Pinewood, a company based in Florida, because it's a strategic fit for our portfolio. They represent a major opportunity for growth because they own beachfront luxury developments perfect for our high-end brand. "Why's Zach not dealing with it?" Real estate, luxury goods, and hotels are his domain.

"Because it's an acquisition, and that's your forte," Dex reminds me.

So it is. Sometimes it feels like I deal with way more than my brothers do. They all have their compact little niches, and sometimes we overlap, but anything related to legal or financial, or mergers and acquisitions is my problem. No wonder I'm always so damn busy.

"This acquisition could turn into a liability because a whistleblower's made allegations of financial mismanagement, and the SEC's flagged their books," Dex continues.

"Fuck."

"Are you serious about her?"

My lips purse together. This brother of mine is psychic. It's unnerving how he can glean so much across the wires. But I'm not telling him anything about me and Cari, not before I talk to her.

"I'll take care of it," I snap, ignoring his question. This isn't something I can take care of over the phone. It's something that requires my presence in Florida for a few days.

"It's something you championed," Dex reminds me. I did. Zach brought it to my attention, and when I looked into it further I thought it could be a great asset to the company. If it falls apart, it will reflect badly on me. "The old man's been trying to reach you, but you've been hiding."

"I've been handling things here, while spending time with Brooke—"

"But it's a working vacation," Dex interrupts. "You need to fix this before it blows up."

I grind my teeth, the pieces clicking together. Our rivals are circling, ready to pounce if this deal falls apart. The SEC needs answers, and it's clear this isn't something I can handle remotely.

"I'll take care of it." I cut Dex off before he can pry further. I fire off a reply to my father's email. *I'll fly out today.*

Throwing on shorts and a T-shirt, I head to Brooke's room to find that Cari is there. She's brushing Brooke's hair, her movements soft and loving. I lean against the door jamb, silently observing. Cari loves my little girl as if she were her own, and Brooke? Brooke has always adored Cari. I get goosebumps when I look at these two together.

The world around me can go to shit, but as long as I have Brooke and Cari in my orbit, things will be fine. They are my North Star and my safe haven.

I want this to be my life .

Cari moves, still focused on Brooke's hair, but the sunlight catches her curls giving it golden highlights. Her skin is all aglow. I feel all warm and fuzzy inside, and something shifts because what if I had this forever?

She looks up, catching me staring. "You okay?" she mouths, just as Brooke notices me.

"Daddy! You're up!"

My little girl launches herself at me, and I scoop her up, burying my face in her hair.

"Can we go to Horses Bay? Zara told me about it."

"Horseshoe Bay," I correct with a smile.

"That one!"

I set her down gently, my mood sobering. "Not today, sweetheart."

Brooke's face falls. "Why not?"

I glance at Cari, who stands slowly, her eyes filled with worry, for me, not for herself.

"I have to go away for a few days."

Brooke's lip trembles. "Where?"

"I'll be back soon, I promise. It's just meetings. Boring stuff."

Cari frowns, her assistant instincts kicking in. "What's going on? Where do you have to go?"

"The Pinewood acquisition. The SEC flagged some financials, nothing catastrophic, but enough to cause a problem if I don't handle it personally. I'll need to meet with their CEO, regulators, and lawyers to straighten things out. So, I have to go to Florida."

I hear the gasp she lets out. "Florida."

I nod. "It sucks, I know."

"Do you need me to pull files or set anything up?" she asks.

"Just keep things running smoothly here, the way you always do."

She gives me a soft smile. "Don't worry. Brooke and I will be fine." She turns to Brooke. "How about we visit Zara this weekend, or ask her to come here?"

Brooke's eyes light up. "Really?"

"Really."

"Why don't you go down for breakfast, sprout," I say to Brooke. When she skips out, Cari stays behind, clicking the door shut. She steps into me, and I wrap my arms around her.

"Thank you for last night," I murmur, brushing my lips against her hair. "But I was supposed to take care of you."

She tilts her head up, a teasing smile on her lips. "I came back to your bed, freshly showered, and in need of attention."

Heat stirs in my belly. God, I wish I could stay. I'd take care of her right now.

"Do you really have to go?" Her voice is soft, tinged with disappointment.

"If I don't act now, the whole deal could collapse. Our rivals are already circling, waiting for an opportunity to swoop in."

She nods, but I see the sadness in her eyes.

"How long will you be gone?"

"Three days. Four, tops." I press a kiss to her forehead, wishing I could promise more.

She tightens her arms around my waist, her touch grounding me. "Hurry back."

"I will." For a moment, we stay like that, holding on as if the world outside doesn't exist.

CHAPTER THIRTY-NINE

CARI

I take Brooke to a play date at Celine's house. She invited us over.

Jett's departure has left both me and Brooke feeling unmoored. We've spent every day together since arriving in Bermuda, and this sudden shift has thrown me off. I know it's harder for Brooke. She's so young, and Jett is her entire world, so visiting her friend is a welcome distraction.

From the moment we step inside, I feel a sense of calm. The house is bright and airy, and has a lovely homey feel to it, rather like Celine herself. It has none of the grand opulence of the other houses I've visited. Wide windows let in the ocean breeze, and sunlight spills over the polished wooden floors. The walls are painted in soft, sandy hues, and vibrant tropical plants adorn every corner.

"I'm so glad you could come," she says, pulling us into a warm hug. "I have Zara here for a few days. Her mom needs time to rest because the baby can come any time now. It will give me a small break, having Brooke over to keep her company."

"You have a lovely place." My gaze takes in her home as she leads me through the house into the kitchen.

"Thank you. We've been very happy here."

"Where's your daddy?" Celine asks Brooke, her voice light.

I shake my head subtly, and she catches my meaning, quickly switching gears.

"He's working." I try to sound breezy. "Hopefully not for too long."

Before Brooke can answer, Zara appears, and Brooke's face lights up.

"Come and play with my dolls!" Zara says, grabbing Brooke's hand and tugging her upstairs.

"They'll be fine," Celine assures me with a wave of her hand. "And don't worry about anything breaking. Brooke's a good kid, she's just like a granddaughter to me. Even if there's an accident, it doesn't matter. Possessions can be replaced."

She leads me out to the back patio, a stunning oasis overlooking the turquoise water. There's a shaded seating area under a pergola draped with bougainvillea, and the air is filled with the soft sound of waves lapping against the rocks. I take a seat as Celine pours two glasses of iced tea.

"Jett's had to go to Florida," I say, breaking the silence.

"Florida?"

"Business. Something about a big acquisition that hit a snag. It's important enough that he had to fly out to fix it."

Celine's wise brown eyes study me for a moment, and my chest constricts. She doesn't miss much, and I worry she'll see through me.

"You know a lot about his business," she says.

"I'm his assistant," I admit, shifting uncomfortably under her gaze.

Her brows shoot up. "You are? Why didn't I know this?"

"I didn't think it was important to bring up," I falter, my voice wary.

She narrows her eyes. "You're his assistant, but you're here?"

"I'm his assistant for about a week after we get back, because I've turned in my notice that I'm leaving."

Her warm brown eyes widen. "Why are you leaving? And why, if you're his assistant, are you here? I'm glad you are, honey. I'm so glad we met." She takes my hand and squeezes it in both of hers. "But whatever happened to the nanny? I'm sure there's always been a nanny who comes along with Brooke."

"She ... ugh. She quit, because it was her sister's wedding and she'd told Jett she needed time off, but he hadn't really paid attention. A week before coming here, she reminded him that she was going to be away and couldn't come to Bermuda, but he'd forgotten. She couldn't miss the wedding and ... well, he didn't like that so she quit. There wasn't time to get a new nanny ..."

"You're talking really fast, honey. Slow down." Celine places a calming hand over mine.

Heat floods my cheeks. Celine can tell. She knows something is going on between me and Jett, but can she tell what we've been doing in bed?

Of course, she can't, but I still fan my face with a napkin that's lying on the table. "Why are you leaving?" she asks softly, her head tilting in curiosity. "You're so good with Brooke. And, honey, I can see it clear as day, you're good for Jett."

The words are like a knife to my chest.

If I can't answer simple questions about me and Jett, how will I ever keep it together in front of his family? In front of his father? And then I realize I'm racing ahead. I'm trying to figure out what will happen when we get back, and I have no clue because I haven't been thinking about it.

"It's complicated." I glance away. She doesn't press, but her look says she knows more than I want her to.

"I've known Brooke since I started working for him, when she was two years old," I explain.

"Ah, we've been seeing her every year, of course. After she was born, Sophia and Jett came here. Sophia rested here and then she came again, I think, just before Brooke turned one. She was due to come here the year after, but then we heard the awful news." She looks pained just thinking about it. "It broke him. Jett was so broken. They were so in love."

It feels like I'm eavesdropping on a secret, private conversation here, but that's all in the past.

"It was an aneurysm in the brain and it was sudden," she tells me. "It was unexpected. Nobody could do anything about it."

"That's so sad. Beyond tragic," I whisper, thinking about Jett and Brooke's world crashing down around them. I feel for Jett and Brooke, but mostly for Jett, because Brooke would have been too young to understand the magnitude of her loss.

"Life has to go on," Celine says, in that steady, determined voice as she looks out onto the ocean. "In life, these things happen. This is why we must make the most of every opportunity we get. Every day is to be savored, and every moment is to be enjoyed. And if you can't make anyone happy, if you have nothing nice to say, don't say anything at all."

"Wise words," I agree.

"You've got a good heart, Cari. I can see how much Brooke adores you. I can see the close bond you both have, and it's surprising, given that you're Jett's assistant."

She has a soft way of asking, and I can see she's curious. I'm not offended. I explain that I've had a lot of interactions with Brooke, because Jett brings her into the office every now and then, and I've seen the little toddler grow into a little girl.

"You smile when you talk of her. It's nothing like what an assistant would do, even if you've been seeing a lot of her. I've watched you with her, and there's something special between you and Brooke."

I chew my lower lip. "I adore her. I love her like ..." I shrug, and our eyes meet. I've given away too much.

"I just want you to be careful, Cari."

The words of warning pierce through the happy bubble I've found myself in lately.

"Jett is a good man, but he's a complicated man. He's gone through a lot. He was just a teenager when his mother died. As you might know, she took her own life. It's all very messy, and it's taken a toll on those boys. As well as the other boys, the family he hid from Aurora for so long. "

"You know of them?"

Her mouth quirks into a knowing smile. "Yes."

She leans closer, her voice dropping conspiratorially. "Their father had a secret life in Italy. Three sons from another woman while raising his boys with Aurora. No one knew until the boys were older, and even then, Paul kept it quiet. They don't come here. I imagine it's another one of Paul's games ..."

"Games?"

"He has ways and means of controlling the boys. He plays with people, as if they're pawns in his chess game. Maybe he doesn't want them mixing with the Bermuda crowd, I don't know. But it's also probable that Aurora's boys, Jett, Dex, and Zach, wouldn't want them here. This is their mother's home. It was a place Aurora loved and Paul had it built for her."

I nod, absorbing the new information. "Jett doesn't talk about them much."

Celine's smile fades. "Paul has a plan. A blueprint, if you

will. He didn't become a billionaire overnight without sacrifice. He's not a man to be underestimated. He's cold, calculating, and every decision he makes is about legacy. Just be careful, Cari. He doesn't take kindly to anything, or anyone, getting in the way of his plans."

I put a hand to my neck, feeling the heat of the warning. "Of course."

"Jett will take care of you, just like he did the other night when he stood up to those vicious piranhas."

I take a sip of my iced tea. It's refreshing and cold, and exactly what I need. "I was really surprised he did that."

"Were you?" Celine asks. "Is he a difficult boss?"

That question is one I can't answer without giving too much away.

She nods. A knowing nod. "I see something different in him this time. Heart."

"Heart?" I echo.

"He's always been cold, closed off, arrogant, a bit, you know, *brutal*, except when he's with Brooke."

"You see that too," I murmur.

"But I see his softness around you. He's protective over you, and when he spoke up for you and told Tiffany and her odious sister what they needed to be told ..."

I open my mouth, getting ready to confess because I feel like I can trust her.

She shakes her head. "Don't tell me anything, honey, not until you're 100% sure."

My fingers brush the condensation on my glass.

"What are your plans after you leave?" She changes the subject, thank God.

I tell her about the florist shop, the one that brought my mom so much pleasure when she was lying on the hospital bed. "I want to do something for myself. I'm an assistant, and a very good one, I know that, but I can do more. Something for me. Something that would bring happiness to people, when their world is filled with misery and pain. It's a small thing, but it's something. I saw how my mom's face would light up each time I walked in with fresh flowers."

"I can see that about you. You're kind and thoughtful, and I can see you doing something that brings happiness to people. That's rare."

Her words settle something in my chest.

"You're also not afraid to stand up for yourself, from what I heard when Abigail and Madison accused Brooke." She chuckles.

"I would defend Brooke with my life. That poor little girl. No one is going to say a mean word to her while I'm around."

"There she goes, Mama Bear." The label makes my heart boom.

I lower my voice. "She doesn't have a mommy, and now she's asking me mommy questions. It's a difficult age."

"Yes, it is," Celine agrees. "I can see she's so happy around you."

"It's been a memorable trip and I'll be sorry to leave."

"Maybe we'll see you again?" Celine asks, and I don't know in which universe that will happen.

I shrug and say nothing.

"Thank you for having us," I say when it's time to leave.

She hugs me tightly. "You can call me anytime, Cari. You're always welcome here."

"If you ever come to New York, please look me up." I pull out a little pocket notepad from my bag and scribble my address and phone number on it.

"I will. Just be careful with your heart, Cari."

CHAPTER FORTY

JETT

Florida.

I've been here three days, and I'm already at the end of my patience. The meetings have been relentless. We've spent hours hashing out solutions, back-to-back with lawyers and executives. I'm running on fumes, fueled by caffeine and frustration, and I've barely had a moment to breathe.

Leaving Bermuda was the last thing I wanted to do. Walking away from Brooke from Cari, from paradise itself to deal with this mess? It grates on me.

Friday night, and I'm finally stepping out to grab something to eat. A quick sandwich will have to do before we dive into yet another session. My phone buzzes, and I glance at the screen.

Update me ASAP.

It's a message from my father. Short, clipped, and predictable.

"Will do when I'm out of here, old man," I mutter, slipping my phone back into my pocket, but not answering his text.

THE WEEKEND BLURS INTO A HAZE OF ARGUMENTS, spreadsheets, and strategy sessions. By Sunday night, the pieces have finally fallen into place. The acquisition is saved, the regulators placated, and the deal secured.

I sit in my hotel room, leaning back in the chair, staring at the city lights through the window. My phone rings, and of course it's my father.

"It's all sorted," I say as soon as I pick up. "You don't need to worry about a thing."

"When are you heading back?"

"Tomorrow morning, after the final meeting."

"Good. But don't forget, there's a golf game at Seminole tomorrow afternoon. You need to be there."

"I'm not going," I reply flatly.

"It's networking. Business. Visibility. You should be there."

My jaw tightens. "I need to get back to my daughter."

His laugh is sharp, cutting. "Since when are you in such a rush to see Brooke?"

"That's not fair," I snap, trying to keep my voice even. "The whole reason I brought her to Bermuda was to spend time with her."

"Is that so? Are we talking about Brooke or someone else?"

The insinuation lands like a slap, and my stomach tightens.

"My daughter. Your granddaughter," I grind out.

There's a pause, then his voice drops into that calculated tone I've despised my entire life. "Have you given any thought to my proposal?"

"What proposal?"

"The marriage of convenience with the Brazilian heiress."

My grip tightens on the phone. "I was going to get back to you about that once I return. I need time to think."

"Good," he says smoothly. "She's perfect for you. Wealthy, connected, and smart. You might not love her, and she might not love you, but that's fine. You can have an open marriage, as long as no one finds out."

The words slam into me, leaving me momentarily speechless.

"What?" I can't believe what I'm hearing.

"You can still have your fun." His tone is as casual as if he's discussing stock options. "Mistresses, lovers, whatever you want. Just keep it quiet. It's how these things are done."

The asshole thinks this is acceptable. This is what he did with my mother. Anger surges through me, sharp and visceral. "I don't do that shit. When I give my heart, I give it. Completely."

"Let's not get overly sentimental," he replies, his voice cold. "A heart is just a muscle. Nothing more."

I push to my feet, pacing the room. My hand grips the phone so tightly I half expect it to crack. "I need to go," I say through gritted teeth.

"Don't forget the golf game," he reminds me before I hang up.

I toss the phone onto the bed and lean against the dresser, staring at my reflection in the mirror.

"I'm not you," I say quietly, the words aimed at the ghost of Paul Knight staring back at me.

I slip on my jacket, smoothing down the lapels.

I'm not him. I'll never be him. I'll never treat a woman the way he treated my mother. I'd rather burn everything I've built than become Paul Knight's shadow.

With one last glance at the mirror, I grab my keys and head for the door.

***

CARI

I SIT CROSS-LEGGED INSIDE THE MAKESHIFT TENT, FAIRY LIGHTS casting a soft glow on the canvas walls.

"This all looks absolutely delicious," I declare, holding up the battered reading book Brooke has handed me as a menu.

Brooke adjusts her tiny apron and stands in front of me, all business. "What would you like to order?"

"Pizza with salad, please," I reply, trying to match her serious tone.

She nods and scribbles something on her little notepad. I lean forward to peek, but her spelling is anyone's guess.

"Did you wanna drink something with that?" she asks, her tiny brows furrowing in concentration.

"Raspberry lemonade would be perfect."

She writes it down carefully, her lips moving as she tries to sound it out. "Coming right up!" she announces, spinning on her heels and disappearing out of the tent.

I glance around at the scene she's created. She's laid out a mat in the middle of the floor, complete with plastic knives, forks, and mismatched plates. Elephant sits loyally beside me, and the dolls, clearly her regular customers, look perfectly content with their empty plates.

This is delightful.

It doesn't feel like babysitting, or work, or any of the countless duties I've had to juggle over the years. This feels like belonging. Like, for the first time in a long time, I'm not drifting aimlessly.

My mom's absence used to feel like an endless void. But now ... now I feel a sliver of something I haven't felt in a while. A connection. A place.

Jett once told me I was never alone.

An unbidden thought of him sneaks in as I stare at my pretend fellow diners, waiting for Brooke to return.

He called last night, his deep voice vibrating through the phone and settling low in my chest. I could listen to him talk for hours. He said he'd be back sometime this afternoon, but something came up and he's still dealing with the "loose ends."

I miss him.

Brooke does too, though I've done my best to keep her occupied. Yesterday, I took her to the park and invited Celine to join us, but her daughter had gone into the hospital to give birth, so Zara came instead.

The girls had the best time. We came home to a picnic in the garden and an afternoon of splashing in the water.

Today, we've been in and out of the pool and the sea, soaking up the sun and keeping busy. It's been wonderful but exhausting. Still, the moment I'm alone at night, when Brooke is fast asleep, my thoughts drift back to Jett.

His voice, even over the phone, ignites something in me. It's not just arousal, although that's undeniable. It's him. His presence. His steadiness. His intensity. The memories of us together aren't fantasies anymore. They're real, tangible, and etched into my mind. But he's not here yet, and it's now late evening. I know we won't see him tonight.

That leaves me with time to think. Too much time.

Celine's words echo in my mind, her gentle warnings about Jett's family, about Paul Knight's controlling ways. About protecting my heart. I know she's right to worry, but I don't want to dwell on it.

Instead, I let myself think about something Jett mentioned last night. He suggested we go away for a few days after he gets back. Just the three of us and the bodyguard.

I laughed when he said that.

But I'm secretly thrilled about it; having time away from everyone on a small private island. It's not the physical side that I miss, though that's part of it. I miss him. I want to lie in his arms, talk to him, and be with him, body and soul. The lines have blurred so beautifully, so seamlessly. It doesn't feel messy. It feels like something new and wonderful, like we're weaving the threads of our lives together.

I don't want this to end.

"Here you go, ma'am!" Brooke's cheerful voice snaps me out of my thoughts.

She hands me an empty plate with a flourish. "One pizza with salad, just for you. Can I get you anything else?"

"This looks divine." I take a pretend bite from my invisible pizza. "Hmm, delicious! Thank you, Brooke." I pat the space beside me. "Why don't you have some with me?"

"I can't," she giggles. "I'm the waitress!"

"Surely waitresses need to eat?"

"Nope!" she declares. "But you can share with Elephant. He wanted pizza too."

I smile as I feed Elephant a piece of the invisible pizza. Brooke's forgotten all about the dolls, but it doesn't matter. Her joy is infectious. And for now, in this moment, I can pretend the rest of the world doesn't exist.

ELIANA CALLS ME LATER ONCE I'VE PUT BROOKE TO BED. HER voice comes through, warm but cautious. "I'm sorry for being such a Debbie Downer when you told me about you and Jett."

I smile at her words, even though guilt pricks at me. I've been so wrapped up in everything here. "It's okay, El. Honestly, I'm just glad we're talking."

"I don't want you to get hurt. Jett Knight has always been your Achilles heel, and I'm scared he's going to hurt you even more. You have this huge heart, and you give it to people who don't always deserve it."

"What's this? A lecture? Should I be taking notes?"

"I don't want to see you crash and burn. I love you too much for that," she says, exasperated but still loving.

I exhale, rubbing my hand over my brow. "I'm a grown woman. I can take care of myself."

"You're also vulnerable, Car," she says, softer now. "Look at the year you've had. Your mom …" Her voice falters, and I feel the grief rise, sharp and raw, like it always does when someone mentions Mom. "I want you to be careful."

I don't respond right away because, honestly, what do I say? She's not wrong. "Okay. I hear you."

"As long as you're having fun," Eliana adds, a little lighter now, "and you're leaving work soon, so he's not going to be your boss for much longer."

The words hit me like a splash of cold water. *Am I still leaving?* The answer feels less clear every day. "Yes, I am," I say to Eliana, but inside, I'm not sure. So much has happened between me and Jett, and I don't know what the next step is.

If there is a next step.

My stomach churns as I look toward the future. What happens when Jett and I return to the office? What if the connection between us fades, and he goes back to being the distant, demanding Jett Knight I've worked for all these years?

Worse, what if he walks in with another tall, leggy and stunning girlfriend, someone more *Knight-worthy*?

Eliana's voice pulls me out of my spiraling thoughts. "Has he been good to you?"

I think back to the trip here, his unexpected vulnerability, the way he's been with Brooke, and how he's looked at me when he thought I wasn't paying attention. How he stood up for me to his rich friends.

"Yes," I say, my voice soft but sure. "There's so much about Jett you don't know. He's … different. More than people think."

"He's also driven you absolutely mad," she quips. "Don't think I've forgotten all the times you've ranted about him."

"That's true." I laugh despite myself. "But right now? I'm happy, El. *Really* happy."

"That's all I want for you. But, you know, I still need details. The nitty-gritty. Don't leave me hanging."

"I'm not going to give you the nitty-gritty," I reply, but can't help adding, "but I think you would be impressed."

"*Impressed?* What the hell did you do, Car? Give him a blow job?"

The silence stretches just long enough for her to cackle on the other end.

"Oh my God, Car, you did!" she teases.

I open my mouth to deny it, but just then, the door to my room creaks open, and Brooke's little face pops in. "I have to go," I blurt, my voice higher than usual. "Talk soon!" I hang up before Eliana can say another word.

Brooke steps closer, her curls bouncing as she tilts her head. "Who were you talking to?"

"Just my best friend, back home," I say, smiling down at her as I quickly toss my phone onto the bed. But my cheeks are still burning, and I swear Brooke's sharp little eyes notice everything.

CHAPTER FORTY-ONE

JETT

WHEN I FINALLY ARRIVE BACK IN BERMUDA, IT'S WELL PAST midnight. So much for tying up loose ends quickly.

Just as I was about to head home, the whistleblower decided to backtrack, claiming he'd been coerced into making the allegations. It set off alarm bells with the SEC, throwing everything into chaos. I spent the entire day in damage-control mode, mediating between lawyers, regulators, and the whistleblower's team. It was a delicate balancing act, and every second felt like walking a tightrope over open flames.

By the time we wrapped things up, it was late, too late, but I was determined to get back. I chartered a flight and land on the island in the early hours of Tuesday morning.

The house is quiet and bathed in moonlight. As I pass Brooke's room, I peek inside. She's curled up under her blanket, her tiny hand resting on her cheek. Peaceful. Innocent. My heart softens as I lean down to press a kiss to her forehead. She stirs slightly but doesn't wake.

The door to Cari's room is open, the bed visible from where she keeps an eye on Brooke. I hesitate, my body itching to go to her, but the long day clings to me like a second skin. I need a shower first.

I head to my room, stripping off my suit and stepping into the hot spray of water. The tension begins to melt away, but it doesn't dull the ache in my chest. It's been days since I've seen her, touched her. And now, our days here are numbered. The sinking feeling stays with me, weighted with grim foreboding. I don't know how I'm going to manage without her in my life.

When I return to my room, the bed feels empty. Too empty. I can't stay here. I find myself standing in the doorway of her room, drawn to her like a moth to a flame. She's lying on her side, her breathing soft and steady, her hair fanned across the pillow. Without a second thought, I slide into bed beside her, putting my arm around her waist.

Her familiar scent washes over me and she stirs, turning onto her back, her eyes fluttering open just enough to register me. "You're back," she murmurs sleepily.

I press a kiss to her lips, unable to resist. "I missed you."

She sighs, her exhaustion evident. "What time is it?"

"Go back to sleep," I whisper. "I didn't mean to wake you."

Her eyes drift shut again. "But what time is it?"

"One in the morning."

"What day is it?"

I chuckle softly, brushing a strand of hair from her face. "You're exhausted."

"We did a lot of things," she murmurs. "I kept Brooke busy."

I lean over her, my body pressing against hers while I prop myself up on my elbow. We're both fully clothed, but my body doesn't care. Desire stirs, swift and insistent. Her arm loops around my neck, pulling me closer. "I missed you," she says, her voice barely audible.

"My little shortcake, you have no idea how much I've missed you." I press my lips against hers, and my cock springs to attention, digging into her.

Her eyes fly open, a sly smile tugging at her lips. "Oh, you *have* missed me." Her hand slips between us to brush against my arousal.

I dip my head, capturing her mouth in a kiss that's all heat and longing. My tongue sweeps in, tasting her sweetness, feeling the warmth I've yearned for. She's everything I want and need. My lover, friend and soulmate.

"Jett," she whispers, her voice breaking through the haze. "We can't. Brooke is in the other bed."

"I know," I murmur, though every cell in my body protests.

She sighs, her head sinking back into the pillow. "And I'm so tired."

I brush another kiss against her temple, then lie by her side. "I'll just stay here for a little while."

Her arms wrap around me, and she snuggles into my chest. "Okay, but then you have to go back," she whispers, as if she's in a daze.

"I will." I pull her closer and imagine what it would be like to have this all night long and into the morning.

THE SOFT PATTER OF LITTLE FEET JOLTS ME AWAKE.

"Daddy?" Brooke's voice pierces the quiet.

I blink, disoriented, and turn to find her standing in the doorway. She's clutching her stuffed elephant, her gaze darting between me and Cari. We're both fully clothed, thankfully, even though we're wrapped up in each other's arms.

I try to untangle us as my mind freezes, scrambling for an explanation.

Cari, however, doesn't miss a beat.

"Good morning, Brooke!" she says brightly, sitting up and smoothing her hair. "Daddy must have been so tired when he got back, he just wanted to say goodnight before going to his room."

Brooke tilts her head, considering this, then nods solemnly. "You should sleep in your room, Daddy. You're too big for this bed."

I bite back a laugh, relief washing over me. "You're right, sprout. I'll head back now."

Brooke climbs onto the bed, throwing her arms around Cari. "Can we have pancakes for breakfast?"

"Of course," Cari replies, hugging her back. She glances at me over Brooke's shoulder, her eyes sparkling with mischief.

I slip out of the room, closing the door behind me. I'm filled with a profound sense of love and relief, and the undeniable realization that I don't want this to end.

CHAPTER FORTY-TWO

JETT

I left Cari and Brooke having breakfast on the terrace this morning and retreated to the study.

It's not how I want to spend the day, but I need to double-check the Pinewood acquisition. Everything appears to be humming along, according to the flood of emails from our legal team. Still, I've learned to trust, but verify.

My gaze drops to the calendar on my desk, and I sigh in frustration. I've burned four days of our vacation putting out fires and now I have such little time left with Cari. I wonder if she's still planning to leave when we return. The uncertainty of that answer makes me uneasy. It's something I don't even want to contemplate, a life without her, when I've seen how life can be with her in it.

Our days in Bermuda are dwindling down fast enough as it is. I feel like there's an hourglass somewhere running out of sand, counting down the minutes until she's gone from my life. And I don't like it.

I deserve this time away, on account of having worked the weekend on the Pinewood deal.

I pull up my schedule and see something that makes my stomach drop. The polo match. Of course. The annual summer gala. The Knight family doesn't skip it if we're on the island. It's practically a commandment.

But we're leaving soon for our private island retreat—something I need to talk to Cari about when Brooke's not around, as it's a surprise for her. Three nights of bliss. Just me, Cari, Brooke, and the bodyguard.

The small, private island is perfection. A remote strip of white sand fringed by turquoise waters, with a modest villa nestled among palm trees. No infinity pool, no ostentatious trappings of wealth. Just raw, untouched beauty. The villa is all smooth wood, glass walls, and salt-kissed breezes. Out there, it feels like the rest of the world melts away.

An alert pings on my phone, snapping me out of my daydream. The polo match looms large. Do I even care?

Before I can dwell, Brooke bursts into the study, running full tilt. "Daddy! Why are you working? You said today was a fun day!" She scrambles onto my lap, her small hands already hammering at my keyboard.

I absently kiss the top of her head, my arms going around her tiny frame. "I'm just finishing up, sprout."

She leans back, squinting at the screen like she's deciphering something important. "Hurry up, Daddy!"

Cari appears, looking devastatingly gorgeous in a strappy summer top and shorts. Her hair is loose, catching the sunlight streaming through the windows. She's the definition of summer, and I have to close my eyes for a moment to stop myself from staring too long.

Focus, Jett. Focus.

"Are you okay?" Her voice is soft but probing.

"Yeah." I shake off the haze. "The Pinewood deal's looking good. Everything's under control."

"And no reason for he-who-shall-not-be-named to blame you for anything?" she teases.

"He'll find something, I'm sure," I mutter, the thought of my father souring my mood. No doubt he'll want to talk about the Brazilian heiress soon. Like I have the bandwidth, or interest, for that.

"What's the plan for today?" Cari asks.

"Blue Hole Park. Brooke's been begging to go. Haven't you, sprout?" I gently set her on the floor.

"I like that idea," Cari says, as Brooke crouches on the floor playing with her beloved Elephant.

"There's also the polo match," I add, reluctantly. "It's a society gala. The whole island shows up for it."

She arches a brow, clearly unimpressed. "You don't strike me as a polo guy."

"I'm not. It's more about appearances. The Knights always go if we're here."

"Well, I'm sure Bryce and Abigail will be there." Her acid tone drips with sarcasm.

"Probably. They love being seen." I lean back, studying her. "Do you want to go?"

"Hell no."

"Good. Because I don't either."

She winces. "But won't your father be angry if you skip it?"

"My father doesn't dictate my life, not anymore." I pause, lowering my voice. "The Vanhelm deal was the first time I trusted my gut with a contract. I did what I believed, knowing the old man would hate it. He was waiting for me to fail, and I wasn't going to give him the satisfaction. I haven't felt the urge to run anything by him since then."

She cups my face gently, her eyes burning into mine. "Jett," she whispers. "I knew it was such a big deal for you."

I take her hands in mine. It's in this moment that I know I'm falling in love with her. I can't imagine going a day without her. "What I want is ..." *The island*, I mouth, not wanting Brooke to hear. I hold up three fingers then motion to each of us. "Three and three. Perfect."

"It sounds like paradise." I see longing in her eyes.

"It will be." The thought of it anchors me. We've gone days without being together, with the Florida trip, and tonight I intend to fuck her and feast on her the way she needs me to.

"Let's start with Blue Hole Park Bay. Brooke's been waiting, haven't you, sport?"

MY HEART IS FULL AGAIN. SPENDING THE DAY WITH MY GIRLS has rejuvenated me. I feel alive, with a buzz of energy that's been missing for a while.

We have dinner together, then get Brooke ready for bed.

I'm already hard when I reach for Cari's hand and tug her into my bedroom.

We kiss long and deep, our hands and mouths a tangle as our tongues duel with need and our desperate hands relieve us of our clothes.

I reach between her legs, my fingers frantic for the feel of her, and when my fingers slide in, I sigh. She's soaking wet. Ready and ripe for me.

"I have something for you," I say, my mouth already starting to water as I retrieve my shorts from the floor and get out my wallet. I pull out a slip of paper which I hand to her.

"What's this?"

I got myself checked and what she's reading is a copy of my

test results. Proof that I'm clean, and I won't put her at risk. We can have sex without a condom, but only if she wants.

I move to the bed and lie on my side, waiting. "Only if you want to," I say, when she looks at me with mischief in her eyes.

"Oh, yes," she whispers, coming for me and reaching for my hardness again, and doing all the things she knows I like.

I savor the intense emotions she elicits in me, but impatient for her, when I can't take it any longer, I push her onto the bed, then flip her over onto her stomach.

"Hey, I was having fun!" she protests, playfully.

"Shortcake, if you continue like that, I'll come in your hands." I adjust her gently so that she's on her knees. Then I pull her from the hips, so her bottom is in the air, face and arms resting on the bed. The sight of her takes my breath away. I glide my hands all over her bottom, parting her cheeks and getting a better look.

She gasps. "Jett!"

"I just want to look." I lick my finger and touch her there.

"Jett."

"Tell me to stop and I will. I won't do anything you're not comfortable with. I just want to look." I wait for her answer.

"Okay." She sounds a little breathless.

"Open for me."

"Wh-what?"

"Widen your legs."

She does. I peer closer, almost salivating at the sight of her dripping. I bend down and kiss her rosette bud. She flinches, clearly not ready for me to kiss her there. I rain tiny kisses along her lower back, my hand skating over her soft silky skin. She seems to relax. I move her hair over to one shoulder, marveling that I have her all to myself for the rest of the night. My cock can hardly contain itself.

My fingers slide to her front where I find her soaked and

slippery, enough to make me lose my mind. I bite out a groan as I explore her silky folds. She sits back a little, giving me better access, and I dip my fingers inside her, making her moan louder this time. Her head rolls back and she gyrates her hips as my fingers pump her.

"Like it?" I rasp, bracketing her hips between my thighs.

"Fuck me," she begs.

Oh, I intend to. She sounds so unlike the Cari I know. I angle her hips higher, then bend down and bury my tongue into her. Just like I knew she would, she flinches at first, then relaxes as I tunnel my tongue inside her. Her scent, her wetness, her readiness for me, hardens my cock. When she jerks and jolts like a woman possessed, I taste her as she comes over my tongue.

"You taste so good," I murmur, lifting back up and kneeling behind her. I need to be inside her.

"Jett." She continues to writhe, but I lift her hips and slam into her, my cock gliding in easily to the hilt.

Throaty, dirty, sensual moans fall from her mouth and she comes apart, jerking as her climax tears through her. She whimpers as her body stills. I try to stroke her clit, but I'm too far gone, and thinking of myself now. Pulling out, I flip her onto her back before slamming inside her again.

I want to see her face when I empty into her. Her eyes close, and she's lost in her own bliss. "Look at me," I beg. Her eyelids flutter open and I go hard, slamming in and out of her. Her muscles tighten around me as she milks me. This feels so fucking good.

I stay like that for a while, buried inside her and she watches me watching her. Dammit if this isn't the most intimate we've ever been. I want to fall asleep like this. We're lost in a haze of sensual fog, until finally, I lay down beside her. We catch our breaths, and lie sated in the sultry heat of the night.

CHAPTER FORTY-THREE

CARI

These last few days of ours are beautiful memories I will cherish forever. Jett checks his laptop every morning and night, but he doesn't go into the study to work. He's adamant that he won't.

We're at Horseshoe Bay where the air smells of salt and sunshine, and the water sparkles like a jewel. Brooke squeals as she splashes in the shallow lagoon chasing minnows, while Jett eyes her like a hawk. He's protective in a way that makes my chest bloom; a man who'll do anything for his daughter.

The day passes in a blur of laughter, swimming, and exploring. Jett even loosens up enough to join Brooke on a makeshift rock slide into the water. Watching him laugh, his hair dripping wet, is something I'll never forget.

Back at the house, we have dinner outside in the gazebo. It's such a pretty place, a wooden structure elevated slightly above the garden, framed by lush bougainvillea spilling over the edges. I wish we'd had more dinners out here, but Jett tells me the private island will take my breath away.

I can hardly wait.

The air is balmy and filled with the clicking of crickets and the occasional rustle of palm fronds in the breeze. It's the kind of August night that feels like it could stretch on forever.

After dinner, Brooke plays on the swings while Jett and I sit with cocktails. Mine is fruity and bright, his is dark and brooding like the man himself. He leans back, stretching his long legs as he looks out at the garden.

"This was a good idea," I say, taking a sip. "Having dinner out here. I wished we'd done more of that."

"We haven't spent much time relaxing around the house," he agrees. His gaze softens. "I wanted to make a few memories."

I smile at that. "You've finally figured out how important those are?"

He looks at me, something unspoken in his eyes, and nods. I feel as if he's about to say something, but Brooke's giggles float through the balmy evening air and grab my attention. She's moved from the swings to the small slide and climbs the ladder, pausing dramatically at the top. "Look at me!" She waves as if she's royalty addressing her kingdom.

Jett and I wave back, our smiles conspiratorial as we huddle close, whispering about our island getaway. It's a delicious little secret, a treasure we're keeping from Brooke until we get there. Just thinking about those three days of peace, surrounded by turquoise waters and quiet, makes me giddy. Like a kid on Christmas Eve.

Brooke sits at the top of the slide, her little legs swinging. She's about to push off when her gaze shifts over my shoulder. Her eyes light up. "Grandpa!" she shrieks.

My blood freezes.

I turn slowly to see if Brooke is imagining things, or if the devil himself has decided to ruin our perfect evening. And there he is, Paul Knight, with his cold, piercing gray eyes locked on Jett. He stiffens beside me, his jaw clenched so tight I'm surprised it doesn't crack. We pull apart, the easy warmth we shared seconds ago is gone, replaced by an icy tension that prickles my skin.

"I didn't expect to see you here," Jett says, his voice flat, controlled.

Paul Knight doesn't flinch. "Good evening to you, too."

No hug. No handshake. Not even a nod of acknowledgment between father and son. It's like they're strangers passing each other on a street corner, the air between them electric with unspoken resentment.

"Mr. Knight," I manage to say, though my voice sounds too thin, too weak. My heart plummets to the depths of my stomach like a rock. The island getaway we were planning vanishes in a puff of smoke.

Brooke doesn't notice the tension crackling around us. She's already slid down the slide and is racing toward her grandfather. "Grandpa!" she squeals again, throwing herself into his arms.

Paul scoops her up with a smile that looks almost genuine. *Almost.* He spins her around, laughing like a doting grandparent. The display is so out of character that I blink, wondering if I've stepped into an alternate reality. Since when does Paul Knight indulge in anything resembling affection?

"What are you doing here, Grandpa?" Brooke's voice bubbles with joy. Jett and I hold our breath, waiting for his answer. Waiting for the motive behind this sudden, unannounced appearance.

"I was passing through," Paul says, his tone vague.

Passing through? Passing through Bermuda? What's next—he casually drops by Antarctica?

"Are you here to check up on me?" Jett's voice is sharp. There's no mistaking the animosity there.

Paul's smile tightens, and he sets Brooke back on her feet. "I had business to attend to, actually." He strolls over to the table and makes himself at home, ruining our evening. Brooke skips back to the swings, blissfully unaware of the dark cloud descending on us.

Gloom settles over the table like another uninvited guest. I glance at Jett. His face is filled with anger layered with frustration, but something heavy lurks beneath the surface. His shoulders are tense, his hands curled into fists on the table. He looks like a man robbed of the last fragile moments of peace he was clinging to.

"How long are you staying?" Jett asks.

"A couple of days." Paul casually reaches for the bowl of fruit on the table. He pulls off a cluster of grapes, popping one into his mouth with the air of a man entirely at ease. "No work today?" he asks. His tone is light, but the jab is unmistakable.

My hands are shaking, so I fold them on my lap. My stomach is a jumble of nerves and anxiety, because Paul is like the harbinger of doom. Nothing good ever comes from him being around.

And now he's here. In paradise, throwing a sharpened machete into our dream trip. Our last few days together.

Jett's jaw ticks and I know he's even more annoyed by this interruption than I am. "I just came back from Florida. I'm taking time for myself, and for Brooke. We've been having fun."

Paul waves at Brooke again, beckoning her over. She skips

to his side, and he hands her a small bunch of grapes. "Have you had fun, sweetheart?"

Brooke beams. "Yes! Daddy and Cari have been so much fun!" She darts back to the swings, giggling.

The mention of my name makes my stomach flip. I hold my breath, praying Brooke doesn't accidentally let something slip, like mentioning the time she walked in on me and Jett in bed. My face burns at the memory.

Paul leans back in his chair, his eyes flicking between me and Jett. "You seem … *relaxed.*"

"Imagine that." Jett replies coldly. "Spending time with my daughter does wonders for my mood."

"And your other responsibilities?" Paul presses. "The family business doesn't take vacations."

"I just spent four days fixing a problem in Florida," Jett snaps, his voice low and simmering with anger. "I've earned a few days off."

Paul's expression doesn't change, but his silence speaks volumes. He's not impressed. He never is.

I sit perfectly still, trying to disappear into my chair. The tension between them is suffocating, and I'm terrified of saying or doing the wrong thing.

Jett stands abruptly, his chair scraping against the stone patio. "Cari, why don't you take Brooke upstairs?"

I nod quickly, grateful for the escape, but I'm worried for Jett. I want to take Brooke out of here, but a part of me wants to stay to offer Jett support. He needs to know that he isn't alone, that I'm there by his side. I'm so torn.

"Come on, Brooke," I call. She skips over, and I grab her hand, leading her toward the house. "Let's go play in your tent."

I glance back at Jett as we walk away. His back is to me, his shoulders rigid as he faces his father. The peaceful evening we were supposed to have feels like it's been ripped apart. There's no point in making plans for the island. No point in looking forward to the joy of being alone together.

Paul Knight has ruined everything. Again.

CHAPTER FORTY-FOUR

JETT

Fuck my life.

We all turn in early tonight, though sleep feels like an impossible luxury. Cari drifted off hours ago with Brooke, leaving me alone in the dark with my thoughts. I should go to Brooke's room to say goodnight, but the thought of running into my father again is enough to keep me rooted here. The man has an uncanny ability to ruin everything.

He knows. I can feel it. He didn't just *happen* to stop by. Paul Knight doesn't operate on coincidence. He thrives on control. The pretense of him passing through on business is laughable.

This is about me. About checking up on me. About me ignoring him. There's possibly some business-related issue tied to this. Maybe about the Brazilian heiress. The old man seems to be in a hurry to get that deal done.

I should have protected this little slice of paradise here in Bermuda, but I made a mistake in canceling our scheduled calls. Pushing him off with vague excuses. Pretending he wouldn't notice when I stepped back to focus on Brooke and Cari. I should've known better. Now he's here, looming over what should have been our perfect escape to the island. Three glorious days of quiet, of being with Cari and Brooke, away from the world and its relentless demands. Now it's gone. Crushed by my father's intrusion.

Cari's face when Paul arrived—she looked shocked and disappointed. I saw the way she folded into herself, trying to seem smaller. Less visible. And Brooke? She's thrilled to see her grandfather, as if he's Santa Claus instead of the man who measures affection in dollars and leverage. She doesn't know better, and I hate that one day she'll realize the truth.

It's just as well that we kept the trip a secret. If Brooke had blurted it out, Paul would've pounced, and that would've been the end of it. Just like that morning Brooke found us in bed together. Fully clothed, but still, it was a close call.

We're going to have to be much more careful around my father. The house feels heavier now, the happiness drained from its walls. One visit from Paul, and it's like all the light has been snuffed out.

His presence suffocates me, and it's a chore dodging his questions while trying to not give away what Cari means to me. I'm left with no choice but to spend all day tomorrow working in the study, dealing with business matters, and keeping my father by my side.

At least I'll have gotten him away from Cari and Brooke. They shouldn't have to suffer him.

CARI

· · ·

BROOKE CLUTCHES ELEPHANT AS I TUCK HER INTO BED. HER tiny arms wrap around the stuffed animal, her big eyes blinking up at me under the soft glow of her bedside lamp.

"What are we doing tomorrow?"

She's been asking this every night, her little world spinning with possibilities. I wish I could mirror her excitement. But I know better. *There's nothing wonderful left here now.*

"Maybe something fun," I say softly, brushing a curl from her cheek.

She smiles, satisfied with my vague answer, and closes her eyes. I sit beside her for a while, her even breaths soothing the ache in my chest. I close her door quietly and make my way to my room. My body feels heavy, my heart even heavier.

Our dream of escaping to the island, of soaking in three days of pure bliss, it's gone. Disintegrated the moment Paul Knight appeared.

He said he's only here for a couple of days, but we fly back soon. The timing couldn't be worse. I already know what Jett's going to do. Without the island as a distraction, he'll retreat into work. It's what he knows. He'll throw himself into meetings and deals while I figure out how to keep Brooke entertained. Maybe another play date with Zara.

Sadness weighs me down. *This isn't how it was supposed to be.*

But there's something else beneath the sadness. A warning, a bitter reminder of the family Jett belongs to. He stood tall against the Bryces and Abigails of this world, but his own father? That's different. He's not just blood, he's the foundation of the Knight family.

Deep down, I know he'll never approve of me.

It makes me wonder if Jett would even tell him about us?

If there even is an "us" to tell about.

The air is thick with tension when I walk into the dining room the next morning. Brooke and I are the last to arrive, and I instantly wish I hadn't come downstairs. Paul Knight sits at the head of the table, a newspaper spread before him. Jett sits opposite, his face hard and unreadable.

Brooke runs in first, throwing her arms around Jett's neck. She kisses his cheek, then offers a small kiss to her grandfather. The sight makes my stomach twist.

"Good morning," I say, my voice brittle.

Paul glances up briefly, his gaze flicking over me like I'm part of the furniture. Jett doesn't look at me at all, which stings more than it should. I know why. He doesn't want his father picking up on *anything*.

I pour juice for Brooke and help her with her plate, filling it with fruit and toast. I barely touch my coffee, the lump in my throat making it impossible to eat.

Jett stands abruptly, the scrape of his chair breaking the heavy silence. "Shall we go?" He's looking at his father, not me.

Paul lowers his newspaper slowly, folding it with precision. "I thought I'd stay here for a while. Spend some time with Brooke." He flashes a smile at her, but it doesn't reach his eyes. Then, almost as an afterthought, his gaze flicks to me. It lingers just long enough to make my skin prickle.

"We have work to do," Jett says, testily.

Paul raises a brow. "Work? Suddenly you're eager to get back to the office?"

Jett's jaw flexes, the tension rolling off him in waves. "Don't you want a proper update on Pinewood? Since you're already here, you might as well."

Paul leans back in his chair. "Someone's awfully motivated this morning."

Brooke giggles as Paul reaches over and taps her nose, but I catch the look Jett shoots me. Quick, almost imperceptible, but charged.

Stay here. Stay safe.

I understand what he's doing. He doesn't want to spend time with his father, but more than that, he doesn't want his father left alone with me. The thought makes my stomach churn. Paul stands, folding his newspaper neatly. "Let's get on with it."

Jett doesn't say another word. He grabs his jacket and storms out, Paul following with an amused glint in his eye. The room feels emptier without Jett, even with Brooke chattering away beside me. I stare down at my untouched plate, Paul Knight's presence engulfing me like a suffocating fog.

Paradise is gone.

CHAPTER FORTY-FIVE

JETT

These last few days have been pure torture.

Instead of soaking in turquoise waters with Cari, and watching my daughter chase sand crabs, I've been trapped in the office with my father. Every second feels like having my nails ripped out one by one.

This man has a gift for draining the very life out of a room. It's unbearable at the best of times, but now? After the days Cari, Brooke and I have shared, and the days we were looking forward to, his presence is like an army tank, heavy and dangerous, running roughshod over all the happy memories we've made.

At night, I lay in bed, staring at the ceiling, feeling the weight of his intrusion. Cari and I haven't risked being around each other since he arrived. The house has eyes, ears, and secrets to guard. But I miss her. I miss the way she fits so perfectly next to me, the way her presence soothes the sharp edges of my life. What we had, what we were building, feels like it's been stolen.

I hate my father so much. This man who cheated on my mother—his wife—had no qualms about having a mistress. He went on to have not one, not two, but three children with her. Now he has the audacity to ruin my plans, to sneak up on me to see what I'm up to. A man who wants me to have an arranged marriage for business reasons.

Who the fuck does he think he is?

What happens when Cari and I return to the office?

Who are we there? Can we go back to being a boss and an assistant, sliding into those roles like nothing has happened? But even there, our time is limited.

We've been so wrapped up in each other here, unraveling feelings and unearthing truths, that the versions of us in New York feel like strangers. I don't even know how to be that ruthless man anymore.

My father leaves tomorrow night, but it's too late. This disruptor of peace and anything that is good has already ruined the fragile, fleeting time I had left with Cari and Brooke.

CARI

JETT'S FATHER IS GONE, BUT IT DOESN'T FEEL LIKE HE'S REALLY left.

His presence lingers in the air, like a ghost hovering just out of sight. I don't think I've taken a proper breath since he arrived.

The black SUV disappears down the driveway, taking him to the airport. Only when it's out of sight does Jett reach for my hand, intertwining his fingers with mine. His touch is warm, steady, but I feel deflated.

It's late on Sunday evening, and I feel sad knowing there are many unspoken words between us. We *need* to talk, but the thought of what lies ahead makes my chest ache. We're heading back to New York tomorrow, and the day after that we're both back in the office. Everything we've avoided discussing looms in front of us.

I've done my best to keep Brooke occupied. Trips to the beach, play dates with Zara, anything to keep us distracted. But the weight of Paul Knight's presence, oppressive and suffocating, has been impossible to ignore.

Dinner is quiet, aside from Brooke's cheerful chatter. She talks about everything she loved on this trip, her excitement about going home, and her sadness at leaving Zara behind, and casually mentioning that Zara now has a baby brother whom she wants to play with. She's an innocent ray of sunshine, blissfully unaware of the tension between me and Jett.

"We'll come again next summer," Jett promises her, his voice soft but resolute.

The words hit me like a sucker punch. I won't be here. By next summer, Brooke will barely remember me, and Jett will have moved on. He'll have another assistant as well as a new nanny. Would I fit into his life anywhere?

The thought weighs heavy on my heart.

THE STARS ARE OUT BY THE TIME BROOKE FINISHES HER bedtime routine. I tuck her in with Elephant, brushing a kiss over her forehead as her sleepy voice murmurs, "What are we doing tomorrow?"

"Going home," I whisper, smoothing her hair. She nods, her

eyes already fluttering shut. I linger by her bedside, memorizing the moment.

When I step out of her room, Jett is waiting in the hallway. His shirt is unbuttoned at the collar, his sleeves rolled up, and his hands stuffed deep into his pockets. He looks exhausted, like a man fighting a battle no one else can see.

"We should talk," he says, his voice low.

I nod, but I don't know where to start. Words feel heavy, unwieldy, and I'm not sure I have the strength to say what I need to. To ask for what I need.

We sit outside on the terrace, our chairs close together. A warm breeze blows, but the air feels different, almost like it's laced with the bittersweet finality of the trip. Jett leans forward, elbows on his knees, his gaze distant. "This wasn't how it was supposed to go."

"No," I say softly. "It wasn't."

"I wanted you and Brooke to have more time," he continues, his voice rough around the edges. "I wanted *us* to have more time."

My lungs suddenly feel too small. "And now?"

He looks at me then, his eyes shadowed but intense. "Now, we go back, and we figure it out."

I nod again, but the ache in my chest doesn't ease. I don't know what *figuring it out* means for us. For me. For Brooke. But I know one thing. This is the last night I'll let myself hope for something more.

Our moods are somber, and I can sense that Jett needs to be alone. I know I do. I can't spend the night with him. There's so much to think about, and maybe it's time to disengage, to uncouple softly.

"Cari." He moves his chair to face me, then takes my hands in his and tugs me forward. He presses his forehead against mine. "I hate that this ended so abruptly."

"Life is full of curveballs." I attempt a smile but fail miserably.

His mouth claims mine and his tongue sweeps in, dueling with my own. We taste each other, kissing roughly with wanton need. I sigh inwardly, knowing how easy it would be to spend the night in his bed, to give myself to him again. But he moves away, perhaps realizing that we need to start disentangling. His fingers trace over my face, and the way he stares at me, with such intensity, makes me shiver.

Is this goodbye? Maybe he feels awkward and doesn't know how to end it. Our vacation is over. The dream has ended.

"I should go," I say, finally.

He nods, and we say goodnight, before returning to our separate rooms.

This is our last night here. Tomorrow, it's back to reality. Back to the office, where I have one week left before my notice ends. Seven days to wrap up my life with Jett and Brooke. Seven days to pretend I'm fine walking away from the man who's been such a big part of my world for three years, even if most of it was imaginary.

But these last few weeks have more than made up for all the fantasies that sustained me during that time. Seven days to slowly sever the bond with the little girl who's become a piece of my heart.

And then what? What happens to us? To Brooke, who hugs me every morning like I'm part of her family? To Jett, who knows me better than anyone, but I don't know if I can I trust him with my heart.

We never talked about it, about what would happen after this trip. We didn't even plan for our return to New York. We were focused on paradise, on the dream of what could be. But now paradise has crumbled, leaving behind nothing but unanswered questions and a hollow ache in my chest.

CHAPTER FORTY-SIX

JETT

WE FLY BACK TO NEW YORK IN FIRST CLASS AGAIN, BUT THIS time it's different. Instead of having Cari and Brooke seated rows behind me, they're close. Brooke is her usual bubbly self, happily coloring, but Cari … Cari is quiet. Too quiet.

We didn't spend our last night together. We kissed and went our separate ways, maybe we're both trying to process what these weeks have meant and what the future holds. It's something we would have talked about had we managed to get away, but my father's suffocating presence put an end to that.

It feels like my father left something behind when he flew out, a heavy lingering shadow that presses down on both of us. All the possibilities that existed before his arrival now seem dead, replaced by silence of what-ifs.

On the flight, I try to make conversation, but it's like speaking into a void. Cari has her nose buried in a book, and while I pretend to work, my laptop stays closed. My focus isn't on the Pinewood deal or anything else, it's on her.

On us.

I glance at Brooke. She's coloring, blissfully unaware of the tension between me and Cari. She doesn't understand what's happened over the last few days, and I envy her innocence.

When we land back in New York, the familiar black SUV is waiting for us when we land, sleek and polished, like a reminder that reality is waiting to swallow us whole. The ride is quiet, save for Brooke's occasional chatter, and when we finally pull up to Cari's apartment building, something heavy sinks in my stomach.

This is it. Goodbye. An ending. This is where we revert back to who we were before. She opens the door, stepping out as Brooke immediately leans over, reaching for her. "Where are you going?" Brooke cries.

Cari freezes, her eyes darting to mine for guidance. I can see her struggling, her lips parting but no words coming out. Finally, she crouches down to Brooke's level, her voice soft. "I have to go back to my place, where I live, sweetie."

"But why? Why can't you come live with us?" Brooke wails. "Don't you like us?"

"I love you, sweetie." Cari cups Brooke's face gently. "B-but, when we lived together in Bermuda it was just for the vacation."

"But I don't want you to leave." Brooke's lower lip trembles.

I step in, my voice firm but careful. "Come on, sprout. Cari's tired. We all are. We have to go back to work tomorrow."

Brooke's shoulders slump, but she doesn't argue. Cari leans in, hugging her tightly. "I love you so much, sweetie. I'm going to miss you, but I'll see you soon, okay?"

"Promise?"

Cari nods, but doesn't make the promise. She straightens, her eyes meeting mine. "So long," I say, the words bitter in my mouth because they're not what I want to say. I want to tell her to come back with us. To not walk away. But I don't.

"I'll see you tomorrow," she replies softly.

Her smile is small, sad, and resigned, and it feels like a punch to my gut. The ache spreads as she turns and walks toward her building, her silhouette fading as she disappears inside.

Brooke leans against me in the backseat, quiet now. She doesn't understand the gravity of what just happened, but I do. Cari is walking out of our lives, and I don't know how to stop her.

The SUV pulls away, and I look out the window overcome by a sense of loss for everything we could have been, and everything we weren't.

CARI

Eliana throws open the door and wraps me in a hug so tight I almost can't breathe.

Her smile is huge, beaming like I've just come back from the trip of a lifetime. I guess I did, until the last few days unraveled everything.

"Why the long face?" she asks, grabbing my suitcase and wheeling it in like it's her duty to carry my burdens.

"I'm just tired." It's not a lie, but it's far from the truth. There's a hollow ache in my chest. That last glance at the SUV, with Brooke and Jett inside, stays etched in my mind. They didn't drive off right away. I couldn't see them through the tinted windows, but I could feel their presence, like an unspoken pull. Their sadness mirroring my own.

"Well?" Eliana prompts, eyes wide with curiosity as I slip off my pumps. "You look beautifully tanned, and there's something different about you." Her gaze flickers over me, scrutinizing.

I force a smile. "I had a really nice time."

"Then why are you so sad?" She narrows her eyes and grabs my hand, peering at me like I've come down with a rare illness. Maybe I have. Lovesickness isn't in the medical journals, but it should be. "Oh, babe." She clutches her chest dramatically. "You've got it bad."

"What?" My cheeks heat under her scrutiny. I feel exposed, as if the sadness of leaving Brooke and Jett has scrawled itself all over me. Coming back here, to this apartment, this version of my life, feels jarring, like I've stepped into a space I've already outgrown. What I had in Bermuda feels too vivid, too alive, to leave behind.

Eliana collapses on the couch and pats a place next to her for me to sit. "I have all the time in the world. Come on, spill it. You're glowing, but not in a *just got a tan* way. This is *I had a life-altering event* kind of glow."

Her words make me think of Jett rubbing sunscreen on me the first time I put on that bikini. My skin tingles with the memory, and I want to go back and rewind to every glance, every touch, every conversation that left me breathless.

She snaps her fingers in front of my face. "See? You're not even here. You're still in Bermuda, with Jett."

"What? No, I'm just tired from the flight." My deflection is weak, and she sees right through me.

"It's a two-and-a-half-hour flight, Car. Did you even sleep? Or were you too busy *doing things*." She waggles her eyebrows suggestively. "Spill. I want details."

"Oh, El."

"What is it?" she presses, her voice softening.

And just like that, the dam breaks. I tell her everything. Not the R-rated specifics, but the broad strokes, the dress, the library, the night we ended up in Jett's bed. Her mouth falls open, her hand clutching her chest like she's about to faint.

"I'm so proud of you!" she exclaims, clapping her hands in delight. "You're finally living your best life!"

"Am I?"

"The sex … so much sex! You lucky girl. Was he good?"

I blush. Heat surges across my skin.

"Well hung?" Eliana pushes.

It shouldn't, but it does, Jett's enormous member, thick and glistening, flashes into my head and I get goosebumps. I cover my face with my hands.

"Oh hon!" Eliana clasps both her hands to her chest. "He must have been beyond amazing. Nothing like Rory."

I look up and chuckle, remembering Jett's comments about not wasting time on boys. "He was … *so* good. I can't even begin to tell you."

"You don't need to tell me, babe, I can see by just looking at you. I've never seen you go so red before. I'm all ears. Tell me."

"I'm not giving you specifics!" I cry. What we shared is buried deep in my heart, memories I will cherish forever.

"How did you do it, get down and dirty with him? You were always falling apart around him. I can't imagine how you managed to be naked in front of him."

Eliana makes me laugh. Given who I was around Jett, before I left, I can see where she's coming from. "It was the dress," I say, though the memory of Jett's hungry gaze when I wore it sends a shiver through me. "And the stilettos. I felt … powerful."

"Dress, stilettos? That dirty, sexy man," she teases, eyes

gleaming mischievously. "What a combo. So, what now? How did you leave things?"

I take a deep breath. "That's the thing ... I don't know where we stand."

Eliana's expression sobers. "You don't know?"

"We had plans to spend a few days on a private island," I explain.

"A private island?" Her eyes grow large. "Car, this is another universe you're living in."

I shrug. "We didn't get to go. His father showed up out of nowhere, and everything fell apart. Jett thinks it was intentional, to keep us from ..." I pause, unsure how to phrase it.

"From being together?" she finishes for me.

I nod. "We stayed away from each other after that. His father's intense. He sees right through you. I couldn't go near Jett, and he didn't come near me. We both just retreated. Brooke was so disappointed in the car just now, and honestly, so was I."

Eliana shakes her head. "That man of yours needs to grow a backbone when it comes to his father."

"He's not mine," I say softly, the words cutting more than I expect.

Her hand rests on mine. "Car, if you think this is over, you're wrong. Men like Jett don't let go of something, or someone, they truly want. I've been so angry with him in the past, for how he's treated you, and how badly you've longed for him. It was painful to see, him with his big shot, arrogant, big dick energy. He had you running around after him—"

"He did not have me running around after him."

"Buying sexy lingerie for his girlfriends? Booking their vacations and dinners. There were times when you came home from work and I could see you were so broken."

She doesn't know what I know, that he did these things partly to keep me at bay. But I love that she's my wing woman and she has my back, no matter what. Billionaire or not.

Eliana pauses, her soft brown eyes glistening under the light. "But looking at you now, something's changed, and I can see he's brought you a lot of happiness. You look so different. Not just sunkissed and golden all over. But you're radiating *something*. All the sadness that sapped your spirit after your mom passed, it's gone, hon. There's no dark cloud hanging over you now, that's not to say you don't miss your mom."

I nod, loving that she's always so careful and mindful when she's talking about my mom. She throws her hands up in the air. "I don't know if it's happiness, or the fact that you've had lots of great sex, or … even if it's love."

I look away and let her words sink in.

Love. My heart swells. I feel the space inside my chest grow bigger and bigger. My mind flickers back to Jett's quiet confession that he had feelings for me for years. How he used his arrogance to push me away, how he buried himself in meaningless relationships to avoid facing the truth.

"Babe, you've gone all quiet."

My eyes well up and I suddenly feel like crying. It feels like we already had our ending, we just didn't know it at the time. It happened the night his father arrived. "I don't know what happens next. I don't know if there is a *next*."

Eliana's eyes soften. "From what you've told me, it sounds like there most definitely is. His daughter is the most important thing in the world to him, and the three of you spent time like a family. He wouldn't do that, risk his little girl getting used to being around you just temporarily. That man sounds lost, and now it feels like maybe you've grounded him."

Her words give me something to consider. She has a point.

"I don't know. I don't know anymore. His father turning up unexpectedly ruined everything."

"He's such a villain."

"He's awful." I agree. Eliana has never met him, but she's heard me talking about him many times.

"I can't see your boss letting his father get in the way of his happiness. It sounds like you had a fantastic time. Jett, too."

I hope so. Last night Jett was pensive. As was I. We both had so much on our minds, a brooding heaviness that overwhelmed us. Making love didn't seem like an option.

Eliana stands up, a grin on her face. "Let's eat. I made your favorite quesadillas."

I love this woman. "You always know how to cheer me up."

She winks at me. "That's what I'm here for. Bianca is coming over later, so you'll have to tell us your dirty bedroom stories all over again."

But as I dig into the familiar comfort of melted cheese and crispy tortillas, my mind is miles away, with Jett, with Brooke, and the uncertain future that faces us.

CHAPTER FORTY-SEVEN

JETT

I couldn't sleep last night.

The apartment feels hollow, stripped of life. No Cari. Just Brooke and me in a space too quiet to drown out my thoughts. There's no Anna either, but that's just an inconvenience. I need to find a solution for Brooke tomorrow, because I'm expected back at work.

As the car pulled away from Cari's apartment building yesterday, Brooke's voice was tiny but relentless. "Why can't Cari live with us?"

"She can't, angel."

"Why not, Daddy?" Her big, round eyes cut through me, full of hope.

"Because she has her own home."

"But it was so nice with the three of us. I love her, Daddy. Can't she be my new mommy?"

I hate that I've given Brooke a taste of something she's

hungered for, but which I can't guarantee. A glimpse of what family could be.

It wasn't my intention.

And yet here we are. Now that I've had Cari in my life like that, woven into every day, her laugh filling silences, her warmth making the world brighter, I don't know how to go back.

When we got home, I kept busy getting Brooke ready for bed. She jabbered on about Cari, her questions chipping away at my composure. The apartment was spotless, cleaned and prepped while we were gone, but it was sterile. It had no soul. It was empty.

I yearn for Bermuda, for the home back there, for the carefree days with my two favorite people.

I don't even know what normal looks like anymore. Cari isn't here. I have no nanny. I texted Anna before we left Bermuda, almost begging her to help me out. Luckily, she agreed. She'll be available to help out, on a part-time basis for a short time, as and when I need her. I need to find her replacement quickly. Until then, I'll be paying Anna double.

My life is going off the rails. There's no plan. No direction. Just a quiet void and questions I don't have answers for. Brooke sits in the tub, her little arms crossed as I rinse the shampoo from her curls. I'm trying, but apparently I'm failing.

"It doesn't hurt when Cari does it."

I pour lukewarm water over her face, shielding her forehead with my hand.

"Sorry, sport. I'm learning."

"Can't Cari come do it?"

How do I explain that Cari won't be around anymore? That I must find someone new, someone who could never fill her shoes?

"Cari's busy now. You won't see her as much, but Anna will be back for a few visits, when we need her."

She pushes my hand away, her voice stubborn. "I don't want Anna. I want Cari. Why can't Cari live here?"

"It's not that simple, princess."

Her little face scrunches up in frustration. "But you love her."

I laugh, but it's hollow. "Why would you say that?"

"Because when she's around, your eyes go all crinkly when you laugh."

Damn. She's perceptive for five.

"Do you love her, Daddy?"

The answer rises in my chest, raw and undeniable. Yes. I love her more than I have words for. But I can't say it. Not yet.

I try deflection. "Do you love her, sprout?"

"I love her so much and Elephant loves her too because she made him new again. We had lots of fun."

"Yeah," I whisper, my throat tight. "We did."

BROOKE STARTS DAY CAMP TODAY, AN ELEVENTH-HOUR solution to my childcare problem because Anna wasn't available.

Savannah, Tobias Stone's wife, recommended it to me when I made a few calls last night. I need to go into the office today, so this is a perfect solution. I drop Brooke off early, then head to the office. It's too early for Cari. Too early for anyone. And that's exactly how I want it.

The elevator hums as it rises. I close my eyes, bracing for the silence of my office, the endless loop of what-ifs in my head. But when the doors open, I forget to breathe.

She's already here. Standing at her desk, a printer cartridge in hand, her back to me. Her pencil skirt hugs her hips, and her silk blouse shimmers under the light. Her hair is swept into a tidy updo, but all I see is her, barefoot in Bermuda, laughing under the moonlight. I want those days back so badly.

She turns, her eyes meeting mine. Time slows.

"You're early." Her voice is calm, but her grip on the cartridge tightens.

"I have meetings all day."

Her brow lifts. "Were you trying to avoid me?"

"No." The word comes out rougher than I intend, but I can't take my eyes off her. She's breathtaking. I'm remembering every second of her beneath me, her sighs and gasps filling the night. The scent of her skin, the taste of her on my tongue.

"You're here earlier than usual." I walk towards her. "Were you avoiding me?"

Chin up in the air, she stares at me defiantly. "I'm leaving and I need to tie up loose ends."

Her words hit me like a slap. "We need to talk."

"This isn't the time or place."

I step closer, my gaze locked on hers. "Is leaving what you really want?"

She straightens, her chin tilting up. "What do you want, Jett?"

Her words slice through me. She's not just asking about her resignation. She's asking about everything. She's asking about *us*. We're inches apart now and the air crackles between us. When she chews her lower lip, I can't stop my eyes from trailing down to the way her blouse clings to her curves. "You look delectable, my little shortcake."

Her lips curve into a faint smile. "And you have no idea what your dark blue Armani suit does to me."

"You know this is Armani?"

She shrugs. "I pay attention."

Just like that the tension disappears. I want her so badly. Every second with her floods me with memories of that vacation. Of her smile. Her moans. I lean in, ready to close the distance between us, but my phone vibrates and snaps me back to reality.

She steps back, her walls slamming back into place, and just like that, the moment is gone.

When I look at my phone, it's that fucking disruptor of peace. The agent of chaos.

My father.

And he wants to see me in his office.

I have no choice but to go. His office is just as I remember, cold and unwelcoming. I step inside, shutting the heavy door behind me, bracing for whatever verbal landmines he plans to scatter.

"Good flight?" he asks, not looking up from the papers he's signing.

"Yes," I say curtly, taking the seat across from him.

He finally glances at me, his cool gray eyes sharp, as if they can cut through every layer of pretense. "I didn't know your assistant was leaving."

My jaw tightens. He's been sniffing around, like he always does. "I didn't think it was something you needed to know," I say, keeping my tone steady. "I informed HR. She's working through the end of the week."

"Hmm." His fingers tap against his desk, the sound grating. "You also don't have a nanny."

"No."

He leans back, studying me. "Will you be employing her for that role?"

"What exactly are you trying to get at?" I ask, the question edged with irritation.

"I'm simply making conversation." His hands form a

steeple, his chin resting on the tips of his fingers. "Why is she leaving?"

"Why the interrogation?" I shoot back.

"It's just a question."

I force myself to relax, though every muscle in my body screams otherwise. He's baiting me, and I won't give him the satisfaction. "She wants to move on," I say finally. "Do something else."

His eyes narrow, as if he's dissecting my answer. "Any thoughts on Daniela Oliveira?"

"Who?"

"Your future wife." My hands grip the armrests of the chair, but I keep my expression neutral. "The Brazilian heiress," he clarifies, his tone far too casual. "Her father and I have come to an agreement. It's a merger, Jett. An alliance between Knight Enterprises and their telecoms empire. A match made in boardroom heaven."

"I don't care what you and her father agreed on. I'm not doing it. Also, how incredibly presumptuous of you to think that I would marry someone just because of a business deal."

"Listen to me." He sits forward, cold eyes pinned on me. "This is business. You need a wife, a mother for Brooke. This is about our legacy. You marry her, and the deal is sealed. You're free to have your mistresses—"

"Stop," I snap. "I don't want to hear this."

"You're turning down ten million dollars? From me?" He scoffs, leaning back like he's caught me in a checkmate.

"Money doesn't buy everything."

He laughs, the sound hollow. "It buys happiness, stability and respect. You're too young and too stupid to see that."

"Don't ever bring this topic up to me again," I say, my tone ice-cold. "*Ever*."

His smile fades, replaced by a calculating look. "You're serious. You won't even consider it?"

"A mother can't be bought. Neither can a wife."

He folds his arms, his posture unnervingly relaxed. "Anything can be bought. You should know that by now."

"Not everything." I give him a hard stare. After everything that's happened in his life, has he not learned anything? He must have loved my mother once. Did he not feel any guilt over her death?

"I'm sure one of your brothers will oblige. The Half-Knights, as you call them."

The mention of Rio, Matteo, and Enzo draws a bitter laugh from me. "The secret sons? The ones you hid from everyone? Somehow, I doubt they'd jump at the chance to clean up your mess."

"They're the same as you, by the way," he says, nonplussed. "You're a Half-Knight yourself, given that your family name and bloodline come through me."

This cunning son of a bitch is trying to rile me up. "At least you were married to my mother, even though you were a terrible husband," I throw back.

My father's face hardens, giving me extreme satisfaction that I've hit him where it hurts.

"Which is probably why you think an arranged marriage can work. You think I can marry someone for their wealth and it will be fine."

The silence is heavy, charged with the reminder of the fractured family he's built. "I'm disappointed in you, boy." *Boy.* I've really pissed him off, but his words don't sting like they used to.

"I've been disappointed in you my entire life," I fire back.

"We have a legacy." It's like he's talking to himself, saying the same old mantra that he's repeated a thousand times. "A name. Our reputation precedes us. We have a brand and an identity to protect."

"Spare me the speech." I stand, buttoning my jacket with deliberate calm. "If that's all, I have actual business to attend to."

His eyes follow me as I turn to leave, and I can feel his disapproval like a shadow stretching after me. But I don't care. I've spent my whole life living under it, and it's done nothing but push me closer to the edge of rebellion.

Let him stew in his disappointment. I have no intention of becoming the pawn he so desperately needs.

I storm past Cari's office, my mood as dark as a brewing storm.

I knew this was coming, the conversation about the Brazilian heiress and my father's ridiculous idea of an arranged marriage. The whole thing is a travesty. I'm not interested. I can't be. My heart is already spoken for, and it belongs to Cari.

I barely sit down in my office, trying to regain some semblance of control, when there's a knock at the door. Before I can respond, Cari walks in, shutting the door softly behind her.

"Are you okay?" Her voice is filled with genuine concern.

"I am now that you're here." The words slip out before I can stop them. I push back my chair and cross the room in a few strides, my hands finding her waist as if they've always belonged there.

She leans into me, her hands sliding up my chest and clasping behind my neck. Her touch steadies me, grounds me. "I miss you," I murmur, tracing her face with my hands. Her skin feels like the softest silk beneath my fingertips and her lips curve into a small smile, her eyes searching mine. "I miss you too."

"Brooke misses you," I add, my gaze flicking between her eyes and her lips. Those lips, I've kissed them a hundred times, and every time I see her it's like falling for her all over again. The freckles dusting her cheeks, her perfect nose, her eyes that always seem to see right through me; everything about her draws me in deeper.

"I miss Brooke." Her voice softens, her lips parting slightly. "I miss you. I miss everything." Her words are a mirror to my own longing. "I keep replaying moments from Bermuda, over and over. It feels like I didn't get my fill. I want more and I feel robbed."

Hearing her words, and the passion in them, seeing her up close, holding her in my arms, I'm done for. I tilt her face up and press my mouth to hers, a quick kiss that quickly ignites into something far more consuming. Her lips are soft, warm, inviting, and I lose myself in her. My hands slide up her back, pulling her closer, her scent taking me back to Bermuda and all the intimate moments we shared.

Her mouth opens to mine, and the kiss deepens. It's all hunger and fire, a desperate claiming. The taste of her, the feel of her, the way she melts into me. It's everything I missed, everything I'm not ready to give up. Her fingers tangle in my hair, and I let out a low growl, pouring everything I can't say into this kiss.

A sharp knock at the door shatters the moment.

We spring apart, both of us breathing heavily, her flushed cheeks and swollen lips giving us away. The door swings open, and Dex strides in, his gaze bouncing between us. He stops short, taking in the scene, the tension, the way we look like we've just been caught doing exactly what we were.

He rakes a hand through his hair, a lazy grin tugging at the corner of his mouth. "Sorry. Didn't mean to interrupt anything," he drawls, his voice heavy with implication.

"I was just grabbing a file." Cari moves quickly, her voice

impossibly smooth as she snatches a folder from my desk. How does she always stay so composed under pressure?

Meanwhile, I just stand there, caught red-handed. My brain scrambling for something, *anything*, to say. But nothing comes.

Dex chuckles, the sound low and knowing. "Right. A file. Got it." He leans against the doorframe, arms crossed. "How was Bermuda?"

Cari glances at me, her expression unreadable, but I know she's thinking the same thing I am. Dex knows. He doesn't have to say it outright, because the look on his face says it all.

"I'll tell you later," I snap, hating that he walked in on us.

"Sure." Dex pushes off the doorframe. "I'll leave you to … your *files*." With a wink, he turns and saunters out, shutting the door behind him.

The silence that follows is heavily charged. Cari grips the folder in her hands like it's a lifeline, her eyes fixed anywhere but on me.

"We should—" she starts, her voice unsteady.

"Cari," I interrupt, stepping closer. "I don't regret it."

She looks up at me, her lips parting like she wants to say something. Instead, she nods, her expression softening. "Neither do I."

But before we can say more, my phone buzzes on the desk. This. This is my life. A constant interruption of people and phone calls. Nothing that's important. I sigh, and she steps back, smoothing her hair like nothing happened.

"Let me know if you need anything else," she says, her voice perfectly professional, but her eyes betray her.

"I always do." I watch her leave, already feeling the ache of her absence.

CHAPTER FORTY-EIGHT

CARI

I still feel the burn of Jett's kiss, the way it left my legs shaky, my mind buzzing, and my heart entirely his. The taste of him, the way he whispered my name against my lips, it's all I can think about.

And yet, here I am, trying to focus on work, pretending my world hasn't just shifted on its axis.

Then an email lands in my inbox. Paul Knight has summoned me to his office. The air freezes in my lungs. It's not a request. It's a command. And the timing isn't lost on me. Jett is out at a two-hour lunch meeting across Manhattan. Why does his father want to talk to me now?

I don't like this. I don't like this because his father waited for Jett to disappear before asking to see me. I smooth my skirt and square my shoulders as I walk down the hallway, and my steps are steady. Paul Knight is the devil incarnate, and I need to be out of his office as fast as I can. I knock.

"Come in," comes his clipped response.

The moment I enter, his eyes land on me, cold and calculating. He doesn't like me. No surprise there. The feeling is mutual, but what really twists my gut is the way he treats his son. All of them, really, but it's Jett I care about.

"You wanted to see me?" I stop just shy of his desk. My hands clasp tightly in front of me, a shield I don't want him to see.

"Sit down."

I take the chair opposite him, my spine straight, chin lifted.

"I hear you're leaving."

"Yes." I fold my hands on my lap.

"Why?"

This is none of his business. But this man has seen things, sensed things, and probably knows things, which is why he wants to talk to me one on one. I must keep my cool and not show him how much his questions rattle me. "It's time for me to move on."

"And yet you went to Bermuda with my son."

"I went to take care of your granddaughter."

His gaze narrows before he leans back in his chair as though he owns not just this moment but my very future. "You need to listen to me. It's in your best interests to take my information, my advice, if you will, and heed it well."

"Okay," I reply slowly as my discomfort grows. I glance at the closed door, but it's a futile attempt because Jett isn't even in the building.

"Men like us, men like my sons, don't marry your type." His words are like a slap to my face, but miraculously, I manage to hold steady, even as the insult cuts deep. "I've spent years building this empire and wealth like ours needs to be preserved and protected. It must be passed down. We are who we are, *where* we are, because of the deals we've done and the relationships we've built. Sometimes, that requires strategic alliances, not *distractions*."

A distraction. Is that what he thinks I am to Jett?

"I expect any parent would want the best for their children."

He gives me a cold smile. "Sweetheart, the best isn't you. Who knows what stock you come from?"

I can't believe my ears. I clench my hands in my lap, forcing my face to remain neutral. I won't give him the satisfaction of a reaction. "It's unbelievable that men like you exist. Men who can say such cruel words and smile so freely."

"Men like me *do* exist, and we run the world." Another icy smile, one that makes me shiver with fear. I force myself to sit taller, to keep my head upright. My heart aches for Jett and the awful time he must have had growing up under the eye of this monster. "My son is destined for greater things," Paul continues, unabashed. "Did he mention the proposal?"

My composure slips, and he sees it. I can't utter a word. "I didn't think so." He sits back in his chair and clasps his hands on the table. "Before he went to Bermuda, there was an offer on the table, an arrangement with a Brazilian heiress. Someone suitable. Someone who would understand his world."

The words hit like a bucket of ice water. *Jett knew?*

"Brooke needs a mother. Jett needs a wife. It's what's best for the family, for the business."

"Why are you telling me this?" It's a futile question, because I already know the answer. This man wants to hurt me. I'll ask Jett if this is true. I don't trust Paul Knight, but I need to know if he knew about this.

"To make sure you don't stand in the way of something important." His tone sharpens. "Someone like you doesn't belong in our world. My son will grow bored of you. Better to leave now than suffer later."

I bristle as my heart beats like a warning drum, and try to

stay seated, try to keep my voice calm and steady. "As you know, I'm already leaving."

He slides an envelope across the desk. "This should help."

I glance at it but don't reach for it. "I don't want your money."

"It's $100,000. All I ask is that you stay away from my son."

"And if I don't?" I snap back, hating that I lost my cool.

"You will. Trust me, only heartache lies ahead for you. You were merely a sliver of fun for him on vacation. We both know that. He recently broke up with his girlfriend and you were simply a convenience. You would do well to remember that."

Bastard. He's such a calculating, malicious and evil man. I swallow, and hate that words don't come easily to me. He's cut me down. Taken a knife and sliced right through my heart. I'm so numb, emotionally and physically, that I don't have the words to throw back at him.

His eyes fall to the envelope. "That's a lot of money for someone like you. Enough to change your life forever. Use it wisely."

"You can do what you want," I say, my voice steely, "but I won't touch your money. I don't need it."

Anger flashes in those cold reptilian eyes. "Take it or I'll deposit it directly into your account."

I stare back at him, my hands lying in my lap. I'm itching to fold my arms, but manage not to. I won't take the envelope. And as for his threat, the whole amount deposited into my account, I will just move it back. "I have no interest in your money. Men like you should realize that some things cannot be bought."

His jaw flexes. The way Jett's does when he's angry. "What is it that you think I'm buying?"

"You tell me." From somewhere, I've found a little strength to look him squarely in the eye even as his words settle heavily on me and my heart sinks slowly to the depths of my belly. Words I can't brush off because I see flashes of truth in them. Maybe I was a convenience to Jett during those late nights in the balmy night air, cocooned from reality.

A vein in his forehead throbs. "You think this is about money?" he snarls. "This is about doing what's right for Jett."

"Then why isn't he here, in this meeting?"

His telltale jaw flex builds my courage.

"He doesn't know about this, does he? You picked a time to talk to me when you knew he'd be away."

"It wouldn't be wise of you to relay this conversation to Jett."

"Oh?" I tilt my head. "Is that because he'll tell me it's all lies?"

Paul chortles. "They're not lies. He knows about this deal. Ask him. Listen, sweetheart." He leans forward, resting his elbows on the table, and steepling his well-groomed hands. "It wouldn't be wise, because you care about him and you care about Brooke. I can tell. From the moment I saw you both sitting out there in the gazebo, it was apparent that you had feelings for my boy. But know that he'll tire of you soon. He always does. That man is a revolving door of relationships. It's physical connection he's craving. Sex, if you want me to spell it out for you."

I bristle and feel the heat rising to my cheeks. I try to steel myself against his verbal attack and try to focus on the man I love.

This man is a monster. And Jett had to suffer him all his life.

"Better take the money and run. Now leave, and get out of his life."

I suddenly remember Aunt Scarlett and my mom, and how they would hate this man. "Why do you meddle with people's lives?"

"I want what's best for Jett, and so should you." He doesn't answer my question.

"Anything else?" I start to stand. My hands are steady even though my insides feel like I've just gotten off one of those spinning rides at the fairground.

He regards me with his snake-like gaze. "Just remember, if you truly care for Jett and Brooke, you'll stay away."

I don't respond. There's nothing left to say to a man like him. He knows Jett and I have feelings for one another. Even Dex knows now. I wonder if Dex snitched on us. Because up until now, his father was only sniffing around, trying to guess if something was going on. Now he seems certain.

This much is apparent; this man wants me gone.

I leave Paul Knight's office with doubts creeping in. He is a slime ball. A snake. I walk back to my desk, his words echoing in my mind.

He'll tire of you.
He's destined for greater things.

What if Jett does tire of me? He calls me his shortcake now, but things can change. I glance at Jett's office, his door still open, chair empty. He hasn't returned, and the silence feels heavy.

Paul's poison is working its way into my thoughts. Did Jett know about the heiress? Did he keep that from me?

I sit down, my hands trembling as I try to focus on anything but the doubts clawing at my resolve.

A few more days. That's all I have left before I leave.

Maybe walking away is the right thing to do. For him. For Brooke. Because if Paul is right, if Jett ever grows tired of me, then maybe leaving now is better than staying and seeing everything fall apart.

CHAPTER FORTY-NINE

JETT

The beer bottle in Dex's hand thuds against the table as he sets it down. It's late in the evening and I'm having drinks with Dex. Zach has disappeared to the washroom.

I've been busy at work, trying to get caught up with everything and these last few days I've been slammed with urgent and important tasks and back-to-back meetings. I slacked off more than I should have in Bermuda and I'm paying the price for it, but I'd do it all again if I had the chance.

Despite this craziness, I can't help thinking about Bermuda and everything we had there. Fun, laughter and togetherness, the things Brooke longed for. But it was also the start of something special with Cari.

I haven't been in the office much since that smoldering kiss with my little shortcake, but Cari has suddenly become aloof. I don't know what I've done. I've been busy, but I plan to see her later tonight and find out. I'll make a surprise appearance at her apartment, because we clearly need to talk and the office is not suitable for that conversation.

Dex leans back in his chair, giving me a look that's all-knowing and too casual for my liking. I've just finished telling him everything about the arranged marriage deal with the Brazilian heiress.

"Damn, bro. That sucks." He drags a hand through his dark hair.

"Understatement of the year." I swirl the whiskey in my glass.

Zach returns, sliding into the booth next to Dex. "What sucks?"

"Nothing," I snap.

"Bullshit," Zach counters, his eyes flicking between Dex and me. "What are you two hiding?"

Dex sips his beer, and I shoot him a glare that screams *drop it.* The last thing I need is for Zach to hear about the arranged marriage from me. He'll hear it from our father soon enough, and I don't have the energy to repeat this all over again.

The silence stretches, heavy with unspoken words, until Zach shifts, restless. "Fine. Keep your secrets. But you know we've got a family dinner soon, right?"

"Joy," I deadpan, tipping my glass back. It falls on the same day that Cari is leaving.

"Don't act like you're not going," Zach says. "You know Dad will guilt-trip the hell out of us if we miss it."

Dex chuckles. "Let's take bets on how long it takes before he brings up the future of the empire."

Zach shakes his head. "I'm putting money on five minutes in."

I grunt, already feeling the oppression of that forced family dinner. Our father's obsession with control knows no bounds. "I don't want to be there," I groan. Coming from paradise, where time seemed to stop and I didn't have to deal with my father's bullshit, to this, is unnerving. Unsettling. And it's even worse because Cari and I are still an unfinished chapter. My father made sure of that by showing up unannounced.

Even here, I haven't been able to get her to myself. Monday is her last day. I shouldn't drag it to then. I should let her go before the weekend but I need whatever time I can get with her because I have so many questions and there is so much I need to say.

There's also a short list of potential nannies to interview, but I doubt she'll have the time to help. She's drowning in loose ends at work. I haven't even started looking for an assistant.

"You sure your assistant can help me out until I get a new one?" I ask Dex.

He nods. "Kirsty's fine with it."

"Cari's leaving soon, isn't she?" Zach chimes in. "Raeanne was talking about it with the others."

I flinch involuntarily. I'm not surprised that office gossip has spread and all the assistants are talking about it. Looking at it now, dragging Cari on vacation with me probably raised some red flags. But I hadn't cared at the time. I'd been desperate after Anna quit and had no one else to turn to.

It was the best thing that ever could have happened.

My heart swells full and bright as I recall the memories forever etched in my heart. I got something priceless. I got her. And now I'm desperate to see her, to fix whatever is bothering her.

"Why's she leaving?" Zach asks.

Dex chokes on his drink.

"What?" Zach looks between us, his brow furrowed. "Why am I always the last to know? What's going on?"

"Fuck me," I mutter, swiping a hand down my face.

"What?" Zach repeats, more annoyed this time.

Dex glances at me, a shit-eating grin plastered across his face as he lifts his beer bottle. "Tell him. Just put him out of his misery already."

Dex and I haven't spoken about it. He hasn't, much to my surprise and relief, mentioned catching Cari and me almost red-handed after our kiss. But he knows. He's not stupid.

"He's in love," Dex declares, rolling his eyes.

"You're what?" Zach's voice pitches higher.

"I wouldn't go so far as that," I snap. I hate Dex for making assumptions about something I haven't even admitted to Cari yet.

"You are in love, brother." Dex leans forward, eyes blazing. "Call it what it is. And this is different." He jabs a thick finger at me. "You know it's different. I was just wondering when the fuck you were going to admit it."

"You knew?" Zach complains, throwing up his hands. "You guys—"

Dex raises his hand, cutting him off. "I didn't know, but I walked in on him and Cari smooching. She looked how I've left plenty of women before, with bee-stung lips, flushed face, and shiny eyes." He smirks. "She's mad for you, brother. She's got it bad."

Dex's words settle the prickling unease in my chest. I needed to hear that. Between Cari's coldness, my father's reminder of the Brazilian alliance, and the chaos of work, I haven't had time to think straight.

But Dex is right.

She has feelings for me.

And damn it, I love her. I love that woman with all my heart.

"Cari? Your assistant?" Zach's disbelief is almost comical. "You and *her?*"

"Three weeks in Bermuda," Dex adds with a wink. "No wonder he wasn't on his A game."

"Fuck you," I growl, downing my whiskey in one go and motioning for the waiter.

"But she's leaving." Zach still looks dumbfounded.

"She is," I admit.

"Is she pregnant?" he asks, wide-eyed.

"Shut the fuck up," Dex snaps at Zach. His head whips toward me. "Tell me she's not."

"She's not pregnant," I grind out, teeth clenched. "She resigned before we left," I add quietly.

"Are you going to let her leave?" Dex asks, his tone sharp.

"I'm not holding her prisoner." I pause, exhaling heavily. "But we're going to figure this out. Her working for me wouldn't be a good idea now."

"You and Cari are sleeping together?" Zach blurts out.

I level a hard stare at him.

Dex chuckles. "Oh, I'm sure they've fucked each other's brains out."

"Shut the fuck up. Don't ever talk about us like that." I snarl, cutting him off.

Dex leans back, affronted. "You're in love with her, brother," he says quietly. "It's written all over you. You look fucking miserable."

"I am miserable," I admit, pinching the bridge of my nose. "Cari's gone cold on me, and the old man …" My voice trails off as my father's looming expectations sit on my shoulders, heavy like bricks. "He's still pushing for me to marry the heiress."

"What heiress?" Zach asks.

"Fuck." I shake my head. "You tell him, Dex. I've got a sneaking suspicion the old man's going to bring it up at the family dinner."

And if that's the case, I need to get my ducks in a row.

Cari's too.

Later, I stand outside her apartment, the city buzzing around me. Cari opens the door, her expression guarded. Her walls are already up, and I haven't even said a word.

She steps aside to let me in, her arms crossing defensively as she leans against the kitchen counter. "What are you doing here, Jett?"

"I needed to see you. I've been out of the office and I miss seeing you," I say, moving closer. Her eyes retain the glimmer of hardness, and she doesn't back down.

"Well, you've seen me. Now what?"

Her cutting tone startles me, but I push forward. "What's wrong?" Has she forgotten our kiss from the other day? Because I sure haven't.

"Nothing."

I lean in and try to put my arms around her to kiss her, but she moves back and out of my reach. It's like this, is it? "Don't lie to me, Cari. Tell me what's bothering you. Or *who's* bothering you."

She looks away, her fingers tightening on the edge of the counter. "I'm leaving, Jett. It's probably best if we leave what happened in Bermuda there. In the past, in our memories."

She just sucker punched me with her words. "Just like that?" I manage to say, feeling winded.

Her gaze locks on mine, and I can see the conflict swirling there, but she holds firm. "We're back in the real world now. We have to face reality."

"We are." I try to reach for her hand again, but she pulls away.

"Please don't make this any harder than it already is," she begs.

Something twists low in my chest and frustration bubbles to the surface. "You're breaking up with me?"

Her voice wavers, but her stance is resolute. "I don't know. How can we break up if we were never really together? We never talked about what we were in Bermuda."

I scrub a hand across my neck, exasperation making me see red. She seems different, more resolute and determined than ever. "Because we never got the chance to. Had my father not turned up—"

"But he did, and he made me see something. I don't fit into your world."

"You absolutely do. You fit perfectly in my world, in my life." I move towards her. "What's happened? You kissed me just the other day like we belonged together."

"What happened in Bermuda was ... special, but it won't work here. We have to be pragmatic."

"Pragmatic? This isn't a business deal, Cari. This is us. This is—"

"It's sex," she says, wearily. "We had feelings for each other, and we acted on them—"

It's sex?

She sounds like a different person. "We made love. Lots of love in the sultry heat of those long, long nights. Nights I'll never forget. We have a connection, Cari. You and I, we finally got to be together after months and years of wanting to be."

Her mouth falls open, just slightly. And then she closes it again. "It won't be enough."

I'm confused. "Enough? I'll get you anything you want, name it." Someone's put things in her head, because this isn't my Cari. My shortcake. "It's more than I dreamed of. It's more than I ever thought I'd get to have again. Someone who understands me like you do."

"It's sex, Jett. We both had feelings for one another, and we got to fulfil them."

I can't believe my fucking ears. "What are you saying?"

"I'm saying that we had a great time and we should move on."

Fuck.

No.

I shake my head. "You don't mean that."

"I do. It's for the best."

Something has happened to her. Something or someone. A gnawing feeling eats away in my stomach and I step closer, my jaw tight. "You don't mean that."

Her eyes glisten, but she doesn't falter. "I do."

"Did someone say something to you?" She looks away, saying nothing. Her silence speaks volumes, and I feel the pieces clicking into place. "It was him, wasn't it? My father. What did he say to you, Cari? Tell me."

"I want the truth, Jett," she snaps. "Did you know about the Brazilian heiress before we went to Bermuda?"

Fuck. That old man has spoken to her, and he's messed with her head. It all makes sense now, Cari being like this. Her question presses down on me and I hesitate. "Yes, but—"

"That's it. A simple yes or no. That's all I need."

"It's not what you think. You need context—"

"No." She cuts me off. "What I need is honesty. That's it."

"That son of a bitch." Rage boils inside me. That man will do whatever it takes to keep his legacy safe. He doesn't care for people, for emotions and feelings. I should know that because of what he did to my mother. Yet, somehow, we've all kept going, living under his rules, working for him, in the family business, needing and wanting the money. But it comes at a price. And now the price is too high to pay. I don't want this. I won't let him dictate who I love and how I live, but I've also fucked up big-time. I should have told Cari about this. It's not just my father's fault. I'm to blame as well. "I'm sorry. I'm sorry that I didn't tell you before, but the truth is, I'm not interested in—"

"You can't keep something like that from me," she cries. "I don't even know if I believe you."

I shake my head, my heart splintering at the thought of her leaving me, of her not believing me. "I have no intention of marrying a woman I barely know. He said I needed a wife and Brooke needed a mother, but my relationships aren't transactional."

Cari's expression is unreadable, but I see the hurt lurking beneath the surface. She folds her arms, her voice soft but resolute. "It's best if you leave."

She hasn't heard me. She's not listening to me. She's already decided she can't trust me. A hollow ache fills my chest. "Is that what you really want?"

"It's what's right," she whispers, and for the first time, I see the cracks in her armor.

I grab my briefcase, heading for the door, my head ready to explode in anger. Cari stares at me in silence, and I know. "He told you not to say anything to me, didn't he?"

She remains impassive. "He made you think that you and I don't belong together, because he has some fucking plan for his legacy. Of who we should marry, of how to preserve and keep the bloodline going. Whatever the fuck that means." She still doesn't answer. "This isn't over, Cari," I growl, as I leave.

Paul Knight getting the better of me? The fuck I'm going to let him.

CHAPTER FIFTY

JETT

All weekend, I'm miserable as fuck.

Brooke misses Cari deeply, asking about her constantly, which only intensifies my own guilt and sadness. It's hard enough coming back from Bermuda, and harder still to walk into an empty apartment. But it's soul-crushing to know that Cari won't be a part of our daily lives.

Even though she hasn't ever been to my apartment, this place feels suffocating without her. Not having her in my life, and in Brooke's life, seems like an impossible situation. This void that now faces me, bleak and bottomless, cannot be my life.

Brooke's questions about Cari are endless, her sadness palpable. "When's Cari coming back, Daddy?"

"She's busy, angel."

"She's always busy now," Brooke mutters, her small voice breaking my heart.

Dropping her off at camp on Monday morning is brutal. She

clings to my hand longer than usual, her eyes darting to the door like she's hoping Cari will magically appear. It's not just me who needs Cari. Brooke does too. But Cari's not coming back.

My father's fingerprints are all over this. He said something to her, something cruel enough to hurt her. He couldn't get me to commit to the arranged marriage, so he's done something to make the woman I love walk away.

I never expected her to do it, to listen to him, but the old man has a way with his words. He's a cunning son of a bitch, and Cari would want to do the right thing by me and Brooke—whatever the "right thing" the old man would have managed to convince her of. He's done it before, manipulated, twisted and broken things he had no right to touch. But this time, he's gone too far because Cari thinks she's doing the right thing by leaving.

For Brooke. For me.

But I know better.

This woman is a part of our lives, and it's not just Brooke who wants her here, I want her here. Not fleetingly. Not for a vacation. For something more. Forever. But she can't see it yet; she's scared and doesn't want to mess things up. But I won't let her go, not without a fight. What we had in Bermuda wasn't just a fling. It was everything. It was real. And I'll be damned if I let my father take that away from me.

There's a strong chance the snake tried to pay Cari off. My father offered me money to marry the heiress, so it's likely he offered her something too. That's the way he operates, calculated and controlling.

But, as I've come to learn, not everything in life is for sale.

Cari may think she doesn't belong in my world, but I'll show her she does. She belongs by my side. Not some heiress that I've never met and don't know. I'm going to make our relationship public, no matter the consequences, because losing Cari isn't an option.

I WALK INTO THE OFFICE ON CARI'S LAST DAY.

A part of me still wonders if she'll change her mind and tell me she doesn't want to leave.

There's a heaviness in the air I can't shake. Ordinarily, I'd make a show of it with flowers and a generous gift, something to mark her years of service. Maybe even a small gathering with the other assistants, my brothers, and some of the other staff.

She emailed me this morning. She doesn't want any of that. She called it "a sad day," and begged me to respect her wishes and not make a spectacle. She's probably going to struggle to say goodbye, just like I will. But unlike her, I'm not ready to let this end. I'm a risk taker. A man who likes surprises.

I have back-to-back meetings for most of the day and I hate that I can't even be around her on this milestone day.

It's late afternoon by the time I see her. She's with the other assistants, saying goodbye with hugs and promises to keep in touch. I watch from a distance as they gush over her, their voices raising with affection.

Then they leave, and Cari stands there, alone, surrounded by the little gifts and tokens of appreciation piled on her desk. She looks sad. I've deliberately kept out of her way lately and I can already see the hurt in her eyes. She thinks I've reverted to being cold and keeping her at bay. That I didn't care about her on her last day.

Nothing could be further from the truth. I walk up to her desk. There are flowers and chocolate boxes and little gifts on her desk from work colleagues.

Her eyes meet mine with hesitation. "Thank you for

respecting my wishes," she says softly, gesturing to the lack of ceremony.

I nod. "Can you come into my office, please?"

"Jett … no. I don't think that's a good idea." She looks smaller somehow, her shoulders tense, her gaze distant. She looks like she's already decided this is the last time she'll see me. I want to tell her everything; how hard it's been to keep my distance these past few days. How much I wanted to pull her into my arms and tell her she's not going anywhere.

But I don't. Instead, I stay rooted to the spot, my fists shoved into my pockets to keep them from reaching for her. "Just come with me."

She follows me into my office, looking unsure as she hovers near the door, clutching her bag, clearly ready to bolt. I'm so tempted to put my arms around her and to reel her close to my chest. I so badly need to feel her lips on mine and I dream about her being back in my life, and in my bed, but I manage to keep my distance, putting my desk between us to keep me in check.

"I need you to do something for me," I say, keeping my voice even.

Her brow furrows. "Jett—"

"Trust me, Cari. Please. Be here. At this time." I hand her a slip of paper. Her fingers brush mine as she takes it, and the heat lingers, shooting straight to my heart.

"What is this?" Her tone is edged with suspicion.

"You'll know soon enough. Seven-thirty. Don't back down. Walk in with your head held high."

Her eyes search mine, as if trying to decipher some hidden message. For a moment, I think she's going to refuse. But she nods, tucking the paper into her bag.

"Okay," she says quietly.

CHAPTER FIFTY-ONE

JETT

We file into my father's penthouse apartment as usual.
Me, Dex, and Zach. We always make it a point to come here
together when it's *that* night.

Our father lives in the most luxurious skyscraper in
Midtown Manhattan. And, naturally, he has the penthouse. Its
floor-to-ceiling windows offer unparalleled views of Central
Park and the New York skyline. But despite its opulence and
grandeur, its whiff of exclusivity and jaw-dropping wealth, this
is a cold place, devoid of warmth and human touches.

Cari's apartment feels more cozy and homey than this place
ever will. But this signals power and wealth, and my father's
imagined place at the top of the world.

I breathe freely only when I leave here.

We head straight for the dining room. Paul Knight sits at the
head of the large, rectangular dining table, the Don, God. A
puppet master presiding over his empire, while the other sons

sit on one side of the table. He's showing them a photo of a woman. I already know who she is. Christ, the man didn't waste any time.

"Just on time," my father says, beckoning us in. I have a feeling as to what he's up to tonight. I fully expect him to continue to plot and make decisions about me and my life, despite what I said to him in the office the other day.

The Half-Knights nod and murmur greetings, and me and the boys do the same, sitting down directly opposite them.

"Isn't she stunning?" Paul asks, passing me a large, framed photo. I immediately know who it is. I instantly know what tonight is about.

This man is so predictable. I pass the photo to Dex and slowly it gets passed around. We're staring at a photo of a woman who has dark, cascading waves of hair and eyes that could set fire to a room. The kind of woman men like my father deem *suitable*, but more so because she comes from a filthy rich family. She will be useful to my father's calculated way of thinking.

"Absolutely beautiful." Paul's voice drips with snakish charm.

Dex smirks, leaning back in his chair. "Looks photoshopped if you ask me."

"No one's asking you," the old man snaps.

Zach chuckles, raising his glass. "She looks pretty good to me."

Paul ignores them, his focus razor-sharp as he turns to me. "Let's eat first. You think it over. I trust you'll make the right decision."

I grip my glass tighter, my jaw clenching. "Oh, trust me, I will."

CARI

I STEP OUT OF THE TAXI AND MY BREATH CATCHES.

Paul Knight lives here. I know because I saw a photo of him in a magazine on Jett's desk. He had a smug smile and this building in the background.

Towering above me is a shimmering, glass monolith that seems to touch the sky. Its sleek, reflective facade gleams under the city lights, projecting opulence, exclusivity, and everything that screams obscene wealth. It's the pinnacle of luxury, and home to billionaires and titans of industry. It's no surprise Paul Knight would live here. He's the kind of man who wouldn't settle for less than the best, or, more accurately, what he deems the best.

Tonight is a Knight family dinner. The other assistants mentioned it and when Jett handed me the address, my stomach churned. It's no coincidence that I'm here. Jett asked me to trust him, and I do, with all my heart, but still, the knot in my stomach tightens as I approach the entrance.

What has he got up his sleeve?

I know what these dinners are like. I've never been here before, but some of the other assistants have been called in on occasion to take notes. I've heard that these evenings are already a minefield on a good day, and after everything that's happened, my insides fill with dread. I'm so tempted to run, but I can't. I won't. For Jett's sake.

The concierge greets me with a sharp nod as I approach the revolving doors. He's impeccably dressed, every button of his uniform polished to perfection.

"I'm here for the penthouse," I say, trying to keep my voice steady. I clutch my bag tighter.

His polite smile barely shifts. "Certainly." He presses a button, summoning a private elevator. As I step inside, the gold paneling gleams and plush carpet swallows me up. My anxiety coils tighter with every floor we ascend. The elevator doors open directly into the penthouse and the space before me takes my breath away.

Marble floors stretch out like a canvas, shimmering under the glow of a massive chandelier dripping with crystals. The windows offer an unobstructed view of the city, the lights below twinkling like stars. Every detail screams wealth, from the grand piano in the corner to the sleek, contemporary furniture perfectly arranged for an artful, yet lived-in feel.

A woman steps into view, dressed in a fitted black dress, her hair swept into a sleek bun. She's regal, poised. For a moment, I wonder if she's one of Paul Knight's girlfriends, but her practiced smile and deferential tone give her away.

"This way, madam," she says, gesturing with a graceful wave of her arm. I follow her, my heels clicking against the marble. This feels like walking into a trap. Blindfolded. I don't know what lies before me, but my anxiety is off the charts. My heart beating as if I've run ten miles, the blood coursing through my veins, my mouth dry.

We turn the corner, and what looks like a dining room comes into view. There is a buzz of low voices. It feels like I'm walking into the Colosseum in Rome, only I don't feel like a gladiator. I'm more like a mouse.

Sleek lilies in expensive-looking vases sit atop a long table. It's dressed in white linen, and resting on it are long-stemmed glasses, silverware, and what's likely the best fine China money can buy. Their plates are filled with food, and they're eating. One of the largest chandeliers I've ever seen, obscenely oversized and shimmering like flawless diamonds, is suspended above. The chairs look plush, a mixture of velvet and wood.

Seated around the table are the Knight men.

Jett is on one side, the closest to his father, followed by Dex then Zach. Across from them sit the three Italian Knights, handsome, dark-haired, olive-skinned, with sharp suits and sharper eyes. They look at me like they don't know why I'm here.

At the head of the table is Paul Knight, his expression unreadable, though the faint tightening of his jaw suggests he wasn't expecting me.

Every head turns toward me and the room falls into an expectant silence. Jett rises immediately, wiping his mouth with a napkin before crossing the room in quick strides. He offers me his hand, and I take it like the lifeline that it is. His touch grounds me in the storm.

"Cari," he says, his voice steady but loud enough to carry across the room. "Thanks for coming. I'm glad you're here."

"What is this?" Paul Knight's voice cuts through the room, cold and sharp.

Jett ignores him, standing beside me as he takes my hand. "This," he says, his voice steady and commanding, "is me taking control of my life. Of my future."

"You're making a mistake," his father growls, his voice full of venom.

Jett squeezes my hand reassuringly. "The mistake would be letting you dictate who I can and can't love. The mistake would be walking away from the one person who understands me better than anyone else in this room."

The silence is deafening.

His father's gaze hardens, his fury barely contained. "This is not how we do things."

"It's how *I* do things," Jett counters. "And if that means throwing your plans into disarray, so be it." He offers me his hand. "You don't belong in my world, Cari. You *are* my world."

He looks at his father, before turning back to me. "This is the woman I love."

I think I'm going to faint. The room erupts into whispers and gasps. I'm afraid to breathe. I don't want to give away the maelstrom of emotions inside me; happiness and shock swirl in a sea of disbelief. I feel giddy. Like this isn't real. Like I'm in a dream and I'm scared I'll wake up to cold reality.

Jett Knight just declared his love for me in front of his family, in front of his tyrannical father. My parched mouth turns even drier and I'm going to choke soon if I don't get any water.

Paul leans back in his chair, slow and deliberate, his gaze narrowing. "What are you playing at?"

Jett's jaw tightens, but his eyes stay locked on mine, steady and unyielding. "I've loved Cari for a long time. I'm done hiding it."

Dex breaks the tension with a low whistle, and walks over. I feel like he's about to give Jett a bear hug, but shifts back a little, as if he remembers where he is. "Well, damn. That's … cool, brother."

His eyes turn to me and he gives me a smile. An approving smile. Not that I need his approval, but it feels nice. Like he's on our side. Jett squeezes my hand tighter, and I squeeze it right back.

Zach gets up, grinning as he saunters over. "Yeah, you didn't have to go full *Titanic* declaration, but good for you, man." He pats Jett on the back, and I think he whispers a soft "Hey," to me. I manage a smile, but feel uneasy on account of the other eyes on me.

This show of support from his brothers gives me a sense of relief for Jett's sake. The Italian Knights exchange intrigued glances. Rio leans back in his chair, assessing me with an intense gaze. With his Mafia energy, and jet-black hair swept back to show off his sharp features, it's clear that he's enjoying the drama. Matteo casually watches us, looking unfazed and bored. He carries the magnetic charm of a rockstar and looks out of place at this table of suited men. Next to him sits the debonair Enzo, a man of few words. The youngest of the entire bunch, he seems wiser than his years.

Paul claps, slow and mocking. "Well, this is touching. Truly."

"Let's sit down," Jett tells his brothers, his tone firm.

Sit down?

What am I supposed to do? Jett makes his brothers shift down a seat, so that I'm now sitting between him and Dex. The table has only been laid for the seven of them, but I'm so thirsty, I quickly reach for Jett's glass of water and drain it dry.

"Love doesn't run empires, boy. Strategy does. Loyalty. And smart decisions." His father picks up his utensils and casually continues eating.

Jett's expression hardens, and under the table, he takes my hand, his grip tightening. "You tried to pay me off. Ten million dollars to marry someone I don't love. Do you really think that's loyalty?"

Paul's face stiffens, his composure slipping.

"Ten million dollars?" Dex cries. "Hell, for that much, I'll marry her."

"Oops," Jett says. "Was that meant to be a secret? Guess what? I'm not for sale. And neither is Cari."

"But, ten *million* dollars? Just to marry someone, on paper?" Dex seems intrigued by the idea.

"Why don't you consider it?" Our father asks. "You are the next in line."

The Italian Knights chuckle amongst themselves. They must find this highly amusing. Then, Rio asks, "Why the hell would you do that? Marry someone just for the money?"

Dex shakes his head. "I wouldn't. I control my future. I don't have it dictated to me."

My insides are in freefall now. Not only has Jett declared his love for me, but he's fighting for us.

"Unlike you," Jett continues, raising his voice, "I hold myself to a higher standard. Love can't be bought. And fake love? It's not worth the time or money."

Paul's gaze darkens, but he says nothing.

Jett turns to me, his voice softening. "Cari has stood by me through everything. She's been my anchor, my confidant, my partner in every way that matters. I love her, and I'm not going to let anything, or *anyone,* come between us."

Emotion swells in my chest, my throat tightening as I try to hold back tears. This is too much, he didn't need to do this in front of everyone but I realize in that moment why he did.

He did it for me.

"Isn't she too young to be a mother to Brooke?" His father's question riles Jett, because I feel him stiffen beside me.

"She's amazing with Brooke, but that's not why I love her. I'm not with her because she serves a function. I'm with her because—" He scoffs. "You wouldn't understand. All you think about is commodities and how you can benefit. How you can make more millions, even when you already have more than you'll ever need, even if you lived forever."

He stands up, and instinctively, so do I. We're still holding hands, and I notice the way Paul Knight's beady eyes fixate on them. "If you'll excuse us." Jett turns to leave.

Dex leans back, smirking. "You're really leaving? Dinner's not even over."

Zach shakes his head. "Bold move, bro."

Jett doesn't respond. He leads me out of the room, his hand warm and steady in mine.

As the elevator doors close behind us, I exhale, my shoulders slouching as I nearly keel over with relief.

"Hey, Shortcake." Jett's arms wrap around me and he holds me close. "Sorry. I know that must have been hard on you." He kisses the top of my head. I'm so exhausted, so mentally drained, that I need a moment to recharge.

The elevator begins its smooth descent, and I stand up straighter, staring up at his now dark eyes. "Did you mean it?" I whisper. "When you said you love me?"

His gaze fixes on me. "With all my heart."

I'm so overcome with feeling, I want to cry. Jett looks at me as if I'm the only woman in the world. I used to dream of such a thing but now this man makes me feel like I'm the only one for him.

He's the only one for me.

As we walk out of the revolving doors, I tug at his hand.

"What?" He turns to me, and immediately, his arms wrap around my waist. Even though I have my thick winter coat on, I feel the spark of his touch. Something happens to my body whenever he holds me. I feel grounded, yet also ready to fly into the air. He nuzzles my nose. "You okay, Shortcake?"

I nod and look up at him. "I love you. I've loved you for the longest time." I sniffle, in typical fashion, dampening the enormity of the moment by falling apart.

Jett's eyes widen as he looks down at me, but it can't be surprise. Surely he knows and has felt what I've felt?

A connection so strong, it seems other-worldly.

It's nothing like a crush.

It's something deeper.

I'm so deeply in love with this man and I'm so profoundly grateful to have met someone who loves me so much. Someone, now that I'm connecting all the little things together, who has been taking care of me, wanting the best for me, helping me through the years and I had no idea about any of it.

He raises his hand to my face, and strokes it gently, waiting patiently.

"It was a crush. A silly crush, as Eliana used to say, but it was something more than that, what I feel for you. It scares me."

"Don't be scared," he murmurs, pressing another kiss to the top of my head.

"It was all consuming, and I've missed you so much since we got back. I thought I had to leave for my sake and yours and when your father …" I hesitate because I don't want this moment and this evening to be about that wretched man.

"I'll protect you from him. You don't have to worry about him anymore." He strokes my face tenderly. "I. Love. *You.* Completely. Unreservedly. Forever."

I open my mouth to tell him that forever isn't guaranteed, but he presses his lips to mine, hushing me. "Don't think with your practical head, Shortcake. Leave your logic and reason, and your excuses and buts out of this. Feel with your heart, because I feel it here." He taps his chest. "I know you feel it, too, Cari. I see it in your eyes. Don't you see the change in me? What you've done to me? Being with you has made me a better man, someone who deserves you."

"Jett …" Words don't usually fail me, but in this moment I'm speechless. He sounds so different to that arrogant, bullish boss who used to break my heart each time I'd see him with a new woman.

But he's picked *me.*

His thumbs trace over my lips. "We'll figure it out. All of it. The Knight legacy isn't important. This … you and me—"

"And Brooke," I add, because the sentence feels incomplete without any mention of her.

"Always Brooke, but you and me, what we have, Cari, this is special. I never thought I'd fall in love again, and this special kind of love, I never thought it would be mine to have once more."

He kisses me again, deeply and feverishly, giving me a taste of our forever, and I believe him with all my heart.

CHAPTER FIFTY-TWO

CARI

This is the woman I love.

We stopped off at a diner just to catch a bite to eat, to catch our breath, because being in the penthouse was intense. I've replayed that moment in my head a hundred times since we left. The way he stood beside me, unflinching in the face of his father's disapproval. The way his hand felt in mine, steady and sure, grounding me when I was ready to crumble. It was as big a moment for him as it was for me.

"Thank you for standing up for me again."

"I'd do it in a heartbeat. I always will."

A warmth blankets me when he says that. "I've spent my whole life feeling like I don't belong. Like I'm not enough. Your father made sure I felt every bit of that when he called me into his office."

Jett's jaw tightens, his fists clenching. "What did he say to you?"

"He offered me money. One hundred thousand dollars, but I refused to take it."

"I knew it." He looks away, but I can tell his tight jaw that he's more angry than he's letting on. I reach for his hand, needing to bring him back to me.

"I would have pushed it back if he'd put it into my account, but he hasn't."

"The fucker."

I stroke his hand. "Let's not dwell on that, Jett. He offered it, but I didn't take it, that's all that matters."

His eyes meet mine. "I always knew you were different. You have a heart that is pure, and you're so amazing. So grounded and sensible and beautiful—"

I hold out my hand, halting his words. "I don't need more compliments."

"It's the truth."

I smile, and inhale a big breath.

"What else did he say?"

"Do we have to talk about this?"

"I just want to know, this once, and we don't ever have to talk about it again."

"He said that I'd never fit into your world. That men like you don't marry women like me. That you'd get bored of me." My voice cracks, but I push on. "And for a moment, I believed him. I let him dig up every insecurity I thought I'd buried in Bermuda."

He exhales sharply, dragging a hand through his hair. "None of that is true. None of it. You know that, don't you? You're not just enough, you're everything."

I blink back tears, his words cutting through my defenses like a blade. "Do you know how hard it is to believe that? When I've spent so long feeling invisible in your world?"

He scoots over to sit beside me, his voice low and firm.

"You're not invisible to me. You never have been. I see you, Cari. I see all of you. And I fucking made each of them see you, too."

The way he looks at me is unbearable, like he's peeling back every layer I've tried to hide behind.

"But what if—"

"No," he interrupts, his tone fierce. "No more what-ifs. No more doubting us. I love you, Cari. I've loved you for so long, I don't even remember when it started. I'm not letting my father, or anyone else, get in the way of what we have."

We sit in silence for a moment, Jett's words sink into my heart and ground me. Giving me strength.

"I still need to leave the company," I whisper, hating the way his face falls. I don't think it's right for me to continue working for him, not when we're together. I want to keep my work and personal life separate.

"I understand, but it sucks."

"There's so much I have to figure out. My next step, us and how I fit into your life."

"Our life," he corrects, his voice firm.

I look away, my heart aching because I'm so deliriously happy, but a part of me is wary too. By being with Jett, I'm stepping into a world I've avoided. A world I got to taste in Bermuda, where some of the people and situations left a bitter taste in my mouth. But then there was Celine. My heart softens as I remember her. She told me to be careful, and maybe I'm trying to do just that. Not jumping into this blindly, but with brakes on. "I need to find my footing first. I can't be the woman you need if I don't even know who I am outside of this."

He leans back, his jaw tightening, but he doesn't argue. Instead, he nods slowly. "If that's what you need, so be it. But I'm not letting go of us, Cari. Not ever."

His eyes settle on mine, like he's looking for confirmation, like he needs to know that I'll be fine. His concern for me, now that I know it came dressed as orders and commands, is as endearing as it is heady.

This man loves me.

Delicious goosebumps break out all over my skin. I'm lucky to have him.

He's lucky to have you, honey. I remember my mom, and a knot forms in my stomach. She liked Jett. Thought he was a good man. She could see that, somehow.

"Shall we go? I have someone at home who's missed you as much as I have." Jett's lips turn up at the corners, and I mirror his smile.

"Brooke." Not a day has gone by that I haven't thought of her or missed her. It was bad enough not having Jett in my life, but Brooke, too? I missed her impish smile, her big, beautiful eyes. I missed being around her, brushing her hair, talking to her, hearing her funny stories, seeing her walking around with Elephant in one hand. It felt as if I'd lost a part of me. "I can't wait to see her."

We return to the apartment to find Brooke waiting for us with Anna who arches her eyebrow as soon as she sees me and Jett walk in holding hands. She gives me a knowing smile.

"Cari!" Brooke rushes to me, her face all lit up as her tiny arms close around my legs. I crouch down, hugging her tightly, my heart swells at the way she clings to me. "I missed you." Her voice is muffled against my shoulder.

"I missed you too, sweetie," I whisper, my throat tight.

"May I go now?" Anna asks. I stand up, with Brooke still glued to my body.

"Of course." Jett moves towards the door, as Anna grabs her things.

"Nice seeing you again," I say, setting Brooke down and going over to Anna.

"I always suspected something," she whispers, hugging me lightly.

"I guess most people did, except for him." I nod in Jett's direction, but he's busy on his phone.

After Anna leaves Brooke pulls me into the living room to show me her latest drawing. Jett watches us, his expression soft. Everything feels right, like this is exactly where I'm supposed to be. But Jett and I exchange a look.

There's a lot to do.

I need to figure out the next steps to start the business I've been dreaming of. He has a shortlist of nannies that he needs me to look through. He also has to manage the fallout with his father.

And yet, even with all the uncertainty, I know one thing for sure: I'm not alone anymore.

CHAPTER FIFTY-THREE

JETT

We knew going public would be a storm, but I wasn't prepared for just how relentless it would be.

The media frenzy starts the moment the first photo of Cari and me leaks. We're splashed across gossip sites, headlines screaming about my "scandalous new romance," speculating on everything from her background to her intentions.

Two weeks after that fateful Knight family dinner, I feel like our lives are under so much scrutiny. I don't care, but I need to make sure Cari is okay with this craziness. It will die down, in time, but for now, whenever we step out together, I keep her hand firmly in mine, meeting every camera flash and whispered judgment head on.

"You don't have to do this," she tells me one night as we leave a restaurant, a wall of photographers waiting outside. "We can deny everything to the press. Just for peace of mind."

I pull her closer. "I'm not hiding you, Cari. Not ever."

She looks up at me, her eyes filled with a mix of gratitude and fear. "What about your family?"

She's always been worried about my family, and I hope my act of defiance, in standing up to my father, proved to her that he's not a factor in my decision making.

"My brothers are cool about it. My father probably has other plans, but he hasn't cut me out at work. It's still very much business as usual."

"What about the heiress?"

"I'm not sure," I chuckle. The boys and I have been waiting for our father to say more about it, but he hasn't.

Dex joked and said that for ten million dollars he'd marry her. I can't tell if he's being serious or just goofing around. He likes his women athletic and strong, like him. I think the heiress would be too fragile, too dainty, and too beautiful for him.

Still, he's a grown man. The only reason he'd ever entertain the idea, though with Dex I can't be sure, is because of the immense pleasure he'd get out of making our father think he's going along with the deal, only to back out at the last moment. That's the only scenario in which I see Dex agreeing to marry that woman. He would never do something just because our father wanted him to.

CARI

I DID IT.

I walk out of the bank, the sunlight spilling over me like a blessing, feeling confident and brimming with happiness. I've managed to secure my business loan and even though Jett wanted to give me the money to start my little flower shop, I wanted to do this for myself. The moment feels monumental, like I'm finally standing on my own two feet. Like the universe has seen me and answered my prayers after the darkest time of my life. It's given me a man I love, a man who loves me, and a new direction in life.

I needed to prove that I'm more than just his assistant, more than someone orbiting his billionaire world. And I've found the perfect place.

In a quirky café on the Lower East Side, not far from Jett's office, I'll be starting with a pop-up shop. Close enough that we could meet for lunch sometimes, though I doubt we'll have the time. He's always swamped, and soon, I will be too. And that thought thrills me.

The café is run by an eccentric woman in her sixties. She's been running it forever; it's her family's legacy. The place is called The Living Room and the moment I walked in, I fell in love with it.

It was like stepping into another world. The place is filled with bookshelves where people can sit and read, with a curated collection of novels and memoirs lining the walls. Add to that the smell of freshly brewed coffee in the air, and you have pure magic.

It's warm and inviting, and brimming with character. It's everything I want my shop to embody, and it's quickly became my favorite place to meet Jett.

When I spoke to the owner, we clicked immediately. I told her about my dream of opening a flower shop, and her face lit up. Her eyes lit up as if she'd been waiting for someone to say those words. "There's a big space at the back," she said. "I've been meaning to do something with it."

That's when the dream was born. The Living Room is perfect for me. The name even feels symbolic, like I'm starting to truly live my own life.

I've done a local course in floristry as well as a few online courses to get certification. I now have hands-on experience in design and flower arrangements. The rest, I'll have to learn on the job. Now, with the loan approved, I'm finally ready to begin. I'm so excited. I've got savings from my job, the small business loan, and additional funding from a Women in Business Initiative. Aunt Scarlett also offered me a no-strings-attached loan. At first, I didn't want to take it. I wanted to prove I could do this on my own. But Bianca and Eliana convinced me not to hold back. They told me I should go all in, and they're right. This loan gives me the freedom to build my dream without cutting corners.

The best part? I've done it without Jett's help. I need to prove to myself that I don't need him for his money. I'm in this relationship on my own terms, standing on my own two feet.

And now I can't wait to tell him.

When I show up at his apartment, the scene that greets me is something I never thought I'd see. Jett is in the kitchen with Brooke, his sleeves rolled up, laughing as she stands on a stool to help him mix something in a bowl.

I have a key to his place, and it still feels odd, letting myself in. But the last time I knocked on the door, he told me off. He said to use the key he gave me, then kissed me, long and hard.

Now his sleeves are rolled up, and he and Brooke are laughing as they work together. "We're making banana bread," he says as if it's the most normal thing in the world for him to be doing early on a Friday evening. There's something like joy on his face, maybe something softer, something I've never quite seen before. It's different. It takes my breath away.

Brooke runs toward me, throwing her arms around my waist. "Cari!" she squeals, grinning up at me with her cheeky grin. I wrap her in a hug, my heart full. Staying here, staying with them, it feels as if this life has always been mine.

It doesn't feel strange or temporary anymore. It feels like home.

"Stay for dinner." Jett glances up at me and his slow, sexy, disarming smile melts away any excuses I might have had. "I gave the housekeeper the night off, so it's just us. I'll even make dinner."

There's no way I can decline that invitation. Nor would I want to. In Bermuda, we had to be secretive, me sneaking into his room at night and sneaking back in the early hours of the morning. Now, we get to spend all night in bed and as much of the morning as early-bird Brooke will let us. We get to stay wrapped in each other's arms, our limbs entangled after hours of lovemaking. It's the only place I want to be.

Brooke pipes up, her voice full of mischief. "Can you help us? Daddy burned the pizza yesterday. It was so bad even Elephant didn't eat it."

I howl with laughter, and she joins in. We leave Jett standing there, arms folded, looking mock-hurt and defensive.

The warmth in this moment embraces me like a cashmere blanket. This is what I've been hoping for. Not just the shop, not just independence, but this feeling. A messy, happy, imperfect life where I get to love and be loved in return.

EPILOGUE

One month later …

CARI

I couldn't be happier.

Having brunch with the girls is one of my favorite things. The October sun beams onto the kitchen table laden with platters of fresh fruit, pastries, and steaming coffee. Aunt Scarlett is fussing over a bowl of eggs, her stern face a stark contrast to her tender hands. Bianca and Eliana sit across from me, deep in a conversation about the latest trends, their laughter a soft hum in the background.

I glance at the clock on the wall, my stomach fluttering with a mix of excitement and nerves.

"Stop fidgeting," Aunt Scarlett says, not looking up from her task.

"I'm not fidgeting," I lie, tucking my hands under the table.

"Yes, you are," Bianca teases. "You've been staring at the clock like it owes you money."

When I told my girls about the Knight family dinner, when Jett stood up to his father and told him, in front of everyone, that he loved me, they were happy, if a little wary. Still.

Aunt Scarlett has been going on about when *we can all meet this Jett Knight and see for ourselves what his intentions are.*

It's like they don't trust me.

Like they think I lost my mind in Bermuda and fell for him. They thought the heat might have gotten to my head.

Aunt Scarlett was worried. Eliana and Bianca, not so much. Now that a few weeks have passed and things have settled down in both of our lives, it seems like the perfect time for them to meet Jett in person. He's coming here. I keep looking at my watch, knowing that he's a stickler for time. He should be here any moment now.

At work, Jett has a new assistant. I was in the interview. She's lovely. In her forties, with a son at college. Jett joked that I didn't trust him so I picked someone older and married.

I do trust him, implicitly. But Deborah is good, and she was the best of the bunch. I also needed someone who would be able to stand up to Paul Knight, because I sense he's placed a target on Jett's back. I'm sure that man hated being shown up in front of everyone. Hated that Jett took a stand, and that even the lure of millions of dollars wasn't enough to sway him.

The doorbell rings and I rush to open it. Jett is standing there looking effortlessly debonair, yet casual. How does he do it? Brooke grins at me, her cheeky smile always lifting me up.

"Hey, sweetie!" I don't even try to lift her, because she's suddenly starting to get too big and lanky for that. I bend down and hug her. "Hungry?"

She nods.

"Good, because we've made a lovely big breakfast." I turn

to Jett, and we lean in and kiss. Brooke giggles. This is still going to take some getting used to for her. "Nervous?"

He shrugs. "Shouldn't be, but surprisingly, yes."

I've been telling him that Aunt Scarlett wants to meet him, and knowing how important my family and friends are to me makes Jett a little nervous. It's something I didn't expect from him. I take him by his hand and lead him into the kitchen.

"Jett and Brooke," I say, announcing them with dramatic flair.

"Hope we're not interrupting," Jett says, a crooked smile tugging at his lips. Brooke, for once, is quiet, surveying the room and everyone in silence. I take her hand, ready to introduce her one by one to everyone when Aunt Scarlett steps forward, her eyes narrowing as she sizes Jett up. "So, *you're* the famous Jett."

He nods, extending a hand. "And you must be the infamous Aunt Scarlett."

She doesn't take it, crossing her arms instead, and I hold my breath, not wanting any drama. Wanting my aunt to love the man I love. "You break her heart, and I'll …" She stops, as if she's only now realized that Brooke is here.

"What will you do?" Brooke pipes up, her eyes wide.

Aunt Scarlett leans down and manages a smile. "I'll be sad."

Brooke gasps.

Then my aunt raises to her full height and whispers to Jett, loud enough for me to hear, "I'll kill you."

He laughs. "Duly noted."

I'm in shock. "Aunt Scarlett!" I cry, relieved that Brooke hasn't heard.

But a slight smile tugs at my aunt lips and she finally takes Jett's hand, giving it a firm shake. "Sit down and eat something."

The kitchen fills with laughter.

Jett sits down to eat with us, and Brooke comes and sits right by my side. She has a new nanny now. Katie, who is in her mid-thirties, calm, and sensible, and perfect for Brooke.

We eat and talk and laughter fills my tiny apartment, and I can't help but notice something unusual: Jett and Aunt Scarlett are deep in conversation. More than I expected. More than what seems normal.

I also notice the way Jett keeps glancing at his watch.

"You have somewhere to be?" I ask, watching him with narrowed eyes. There's a restlessness to him, something I don't understand. After all, the plan for today was simple—he and I were taking Brooke out. A movie, the park, whatever she wanted.

But then Jett and Aunt Scarlett exchange a knowing look, and my stomach tightens.

What the hell is going on?

Jett clears his throat and leans forward, his blue eyes locking onto mine. "While everyone's here, I wanted to let you all know about my plans for the day."

Something flutters low in my stomach, but I force myself to stay calm. Jett making an announcement, here and now? That can't be good.

My gut is right.

"Once upon a time," he says, his eyes piercing into mine. "I may or may not have been the reason my girlfriend missed a concert she'd been waiting years for."

The word "girlfriend" lands like a spark against my skin. It's the first time I've heard him call me that. My breath catches, warmth surging through me like a slow-burning fire. God help me, I love this man.

"So," he says smoothly, stretching an arm along the back of

my chair like this is no big deal, "today, I'm flying her to see The Mayflies."

My hand flies to my lips as realization crashes over me. I look at Eliana. Then Bianca. Then Aunt Scarlett. They're all staring at me.

Like they know.

Oh my God.

I've been set up.

"What?" The word barely leaves my mouth before my heart slams against my ribs.

"The Mayflies!" Eliana squeals.

"But ... they're playing in *Canada*." My voice is breathless, and my brain struggles to catch up.

Jett's eyes glint with amusement. "That's where we're going."

My stomach does a full-on nosedive. "B-but *Canada?*" I echo, still not quite computing.

"It'll be a weekend trip," he says casually, as if he's discussing dinner plans. "We could fly back right after the concert, but—"

"But we have plans," I murmur, glancing at Brooke. I'm still trying to process what's happening, still trying to figure out if this is real life or a dream.

Eliana lets out an ear-piercing squeal. "You get to see them, Car!"

I spin toward her. "You knew about this?"

"You have backstage passes!" she shrieks. "And VIP access! You get to meet them!"

Bianca nods enthusiastically, grinning like a fool.

Aunt Scarlett, looking suspiciously like the Cheshire Cat, beams at me. "You're welcome."

I gape at them. "You *all* knew?"

"Of course we did," Aunt Scarlett says smugly. "Your boss,

sorry, your *boyfriend,* wanted to check if you were free this weekend."

I turn back to Jett, overwhelmed. "You could have just asked me."

He grins. "Where's the fun in that?" Then, as if dropping the biggest bomb of all, he turns to the others. "Oh, and you're all coming too."

A stunned silence.

Then:

"What?" comes a chorus of gasps.

Jett nods toward Aunt Scarlett. "She assured me that you were all free. That includes you too, Scarlett."

I see an unfamiliar expression on my aunt's face. Surprise. Shock. Awe. I turn to Jett, feeling giddy with happiness. "You planned all of this?"

His smirk deepens. "Guilty."

Brooke's eyes are huge. "We're going to Canada, Daddy?"

Jett pulls her onto his lap. "We sure are, sprout."

"To see The Mayflies? All of us?" Eliana asks, feeling the same disbelief that I feel.

"Yes, really."

She makes a strangled noise like she's about to combust. "T-thank you, Jett, this is—" She throws her hands in the air, utterly speechless.

Aunt Scarlett shakes her head in disbelief. "To Canada and back in one day?"

Jett shrugs. "Not just that. We're going to the after-party too."

I choke. "What?"

Bianca lets out a low whistle. "Well, damn. Money really can buy anything." Then, as if realizing how that sounds, she tacks on, "Not that I'm complaining."

Jett chuckles. "Didn't think you would."

Aunt Scarlett lifts her coffee cup in a toast. "Jett, this is… wonderful. Thank you. I don't know what to say."

"It's a pleasure, Scarlett. No need to say anything, but I suggest you all get packed quickly."

His eyes settle on me, like I'm the only one in the room.

Like I'm the only one who matters.

"Jett," I murmur in a low voice. I'm overcome with emotion, and I would seal this moment with a kiss were it not for Brooke sitting on his lap. I tap her on the nose gently. "We get to go on the plane again, Brooke. We get to spend a weekend together!"

"Yay!" She hops over to me and sits on me, her arms encircled around my neck.

"Thank you," I mouth to Jett.

***

The low hum of the jet is almost hypnotic as it cuts through the sky.

I still can't believe this is happening. I don't know what's more surreal, finally getting to see the band I missed, or the fact that my entire world is here with me. My friends, my aunt, Brooke and Jett.

Bianca and Eliana sit across from me, wide-eyed, their gazes bouncing around the cabin like they've stepped into a dream.

"This is insane," Bianca murmurs, running her fingers over the butter-soft leather armrest.

Eliana nods, voice hushed. "Is this real life?"

"You'll get used to it," I tease.

Jett leans in, his hand brushing mine. "See? You belong here." Then softer, just for me. "With me."

EXCERPT FROM DEX

DANI

This place reeks of decadence. It's discreet and stylish. Filled with the type of people who came to Paul Knight's soiree.

Dexter picked me up earlier, not from the hotel door, but from the car. He called me, and I went downstairs. I'm dressed more appropriately this time. A sleek, navy jumpsuit. Simple, yet flattering.

He gave me a casual glance, his eyes not even taking in what I wore. Not that I wanted him to. I don't. But this is why he's different.

We drove in complete silence for twenty minutes.

Interesting.

Now we're sitting in a place called The Midnight Lounge, in a booth of thick and luxurious blue velvet seats. This place reeks of elegance and luxury. I find myself admiring the rich textures of the furniture and furnishings, while the scent of money hangs in the air, along with the spicy floral notes.

This place has the same floor-to-ceiling windows as Paul's penthouse. With sweeping views of the skyline.

"You didn't have to impress me, Dexter."

He barely lifts a shoulder. "We need to put on a front. I'm obeying my father's orders."

"Do you always "obey?" I find his choice of words interesting, but I've learned a lot about the Knight family dynamics in my short time here. Dexter flashes me a smile that is cold and detached. It sends a strange shiver down my spine.

I study him, taking in the way his dark hair is styled. The slightly longer curls on top, styled just enough to have a natural wave. The dim lighting makes his sharp jawline more defined. And those eyes; dark and intense bedroom eyes. He's good-looking. Frustrating as hell, but good-looking, and I find myself staring at him for longer than I should. I find it harder to look away. Maybe because he isn't fawning over me, the way most men do. This man seems completely uninterested.

I just wish he liked me. It would make things easier.

A tall and smartly dressed man comes over, all in black. He and Dexter shake hands and Dexter introduces him as his friend, Luke. "This is my fiancé, Daniela," Dexter says, smiling at me with such warmth, it makes my skin prickle with goosebumps. He can be charming when he wants to. I immediately hide my left hand, the one that doesn't yet have a ring.

"You got engaged? Congratulations!" Luke exclaims. "I never thought I'd see the day when you'd want to settle down, but I guess you found the right woman."

Dexter flashes a wolfish grin. "I sure did."

"You never let them go, once you find them," his friend says, smiling at us both.

Dexter reaches across the table for my hand, making a show of our togetherness. "That's why I put a ring on her finger. I don't plan to *ever* let this one go." His words send goosebumps running down my skin. He says it like he means it, but I know better. He's so smooth. So charming. Such a good liar. I just pray his friend doesn't ask to see the ring.

"I'll leave you to enjoy your evening. Congratulations to you both. Nice meeting you, Daniela."

After he leaves, Dexter and I immediately withdraw our hands. Then a server brings over an ice bucket in which lies a bottle of champagne.

"With compliments, from Luke," he says.

"Jeez. He's really pulling out the stops." Dexter's voice drops as he pulls out the bottle. "Cristal. This is one of the most prestigious champagnes in the world."

I wince. "I hate lying to people."

He grimaces like he's in pain. "Me too. Luke's a good guy, but if we send this back now—"

"We can't."

"What would you like to drink?" he asks, scanning the menu.

"How about this expensive champagne?"

"We can open that later. I'm not really a champagne type of guy."

I can see that about him. "I'll have a cocktail. Something light and fruity. The Bluebell," I say, opting for the signature drink.

He orders scotch, and after the server has taken the order, he leans back, lacing his fingers together on the sleek and shiny table. "I guess we need to decide how we met."

I sigh, that is the task for this evening. "We should try to keep the story close to reality."

"You've done this before, haven't you?" His voice is suspicious.

"No. Have you?"

"No. But you seem pretty eager about it."

I roll my eyes. "Look, I don't want to keep repeating this. I only want to help my father. You're suspicious of me, maybe you're wondering why I haven't met anyone, but you're not a bad-looking man and I'm not bad-looking either—"

He cuts me off. "What? Did you just say you're not *bad looking*?" He shakes his head. Then, he schools his surprise, nodding. "Yeah, I guess you're not bad looking."

It's strange. In this moment, I like him a little more. "Thank you." I tilt my head and give him a wide smile. "No food stuck in my teeth? No mustache?"

He exhales a laugh. "No."

"No booger up my nose?"

"Jesus, Daniela."

"Just checking." I grin. "So, I must be presentable."

"This is definitely better than what you had on the night we first met." His eyes casually sweep over me.

I freeze. "Excuse me?"

"You weren't wearing anything," he reminds me.

I blink. "*What*?"

"When I came to your hotel room, you could've been naked behind that door, for all I know."

"I was holding up my dress!" I cry out in exasperation.

He shrugs. "Exactly. You weren't *in it*."

I narrow my eyes. "Were you curious?"

"Nope."

"Not even just a little?"

"Absolutely not."

I sit back, studying him. "You really don't fancy me, not even a little bit?"

He leans forward and whispers, "Daniela, you're the last person I'd want to marry. What we're doing now, pretending to be madly in love, it's all lies. You know that."

I arch a brow. "What if I were the last person on earth?"

"Same. There were two other women at the soiree that

night," he says smoothly. "Both in their fifties. Both wearing trousers. I'd have picked them over you any time."

I gasp. "You're dead serious?"

"Damn straight."

I burst out laughing. It's so unexpected, because I've never had any man say that to me. While his words feel refreshingly different, they also leave a sting. Because at last I've met a man who interests me, but has no interest in me.

Our drinks arrive and Dexter lifts his glass. "Let's toast to something."

I pick up my cocktail. "Like what?"

"Our impending wedding."

"Our surprise wedding."

"That too." He lifts his glass and drains it completely dry. Shock lances through me. He must be stressed. Maybe he's uncomfortable being with me, and that's why he's drinking so fast.

I groan. "We need to work on our stories."

"We do," he agrees. "People always ask how people met. What are you going to tell them?"

I take a slow sip of my drink, thinking. "I'd say we were both at a carnival," I begin. "I won a giant stuffed panda, but I couldn't carry it, so you, being the chivalrous man you are, offered to hold it for me."

He narrows his eyes. "I'm already regretting this story."

I grin, feeling the tension between us soften. Feeling slightly more at ease with him. "And then, just as we were standing under the Ferris wheel, bam! You asked me out on a date."

He shakes his head. "Absolutely not."

"Why not?"

"Because which Ferris wheel? Which carnival? Why would someone you like and me meet at a place like that? We live in different countries, also, I can't remember the last time I went to a carnival. And, did you go alone, or with friends, if so, where were they?"

I'm impressed that he's giving this such careful consideration. "Maybe we should work on our proposal story instead? How did that come about?"

He shrugs. "The usual. We went out for dinner. Had a lovely time."

"What did we eat?"

"Truffle risotto. It was out of this world."

"I love truffle risotto!"

He nods. "Good to know. At the end, I ordered you a pudding, and inside was a ring."

I wrinkle my nose. "Boring."

"Predictable," he admits.

"Have you ever actually come close to actually proposing?"

"No. Never."

"Good thing this marriage is fake, then," I mutter.

He exhales a laugh. "We probably shouldn't be saying that out loud."

I'm more curious than ever now about his former girlfriends. I swirl my cocktail, feeling a little flirty. "Maybe we should've done this 'getting to know each other' part at your apartment instead."

He cocks a brow. "Are you coming on to me, Miss Oliveira?"

I roll my eyes. "You wish."

"Soon to be Mrs. Knight."

I stiffen. "Nope. That doesn't work."

"Why not?"

"Daniela Knight?" I shake my head. "It's like chalk and cheese."

"That's because we *are* like chalk and cheese."

I sigh. "Okay, fine. We're getting to know each other." I rest my chin on my palm. "Tell me something about you."

"I like to have a lot of sex."

I blink. "Did I need to know that?"

"You're going to be my wife, aren't you?"

I straighten up, feel the heat inching along my cheeks. I can tell by the way his eyes twinkle, that he's noticed.

"I'm joking!" he cries, probably because he's realized how awkward I feel. And why do I feel awkward? He was joking.

I frown. "Why tell me, then?"

"So you understand what this isn't."

Ouch. Way to put me back in my place. Not that I was harboring any ideas. I just liked that we were starting to feel comfortable around one another.

"I understand that this isn't a real marriage," I say, carefully choosing my words. "It's a marriage on paper only, and neither of us will become romantically involved with one another or with other people, for the duration of this alliance."

He nods. "You understand completely."

A beat of silence. I want to know what a man who likes to have a lot of sex will do in the sandy desert of a one-year loveless alliance.

"You asked me about my previous relationships, but I didn't get a chance to ask you about yours."

"What do you want to know?" He picks up the second glass of scotch he's ordered. I've only taken a few sips of my cocktail. But I can tell this man is buying some time. He's hiding something.

"Tell me about your relationships."

He brushes something off his dark shirt. "Don't have one at the moment. I tend not to go for relationships, per se. I'm more of a friends-with-benefits type of guy."

A gasp falls from my lips. I pray he didn't hear it. "Why?"

He lazily puts his arm up along the top of the booth. "I don't like getting involved. I love sex, and I already told you that, but commitment scares the shit outta me."

"Why?"

He inhales a long breath, stares down at his drink. Wraps his palm around it, as if deep in thought, then fixes me with a cold stare. "We don't need to become each other's therapists. You don't need to psychoanalyze me."

Touchy.

The cutting sting of his barbed wire words is a subtle warning to stay away.

"But you asked, so I guess you deserve an answer about my previous hookup." He clears his throat, eyes averted. "She's abroad. Working in Europe. Has been for a few months and won't be back for a while. Don't worry. I won't even look at anyone while we're married."

I clench and unclench my hands which are on my lap. What do I say to that? Thank you? I appreciate that?

"Your turn. Tell me something about you," he prompts. "What's your favorite color?"

"Green."

"What shade of green. There must be a gazillion."

"The shade of green that's earthy and solid, like the one we have at home."

He peers at me. "What color is that?"

"You'll see when you come over."

He chortles. "I get to ask another question because your answer is so vague. Tell me something else."

I sip my drink. "I'm a black belt in jiu-jitsu."

He sits up straighter. "What?"

"You heard me."

"You're a black belt? In jiu-jitsu?"

I nod.

He stares like it's the most impressive thing he's heard. "That's … fucking *awesome.*"

I raise a brow. "You sound surprised."

"Because I am." He leans in. "What else?"

I hesitate. "I go to the gym. I run."

"Big deal. So do most people I know."

"I've also run marathons."

His eyes widen. "F—" He stops himself. "You've run marathons?"

"Yes."

He exhales. "You really are full of surprises. Where?"

I sip my drink, watching him. "The São Paulo International Marathon, the London Marathon and the New York City Marathon."

"Color me shocked." He slumps back against the velvet booth, but this time when he looks at me, there's admiration in his eyes. "You love your parents," he states.

"Doesn't everyone?"

"No." We stare at one another in silence. He doesn't want me to probe, yet he's digging deeper. "You adore your father."

"I do. He's a wonderful man."

He shakes his head. "Yeah. We really are nothing alike." He doesn't smile this time, and it feels like the air has suddenly chilled.

"Serious question. What's your biggest weakness, Dexter?"

His lips tug up at the corners. "Women who ask too many questions." Then, softer, his voice dropping lower. "And people I can't protect." A server passes by. "Another round of drinks?" Dexter asks me.

"Maybe we should open the champagne? It was nice of your friend to offer it."

"I guess it was."

I sit back and watch Dexter pour champagne into our glasses. This evening isn't as bad as I thought it would be.

DEX

I sit back in my chair, taking a sip of champagne as Daniela tells me about her college life here and then about her life in Brazil.

My gaze drops to her outfit. It's a slinky dark blue jumpsuit and it shows off her curvy hips and small waist, and with a neckline that reveals nothing, but hints at plenty. She's luscious, no way about it.

This evening could have gone worse. So far it's not been too bad. It's not like pulling out my toenails with a pair of pliers, which is what I feared.

When I told her I'd have picked the other women at the soiree over her, the way she threw her head back and roared with laughter, it hit me then. She's beautiful. I found myself staring at her, mesmerized by the soft, bare expanse of her neck, and by her sense of humor. This woman has the confidence to laugh at herself.

She's like no other woman I've met.

When the drinks arrived and we made a toast, I had to knock back my scotch to steady my nerves and quench my suddenly dry throat because Daniela is so utterly captivating when her defenses are down.

Then she had to go and tell me that she's a black belt in jiu-jitsu and my opinion of her went up a notch. And then she had to throw in that she's run marathons around the world.

Of course she has.

She just caught my eye in a way I didn't expect. And not

only that—she's funny. She's sarcastic and sharp, and I like that.

I *really* like that.

But something still feels off. A woman like her has everything. She is everything. So why is she still single?

Then again, I already know the answer. She told me herself.

And this is an alliance. It's not about love. This is business.

And I can't let myself forget that.

I do not fall.

I refuse to fall.

I glance past her, toward the bar, wanting to see what Rio is up to. The dude is propped against a stool at the bar at the far end, watching me. Every now and then, he turns slightly and winks. He's perfectly positioned. Daniela's back is to him, so she has no idea my wingman is here. I told him to join us, but he refused. Said it would seem like we were ganging up on her.

"Dude," he said, "this is supposed to be an intimate date. You don't want me in the way."

I told him never to use the word intimate when talking about me and the heiress. But now … I'm starting to wonder.

I shake the thought out of my head, as quickly as it landed.

We're not going there.

She's agreed to an arranged marriage. I don't care that her family is wealthy. I don't care that she has a charming smile or that she laughs at my sarcasm.

I don't care. And yet, this isn't as bad as I expected. She's saying something. I blink, realizing I haven't been paying attention.

"You're not listening to me," she says, giving me an accusatory state.

"I'm sorry."

"Are you waiting for someone else?"

"What? No."

"Then why do you keep looking around?"

I almost tell her about Rio, about how he's perched at the bar with a smug grin, watching all of this unfold. But I don't.

Instead, I clear my throat. "Look … this is an awkward situation for both of us." I pause, tapping my fingers against the table. "I need to tell you something. After our meeting with my father this morning, he called a meeting with my brothers."

"And?" She shrugs like it's nothing.

"He told them we were getting married soon, within a few weeks."

Her lips press together. "Best to get it over and done with."

I exhale. "Right?"

"He sent me an agenda."

That makes me laugh. "Of course, he did."

She sighs. "My parents need to make arrangements. Your father is taking control. It all feels so … impersonal. Not like how a wedding should be."

"That's because it's not a wedding," I say, my voice low. "We don't love each other. Jeez, we don't even like each other."

Her gaze sharpens. "You don't like me?"

I wince, choosing my words carefully. "You picked me, Daniela, and I'm not sure why. I wasn't exactly my charming, best self."

"You have a charming, best self?"

I laugh. I actually laugh, not just at the way she says it, but because of her deadpan expression. Her delivery is perfect. "Tell me," I say, crossing my arms. "If this were a real date, what would have happened by now?"

She stares down at her drink. "I don't really go on many dates."

What the fuck? "What do you mean? Because you're too pretty for most guys?"

She looks up, and the hurt in her eyes makes me feel like a douchebag. "No. Because men only want one thing."

I blink. "You really believe that?"

"In my experience? I *know* that."

Something sharp twists in my gut. I don't like the sound of that.

She shrugs, her expression nonchalant. "Men expect something after dinner. I've never really met someone who sees me for who I am." Her voice is casual, but there's something in her tone that makes me pause.

I study her, really look at her. The way the light hits her face. The way her eyes shine with something I can't quite place. Then it hits me like a slap to my face.

This woman has a fear of being seen.

The way she looks, she turns heads. She gets noticed. I know, because I saw the reaction to her that night at the soiree. Just like I've seen the reaction to her as we walked in here. She meets my gaze. "I don't know you, Dexter."

"But we're getting to know one another," I say softly, starting to see the real Daniela.

"You know that I'm more than just my hair, or my smile, or my eyes, or my body, don't you?"

I shift in my chair. "You're so much more than that." The air between us lightens even more. "Tell me more about the jiu-jitsu."

Her brows push together, like she's trying to figure me out. Then she launches into a story about how she started training.

"What made you start running marathons?" I ask.

"A friend of mine got me into it," she says. "Raquel. She started running in college, and I joined her."

I sit up. "Raquel?"

"She's my childhood friend. My wing woman."

I chuckle. "What are we going to tell her?"

Daniela hesitates. "I told her about you."

"Already?"

"She's inquisitive."

"Her reaction?" I ask.

"She's shocked."

"Why?"

"Because I haven't mentioned any guy in a long time and—"

I arch a brow. "You haven't been dating?"

"Not for a while."

"Why?"

She shrugs. "I dated in college. Had a couple of boyfriends. But I was more focused on my studies."

Studious, too. The more I get to know this woman, the more I'm starting to see that Daniela Oliveira is the dream package.

"After college, I went back home to Brazil," she continues. "I didn't really date after that. Just focused on helping my father with the business."

She hesitates. Just slightly. Like she was about to say something else, but held back. I lean forward. "You'd tell me, right?"

She frowns. "Tell you what?"

"The real state of your father's company." Her eyes flick to mine and we just stare at each other. I don't know what it is, but something shifts in my stomach and I force myself to look away. "More champagne, or another cocktail?" I ask.

"Another cocktail would be nice. Champagne goes straight to my head."

I almost tell her we could order food. This wasn't supposed to turn into dinner, but … it really isn't such a bad way to spend an evening.

"We haven't decided on our proposal story. We should, because people always ask that question."

She's right. "We do need to figure that out."

"Do we need to take this back to your place?" This is the second time she's hinted at that. Maybe she's testing me.

I glance at her. "Are you coming on to me again, Daniela?"

"Don't flatter yourself."

I chuckle lightly. I really do love her humor. "Let's say we met through a friend."

"That won't work. Raquel has the nose of a bloodhound. She's a corporate lawyer and she'll find holes in our story."

"Will I have the pleasure of meeting this friend?"

"Of course you will. I've known her all my life, and she'll be at the wedding."

I pull a box out of my pocket. "I forgot." I lower my voice. "The ring."

Her mouth falls open. I feel like a jerk now, because I bought a cheap little thing. Nothing exclusive or special, not from an upscale jeweler. No Tiffany or Cartier here. I spent ten thousand dollars on it. It's a large square pink diamond set in a chunky rose gold band, with small diamonds all around. I slip it under the table, looking around the room. People are talking in hushed tones. Rio seems busy. He's talking to someone.

"You should just slip it on under the table," I whisper.

"Okay." She reaches under and our hands meet. The first touch of her soft, warm fingers, make me jolt. Not with fright. With an electric tingle. Like something inside me has awakened.

"I've got it." She sits back. I sit back, slip the ring box back into my pocket. "Why, thank you, darling." She waves her hand at me, showing off her ring proudly, before flashing a smile that has more megawatts than the pathetic two carat ring on her finger. Looking at it now, it's flashy, and totally impersonal. The kind of ring that screams "this is for show" rather than "I care about you."

"You like it?" It seems like the appropriate thing to say, even though I feel like I should have given her something classy.

"It's lovely, Dexter. A little too big, but it will do, also, I don't like ostentatious things, but, as you say, this isn't for real. But thank you."

She doesn't like bling. "Noted." I lean back in my seat, watching her, and I forget that this is just business. In fact, I'm starting to feel a little off kilter the more I get to know this woman.

Most of the women in my circle are materialistic, and they don't even bother to hide it. The more expensive and gaudier a trinket is, the better.

Daniela's genuine appreciation and joy surprises me again. More than that, she calms that unsettled feeling I've been wrestling with for too long. Being with her does something to me and I feel like I can breathe and be still for the first time in a long time.

There is so much more to her than I first saw, and as I start to pull back the layers slowly, a sizzle of excitement zaps through my veins. I want to discover more about who she is underneath her beautiful exterior.

Because I have a sneaking suspicion that her beauty goes all the way through to her core.

And if that's true.

She's unique.

Truly one of a kind.

Which means, what the hell am I doing?

Dex is available from all retailers.

BOOKLIST

Buy direct from Lily and save!

NEW SERIES

Knight Empire: A series of steamy billionaire romances based around a family of six brothers and their tyrannical and controlling father.

The Darkest Knight (prequel)

Jett

Dex

Rio

Zach

The Seven Sins: A series of seven standalone romances based on the seven sins. Emotional, and angsty romances which are loosely connected.

Underdog (prequel)

The Wrath of Eli

The Problem with Lust
The Lies of Pride
The Price of Inertia
The Other Side of Greed
The Seven Sins, Books 1-3

The Billionaire's Love Story: This is a Cinderella story with a touch of Jerry Maguire. What happens when the billionaire with too much money meets the single mom with too much heart?

The Promise (prequel)
The Gift, Boxed Set (Books 1, 2 & 3)
The Offer, Boxed Set (Books 1, 2 & 3)
The Vow, Boxed Set (Books 1, 2 & 3)

Indecent Intentions: This is a spin-off from The Billionaire's Love story. This two-book set consists of two standalone stories about the billionaire's playboy brother. The second story is about a wealthy nightclub owner who shuns relationships.

The Bet
The Hookup

Honeymoon Series: Take a roller-coaster journey of emotional highs and lows in this story of love and loss, family and relationships. When Ava is dumped six weeks before her Valentine's Day wedding, she has no idea of the life that awaits her in Italy.

Honeymoon for One
Honeymoon for Three
Honeymoon Blues

Honeymoon Bliss
Baby Steps

Italian Summer Series: This is a spin-off from the Honeymoon Series. These books tell the stories of the secondary characters who first appeared in the Honeymoon Series. Nico and Ava also appear in these books.

It Takes Two
All That Glitters
Fool's Gold
Roman Encounter
November Sun
New Beginnings

A Perfect Match Series: This is a seven book series in which the first four books feature the same couple. High-flying corporate executive Nadine has no time for romance but her life takes a turn for the better when she meets Ethan, a sexy and struggling metal sculptor five years younger. He works as an escort in order to make the rent. Books 4-6 are standalone romances based on characters from the earlier books. The main couple, Ethan and Nadine, appear in all books:

Lost in Solo (prequel)
The Proposal
Heart Sync
A Leap of Faith
Misplaced Love
Reclaiming Love
Embracing Love

Standalone books:

Tomorrow Belongs to Us
Love Among the Ruins
Love, Inc
An Unexpected Gift

ACKNOWLEDGMENTS

I would like to thank Maria at SteamyDesigns for creating this awesome cover. A huge thanks to Nicole McCurdy at Emerald Edits and Emily McNish at Fairy PlotMother for editing.

As always, a huge 'Thank You' to my wonderful team of proofreaders:

Charlotte Rebelein
Dena Pugh
Marcia Chamberlain

ABOUT THE AUTHOR

Lily Zante lives with her husband and three children somewhere near London, UK.

Connect with Me

I love hearing from you – so please don't be shy! You can email me, message me on Facebook or connect with me here:

Buy Direct from Lily and SAVE
https://shop.lilyzante.com

TikTok |Instagram | Website | Facebook Email

Newsletter sign-up:
http://www.lilyzante.com/news
Follow me on Bookbub
Follow me on Goodreads

facebook.com/LilyZanteRomanceAuthor
instagram.com/authorlilyzante
bookbub.com/authors/lily-zante
goodreads.com/authorlilyzante

www.ingramcontent.com/pod-product-compliance
Lightning Source LLC
Chambersburg PA
CBHW050603170726
48283CB00001B/87